More Praise for

The Queen's Pawn

"*The Queen's Pawn* is a powerful portrait of two dynamic royal women and the men who controlled their lives—or is it the other way around? Treachery, betrayal, lust—and an unusual and compelling love story, beautifully told." —Karen Harper, author of *The Queen's Governess*

"*The Queen's Pawn* by Christy English resurrects from misty legend Eleanor of Aquitaine, Henry II, Princess Alais, and Richard the Lionhearted. I knew the outlines of their stories, but now I have come to know them as fully, emotionally human, both flawed and magnificent. The French Princess Alais comes as a child to England to be raised by Eleanor for marriage to Richard, the queen's favorite son. But the child becomes a beautiful woman and catches Henry's eye, starting an ever-escalating palace war of intrigue, betrayal, and passion. Almost 850 years have passed, but Christy brings the complex time of unrest and deceit to full, lyrical life for us. A captivating love story of Richard and Alais beyond the story I thought I knew of a young woman trapped between Eleanor and Henry in their lifelong struggle for mastery over the English crown and each other. A jewel of a novel." —Jeane Westin, author of *The Virgin's Daughters*

"Told with simple grace and from the heart, *The Queen's Pawn* is a moving evocation of two women, deep friends but destined to a tragic rivalry for royal power and two men's love." —Margaret Frazer, author of *A Play of Treachery*

continued . . .

"What a promising debut! With deft strokes, Christy English transforms Alais from the innocent child her father sends to England into the cunning woman her surrogate mother, Eleanor, teaches her to be—while the crafty and sophisticated Eleanor is ensnared and nearly brought down by helpless love for her adopted daughter. The complex love-hate quadrangle between Eleanor, her husband, Henry, her son Richard, and the ever more wily Alais is a fascinating and original take on this juicy historical footnote."

—Ellyn Bache, award-winning novelist of
Safe Passage and *Daughters of the Sea*

"An astonishing debut! Christy English spins an unforgettable tale of dangerous splendor, evoking the stone and tapestry of the Plantagenet era, and the fierce rivalry of two equally fascinating and determined women, whose ambitions threaten to overturn their world."

—C. W. Gortner, author of *The Last Queen*

NEW AMERICAN LIBRARY
Published by New American Library, a division of
Penguin Group (USA) Inc., 375 Hudson Street, New York, New York 10014, USA
Penguin Group (Canada), 90 Eglinton Avenue East, Suite 700, Toronto,
Ontario M4P 2Y3, Canada (a division of Pearson Penguin Canada Inc.)
Penguin Books Ltd., 80 Strand, London WC2R 0RL, England
Penguin Ireland, 25 St. Stephen's Green, Dublin 2,
Ireland (a division of Penguin Books Ltd.)
Penguin Group (Australia), 250 Camberwell Road, Camberwell, Victoria 3124,
Australia (a division of Pearson Australia Group Pty. Ltd.)
Penguin Books India Pvt. Ltd., 11 Community Centre, Panchsheel Park,
New Delhi - 110 017, India
Penguin Group (NZ), 67 Apollo Drive, Rosedale, North Shore 0632,
New Zealand (a division of Pearson New Zealand Ltd.)
Penguin Books (South Africa) (Pty.) Ltd., 24 Sturdee Avenue,
Rosebank, Johannesburg 2196, South Africa

Penguin Books Ltd., Registered Offices:
80 Strand, London WC2R 0RL, England

First published by New American Library,
a division of Penguin Group (USA) Inc.

First Printing, April 2010
1 3 5 7 9 10 8 6 4 2

REGISTERED TRADEMARK—MARCA REGISTRADA

Library of Congress Cataloging-in-Publication Data:

English, Christy.
The queen's pawn/Christy English.
p.   cm.
ISBN 978-0-451-22923-6
1. Alix, de France, 1160–ca. 1220–Fiction.   2. Eleanor, of Aquitaine, Queen, consort of Henry II,
King of England, 1122?–1204–Fiction.   3. Great Britain–History–Henry II, 1154–1189–Fiction.
4. France–History–Philip II Augustus, 1180–1223–Fiction.   I. Title.
PS3605.N49Q84   2010
813'.54–dc22   2009040457

Set in Post Medieval
Designed by Alissa Amell

Printed in the United States of America

THE QUEEN'S PAWN

CHRISTY ENGLISH

NEW AMERICAN LIBRARY

For my family

Acknowledgments

My thanks to all who read and critiqued my work in various drafts from the eighth grade onward: LaDonna Lindgren, Laura Creasy, Tammy Monfette, Ellyn Bache, Hope Johnson, Audrey Forrester, Amy Pierce, Philip Drew, Kat Vernon, Alice Osborn, Alisa Roost, S. J. Stratford, and Beth Seltzer. Special thanks must be given to my fabulous agent, Margaret O'Connor, who believed in this book from the first time she laid eyes on it. I thank my brilliant editor, Claire Zion, who took an early draft into her experienced hands and, with the clarity of her vision, helped me to discover the novel as it was meant to be written. I would like to thank all the wonderful people at New American Library, especially Jhanteigh Kupihea for her insight during the revision process, Michele Alpern for the excellent copyediting, the publicist Kaitlyn Kennedy for spreading the word, and Maureen O'Boyle and her team for the amazing cover art. I thank all who believed in me from the day I first picked up my pen: Karen English, Carl English, Barry English, Vena Miller, Susan Randall, Marianne Nubel, Chris Nubel, Ellen Seltz, Susan Hurst Alford, Jenny Morris, Nicole Garrett,

Janie Lam, and my Internet consultant, Andrew Seltz. And I thank Eleanor of Aquitaine and Alais of France. Though it has been my honor to convey one possibility of who these women were, I have no doubt fallen short. Alais and Eleanor live on when we remember them, no matter how imperfectly.

THE
QUEEN'S
PAWN

PART I

⚔

CHILDHOOD

Chapter 1

ॐ

ALAIS: PRINCESS OF FRANCE

Île-de-France
February 1169

My mother died the day I was born. I now know that this was in no way unusual, but for the first years of my life, I felt quite singled out by the hand of God. She was a great loss to me, my first loss, though I never knew her. My nurse often told me that I have her bright eyes.

On the day I was born, the King of France gained only me, another daughter who was useless except for the alliance my marriage might bring. The day that brought me also brought the death of his queen, so that after a decent period of mourning, my father had to go about the tedious business of finding a new one, and starting all over again.

My mother was Spanish, and a great lady, or so everyone said. Of course, they would have told me no different, even if she had been a shrew. My father, King Louis, the seventh of that name, never spoke of her.

So my nurse, Katherine, brought me up on stories of my mother's beauty, of her graciousness, of her unyielding courtesy. According to my nurse, my mother was a sort of saint on earth, a woman who never got angry, who never spoke a harsh word, neither to man nor woman nor servant. A woman who bred quickly and died quietly, her only fault delivering my father two girls, who could inherit nothing but pain.

This paragon was held up before me always, so that I, too, learned silence and stillness. I learned that quiet in a woman is prized above gold, and that obedience was not only my duty but my honor. For in obedience, I best served my father and my king.

My father was tall and thin, with the face of a monk. In a better world, he would have been free to spend his life in holy contemplation, serving God.

That was my father's true gift: to sit in silence and feel the presence of God. Sometimes, when the business of state was done, and no one else had claim on his attention, he would let me sit with him in his private rooms, and kneel with him at his private altar. This altar was beside the bed of state, where my sisters and I had been conceived.

My oldest sisters did not know me, for they had been married away from France long ago. They were also cursed, I was told, because they had been spawned by my father's first wife, the wicked Queen Eleanor, the woman who had abandoned my father for a younger man years before. No one spoke of that queen except in whispers. My nurse would summon her memory when she sought to remind me to be a good girl, when she sought to turn me from wickedness. I spent my childhood in horror of that mysterious queen, a woman who was never obedient, a woman who had gone on Crusade against the infidel and ridden astride a horse like a man.

I later learned that Eleanor was not dead and with the devil, but had married the King of England, who was another kind of devil, or so everyone at my father's court said.

Just before my eleventh birthday, my marriage was arranged, now that it looked certain that I would live. During this time, my father called me to him.

The ladies of the court brought me into a large room made of stone. The windows far above us held clear panes of glass, and sunlight shone in through those high windows, catching the dust that danced over all our heads. The ceiling was made of a latticework of stone so delicate that it looked almost like lace. I craned my neck to look at it.

My father stood with his men-at-arms and gentlemen-in-waiting beside a great wooden chair with cushions and gilded arms. I smiled when I saw my father, but he did not smile back, not because he could not see me, but because this was a solemn occasion. I did not know why I was there, but I knew that I was expected to walk to the king.

For the first time in my life, I walked alone in a room full of men. The court ladies followed me a few paces behind as I moved among my father's courtiers.

When I came to the dais, which seemed to take an eternity, I curtsied to my father, then knelt before him, as if I were his vassal.

There was a murmur in the room, like wind in a field of barley. Then there was silence. It had a different quality now, not one of people waiting for a task to be completed, but one of people watching a play. I must have done the right thing unprompted. Though my father wore his heaviest robes of state, trimmed in gilt and ermine, now he smiled down at me.

I had never before seen him crowned. He looked like a different person, until he smiled, and I knew him again.

My father raised his hands and blessed me, speaking words I no longer remember. The substance of his speech was that from that day forward I was to be known as the Countess of the Vexin. I would hold the county of the Vexin in my own right, a valuable sliver of land that lay between Paris and the great duchy of Normandy. I swore to serve my king in all things, and to serve the throne of France.

When the ceremony was over, I saw a man standing behind my father's throne. He was a small, ferret-faced man with eyes that gleamed. I was told little in my father's court, but I knew how to listen. I knew he was one of the minions of King Henry of England. I also knew his name: Sir Reginald of Shrewsbury; even in my nursery there was talk of him when he first came to Paris as ambassador for the English king.

I wondered why he had bothered to come to my investiture as countess, when even I had not been told of the proceedings until the day they were upon me. Then I heard one of my father's women speak to another as they moved to lead me away.

"God help the girl," she said. "Going to the court of that devil's spawn."

The "devil" meant only one thing to me: the wicked queen who had been my father's wife.

I froze in midstep, the old fear of my childhood rising from the ground to grip my throat. Its bony fingers closed off my air, and I had to fight to breathe. It was not the first battle I had had with fear, and won; nor was it the last.

I said a prayer to the Virgin, and She heard me, for my breathing calmed and my fear of that evil queen receded. I stood alone in my father's court, and I knew why the ferret-faced ambassador was there. My marriage had been arranged already; I was to marry one of the devil-spawn princes, a son of my father's former wife.

I stood still as the rest of the court moved around me. I could feel the eyes of King Henry's ambassador weighing and judging me, finding me lacking. I was small for my age, but I drew myself up straight. I would not have a servant of my husband-to-be carry tales of me, unless they were tales I placed in his hand.

I did not follow the court ladies to the door, as I was meant to do. I turned back, and the women standing by did not have the sense to catch me. They thought me truly one of their dogs by that time, and did not know until too late that I had slipped the leash.

My father still stood where I had left him. He sensed somehow, as I did, that more needed to be said, words that had been left unspoken. He was a good man, and a good king, but he was never one to speak before crowds. I saw that it was left to me to do it for him.

I met my father's eyes and stood before him, seeing only him, while his courtiers paused at the door. They had thought to leave, the ceremony over, but I was not done with them. Not yet.

When I heard the courtiers turn back from the outer hall, I knelt slowly, solemnly, my eyes on my father's. The room fell once more into a hush, until the only sound was the court ladies cooing like doves by the door, until the chamberlain's harsh voice shushed them.

I raised the hem of my father's robe, and kissed it. The men around him drew back, but stayed close enough that they might watch my impromptu performance as it unfolded. I did not look at them, but only at my father's face. In that moment, I took my true oath, one that I kept for the rest of my life.

"My lord king," I said. "It is for me to serve the throne of France. If you call on me to travel to the farthest reaches of the world, even into the outer darkness, I will go. If France needed me to marry the devil himself, I would do it. It will be my honor to marry King Henry's son."

I did not know which hell-spawn prince I was meant for, so I did not use a given name. I knew that King Henry had so many sons, when all God had seen fit to give us was my younger brother, Philippe Auguste, the child of my father's third wife.

My father looked down at me with such pride that I thought he might weep. I saw in his face regret that he had not called me to him alone before my investiture as countess, before my marriage had been arranged. He saw for the first time that I was old enough to understand what my duty was. Tears filled his eyes as he stared down at me; then he blinked them away.

My father raised his hand once more to bless me, placing it on my veil where it rested on the crown of my head.

"Daughter, when spring comes, you will be sent to marry the Lord Richard, Prince of England, son of our esteemed vassal Henry, King of England and Duke of Normandy. You are the pride of my house, the flower of France. King Henry will welcome you, and honor you, as we honor you here."

I did not speak again, for already I had said too much. A French

princess lives her life in silence, as my mother had done before me. I
was not naturally silent, but I was obedient. I knew that I would serve
my father better now by holding my tongue.

I thought that he would dismiss me then, my duty acknowledged, all gossip of devils and their spawn cast aside. Instead, my father raised his hand from where it rested on my veil and, with a
gesture, dismissed the courtiers around us, and King Henry's vassal
with them.

"Leave us," my father said.

The room was cleared in a moment. The ladies who had brought
me were the last to leave. They were scolded by my father's chamberlain for letting me get away from them in the first place.

Once we were alone, my father sat down, not on his throne, but
on a cushion on one of the dais' shallow steps.

I realized that the cushion had been set there for me to kneel on.
I had knelt early, not having been coached. The ceremony making me
countess, and all that came after it, had been accomplished below the
dais altogether.

My father gestured to me, and I went to him. He took my hand
in his. His skin was like old vellum, soft and almost yellow. I prayed
to God, standing there before him, that he would live long enough to
see my brother grown and strong.

"Daughter," he said. "What have you heard of the devil?"

"The ladies said that I was to marry among the devil's spawn. I
knew at once that they meant a son born of your other wife."

To my surprise, he smiled. I was glad to see a little light come into
his face. But his expression turned grave once more, and I moved
closer to him.

"Eleanor is not the devil, Alais, and neither is her husband. They are both just sinners before God, as we all are. Sinners who do not repent."

I was not convinced. I would marry the devil himself if it would serve France. He saw this truth in my eyes, and his hand brushed my cheek. He searched for his next words. He was a man who did not speak much, except to God, and then only in his thoughts.

I waited, for when my father spoke, he always had something to say. At the time, I thought that was because he was king. Now I know that it was the way his soul was made. He spoke carefully in order to do the least harm. It was his sorrow all his life that, as king, harm came from him as often as mercy.

"Daughter," he said. "You are a good girl. You are the pride of my house. I have made you the Countess of the Vexin in your own right, though this title has never before fallen to a woman. Do you know why I did this?"

"Because I am strong enough to bear it," I answered.

I thought again that he would weep, but he was a man. Though he was not great in battle then or ever, he was always in control of himself. I have known many renowned in battle who could not say the same.

He pulled me onto his lap, and kissed me. I could not remember a time before when his lips had touched me. Though he loved me, and though I always knew it, our family was bound by tradition and necessity. There was little time for kisses or for tears. I remembered that, even as I felt his tears on my hair.

Once a daughter of the house of Capet is betrothed, she is sent to live among her future husband's kin. I was ready to face a life in exile among my father's enemies, for his sake, and for the sake of France. Because I knew King Henry was my father's enemy; his power stretched far, surrounding my father's lands. While king in England, Henry was also duke in Normandy and, through his wife, in the Aquitaine. Henry was my father's vassal, but he was strong. My betrothal was one way to contain the threat of the English king and his many sons, one more way to keep the fragile peace.

My father drew out his prayer beads, for a set of them was always with him. Today he carried gold beads set with diamonds, pearls, and amethysts, leading down into a crucifix of gold where Our Savior lay, His agony made beautiful. My father gave me these beads, and pressed them hard into my palm.

"Keep these with you always, Alais. Use them to pray for me, and for France. In this way, you will always remember where you come from, and who your father was."

He kissed me once more. I heard his men-at-arms begin to gather by the door. They had come to fetch him away, for he was needed elsewhere, as a king always was.

He did not turn from me even then, but held me. I looked up into his face and saw that my father was already old. It would be many years or never before I would see him again.

He stroked my hair and dried my tears with the sleeve of his brocaded gown. The brocade was harsh, and scratched me, but I would not have traded those scratches for kisses from anyone else.

"Be a good girl, and serve your house always. We will see each other again, at the foot of Our Savior in heaven."

Looking into my father's face, I saw that he believed what he said. When life was dark, and the road of duty and honor was rocky and long, I remembered my father's face on that day. I remembered how he loved me, and how he was a man good enough to see beyond the evils of this world into a certain paradise.

Chapter 2

⚜

ELEANOR: FORGOTTEN QUEEN

Winchester Castle
April 1169

The day Louis' daughter came to me, I was not prepared for her. Louis, my ex-husband. My old lover. My old enemy. The only man I ever left weeping who was not strong enough to hide his tears. Or, perhaps he was simply too strong to feel the need.

She came to me and stared up at me out of Louis' eyes. The color was her mother's, a light brown tinged with yellow. But her serious- ness, her gravity, she had learned from him.

I was alone when she arrived at Winchester Castle. I was sur- rounded by women, but none of them knew me. They feared me, and loved me, the way a worshipper in a cathedral claims to fear and love the Christ. But none of them saw behind my mask; I would never allow it.

My son Richard was at my castle at Oxford, as were the rest of my living children, until we left in a few months' time for Aquitaine. I had borne nine children for Henry, the daughters for foreign marriages, the sons to follow their father. But in my heart, Richard was mine, born for me alone.

My husband, Henry, had left me years ago in all but name, following the skirt of Rosamund. She was nothing but some knight's daughter born of a family that had held their obscure strip of land an hour, while my family, descended from Charlemagne himself, had held the Aquitaine for centuries. The thought of that woman, her blond hair coyly displayed, her beguiling, vapid eyes, raised a taste of acid on my tongue. It was said Henry found peace with her, that he loved her silence as much as her chatter. Perhaps he did. For a certainty, he got neither peace nor silence from me.

From the day we met, all Henry got from me was fire. A fire that never burned, but warmed, and singed his fingertips when he touched me. A fire that kept him in my bed for years longer than anyone said I could, for I was older than he by more than a decade, too old at twenty-nine to catch the eye of a king even when we met.

But Henry was no king then, only a hardscrabble warrior who would wrest a kingdom away from his mother's enemy. He was a caged lion, pacing through Louis' court like some apparition from another world. When I met his gray-eyed gaze for the first time, my husband, the King of France, stood beside me, but I knew that Henry would love me for the rest of my life. Well, I was wrong in that, too.

But the day he saw me, Henry wanted me, as he has wanted no other woman since. I know this, because I know him. The fact that

I know him better than anyone alive on earth is why he took up Rosamund, and even now stays away from me.

I was thinking of Henry when Louis' daughter arrived. I often think of Henry, when neither the speech of my women nor the songs of my men can beguile me into forgetfulness. I remembered his great, booming laugh, and his wide peasant hands that could span my waist and lift me as if I weighed nothing, though I am a tall woman, filled with strength. That was why I had loved him well; his strength matched mine, when he chose to use it.

I was sitting with my women when Alais came to me. My spy brought word from Southampton when she landed, and another brought word that she would arrive that day. I waited, watching out my window, enjoying the light breeze that rose past the castle walls to caress my face. The rain had finally stopped, and it seemed I could catch the scent of spring, damp earth, and sweet new grass.

Amaria, my favorite servingwoman, was reading to us from the Book of John. None of my women in England understood the irony of the Gospels being read aloud in my court. Few of the women here would return with me to Aquitaine, where the Court of Love was born, where I had been raised. But if Henry had heard the Gospel read in my court, he would have understood. He would have laughed with me, had he been there. Henry knew better than anyone how little stock I put in religion, and all its false trappings.

My women were the most educated in Christendom. I liked to remind myself, as well as them, of that, so I had them read aloud in Latin. They read the Gospels, and took in the word of God, and thought me pious, which was the ultimate irony. I simply enjoyed listening to the third language my father called on me to learn, after my native tongue, the langue d'oc, and, of course, Parisian French.

I loved most listening to the voice of a woman as she read aloud. In a world where most priests could not read, it meant something to me that my women, weak creatures that they were, could do what so many men, with all their strength and power, could not.

Though my father was long dead, his cathedral still stood. As Amaria read, my other women embroidered a great tapestry that would serve as the new altar cloth at his cathedral in Poitiers. They did fine work, better than any guild could produce, and it kept their hands busy and their minds out of mischief.

As the afternoon wore on, and the light began to fade, I thought to call on Bertrand, my favorite troubadour, to come abovestairs to give us a song. But I had yet to speak this thought aloud when the castle servants came to light the evening candles, taking the day lamps away.

It was late that afternoon when one of Henry's fools brought the girl to me. Her wimple was filthy, her silk gown so wrinkled and soiled from travel that she could never wear it again. She stood blinking even in the soft, fading light of my solar.

My women knew better than to laugh at the girl's disheveled appearance outright, at least until I gave them leave. But I heard their laughter, tucked behind their teeth, waiting to come forth at the first sign of permission from me. I did not give it.

The princess looked as if she knew that they mocked her behind her back, that they would mock her to her face if I would allow it, but she did not heed them. She did not even give my ladies the courtesy of a glance. She kept her eyes on me.

I rose from my chair and faced that girl, looking into my old lover's eyes. She did not flinch from my gaze, or cower, as I would have expected a child of Louis' to do. Instead, her brown eyes met mine with a frankness that I have rarely seen, a steadfast gaze that seemed to take my measure, as if she thought to find me wanting.

The child was Louis' daughter, but she was as strong as I was. The sight of that strength in another struck down all my defenses. I smiled at her.

The girl rose from her curtsy. She was a small child, but some woman had had the training of her, for she moved gracefully. I wondered for a fleeting moment if someone had had the sense to teach her to dance. I vowed that I would, if no one had done so already.

The sight of my smile brought a light into her eyes that had not been there before. She looked on me as a friend, as an equal, though no one had had the effrontery to look on me like that since the day Henry first saw me in Louis' court. Yet this child met my gaze with the strength I never found in my own daughters, the strength I had always looked for in them but had never seen. I saw it now in her.

"Welcome, Princess Alais."

She curtsied once more, this time not as deeply. I turned my eye on Henry's fool, and stared him down.

"You bring to me the Countess of the Vexin, a princess of France, covered in dirt from the road, and blinking with exhaustion."

Sir Reginald, although he was a knight of Shrewsbury, did not have the sense to bow again, and I saw that he was one of the men Henry kept about him who thought I should never have been queen. That a mere knight would seek to judge me caught my fancy, when it should have stoked my temper. I almost laughed in his face, but I thought better of it and decided to frighten him instead. In swallowing my laughter, I met the princess' eyes.

Princess Alais smiled at me, as if we were conspirators and this man was our dupe. When she smiled, it was as if the sun had risen there in the room. As she watched Sir Reginald squirm before me, I saw that she hated him, that he had done nothing to comfort her on her long journey from her home. He had probably not even had the sense to give her care over to a woman in the evenings, just as Louis had not had the sense to send a woman with her.

The stupidity of men made my smile widen, and as I watched, the princess covered her mouth with her hand. She tried to catch her laughter, to swallow it down, but as we looked at each other, conspirators together, she failed.

Her laughter rang out like the sweet peal of a bell, the bell that had once rung from my father's chapel in Poitiers. I seemed to hear my own laughter in hers, the laughter my father had always drawn from me, as no one else but Henry had ever done. That old carefree laughter rose in me, after many years of silence. I could not catch it, or hold it back.

Sir Reginald knelt before me then, frightened in truth, as well he should have been. But as the daughter I should have had stepped close to stand beside me, I knew that I would let him go.

"Get out," I said. "And don't ever come into my sight again."

The sound of these words gave my new daughter pleasure, and she laughed again.

My ladies, shocked at my behavior, for once did not laugh to placate me or to join in a joke they did not understand. When I waved one hand, they left, too, so that the little princess and I stood alone.

"You made him afraid," Alais said, awe in her voice, as if I had worked some feat of magic.

I gave her my hand, and she kissed it with reverence. I could not let her fall into reverence with me. I would take worship from anyone else, but from her, I wanted love.

"No, Alais, no hand kissing, if you please. The man is a fool, and all fools must be laughed at."

"It is not so in France."

I met her solemn eyes, and drew her ruined wimple from her hair. Her curls were a riot of brown and auburn and maple, soft and fine, but full, with a life of their own. I smoothed her hair back from her face, and almost leaned down to kiss her. I stopped myself, in case I might frighten her with too much affection, and from a stranger.

But we were no strangers, not from the first. Alais stared back at me with the knowledge of my soul in her eyes, as if she could see through my mask, not only to the woman I was, but to the woman I wanted most to be. I did kiss her then, the skin of her cheek soft under my lips. She smelled of sweat and road dust, and I knew I must see to her comfort. I would leave her well-being to no one else.

"Come with me," I said, taking her hand.

She did not move to follow, but stared at me, all traces of laughter gone from her eyes.

"You were my father's wife," she said.

She spoke with such sudden horror that I faced her once more. This matter would be dealt with, before we could go on. "Alais, it would be better if we both agreed never to speak of the past."

She did not obey me blindly. She did not nod to placate me, as anyone else might have done. She gazed at me solemnly, taking me in as few ever had in my life, only Henry and, before him, my father. I saw the wheels of her mind turn as she considered what I said. I watched her love for her father war with her newborn love for me. I did not win that battle, but neither did I lose it.

"All right," she said. "I will forget."

She gave that concession freely, and I had not even asked it of her. I kissed her again, and she leaned close to me, like a bird taking shelter from a storm. I did not draw her from the room as I had meant to, but held her close, kneeling beside her, as if she were my daughter in truth.

We went, hand in hand, down the long dark corridor to my rooms. The torches were not lit at Winchester when the king was not there, and I liked it that way. The whitewashed walls were still wet from the rains we had had the day before, but even now the damp was rising off the stone. The days were growing warmer, and I welcomed the spring.

I had a boy to lead me with a lamp, as down a long and winding street. He left us outside my rooms, and when I opened the door, I found my women waiting for me.

My ladies-in-waiting stepped forward, or rose from their chairs to curtsy to me.

"Your Majesty," Amaria said. "You come here unattended?"

"No, indeed. I come here with the Princess of France."

Amaria heard the unspoken order in my voice, and she curtsied at once to Alais.

Alais stood beside me, her hand still in mine, taking my lady-in-waiting's offering as her due, as indeed it was.

The rest of my women saw my face, and followed Amaria in

their obeisance, before I raised my hand once more to dismiss them. As they left, I instructed them, "Ladies, please tell His Holiness the bishop that I will not be attending tonight's feast."

"As you say, Your Highness." Amaria bowed, looking to Alais once more.

The little princess met her eyes, but her face was inscrutable. Once again, I saw Louis in her.

My women left us alone with the castle servants, who knew my habits, and had already begun to prepare my bath. Alais watched them with wide eyes as those women brought an almost endless stream of hot water from the kitchens, water that I had them heat every day, whether they thought me a witch or not. Of course, no one would have the temerity to name me a witch aloud, not even to whisper it. Though I was separated from Henry, I was still queen.

The women left the heated water standing in its tub, and my dressing women came forward to take my gown. I raised my hand, and stopped them.

"The princess will bathe first."

Her eyes lit with fear. Alais would have run had I not been holding her hand. As it was, she stood caught, like a boar in a net, like a deer that first scents the hunter.

"I must bathe?" she whispered to me.

"Every day, little princess. As I do."

She turned her eyes on me, the light maple brown that took me in and held me as no other eyes have, before or since. She measured me and my words together.

"You bathe?" she asked, as if to make certain she had heard me right.

"I do."

"Every day?"

"Yes," I said. "And so will you."

I do not know what nonsense the child had been taught at Louis' court about the dangers of getting wet, or the Church's strictures about mortification of the flesh. I could only imagine what had been wrought in Paris since my time. Even when I was queen in France, only a handful of courtiers had been brave enough to bathe weekly, and those few did so only to please me. I had been the only one to bathe daily, except early in my marriage, when I tempted Louis into the bath with me.

I turned my mind from such musings. I could not think of my ex-lover as I looked upon his daughter.

She was braver than many French before her. She stared into the tub as if it were filled with acid and not with water. She stood still and staring as my women stripped her down to her shift.

They saw that she had no baggage with her. I discovered later that Louis had sent a paltry bag of gowns and shifts, things I would not give a servant, much less dress my daughter in. As soon as I saw that bag, I had them take it away. I would order new gowns made for her myself.

My dressing women stepped forward and offered their hands to her, which she took, raising first one foot and then the next into the bath. The warm water was an unexpected delight, and her eyes darted to mine. I saw that she had never had the pleasure of submerging herself in warm water before. Once more I cursed Louis and all Parisians for fools.

Alais stood still and let my women wash her, their hands gentle beneath her shift. They knew that she was far too modest a child to bathe naked, as I did. The largest of my women washed her hair gently, then lifted her from the tub as if she weighed nothing.

The princess clung to her as a little monkey might, but always, she kept her eyes on me. My women drew her wet shift from her so swiftly that Alais had no time to protest. They dried her in warmed linen sheets, then wrapped her in a fur cape I ordered brought from my trunks.

Alais would not let me out of her sight, but sat on a little stool beside the tub as my women stripped me to the skin and helped me step into my bath.

"Very good, Alais. You were very brave."

Tears rose in my new daughter's eyes, and I saw that praise came to her as rarely as bathwater. I reached out from my tub and took her hand, soap from my skin wetting the fur of her borrowed cloak.

"You must give no man your tears," I said. "Nor woman, either. Always, their strength belongs to you."

She nodded and swallowed hard, her tears receding through sheer force of will. I watched her battle with herself, and knew that I would love this child every day for the rest of my life. And beyond, if the Church was right.

If I lay in torment after death, my memory of this girl would be one bright, cool spot in hell.

We sat together, our meat and bread finished, and Alais looked at me. "Is King Henry the devil?" she asked, as calmly as she might have asked me to look out the window for the weather.

I choked on my wine, and sat gasping.

Still, she looked at me, as still as death, as calm as a priest.

"Did your father tell you that?"

"No, Your Majesty. But everyone else said it at my father's court."

No doubt the child was referring to one of the old Angevin tales that spoke of Henry's great-grandfather rising from the ground like a demon to torment all his enemies. I laughed again; no one had had the temerity to speak of those old stories in years. And now this child, a little girl from Paris, had the audacity to meet my eye and ask if the man I had loved and the children I had borne him were devil's spawn.

"No," I said. "Henry is not the devil. That is an old and foolish story."

I could see that she did not quite believe me, but that she was going to try to take me at my word, for my sake.

I smiled at her, and smoothed the curls that rose in waves along her brow. "You must never speak of it again," I said. "At court, the walls have ears."

"I know," she said, fingering a piece of bread that she did not intend to eat. "My papa told me."

"You papa was right," I said. I could not bear to think of Louis, much less speak of him, so I changed the subject. "Shall we play a game?"

Alais' face lit like a sunrise, and the simple joy in her eyes pierced my heart. I wanted to clutch her to my breast, to ask if she had never been allowed to play at games in Paris. I suppressed this longing, and held myself very still until it passed.

I raised one hand, and my women brought forth my chessboard, the board I had not played on in years, since Henry left me for Rosamund. The pieces were finely wrought in gold and silver. I had brought them back in my retinue from the Holy Land. Louis had given them to me.

I had always meant to teach Richard to play, but while military strategy fired his mind as nothing else, he could rarely sit still long enough to indulge in a game with me. I missed my son, and my sickness for him pierced me. I looked at my new daughter.

"This is a chessboard," I told her.

Alais reached for the silver queen, but when I said the word "chess," she drew her hand back, as if the board had caught fire.

"That is an infidel game," she said. "My papa told me."

I almost laughed, but I saw the earnestness in her face, and I held my tongue. I picked up the gold queen from my side of the board, and fingered it lovingly. I thought of all the times my old lover Raymond and I had whiled away the hours, playing at this very board. No wonder Louis cursed the gift he himself had given me.

"Well," I said, "your papa is right. Arabs began this tradition. But it was a Christian knight who designed this board, and who cast these pieces for me."

"Has it been blessed?" Alais asked.

Again, I did not laugh at her. I knew of Louis' superstition, of his devotion to the Church. I could only imagine how much of that blind belief he had passed on to her. I knew, no matter how long it took, that I would cleanse her of religion. I would teach her to think.

In honor of future teachings, I swallowed a scathing reply. Instead, I lied. "Yes," I said. "My confessor blessed it yesterday."

Alais looked at me suspiciously. Though she saw the gleam of mirth in my eyes, she decided to trust me. She lifted the heavy silver queen, a piece so large it filled her palm. On the board of inlaid ivory and ebony, trimmed in gold and lapis, that queen stood three inches tall.

"She is beautiful," Alais said, all thought of infidels forgotten. She knew at once that the piece in her hand was a woman. She knew, without my having to tell her, that in this game it was not the king but the queen who ruled. Alais was the daughter of my soul before she ever knew it, a girl to match my mind as well as my spirit.

I set my own queen down, and she did the same. I raised my first pawn, and spoke. "Let us begin."

"I do not know how to play," she said.

I smiled as her clear maple eyes met mine. "I know, little princess. I shall teach you."

Chapter 3

⚭

ALAIS: A STOLEN SEASON

Abbey of St. Agnes, Bath
May 1169

I cannot tell you how I loved Eleanor. From the first moment I met her, I knew I would love her all my life.

Eleanor took me in and sheltered me when I had nothing and no one. The food I eat, the wine I drink, the way I bathe, even my strategies at chess, were all learned at her hands. She kept me with her for months when I first came to England, though she and the king had planned to send me to a nunnery to be raised by the sisters until the time came for my marriage to their son.

Eleanor kept me by her far longer than she was meant to. I believe that once I was with her, once we had found such kinship unlooked for, she did not want to let me go. Perhaps she hoped that King

Henry would simply forget that I had come, and she could keep me with her indefinitely.

During our time together, Eleanor taught me a little dancing, how to play a lute, how to smile graciously at fools. She taught me all these lessons and more.

Her hair was the color of burnished bronze where it peeped out from beneath her wimple. She let me brush it every night, after she sent her women away, when we were left alone. And always, from the first moment I saw her, I knew why my father once had loved her. For she was the most beautiful woman in the world.

It was her bones that held her beauty, the strong cheekbones and chin that were softened by her hair and the folds of her wimple and gown. Her slanted eyes were a deep green, and they flashed at me from the moment I met her, as if to say she knew me already.

Our stolen season could not last. I knew, even as a child, that it would not. The devil queen of my childhood fancies had long since vanished from my mind, to be replaced by Eleanor in all her power, her musical, wicked laugh, her way of seeing the world, so different from any other I had ever known.

The letter from the king came one day when she was teaching me a dance by the fire. The king wrote that it was time for me to go to the nunnery they had long since chosen for me; the abbess, Mother Sebastian, waited for me. Eleanor tossed his letter into the fire with a laugh and a contemptuous flick of her wrist, but I knew that she would have to let me go. For Henry was king. Even Eleanor could not stand against that. And I knew that she had stayed away from her lands in the south, for love of me. She would take her children and return there once I was tucked safe away in my abbey.

So that spring, in late May, Eleanor and I rode together in a litter to the Sisters of St. Agnes outside Bath. Those old Norman stones had stood a hundred years when I first knew them, and would stand a hundred more after I was gone. Eleanor spent that first night with me, her hand on my hair. I hoped that she might stay with me longer, but I knew she could not. Though she was my mother, elsewhere, she was queen.

So the next day we stood in the stone courtyard of that nunnery, Mother Sebastian waiting patiently while I took my leave. Eleanor was clothed from head to foot in emerald silk, her linen wimple white against the drab gray stone. I was dressed in the black wool of the nunnery. Already I missed the fine silk dresses that Eleanor once had given me, the dresses that now she was taking away with her. I could not wear such things in the house of God.

The queen drew me close, ignoring all the sisters who stood staring at us, and the men-at-arms who would take her back to her castle at Winchester. She knelt beside me there on those stones, and drew me close to her heart.

"I will come back for you, as soon as I am able." She kissed me, and drew a ribbon from the sleeve of her gown. She pressed the silk into my palm. "Take this, so that you have something pretty to remember me by."

She watched me, and I stood without weeping. She had taught me well; already I was strong enough to heed her.

"Good girl," she said, and kissed me. "Remember, you are a princess of France."

I stood in the courtyard and watched her litter disappear down the road that had no turning. I watched until she was too small to see any longer, vanished into the dust of the horizon. The Mother came to me then, and hugged me close, telling me that it was time for prayers.

I drew out my father's prayer beads, the only beautiful thing I still had with me. That and the silk ribbon from Eleanor's gown.

I slept with that ribbon clutched in my palm for a month, but as I settled into life at the nunnery, I laid it by. I used it during those years to bind the letters that Eleanor sent to me without fail, at Christmas, and on my saint's day.

My years at the nunnery were more peaceful than any I have known before or since. We were called to prayer each morning by the bell in the churchyard. The abbey did not ring many bells at once, as I was used to hearing at home in Paris. Instead we answered to the sweet, high sound of one bell echoing, like a woman's voice, calling us to God.

Our time was meted out to us by the sound of that one bell: time for mass, time to eat, time to pray. The abbess, Mother Sebastian, looked after me.

I lived with the nuns of the abbey, but their days were not my days. While the sisters worked, tutors saw me, closely chaperoned by the Mother in my rooms. Language instructors came to teach me Spanish, and a traveling priest came to teach me better Latin. Latin was the only language I had learned to read and write well, and I improved greatly under Father Anthony's tutelage. After a year he declared that he had no more to teach me, and he went away. So my only instruction in Latin after that came from the Mother herself.

When I passed twelve summers, the Mother took me into the simples garden and showed me how to tend the herbs and plants that lived there. She had given me all of her Church Latin, so now she taught me the names of plants, what they were good for, how some were aids in healing, and others aids in death.

There was a fountain in this garden, a small one that never ran dry. Sometimes when we were done working, the Mother and I would sit beside it, sipping cool, clear water from a dried gourd.

My favorite of all my work, what I loved more than the garden, more than prayer, was to sit in the small library and work with Sister Bernard on the illuminations.

We were a small house, but we had the queen's favor, so others who sought her favor as well would often send us requests for small books. They would ask for a woman's prayer book very rarely, or sometimes for a Gospel for a small church that had just received an endowment from the Crown.

It was considered odd for women to paint illuminations, but Sister Bernard had a gift, and what little she could teach of it, she gave to me.

The day I first found her painting, I gasped to see the colors take shape under her hands. She was working on a small book, its vellum old, scraped many times. But Sister Bernard worked as if the words she drew would last into eternity. Being the Word of God, I suppose they will, though not the ones drawn by her hand.

I watched her for hours, not returning to my rooms or even to the simples garden to meet the Mother. Mother Sebastian came to find me, and when she saw the look on my face, I did not have to ask permission to stay. She granted the requests she could, for I asked for very little.

So time was taken out of my day to work with Sister Bernard. At first, I could do only the calligraphy, for we could not risk the costly colors on my lessons. But even the Mother agreed that no one seeing the book when it was finished would be able to tell that it had not been written by a man.

After a few months, I was allowed to paint with color. Sister Bernard stood next to me by my high table and stool. We sat in full sunlight when we could and brought lamps when it was raining. We needed light for our work, as the rest of the nunnery did not.

I dipped my brush in the vermilion paint, and began the first word of the Gospel of Saint John. I felt as if the hand of God guided me, keeping me from any mistake. The first letter was done last, after the rest of the calligraphy had dried. It was a testament to the rest of the work, one that would draw the eye and bring the reader's mind to God. This was a simple Psalter, with no other illumination than the first letter of the first page. Some country squire had ordered it to further his place at court, and it was deemed a good book for me to begin on.

The Mother came to see the book after it had dried. Sister Bernard and I had worked on this one Psalter for months. We were sorry now that it was done and would go out into the world, away from us.

I stood by the Mother and looked down at my work. It seemed to me that it had been done by another. How could the hand of a princess, born only for marriage, draw even a shadow of the mind of God? The Mother answered this question for me, though I had not asked it out loud.

"Our gifts come through us from God, and go back to God from whence they came. We are only their keepers for a little while, sometime stewards of God's inward grace."

Sister Bernard nodded, and I found myself comforted. This Psalter, and every illumination I did after it, belonged to God. It was for me to let them go.

I was at the work of painting illuminations, on a day in my fourteenth spring, when the queen came back for me.

I sat at my high table, the sunlight warm on my hands. The light brought out the auburn hidden in the brown of my hair.

"You have grown beautiful, little princess. I would not have known you."

Eleanor stood in the doorway of the cloister garden, her eyes on me. Her bronze hair was hidden under her wimple, but I could see her green eyes glinting. She had not aged a day. It was as if she had prayed to the Virgin to stay ever youthful, ever beautiful, the better to hold all men in her sway.

I sat there, thinking these things, caught, as all men are, by the power of her eyes. Then she smiled at me, and she was the woman I remembered, the woman who had made me welcome when I had nothing, and no one. The child in me wanted to run to her, to feel her arms around me. But I was a woman now, and it had been almost three years since I had last seen her.

Then, too, as always, she was queen. The court manners I had mastered as soon as I learned to walk called to me from my childhood. Long ago, I had known when to bow and when to kneel, and had done so as thoughtlessly as I drew my next breath.

I laid my paintbrush down, knowing that I might never take it up again. Eleanor had come for me, and I must follow her. I had not come among my father's enemies to become a woman of God. I had come to marry, and to hold the English king to our treaty, if I could. I had come to give my life, and the lives of my children, to keep the fragile peace.

I climbed down from my stool gracefully, and curtsied to Eleanor.

The queen bent close to my table to better see my work. After looking at the parchment for a long time, Eleanor raised her head and stared at me.

"I did not know you had such work in you, Alais."

"Neither did I, Your Majesty. Until God showed me."

At the mention of God, Eleanor stepped away from my work-table. "I am glad that you have learned this art, Princess, but what of the other things I ordered you to learn? Do you practice your Latin and your Spanish?"

"Yes, Your Majesty."

I moved toward her, feeling her eyes on me as if they were hands, reaching out to trip me. I did not falter. I stood beside her in the sunlight and let her look her fill.

Eleanor took my chin in her hand and turned my face to the sunlight.

"You move well," she said, "though I would teach you different ways of walking. I did not send you here to make a nun of you, but a strong woman who will be the mother of my grandsons."

"Yes, Your Majesty."

She looked at my skin, at the youthful flawlessness of my complexion. I bathed my face in goats' milk once a day at the Mother's insistence. I had always thought it a foolish practice, but now, as I stood under the queen's scrutiny, I was glad that I had.

I stared into Eleanor's eyes, and wondered if she had become a stranger. It was then that she smiled at me, and I knew her once more.

"I missed you, Alais. More than you know."

Even then, I did not wrap my arms around her, but waited. I knew it was not my place. It was for her to bring me close, if she wished it.

Eleanor raised her jeweled hands. She took my face between her palms so that I could not look away.

"I will bring you to my son. But for as long as I can, I will keep you with me."

She kissed me then, and I clutched her as I had longed to do for all the years we had been apart. Eleanor held me close, her strength flowing into me, so that I felt truly myself once more for the first time since she went away.

Chapter 4

ॐ

ELEANOR: THE LARGER WORLD

Winchester Castle
May 1172

The first thing I did, once I took Alais out of that nunnery, was to arrange decent dress. I could not stand to see her in the rags they clothed her in. I thought I had been clear when I left her there, regarding what was due a princess of France. She was not there to take vows, after all, but to be held in safekeeping for me.

Well, Alais was safe, after all, and clothes could be changed. The first day I came to her, finding her dressed in those black rags, unevenly dyed, I had to make an effort to hold my tongue. I saw how much she loved the Reverend Mother, and how a harsh word from me to that old woman would hurt her. It was one of the first times I held my tongue for Alais' sake, and stayed my hand. It was not the last.

I held myself apart from her at first, to see what she was made of.

Though I loved her, and would always love her, until darkness took me from this earth, I did not tell her so. I watched her walk and stand in the sunlight. I met her gaze as she searched my cool green eyes.

She saw nothing of my feelings until I allowed her to, but my heart swelled at the sight of her, sitting there in the sunlight of that cloister garden. As she bent over a clerk's task, the vellum under her hand became something else, not a book to be read by fools, but a work of art. I stood looking over it a long while. I am not sure whom that prayer book was meant for; I had it bound and wrapped in silk. I took it away with me.

I do not read it, of course. Hearing the Gospel once, I found, was enough for me. I never listen to the words even when my women read them. But the paintings in that book were a miracle, so small that the largest one fit into the palm of my hand. Those paintings I look over every day. I marvel that the hand of a princess, meant only for what tasks men ordered her to, could make one of these. That first day, as I gazed down at those paintings, the brush still in her hand, I considered what other wonders lay within Alais, undreamt and unlooked for, but by me.

There were many things to be proud of in my daughter. Her newfound skill at painting was only one of them. She spoke low, her voice soft and resonant. When she laughed, I heard the siren song; it was music to bring men to their knees.

I knew when I first saw her that she would fit with my plan as smoothly as the next piece of a puzzle fits into its joints. For the child I had left behind me was gone as if she had never been. In that child's place stood a woman.

As I looked into the quiet depths of Alais' eyes, at first I wondered if by sending her to that forsaken place I had gotten only a beautiful nun out of her. I remembered well how she had clung to her father's religion when I left her there. I was thinking already of how to break her of it when she smiled.

That first smile was like a curtain lifting before an altar that hid precious things. I got a glimpse of heat beneath that smile, a sense of layers beyond the heat, and strength underlying that.

I thought of myself at the age of fifteen, how, even then, men had written songs in my honor. I thought of how my father had seen my strength and had left the duchy to me, when my male cousins would have taken up the Aquitaine, and gladly.

I saw that if I gave my son to this woman, she would know what to do with him. She was strong enough to hold Richard, even then.

Richard was a man for strong women, as his father had been before him. As indeed, his father still was, though Henry fought to deny himself, and lay down among fools. I took a sort of perverse satisfaction in the thought of Henry taking his first look at Alais, once I had her dressed from head to toe in silk again. It gave me pleasure to know that Henry, too, would fall under her spell, for he loved strong women, especially strong women who knew how to hold their tongues, and who knew also when to speak. Alais was such a woman.

Alais and I broke our journey to Winchester at an abbey also loyal to me. The abbot fawned on us, offering me his own rooms. Alais looked askance at those fine stone walls, with their brocade tapestries and their sconces of bronze. We ate off gold that night, and Alais was shocked to see such things in a house of God. She did not say so, for my sake, but even after the years we had been apart, I could read her eyes.

"Alais, surely you know by now that most religious houses are not like the one you come from," I said.

"No, Your Majesty. I did not know."

"Most royal abbeys are like this one. Full of gold plate, and tapestries, and beeswax candles."

"And fat abbots," she said, her smooth voice belying the glint in her eye.

I smiled at her. "Yes."

The knife she had been given was almost not sharp enough to spread butter on the bread, much less cut the meat. Soon she would have to tear the food with her teeth. I saw her annoyance and laughed, drawing another dagger from my sleeve. "Here, Alais, use this one. The monks did not give you a decent knife because they don't want you to assassinate me."

"I would as soon cut out my own heart."

I touched her cheek. "Well I know it. Do not trouble yourself over the assumptions fools make."

My acknowledgment that the abbot was a fool calmed her at once. She picked up the dagger I had given her, and started to eat.

I smiled, watching her devour her meat. The squab was good; in that house, the abbot's table was always well stocked, as anyone could tell from his ample belly. But I would have known that without seeing him, for I paid the abbey's bills. Such trifles were the foundation of my spy network. I was always amazed at how easy it was to buy a man's soul, and how cheap.

"You might be a spy for France, you see," I said, sipping my wine. "Your betrothal to my son might be a ruse. You might be here only to kill me."

"Why would they send a girl?" she asked.

I laughed, and though she smiled with me, I saw that she did not make a joke. She was not quite easy enough with me for that. Not yet.

"I do not think this, Alais. I only tell you what others think. Those who are not trained to kindness and obedience as you are."

Alais met my eyes when I said this, to see whether I teased her, which, of course, I did. Though kindness and obedience had been bred into her from birth, much more lay behind the maple brown of her eyes, and she and I both knew it. She smiled wryly, and the light in her eyes did not dim.

"You will find that the world is not the place you were told it was in the nunnery. Men are cruel, and women are their playthings."

"I am not afraid," the French princess said, all light of mirth going out of her eyes. Her strength was revealed to me then, unsheathed, like a weapon used in war. I knew she never dropped that mask before another, and I was gratified.

She looked away from me, her eyes cast down at her plate. She did not eat another bite, nor did she move, but sat frozen, as if waiting for an assassin's knife. I found myself holding my breath, taken in by her reverent silence, until she looked up once more at me.

"Where were you just now, Alais?"

"I'm sorry, Your Majesty. I was saying a prayer for my father, and for France."

I do not know what I expected. I myself had left her in a religious house, and one where the abbess had a true calling. Had I wanted to wean her from her father's religion, I would have done well to send her someplace else.

I would have her for my own, Louis and his religion be damned. But clearly I would not have her for myself that day. I would lay siege to her piety; I would find a breach in the wall, or perhaps a door. Piety was something I had never understood. In spite of my best efforts, and Henry's, it had taken root in Richard, too.

"It is kind of you to pray for Louis. No doubt he needs it," I said.

Two lay sisters came in then to clear away the plates, and a third to lead Alais to her room. I took my daughter's hand as she stood to leave me, and when she met my eyes, all thoughts of religion fled.

"The world is hard on women," I said. "You must prepare yourself."

For all her religious leanings, she was the girl I remembered, the girl whose strength had called to me from the first, my daughter in truth, grown now into a woman. Her strength shone out of her face, from the depths of her maple eyes, a light that surrounded me.

"I am ready," she said.

I could not bring myself to speak again, but I drew her close and kissed her. She did not cling to me, for as I have said, she was a woman already, but she seemed to know that I needed her touch. Alais held me until I rallied my own strength, and let her go.

When we arrived in Winchester the next day, Richard was there before me. I took joy in seeing his standard flying above my keep. I knew that soon I would give him a different standard, and he would be able to fly that as well, wherever he went.

Winchester gleamed white in the morning sun as we rode up before it. Though our litters were slow, I savored the time it took to reach the castle. The white palace rose on its hill like the city of Antioch, where I had first loved Raymond, so many years ago.

The castle of Winchester never failed to soothe my nerves, or to give me hope for the future. Always it reminded me of my youth, a time when everything seemed possible, and the love I had given up to keep the crown of France.

Raymond was long dead, and my marriage to Louis of France long over. As we rode into the keep at Winchester, I turned my mind from the past. Memories were like sirens; I might dash myself upon their rocks and sink beneath the waves. Better by far to live in the present, and to take what comes.

I set aside all thoughts of the past, and went to find Alais. I had given her rooms with a view of the rose garden. Fresh clean air came in from two tall windows, and the tapestries were well brushed, clean of dust. I wanted to make her welcome, to make her feel at home with me.

We had come to Winchester only an hour before, but I would not wait to call Richard to me, to introduce him to his fiancée. My son's early arrival was an omen, one that I would heed. I would make my move before my trunks were even unpacked. I had no religion but politics and the power it brought me. That day, I would worship in my own church, beneath my own god, and I would bring my son and my adopted daughter with me.

I would take action that day, moving finally in the direction I had planned months before. This move was risky, but risk was a part of the game of power, as was passion, and the ability to lead. These were all traits I excelled in; all reasons why Henry still loved me, in spite of

himself. Though Henry was in Anjou, I would make my move in
Winchester, and by sunset the next day, Henry would know of it.

I scratched at Alais' door and came in without waiting for leave,
followed by a retinue of ladies. Alais bowed, half-dressed in one of my
own gowns, which I had sent to her so that she might wear it to meet
my son. She had been looking out the window at the rose garden
below, and the laces were still undone, dangling from her hand.

My women saw at once that I had lent the princess my favorite
gown. I saw them take this in, exchanging glances. I thought for a moment that Angeline, the least discreet of my ladies, might even com-
ment, but her sister Mathilde laid a hand on her arm in warning, and
she said nothing.

I laughed to find Alais half-dressed, and reminded myself to send
a woman to see to her needs. I moved across the room at once, and
helped her lace her gown.

"Look, ladies, the flower of France has learned to dress herself
among the sisters."

I used my brittle, public voice, and Alais met my eyes. She smiled
wryly, making sure that my women could not see her do it. I would have
kissed her, but with half my court present, I simply tied up her gown.

The ladies laughed at my gibe even as I finished lacing her. Alais
could not care less what my women thought of her.

"Well, Alais, I have good news. You will be fitted for new gowns,
and the first just waits for the seamstress to take your measure. It will
be ready tomorrow."

"Thank you, Your Majesty."

"I have even better news today."

My ladies leaned in closer, though I still spoke in my public voice, which could have filled a room much larger than this one.

"This simple dress will have to do. Today Richard has come here to meet you."

My women laughed again to hear me call my own gown simple. Just as I had known it would, its deep emerald green went well with Alais' rich brown hair. I stepped back and took stock of her. Richard would no doubt be on his knees.

My ladies watched her, as if their eyes would drink her in. Alais stood as unruffled as a glassy lake, her calm rising from the depths of her soul. In the last day, I had realized that this calm did not come to her from Louis, or from me. I wondered who had given it to her. Perhaps it was her religion, or her mother, or something else altogether that I had yet to learn of. As well as I knew her, some facets of her heart were still a mystery to me.

She curtsied to me, her curls falling in a curtain to hide her face. "As you say, Your Majesty. I serve you in this, as in all things."

I almost laughed out loud that she would take a servant's tone with me. I would reprimand her later; I would remind her that whatever honor was due to me was due her as well. She was a princess of France.

"Very good," I said. "I will tell Richard that you are eager to meet him. We will all come together in the solar in an hour, if that suits you."

"As you wish, Your Majesty."

I saw only then that she was pale and frightened. I remembered that she had seen little of men in the nunnery I had sent her to. Only a few priests, and to call such milksops men was generous.

Beneath her fear, I saw her determination. Her strength would always outweigh her fear, and always conquer it. It had been many years since fear had touched my heart, but I remembered. I once had to face and conquer my fear, too.

If we had been alone, I would have said something to comfort her. But I had made the first meeting between the princess and my son a public matter, as it must be. I could show her no sympathy before my ladies. Always, especially in front of the court, I was queen.

My solar was full of women when Alais arrived, but none of them sewed or embroidered or gossiped, their usual pastimes in my keep. They watched the door, waiting for the princess. Richard stood beside me, fresh from the tiltyard, his chain mail visible beneath his tunic. I loved to see him dressed in armor, his red hair falling around his shoulders like a lion's mane.

My son was fifteen summers old, and towered over me, as Henry had the day I met him. His eyes were the same bright blue my father's had been, and they shone with love for me, just as my father's always had. His shoulders were broad, and the planes of his cheekbones high in his face, cheekbones that were so like mine. Alais would be pleased with his beauty, I had no doubt.

His power rose off him in waves, waves held back by a wall of protocol and honor. As I watched him, he took in the room and all the women in it, looking for ways to defend it, or ways to conquer it. It was my solar, a room built for women taking their leisure in times of peace. But always, Richard's mind was made for war.

Richard was like a lion in a room full of forbidden sheep, uncomfortable surrounded by so many women. I could see in his stance, in his utter stillness, that he would rather be anywhere but here. He would rather be outside in the fresh air, a man among men. The women's solar was a place he came only out of love for me.

Alais stepped into my rooms with only the one woman I had given to attend her. She moved with grace, and curtsied to me as she always did, the smoothness of her motion belying any fear I had seen when we were in her rooms. Her eyes were downcast, hiding even her strength. Her hair fell in long curls to her waist against the deep green of my silk gown.

I saw her in that moment as a man would see her, a fresh young thing just out of the nunnery, ripe for whatever pleasures a man might devise. Her breasts rose with her breath beneath the borrowed silk. The skirt of my gown had been drawn up in a leather belt worked in gold, so that the emerald ribbons of her shift showed at her ankles. She smelled sweet, like spring rain. Her cheeks were fresh and smooth, and only faintly tinged with a blush of pink.

Richard stared at her as if he had never seen a woman before, and I was gratified. All my work in raising and sheltering her had come to this moment, when she faced my son, with my blessing.

"Richard, this is your bride-to-be, the lovely Alais, Countess of the Vexin, and Princess of France."

Alais curtsied again, deeply, and Richard bowed back, courteous but distracted. As I watched, he tried to meet Alais' eyes, but the princess was inscrutable—the sphinx all men adore, and thrill to possess. I had been one myself, once upon a time. As amusing as it was to remember, I drew my mind to the here and now, and the move I was about to make in my constant game against Henry.

"Alais, this is my son Richard, Prince of England and Duke of Aquitaine."

My women gasped, and I felt Richard tense beside me. I had just announced that I was giving the duchy of the Aquitaine not to my eldest son, as Henry would wish, but to Richard.

Richard was shocked, but knew that Alais did not fully understand the significance of what I had just done. I saw that he thought only of the princess, of putting her at ease as best he could. He was a man of courtesy always, as I had raised him to be. His blue eyes met hers as he bowed once more. "It is my honor, Princess. Welcome to England."

They smiled at each other, and it was as if the duchy of my fathers, the land my family had held unbroken for generations, was as nothing to Richard, and the princess, everything. Even while I understood why Richard had done it, jealousy rose in me, as green as the gown Alais wore. I fought it down, and almost won.

I waved my hand. "Thank you, Alais. That will be all."

She curtsied to me, not offended that I had dismissed her like a servant. Her glacial calm was in place once more, but for her eyes. She drew her gaze from Richard's reluctantly and moved to go, with her woman beside her.

At the door, Alais turned back. Richard still was watching her. The bitter taste of dread joined the sour tang of jealousy in my mouth. I was surprised to taste it.

I loved both my son and Alais. I wanted them to make a good match; with it, they would shore up my power. With the two of them holding the Vexin as a wedge between France and Normandy, and with Richard as duke in the Aquitaine, my position would be stronger, no matter what passed between myself and Henry in the future.

But something in their eyes gave me pause. More than that, something in their shared gaze frightened me, an emotion so alien to my being that I barely recognized it. But I saw that they looked at each other almost as Henry had once looked at me, the day we first met.

I raised one hand. My women retreated at once, closing the door behind them, shutting Alais out. My son and I were left alone.

"Richard." My low voice caught his attention. I touched his arm, and drew him with me toward the window.

A light breeze moved my hair against my cheek. As I watched, Alais' face faded from his mind, and he remembered. I had gifted him with the Aquitaine.

The Aquitaine and my father's castle at Poitiers were the only true homes Richard had ever known. He had learned there at my side, through all the sunlit summers of his childhood, what it meant to be a man of war and of poetry combined. I had given him more than just a political gift when I handed him my father's duchy, and he knew it.

"Mother, I am in your debt."

Richard knelt to me there in the sunlight, as if swearing fealty. He kissed the emerald ring on my hand, as if I were his bishop. His hair was like burnished bronze, less red in that light, less like Henry's, and more like mine. I wanted to kneel with him, to draw him to his feet, but I knew that I could not. Alais had made her impression; now I must make mine. I must bind him to me with yet another thread of gold.

I let him hold my hand in his great one. I raised the other, pressing my palm to his crown in blessing.

"Richard, rise. There is no need for such demonstrations between us."

He stood, and drew me close. I allowed myself the weakness of leaning against him.

"I love you, Mother. And not for the Aquitaine."

I turned from him, and drew my handkerchief from my sleeve. I pushed away all strong emotion, for it never served me.

In spite of my joy in giving the Aquitaine to my favorite son, I knew that the ceremony three years before that had acknowledged Richard as the future duke would not be enough. That treaty had been drawn between Henry and Louis of France, stating that Richard would one day be given the duchy of the Aquitaine. The same treaty arranged Richard's betrothal, and brought Alais to me.

That agreement had been made and oaths sworn; three years later, Henry still held the land. I knew Henry thought to ignore the oath he had taken as if it had never been. He wanted to give our eldest, Henry the Younger, the Aquitaine as he had already given him Normandy. Louis of France was weak, and could do nothing to make the treaty hold, even though his daughter Alais stood to gain from it with her marriage to my son. Richard would have to take the Aquitaine now and hold it against his father.

"Even now, Richard, a rider has gone to Henry, who is with your brother Geoffrey in Anjou. The king will be at Windsor in less than two weeks' time."

"I know."

"Henry will stop off to see Rosamund, that woman he values so highly."

Blood rose in his face at the sound of our old enemy's name. Not because she was the king's mistress; it was Henry's right to take lovers where he would. Richard hated that woman, as I did, because Henry loved her beyond all reason. She had taken what was mine, Henry's genuine affection; he had never loved me the same way since he first laid eyes on her.

Richard did not spit, but I saw the desire to do so cross his face. This sign of spleen made me smile once more; it was yet another proof of my beloved son's loyalty. All thought of Princess Alais was banished from the room.

"So we will have time to send word to Louis, and to make plans for your official investiture as duke in Aquitaine. A ceremony in Limoges to seal the beginning that we made three years ago."

"The king will not be pleased."

"No. Henry will be furious. You must be cautious. We will tell him simply that we thought it understood that once you were old enough to defend it, you would take your inheritance in hand. King Louis will agree with us, with his daughter promised to you, and your father will be forced to concede."

Henry had never made a concession in his life, which was why he was still king. My son knew this, as well as I.

"Or he will not," Richard said.

I smiled my cat smile, relishing the thought of combat with Henry on open ground.

Henry and I had been separated for years, ever since he had first taken Rosamund to his bed. We had met a few times for politics' sake, and for some holy days, but even at those times, Henry had not shared my bed. He had taken many women over the last few years, but he had loved only her. The thought of that woman still rankled, even now. I set it aside. I would forget her, and deal only with Henry.

"We will cross that bridge when we come to it. For now, you will make ready to leave for the Aquitaine in two days' time. I have already sent word to the bishop in Limoges. He will be ready to receive you."

I knew that, in this, Richard would obey me. He would go to my holdings in the south and swear the final oath making him duke, with Louis of France as his witness. Once he had taken possession of the Aquitaine, even Henry would not be strong enough to wrest it from him.

I stepped close to my son and laid my hand against his cheek. My confidence drew him to me and held him, as it always did, as it had always done, no matter who else was in the room.

"Trust to me, Richard. I have all in hand."

Chapter 5

ॐ

ALAIS: PRINCE AND TROUBADOUR

Winchester Castle
May 1172

On my first day in Eleanor's court, she made me welcome but kept her distance, as if to avoid encouraging her ladies-in-waiting to envy. I saw behind her eyes that she loved me, even as she dressed me with her own hands, in her own gown. It was made of emerald silk, the finest dress I had ever worn in my life. My shifts were all plain convent wear, and Eleanor would not rest until she had had her seamstress sew a ribbon of emerald silk around the hem of the shift I wore.

Eleanor made a brief show of presenting her women to me, each in their turn. They were all beautiful, and all only a few years older than myself, save for Eleanor's chief woman, Amaria, who was of an age with the queen. They left with Eleanor almost as soon as they came in, and I was left alone to take in the beauty of my rooms by myself.

The bedchamber had wide windows that looked down over a rose garden. The flowers had begun to bloom early, and I took in the scent of their perfume. There was a dressing room with a fine clothes-press, though as yet I had no gowns to place in it.

The tapestries on the walls were old but well brushed, and the bedstead was large, its rosewood posts carved with trailing flowers. I fingered the carving, and felt the polish of the years beneath my fingertips. The bedstead, too, was old, but it had been cherished, just as Eleanor cherished me.

I had little time to admire my rooms or the gown the queen lent me, for her lady-in-waiting came for me almost at once, and took me in to meet the prince.

Marie Helene, one of Eleanor's ladies who had not been presented to me before, was a quiet woman, always watchful, a woman who thought long before she spoke. She reminded me of my father in that, though in no other way.

Her hair was a soft blond, like wheat when it first turns from green to gold. Her hair was as fine as silk, and she often kept it hidden beneath a wimple. Her blue eyes were bright but steady. Marie Helene was worldly enough to see deception in others, but she did not lie herself. She never lied to me.

The day I met her, Marie Helene curtsied to me with as much respect as if I were married to her prince already. She honored me from the first.

As young as I was, I saw her good sense shining out of her eyes. She saw me fiddling with my borrowed gown, for I was six inches shorter than Eleanor, and the hem dragged the floor.

"May I help, Your Highness?"

I smiled at her soft tone of diffidence; it was clear that she did not
want to overreach herself, and offend me. This evidence of reserve, the
only such I was to see in Eleanor's court, pleased me, as it was tinged
so heavily with respect.

"Yes."

I stood still under her capable hands. Marie Helene drew my
skirt up and tucked it into the belt I wore so that the ribbon on my shift
showed beneath the emerald of the gown.

"Thank you," I said. "I have no clothes of my own."

"You will." Her blue eyes met mine, and I saw her kindness as
well as her restraint. "The queen will see to that. I have heard her
speak of it already."

"Is it time to meet the prince?" I asked.

She hesitated, as if afraid to frighten me. "It is."

I smoothed the silk of my borrowed gown. "I am ready."

I remember little of my first meeting with Richard. Eleanor's ladies
were there as witnesses, and Marie Helene stood waiting for me by
the door. Beyond that, I remember fragments. Only that the sunlight
came in from behind him, and touched his red hair with gold. And
that his eyes were the deep blue of France, so that I felt I had come
home when I looked into them.

We barely spoke, and the prince was as courteous as I could
have hoped for. Behind his eyes, I saw his joy in me and in my beauty,
and I felt the same joy at the sight of him. I remember the tone of his
voice, if not his words, as he welcomed me.

The queen called us together to announce that Richard was taking on the duchy of the Aquitaine in his own right. No sooner had she made this announcement than I was dismissed, and her seven ladies with me. I saw from her eyes that she wished to take counsel with her son. I turned back at the door to look at him once more, and caught Eleanor watching him, and me.

I reminded myself of my duty and followed Marie Helene back to my rooms. I looked down at the rose garden below, wishing I might walk in it, but I stayed in my room, and waited on the queen. I knew that, before long, she would call me to her.

Later that afternoon, when I came into the queen's rooms with Marie Helene at my side, all her ladies were in place once more. I saw that they were celebrating Richard's rise to the duchy, but Richard himself was nowhere to be seen.

As soon as I came in, Eleanor rose from her chair and smiled, crossing the room to meet me. Her ladies saw this sign of favor, and stopped their conversations, turning instead to look at me.

I curtsied and Eleanor helped me rise, her hands on mine. I caught the sight of Angeline's resentment, her jealousy clouding the blue of her eyes. I remembered her name from the time I had met her briefly in my own rooms. I had no doubt in that moment that she had been the favored lady before I first came to Eleanor's court.

"Alais, you are welcome to this place."

The queen kissed me. The silence deepened, so that birdsong could be heard beyond the windows.

"Thank you, Your Majesty."

"Have you eaten? There is fruit here, and bread."

"Fruit would be welcome. I thank you."

Eleanor drew me with her across the room. At a gesture from her,

Mathilde, Angeline's sister, rose and offered me her chair. She was better at hiding her jealousy, and managed to smile at me. I sat at once, and the queen sat beside me, while fruit was brought to the table between us, and fresh wine.

Eleanor offered me a goblet from her own hand. I sipped the wine, and found it fresh and sweet, with a hint of the flavor of pears. The cup I held was cast in gold, and glinted in the afternoon sunlight. This room was her solar, and there were windows to the west as well as to the east, so that the sun always fell within those walls, and warmed them.

I looked around at the queen's ladies, all of whom had taken up their embroidery once more, and were talking among themselves, though I saw that they still cast their eyes on me. They noticed the high favor the queen showed me, and wondered at it. I knew that Eleanor liked to keep her women, and all those around her, guessing. Though this public welcome was gratifying, it was calculated. Our real time together would come later, when we were alone.

"I would have my troubadour sing for you, Princess, if you are willing to hear him."

"It would be my honor, Your Majesty."

"No, indeed, little princess, it will be his."

Amaria, the chief of Eleanor's ladies, called for Bertrand, and when he stepped into the room, there was a flurry among the women. Angeline and Mathilde, both blond and fair, turned bright pink at the sight of him. The girls rose at once, straightening their gowns and simpering. The voices of all the women rose in pitch, as did their laughter. The man was young and as tall as Richard was, but not as beautiful. He bowed first to the queen, and then to me, before casting his eyes upon the ladies.

As I watched, they fawned on him. If I had not known the queen's ladies to be virtuous, I would have thought a lascivious glance passed between Bertrand and more than one of the queen's waiting women. I raised an eyebrow, only to find Eleanor watching me, a sardonic smile on her face.

She was offering her women up in all their foolishness, for me to laugh at. I swallowed my mirth, but my eyes still sparkled. My suppressed mirth was enough to soothe Eleanor's need for mischief, for she turned at once to Bertrand, and called for a song.

He bowed low, his hose displaying his leg to advantage. Convent-bred as I was, even I noticed the fine line of his thigh in his rose-colored hose. He caught me looking and winked, and I laughed in spite of myself.

"The princess has not heard enough music, locked away in her nunnery. Play something for her now."

Bertrand might have amused himself by smiling at me, but he knew where his duty lay. He strummed his lute, all sign of laughter gone, and sang a song for the queen that was so beautiful, it brought tears to my eyes.

He sang of beauty that endured forever, and of a queen that held all men under her sway. His voice wove a spell over me, and over all the women there. I knew that he was desired not only for his fine leg but for his voice, and the spell it cast.

When he was done, the queen applauded him, and her women followed suit. I clapped as well, a beat late, for I had to wipe tears from my eyes.

Eleanor, always one to chastise me for weeping, reached out and took my hand. She pressed a handkerchief embroidered with her crest

into my palm. She drew it from her sleeve with a flourish, so that all
her court ladies could see. This sign of favor granted to me, she turned
to Bertrand, her public voice ringing in the room like the peal of a
bell.

"You have moved us all to tears, Bertrand, and given me much
pleasure."

"Your Majesty, the pleasure is all mine."

Eleanor's smile turned wicked. "Indeed, Bertrand, that is not what
my ladies tell me."

Laughter filled the room. As I watched, Mathilde and Angeline
blushed, and a few others raised their hands to their cheeks, or to their
mouths, to cover their laughter. Bertrand said nothing, but took the warm
laughter as yet more applause, and bowed once more to the queen.

Shocked, I met Eleanor's glance, and she smiled at me. I realized
that she meant to tell me that her troubadour sampled the favors of
her women, and she approved.

I knew little of the pleasures of love. The Reverend Mother in
the abbey had instructed me on my duties in my marriage to the
prince. Now that I had seen Richard, I hoped that those duties would
be sweet. But the queen's women were not married to her troubadour,
and some were not married at all.

I saw that adultery and lasciviousness were things that Eleanor
winked at among her women, but I knew she would not wink at them
in me. She sought to teach me this, as she sought to teach me everything. While these women might sport with lowborn chanteurs, she
and I could not.

I set aside my maiden modesty, and looked once more on the
troubadour. He had risen from his bow under the gaze of all those

women. While he smiled at them boldly, he had the courtesy not to turn his gaze on me.

"Ladies, I find myself growing tired," Eleanor said. "Please leave me. I will see you all in the great hall for this evening's feast."

Her women rose, some still laughing, and as one they bowed to her. Amaria, Eleanor's chief lady-in-waiting, made a gesture, and the other women filed out, as orderly as the nuns in the abbey I came from, and I saw once more the queen's power. Eleanor held these women with such authority that they did her least bidding without question, without hesitation.

I thought to go as well, but she held me there, her hand on mine. Bertrand bowed to her, but when she raised one hand, he stayed.

Marie Helene met my eyes across the room. She was the last lady to leave, and she caught my gaze before drawing the door closed behind her.

"Do you like the woman I have asked to attend you?" Eleanor asked once we were alone.

"Yes, Your Majesty. I thank you. She has taken very good care of me."

"As she should. Very well, then. I will let you keep her."

"Thank you, Your Majesty."

I glanced at Bertrand. He had taken a stool along the far wall, a simple stool that one of the ladies had abandoned in her flight. He did not look at us or seem to listen as we spoke. He simply strummed his lute quietly, his soothing music underlying our talk.

Eleanor did not heed him, so I did not. In this, as in all things, I took my cue from her.

"Do you like your gown?" Eleanor asked.

Of their own accord, my hands moved down to the skirt of my dress, to the smooth emerald silk. I ran my fingers over its softness. "It is the most beautiful dress I have ever worn," I said.

"It is my favorite."

I had been fitted for my own gowns in my room, before Eleanor called me to sit among her ladies. The seamstress had assured me that I would have at least one of my new dresses the next day, though how any woman could work so fast, I could not comprehend.

"You will have your own tomorrow. For now, you will have to make do with mine."

"It is my honor, Eleanor."

The troubadour, whom I had almost forgotten, stopped strumming in midnote, and the silence held for a full beat before he resumed his music once more. Later I learned that he was shocked into silence; no one else used her given name, save perhaps the king.

"My father chose my name, you know," was all she said. "In the langue d'oc, it is Aliénor. The only name I ever heard spoken before I moved to Paris."

"Before you married my father," I said.

"Yes. Louis could not say 'Aliénor,' so 'Eleanor' it has been ever since."

"I am sorry."

"You will find, little princess, that with marriage a woman often loses more than just her name. You would do well to heed it."

"Richard would take nothing from me," I said.

Eleanor's eyes sharpened, and her gaze held mine. "Richard is a good man, but always remember that he is a man. You like him, do you?"

"I am honored to marry so fine a prince."

She must have seen something in my eyes, or heard the joy in my voice, for her face softened. She loved him well. "I am glad that you are matched," she said. "You will make beautiful children."

"I hope to give him many sons," I said, my eyes cast down.

Eleanor raised my chin so that I was forced to meet her gaze. I remembered that though it was proper for a nun to keep her eyes on the ground, a princess must face the world. Eleanor had taught me that. I would not shrink from her again.

It seemed that she would speak of Richard, and our many sons, but instead she said, "You are a brave girl. I am proud of you."

Her unexpected praise warmed me more than mulled wine. My heart swelled with my next breath, but I did not weep. Eleanor had taught me that, too.

"Shall we have another song before we go down to dinner?" she asked.

"I would sing one for you," I said.

Eleanor's eyes widened. "Such talent, little princess. How is it that I did not know of it?"

"It is a small gift, but I would give it to you."

"You must never hide your talents, Alais. Only your failings."

I smiled wryly, my eyes sparkling. "But, my lady queen, I have none."

Eleanor laughed at that, as I had meant her to. I sang for her a sweet song my nurse had taught me at home in Paris, before I was sent away.

The queen then honored me by taking me down to the great hall herself, her hand on my arm. All the court bowed to us as we passed, and parted before us as we strode to the dais, where the high table stood. Richard sat at the head of the table already. He stood when he saw us, and bowed as the others did.

I ignored the people below the dais, but to Richard, I offered a curtsy.

"Welcome, Mother. Princess Alais."

His voice thickened a little when he spoke my name. I met his eyes, and saw warmth in their blue depths as well as his honor for me.

"Good evening, Richard." Eleanor raised her cheek for his kiss. "It is good to have my son here before me, to welcome me to my own table."

"It is good to sit with you once more, Mother. There is no gracious spot in England unless you are there."

Eleanor laughed and leaned close to me. "You see, Alais, he will charm you before you know it."

"He already has, Your Majesty."

I spoke low, my tone soft, but my bold words shocked him. Richard almost turned from me, but managed not to. A hot blush crept up his cheeks, and into his red gold hair. For the first time, I was reminded that he was only fifteen.

Eleanor laughed again, and I sat in the chair that Richard drew out for me. Unlike my father's court, where all but the king sat on benches, everyone at Eleanor's high table had a chair and cushions. I sank into this luxury, grateful that I was no longer eating on a bench in the nunnery, listening in silence while the Word of God was read aloud. I loved the Scripture, but in Eleanor's court, I had already learned that I loved music more.

Eleanor sat beside me, and Richard took the chair on her left hand. He set about cutting meat for both of us, and was as gracious and charming as any man I have ever known. He spoke of the company, and of how the court was glad to welcome me among them. I knew that Eleanor's ladies were not particularly pleased that I was there, as she forced them all to give precedence to me, but I did not correct him.

The queen knew my thoughts without my voicing them. She smiled her wicked smile, and changed the subject to the duchy of the Aquitaine, and of how Richard would be a credit to her there.

I did not listen close to this talk, for the meat was good, and still hot from the spit. I had not eaten much meat in the nunnery, only at Christmas and at Easter. The venison was succulent, its juices threatening to drip down into my borrowed sleeve. As I licked my fingers, I found Richard staring at me.

Eleanor tapped my hand, offering a bit of meat from her own knife. Though she smiled, her eyes were cool, her thoughts shuttered so that I could not guess at them.

Before I could wonder at the sudden change in her demeanor, Richard rose from his place. He laid his hand on Eleanor's arm, and kissed her. "With your permission, Mother," he said, his low voice courteous.

She waved her hand without answering him, which Richard took for assent. I watched her, though, and wondered if he was right.

I heard the strum of a lute and I turned, surprised, for the fruit had not yet been brought out. We were still eating the meat.

Mother Sebastian had taught me the manners of the court, as she had known that one day I would go there. She told me quite clearly that no musician came into the hall until the fruit had been served.

I met Richard's eyes, where he stood at the edge of the dais. I felt the warmth of his gaze on my skin. Perhaps there were different rules in Aquitaine, and Eleanor had brought them to her own court at Winchester.

The hall fell silent as soon as it was seen that it was the prince who stood to sing and not a troubadour. Even the simpering women at the queen's table stopped their gossiping.

Richard looked to his mother as if for permission again, and Eleanor bowed her head. The hall filled with applause at once, the polite applause that was required when a prince stood to raise his voice in song. Such a thing would never have happened in my father's court. Even as a child, Philippe Auguste would sooner have cast himself into the fire than raise a song in company.

I leaned back against the cushion of my chair. I was shocked when the prince took up the lute himself.

"I would sing for my betrothed, if you would indulge me."

I felt all the eyes in the hall on me then, but I did not heed them. I kept my gaze on Richard's face. My breath lodged in my chest, and I thought I would not draw another.

Richard's voice was sweet, the sweetest I had ever heard. A true silence fell over that hall as he sang. The nattering women and loose-moraled men stopped dead in their talk, and not because Richard was prince. When Richard sang, even those people could not turn away.

The song he sang for me was in the langue d'oc, the language spoken in the Aquitaine. I could make out only one word in three, but I knew that he sang of love.

When his song was done, Richard fell silent, and his hand drew out one last note on his lute. That note filled the hall, and hung there, mesmerizing all of us, so that we forgot to move.

Then he bowed, his eyes seeking mine. I wiped my tears away with the kerchief Eleanor had given me, the soft linen cloth that bore her crest. Richard did not smile, for the moment between us was too solemn for that. Instead, he turned to the queen, and smiled on her.

Eleanor led the applause. In spite of my tears, I had the sense enough to join it.

"My son," the queen said. "You surpass us all in honor."

Richard bowed once more before taking his place beside her. He did not look at me again.

"You see, Alais, I do not lie. My son will turn your head, before you even know he's done it."

Richard, who had stood before all the court and sung from his heart, blushed now to hear his mother speak of him to me.

"He has already done so, Your Majesty."

Eleanor turned from Richard, and looked at me. "So I see, little princess. So I see."

That night I dreamt of Richard's song. His voice followed me into my dreams, so that even as I woke, the last note of his song was still with me. It made my sleep sweet, and my heart light, to know that such a man had been chosen for me by God.

But when I looked to Marie Helene in the morning to bring my breakfast and to laugh with me over the cattiness of the queen's ladies, especially Angeline, Marie Helene could not speak. Her throat had closed up overnight with a swift cold that she assured me with croaks would soon fade. I sent for teas to soothe her, but the water the servants brought was lukewarm, and the tea only some valerian root from the simples garden.

Since my own gowns had not yet come, I drew on Eleanor's beautiful emerald silk once more, and set out to find the simples garden myself. I knew enough of herb lore from my time in the nunnery to help my friend.

For such a large castle, Winchester had very few servants. Or perhaps, more likely, they simply saw me coming and ducked out of my way. It took me almost an hour to find a door that led out into the sunshine of the morning.

When I stepped outside, instead of the kitchen garden, I came upon roses in the center of a walled courtyard. It was a small garden, the same garden I could see from the window in my room. Though surrounded on all sides by stone and damp, there was enough sunlight for a few hours a day for the roses to flourish, red ones, and pink ones, and even some roses of white.

I marveled at how such beauty could grow in the midst of such dark confinement.

I stood among the flowers, breathing in the scent of their perfume. Most were open, though spring had not yet turned to summer. I lifted my face to the sky, to take in the rays of sun that came down over the high walls.

Richard found me there, when my thoughts were turned on nothing but the way the warm sunlight felt on my face.

"Good day," he said.

Richard stood just a few feet away from me. Either he was very

quiet when he moved, or my thoughts had been far away, for I never
heard him until he spoke.

"God be with you," I said. The warmth of my dreams came upon
me then, and the joy he had brought me with his music.

His blue eyes met mine, and it seemed he, too, was remembering
his song. I savored Richard's tall, proud grace, the way his stance spoke
of who he was and what he was born to. It was a pity that he was a
younger son, and would never be king.

"Where is your waiting woman?" he asked.

I thought of Marie Helene, alone in my bed. I realized then that
I should have called another of the queen's women to walk with me.
A princess could not walk alone unencumbered.

"She is in bed," I said. "Her throat is sore."

Richard did not chide me for my folly in walking alone, though
he had the most to lose if I was accosted. He nodded and said
nothing.

The warmth between us was still there, as it had been the night
before, but now, as we stood alone with no one else watching, he was
too shy to speak. So I spoke for both of us.

"I am looking for the simples garden," I said. "I must make Marie
Helene a tisane to help her throat heal."

He smiled at this, thinking that surely I knew nothing useful,
nothing that could heal another. It also seemed to amuse him that I
was out of my rooms, in service of my waiting woman. But Marie
Helene was my friend, my only friend besides the queen at this court.
I would not watch her suffer and do nothing.

"I know of the simples garden," he said. "I can take you there."

The sun on the roses made their petals look like velvet. I thought to take a flower with me, my fingertips brushing the petals of one red rose. In the end, the stem was too thick for me to break, and I left the rose in the sun. I promised myself that I would come back, and look at them again.

Richard led me back into the castle keep, and as we walked together, he shortened his strides to mine. "You seem to have a care for your servants," Richard said.

"I have never had a waiting woman before, not one that was all my own. I had a nurse in France."

I thought of Katherine, of her sweet smile and warm hands. "But she was responsible for me."

"And you feel responsible for your woman here," he said, as if to finish my thought.

"Yes. Marie Helene is in my charge, for however long she serves me. I cannot leave her to suffer."

"You could call for a new lady to wait on you," Richard said. "My mother would give you one."

"I would not turn Marie Helene away. She is my friend."

"It is good to have a friend in a new place," he said.

I saw his loneliness then, and it called to the loneliness within me. Just as I had been alone all my life, sent to marry among my father's enemies to serve the throne of France, so had Richard been alone, except when his mother was with him. He, too, served as I did. He worked always for the good of Eleanor, placing her needs and the needs of the duchy of Aquitaine above his own.

He met my eyes then, and I did not look away. Our gazes held, and he seemed to see behind my eyes into my thoughts. I felt, in that brief, blessed moment, that he understood me. Since I was a child, I had known that I must marry this man, and part of me had feared it. Now I saw that we might build something together, something that politics and all its harsh necessity could not touch. Together, we might build a home, and find some peace amid the constant furor of royal courts, with their backbiting and their shadows. Together, we might love each other as a man and woman, not as a prince and princess.

Richard took my hand, and held it in his own. "My mother is also your friend, as I am."

I did not know what to say, for my breath had gone. Tears rose to my eyes unbidden, though Eleanor had taught me never to cry. But my heart wept at the thought of finding a haven in my new life, a haven with my husband; my eyes wept, too.

Richard stood beside me, my hand in his. He did not speak of my tears, and I felt that to him they did me honor. He reached down and wiped them away gently with one large finger. The sweetness of the gesture moved me more than anything else he might have done. I wiped my eyes with my free hand, and I smiled.

"Eleanor has been like a mother to me," I said. "All I am, all I will ever be, I owe to her."

His smile lit his face, as if dawn had broken over a plain of darkness.

"It is so with me as well," he said. "In all the dark places of my childhood, my mother was the only light. My music, my poetry, even my prowess in war, all were gifts from her hands."

I knew this was an admission that he would never have given to anyone else. Anyone else would have questioned that: a woman giving a man the gift of war. But I knew what he meant, for even in my cloister, I had heard of Richard's heroism in war. He meant that Eleanor had taught him the art of war by teaching him to nurture art within his soul. His music, his poetry, and his flair for battle, all came from the same place, the creative fount that Eleanor had nurtured, as she had left me nurtured in the Abbey of St. Agnes. Nowhere else would a woman have been taught to paint as I had been. No other nunnery would have allowed it. Always, Eleanor gave the best to those she best loved, holding nothing back.

We walked on, and I felt close to him, closer than I had felt to anyone but Eleanor in many years. I thanked God once more that He had seen fit to give me this man as a haven for the rest of my life.

We came to a part of the castle where people were stirring. As we passed, people bowed to Richard, then looked twice when they saw me. Some did not even think to bow, but stared. Richard did not acknowledge any of them except to nod to a few, the ones who were high ranking, the ones he could not ignore.

He spoke to none of them, but dropped my hand as he led me to another door. This one opened onto a much larger courtyard. I could see the buttery in the distance, and somewhere I heard a wheel turning, drawing water from a well.

Richard bowed to me in the middle of a simples garden that was not much larger than the one at the abbey. Winchester was a royal palace, as well as the bishop's seat, but it was not as large as my father's palace in Paris. No one else was in the garden, though I could hear women working in the kitchen not far away.

"I will leave you here," he said, his face closed to me. The easiness between us had fled. We had started gossip by walking in public unescorted, and he did not like it. For me, he had broken every rule of the honor we had both been raised to. Behind his displeasure at the talk we had started, I saw in his eyes that he wanted us to build our own alliance, a love born from our common loneliness. Richard hoped that we might make our own rules, and be a haven for each other.

"I must thank you." I touched his arm. "I would not have found this place without you."

His face softened, and the shutters fell from his eyes. Before he could speak again, Marie Helene found me, her wimple askew where she had drawn it on by herself.

"Your Highness, where have you been?" she asked. "When you did not come back, I was worried, my lady."

"You see, my lord," I said. "She is my friend who fears for me, so much that she would scold me in front of my betrothed."

"It is a good friend who will scold you, though you are a princess. Keep her by you always, for friends like that are rare."

We stood looking at each other, Marie Helene forgotten until she cleared her throat.

Richard bowed to us, and we curtsied. "I hope to see you again," he said to me, lowering his voice slightly, as if to give us privacy that we no longer had.

"I fear you will have to, my lord."

I quirked an eyebrow at him, and he laughed. "Yes. Well, it is a charge I would not turn from."

"Nor I."

Marie Helene stiffened, but neither of us heeded her.

As we stood together, Richard's page came running to us. He bowed first to me, then knelt to Richard on the damp ground. Richard smiled, his face softening still further at the sight of the boy. He touched the crown of the boy's head, and the page rose to his feet.

"My lord prince, the queen calls for you to go on a hunt."

The child invoked Eleanor as if she were a pagan goddess come down to earth. I hid my smile. I had always loved her. My awe had been married to my love. With others, she was always above them, beyond their reach.

Richard turned to me. "Shall we ride out, my lady?"

I had never been on horseback in my life. I ate meat, but never had I seen it dressed or killed. But I would not let them leave me behind.

"I would love to, my lord prince."

We left the garden then, trailing behind Richard's page, who ran ahead like the child he still was. I remembered to take up herbs for Marie Helene, and when I returned to my rooms to dress in a new gown that the seamstress now had ready for me, I found steaming water waiting, so that I might brew Marie Helene's tea. No doubt Richard had spoken to someone, and had seen it done, before I could ring the bell myself. His kindness touched me, as had the deep blue of his eyes.

I dressed in royal blue, and wrapped a new leather belt around my waist. I would ride out on horseback for the first time in my life, with Richard beside me.

Chapter 6

ॐ

ELEANOR: A BALANCE OF POWER

Winchester Castle
May 1172

"Your Majesty," my spy said. "There is news."

I suppressed my smile, for he would not have sought me out otherwise. My women were already dismissed. I raised a bell to call Richard's page to me, that he might deliver a message of my own. I lowered my hand, and the bell stayed silent on its stand.

My man knew better than to keep me waiting.

"Your Majesty, the prince has been seen in the rose garden."

Why this was deemed important by the network of men I kept was beyond me. I held my patience, and waited to see if this was a fool's errand, or if something was afoot.

"The princess is with him," he said.

I did not respond, but took this information in. I remembered how Richard and Alais had watched each other the night before, how he had sung to her in front of the court, as he once would have done for me. It was as if my son had never seen a woman before, as if his other lovers had never existed for him. I, of course, knew better.

When I did not speak, my man's voice went on, low in my ear. "He was with the Princess Alais, Your Majesty. And in the kitchen garden, too."

I laughed out loud at that, the thought of my son following a skirt into the bowels of the servants' quarters. My man looked shocked at my levity, and I calmed myself. Fools very seldom laugh, and they seldom tolerate laughter in others. I did not pay this man for his mind, but for his information.

"I thank you," I said.

He blushed, and lowered his head almost to the floor in supplication. I never offered thanks to my men, only gold. He knew then how valuable his information was to me, or at least, how valuable I meant it to seem.

I raised one hand and rang my bell. Amaria came forward at once from a hidden door, where I had kept her waiting once my other women had gone. She knelt to me, too, and offered her hand. I took it, as a sign of favor, before I spoke. "Pay this man in gold, double the usual fee. Then send Richard's page to me."

"Yes, Your Majesty."

Amaria bowed, and took my man out of the solar the way she had come. I had not long to wait, for Richard's page came almost at once, as if I had spirited him there myself. I was gratified to see that my network was quick as well as silent. Soon I would need to call my women back to sit with me; I had been alone too long already.

When Richard's page came in, he found me kneeling at the window, as I had seen Alais do in her own rooms. I knew the picture was a pretty one, my slender figure in cloth of gold, kneeling before God in the sunlight. The boy did not have to know that the gold beads in my hand were not a rosary but a necklace that Raymond, my old lover, had given me, many years ago.

I finished the semblance of my prayers while Richard's boy waited for me. I crossed myself as he watched, his breath bated. I knew beyond a doubt that he was taking in all he saw, to report to Richard.

I rose then, and turned to him almost as if I had not known he was there, as if I had not called him myself. The boy was too young to see through this obvious subterfuge. He was barely ten summers old, the down on his cheek not yet replaced by whiskers. The boy's eyes shone still with worship, the innocent worship that only a child can harbor.

I raised my hand, and he took it, kneeling before me. "I would call your lord to a hunt this afternoon, if he is willing."

"Yes, Your Majesty."

He did not move, as anyone else would have done. He did not hear the dismissal in my tone, so I was forced to repeat it.

"I would hunt with my falcon," I said. "Ask him to bring his hawk."

"Your Majesty, I will."

The boy spoke as if it were a solemn vow he was taking, as if he were swearing an oath, not to deliver a message, but to protect me for the rest of his life. I saw at once that he would remember this day, and these moments alone with me, on into his old age, if he was so lucky as to have one. Were he to stay in my son's service, no doubt he would die in battle, as so many men did, praising my son's name. Richard inspired the men he led with his prowess on the field. By me, men were simply inspired, as if their god had spoken to them through the glint of my green eyes.

He left me then, and my women returned. I did not fasten Raymond's beads at my waist, as I once would have done, but handed them off to Amaria. She palmed them without question, and hid them in her skirts, as I stepped forward and called my women to take up their tapestry once more.

I heard from three more sources that Richard had helped Alais find the kitchen garden. He was with her there when his boy found them together and brought my message, offering to take them on a hunt. Alais agreed at once, though I knew she had never been hunting before.

We set out, just as the afternoon sun was beginning to make its way in the west. It was a terrible time to go hunting, as Richard knew full well. He did not contradict me, but helped me mount my horse himself.

Alais did not turn a hair when he offered to lift her onto her own. I knew she had never ridden before, but she watched how I held the reins for only a moment before he raised her into her saddle. The skirts of her new gown got in her way, and Richard turned his back as she and her lady-in-waiting set them to rights once more.

I sat my horse, as still as stone, and smiled at her. If I had thought to catch her at a disadvantage, I did not. Alais met my eyes over Richard's head, her laughter barely suppressed for his sake.

I raised one hand and we rode out together. I let the children lead. I watched them, their heads together, as Richard pointed out first one thing and then another along our path. Winchester is lovely in the spring, and there was much beauty to see, though I saw none of it. Instead, I looked only on my son and his betrothed, the daughter I had raised to become a woman like me.

Her dark hair glinted with auburn in the dying sun, and Richard's fiery mane shone. I listened to my daughter's low voice as she drew my son ever closer into her web.

Jealousy ate at my stomach, and threatened to gnaw on my spleen. I did not fight it, but watched my own emotions, as I did all my weaknesses. They would remain my secret, as long as I did not act on them.

To see my son favor Alais tore at my heart, but I knew that he loved me still, and always would. As we rode, I wondered whether I could let their betrothal continue. They were marrying, not for Henry's power and wealth, but for mine.

With Richard duke in the Aquitaine and count in the Vexin, I stood to control key parts of the Continent. Those holdings would shore up my power, no matter what else Henry thought to do in the future. Though I had lost Henry's ear years ago, I still had Richard's. As I watched him speak to Alais, leaning close to take in the scent of her hair, I wondered how long past their marriage I could hold him.

Richard's squire rode beside him with his hawk. As I watched, Richard turned to take his hawk onto his arm. He offered the bird to Alais so that she might caress his feathers.

My daughter did not shrink from that bird of prey, but touched him gently, lovingly, as she might someday touch my son. I had taught her nothing of the love that sprang up between a woman and the man who wooed her. Perhaps I would not have to. Richard seemed determined to teach her himself.

As I retrieved my own bird from my man, Alais laughed, her soft voice rising, its low cadence making Richard draw near, and heed her. I had not taught her to do that, either.

Richard set his hawk free, and I did the same with my falcon. Our birds of prey rose into the darkening sky, their eyes sharp, settling almost at once on their quarry.

They brought down two doves. Alais made not a sound, but when our birds struck, she paled. Richard did not notice, but raised an arm so that his hawk could return to him. The bird landed on his arm as it dropped the wounded dove into Richard's outstretched hand.

The squire took the hawk from Richard then, and my son cut into the dove's flesh. He offered his hawk the heart of its prey, even as it still lay beating.

Alais grew even paler. I knew she would not swoon, because she was strong, but I took hold of her arm just the same. I moved my horse close beside her. "Daughter," I said, "that is enough hunting for one day. Come away from here. My groom will take my falcon, and its prey with it."

The relief on her face was clear to me, as it would have been to no one else. She might hide her thoughts from my women and from Richard, who even in that moment praised his hawk's prowess. From me, she could hide nothing. She turned to me in her distress as she always had, as if I was her only refuge in the world. As indeed I was.

Alais had been schooled by Louis in obedience and silent stoicism, but I had raised her to love me. When she turned her face to me, away from that dove's death, I saw that I need not fear the love blooming between Richard and the princess.

I would stay my hand. Let them marry, once Henry had blessed them. Let them love each other. Pray God they would be happy longer than Henry and I had been.

Richard loved her well, but she loved me more than any man. Between the two of us, we would hold Richard in our sway. I would have the power I craved in the Aquitaine and in the Vexin. I would take one more step on the path that had no turning. If it ever came to a contest between Richard and myself, Alais would choose me.

I saw in her eyes, as I drew her horse away from Richard's bloody kill, that she would love me for the rest of her life, more than any other.

Chapter 7

༒

ALAIS: A ROSE WITHOUT THORNS

Winchester Castle
May 1172

The sable Eleanor had given me was warm around my shoulders, but I could still feel the cool of the evening where it came in at the window. I drew the queen's fur close over my shift and went to look down into the garden where I had first seen Richard alone. The darkness below was deep; only the scent of roses drifted up to me. From somewhere in the keep, I could hear laughter at the feast.

"My lady, come away from the window."

Marie Helene heated mulled wine for me in a bronze goblet. I drank it, but it did not warm me. I saw once more the gray dove in Richard's hand, and the glint of his knife.

Marie Helene had listened to my story of the hunt, but said nothing. Now we stood alone in silence as the feast went on below. Eleanor had brought me back to my rooms herself, and left me there, saying that I need not dine in the hall that night.

Indeed, it would have been too much for me to sit among her courtiers with Richard on one side of me, the knife he had used on that bird fastened at his wrist. I had never seen an animal killed before, though I had eaten meat all my life.

I told myself that I was simply being squeamish, that my delicate folly was not worthy of a princess of France. Still, my mind would not let go of the sight of that gray dove; over and over again it bled to death on Richard's glove, while Richard's bird of prey ate its warm heart.

I set the bronze goblet down, and reached for my prayer beads. Though I prayed to the Holy Mother, She had not taken the sight of that bird's death from my mind. It lingered, so that I wondered if that creature's death contained a message for me, one that I must heed.

"Marie Helene, the prince hunts often, does he not?"

"Yes, my lady. As does the queen."

I sat on one of my room's chairs, its curving arms and soft cushions supporting me as my mother might have done, had she lived; as Eleanor did with her very presence, when we were alone.

"I saw that dove in my lord's hands, small and helpless, and I thought, dear God, will they deal so with me? Am I the dove, and they the hunter?"

Marie Helene sat down close beside me. She did not turn from me, nor did she speak. She took my hand in her own.

I expected her to tell me that my mind had taken on a morbid fancy. Convent-bred, I was simply not used to such sights, and to the actions of a man, a real man, such as my betrothed. But she said none of these things.

"The Lord Richard hunts for sport, as does the queen." She leaned close to me, and whispered so that the walls with their many ears would not hear. "But know this, my lady. Never has the Lord Richard looked on a woman as he has looked on you. He honors you, as he has honored no one else."

Her words rang in my ears, and the silence that followed seemed to smother them. I held them close to my heart, for they held my own hope. I prayed to the Virgin, and this time found a touch of peace, Her hand on mine, just as Marie Helene's was.

Once more, I heard from afar the laughter in the great hall. Eleanor expected me to face what came, and so I would. I would put my trust in her, and in my husband-to-be, and in God, who had led me to this place for the good of France.

I woke the next morning to sunlight falling on my bed from the windows over the rose garden. The servants came in to light the braziers as I reclined on my pillows. It was cool and damp in the castle at Winchester, and braziers were always lit to ward off the chill.

My fears of the night before had faded with my sleep, but the taste of them lingered. I washed that tang away with watered wine, and stood still as Marie Helene dressed me in fine blue silk. A gift, as all things were, from the queen.

A summons came early from Eleanor. I knew that Richard was leaving that morning for the Aquitaine. She called me to her, that I might see him once more.

In the antechamber of the queen's solar, three stone walls were warmed by tapestries. The fourth was dominated by windows.

These were not narrow windows that would be shuttered against the cold come winter. They stretched to the ceiling and were covered over with glass, so that the sunlight shone through in wavy patterns.

Instead of walking into the solar to see the queen, I stopped at the windows, and reached out to touch them. The glass was warm under my hand.

I heard the lady with me draw in her breath. I knew then that he was there.

I turned to smile at Richard, and bowed low to him. He did the same to me, then stood looking at me from the doorway of his mother's solar.

He was dressed for the road, with a breastplate of worked steel, and chain mail beneath that. His hair fell to his shoulders in waves of reddish bronze. His large hands were covered in heavy leather gloves that made them look that much larger.

Richard held a rose between the first fingers of his right hand. He held it carefully, delicately, as if he was afraid to crush it, as if he did not know his own strength.

Something in his stance reminded me that he was a warrior. It was not just the armor he wore but the way he carried himself as he wore it, as if, were we overrun in that moment by some unknown enemy, he would stand before me and defend me to his last breath. Had an unknown enemy stormed the castle keep, Richard would have been ready to face them.

I had always known he was a warrior; he was famous for his prowess in war, as young as he was. But I had seen only the poet and the gentleman, the man of courtesy who had bowed over my hand with his mother watching us. This man was more than that. More lay behind the blue of his eyes than I had dreamt of.

Richard knew by now that I had been frightened by our hunt. He stood in silence, as if he feared me, or as if he feared to frighten me once more. I saw compassion in his blue eyes, where the day before I had seen the thrill of the kill. His compassion warmed me as all Eleanor's furs and mulled wine had not.

Richard crossed the room to where I stood beneath the window. My breath caught as he came near, and his broad shoulders blocked out the rest of the room, so that Eleanor's woman was hidden from me altogether. His gaze lingered on my hair, where my dark curls caught the sunlight. My veil had slipped down to my shoulders, and I had not bothered to put it right again.

"Alais, I am glad to see you before I go."

His heavy leather gloves dwarfed the flower he held. He offered it to me.

"I know that you love roses. I had hoped to see you this morning, so that I might give you this."

I ran my hand along the stem. It was smooth, with no thorns. I breathed in its scent, a perfume that was heavy but not cloying. The rose was dark red, a darker red even than one of the silk dresses I had been fitted for.

"Thank you."

I would keep that flower, long past the time when its scent was gone. I would dry it, pressed between two pieces of silk.

"I would like to write to you," he said, "while I am in the Aquitaine. You can have one of my mother's ladies read my letters to you."

"Oh, no," I said. "I can read Latin for myself."

Richard smiled at my pride, and I did nothing to hide it.

"Then I will write to you in Latin," he said. "And no one but my father's spies will read it."

I laughed. "Surely no spies care what a betrothed couple has to say to one another."

He smiled as if he did not believe me. "Perhaps you are right. Perhaps we will be immune to spies and their poison."

"God grant it." I crossed myself. "I will pray for you," I said, "while you are away."

We fell silent then, neither knowing what to say to the other. The silence in the room grew heavy, and I knew Eleanor's woman still watched us. For all I knew, by now more women might have gathered at the door. As I stood looking up into Richard's eyes, I found that I did not care if all the court looked on. For a long moment, he stood sheltering me from the rest of the world.

Richard lifted his hand, and the heavy leather of his glove touched my cheek. The warmth of it made me lose my breath. I found that I did not want him to take his hand away.

I thought for a moment that he might kiss me, but Richard withdrew his hand, and stepped away.

The loss of the warmth of his body so close to mine woke me as from a dream at morning. I remembered myself, and curtsied at once, wishing that I could feel his touch on my cheek without his glove between us.

Richard turned and was gone without another word. I watched him go, heedless of the waiting woman who stared at me, the rose without thorns still clutched in my hand.

Only then did I notice Eleanor standing in the doorway of her solar. She did not step back and invite me in, but stared at me in silence, her eyes fastened on the rose I held.

"Strange, Alais. When my son came to bid me farewell, I thought that rose was for me."

I met the eyes of the woman who had defended me since I had come away from my father in France. I saw sorrow in her face as well as jealousy; for love of me she did not hide it, as she would have with anyone else. I stepped forward, mindful of all who watched me.

I did not kneel, for she was my mother as well as my queen, but I bowed low, and rose only when she bade me. I saw the pain in her eyes, and was reminded of how lonely her life was, of how lonely her life had always been, except when Richard or I was near.

Without warning and without thought, I moved then to take her into my arms. I pressed myself against her, drawing her close to me. I felt the surprise in her bones, in her muscles and sinews, but she raised her arms to embrace me without thinking.

I spoke, heedless of all around us, heedless of what her women might think, or how they might judge me for my impertinence. She was in pain. I would not stand by and do nothing.

"I love you, Eleanor."

I whispered her name low, so that only she could hear. She drew me closer still, and kissed me. We stood that way a long time, as the women in her solar and the women in her antechamber stared at us as if we had both run mad.

She laughed then, the music I had missed all the years I had been in exile at the nunnery.

"You are my daughter, Alais, married to my son or not."

I did not understand her; my marriage to her son had been decided long ago, by kings, before I had ever stepped foot in England. So it was as a daughter and not as a princess that I reassured her, taking her hand in mine even as she pulled away.

"Yes, Your Majesty. I will always be."

We traveled to Windsor the next day. The queen did not stand on ceremony, but went to the king's court before the king himself had made landfall at Southampton. I knew that Eleanor wished to entrench herself in her husband's keep before he could reach it. Eleanor would face him, and all that she and Richard had wrought, as fearlessly as she ever did anything. Her courage was only one more reason to love her.

Windsor Castle was a great keep, with a deep moat and a spike gate that seemed to dwarf all who passed under it. I shuddered as we entered its gray stone walls. It was old, one of the first Norman strongholds in that land. The man who held Windsor held the kingdom.

Armies of servants greeted us as they had not at Winchester. They descended on our baggage train like locusts, taking away my trunk before I had even stepped out of my litter.

I met Eleanor's eyes across the bailey. She smiled to see my pride, and the fact that I would let no army of servants, and no great gray walls, intimidate me.

She raised one hand, and her women surrounded her. Angeline and Mathilde were quick to flank her, as if jealous of another taking their place. Amaria led the rest of the women into the castle, but I did not follow. Marie Helene and I waited, and walked in alone.

I had no word from my betrothed, though I hoped that he might write me as he said he would. The queen got a letter from him just after we rode into Windsor Castle. Jealousy came to me now in my turn; I found it took my breath away.

Eleanor did not let me read his letter, but she said that Richard sent his love to me in its first lines, after wishing her good health. I had her word on this, and I hoped she was not lying to soothe me. I prayed to the Virgin that Richard had not already forgotten me, when we had been apart only one day.

My rooms in Windsor palace were small but very fine. The stone floor was well swept and my bedstead was covered in fine damask, as green as the forests we had ridden through.

I had two great windows that looked down on the river, not the garden, as they had at Winchester. An army of women unpacked my new clothes and placed them in the press that stood in my dressing room. My gowns hung on hooks, ready to be pressed once more, gowns in a dozen shades, all made of the same soft silk, all made in the same fashion as the blue gown I still wore.

Marie Helene found me looking at my clothes, and she smiled for the first time since we had arrived at King Henry's court.

"I am glad you like your dresses," she said.

"They are beautiful and elegant, as good as anything I ever saw in France." That was the highest praise I knew, and Marie Helene smiled even as she looked over her shoulder.

"You must not mention France here, my lady. The king does not approve of France."

"Well, France does not approve of him, so that is just as well."

"My lady," Marie Helene hissed a warning, but I only laughed. I knew that though we were alone, the walls had ears.

"God save His Grace the king," I said. "He is a good man who need not think on France."

Marie Helene relaxed to hear me say this, and quickly changed the subject back to my gowns. It was not long before some of Eleanor's women found me, and led me down to the great hall, for it was time to eat again.

I looked down the table and saw the place for the king was bare. He was not at court yet, but it seemed that everyone else was. Strange men eyed me as I took my seat among the queen's women. Though I was still well favored and seated at the high table, I was not served off the queen's trencher that night.

As I ate from the platters of venison and squab, I listened to the gossip all around me. Men were seated at our table, one for every woman, and while they did not speak to me directly for fear of the queen, they spoke around me as if I already knew the gossip, and was only hearing it repeated from their lips.

The men speculated about Richard's sudden rise to power. Here, at the king's high table, sat his ministers. These men helped with the ruling of the kingdom. They served the king closely, and knew well his mind.

"He wanted that duchy for Henry the Younger," one man said.

The taller man beside me took another piece of venison, and drank deep from his tankard of mead. "Indeed, there is no end to the honors the king would heap on his eldest son. He wanted young Henry to have the Aquitaine, and Normandy, and England, too."

"Well, it remains to be seen how it will play out. God knows, the king has waited long enough for his sons to honor him. All they do is take, then ask for more."

My color rose when I heard this, for I knew Richard was no grasping prince. But I knew when to hold my tongue. I ate my meat in silence. Richard did not need me to defend him.

"This matter of the Lord Richard puts me in mind of Thomas Becket," the first man said.

They both fell silent, and crossed themselves.

The Reverend Mother wept on hearing the news of Becket's death when I was a child. She had never told me how he died, but there, sitting at the king's table, I was soon to learn it.

"We know the king's tolerance for challenges to his authority," the other replied. "The king's knights murdered Becket, and in his own cathedral."

"His Majesty had no knowledge of that and will one day do penance for it," one young man said. "My father told me."

The two older men locked eyes above the young man's head. They did not acknowledge in any other way that the boy had spoken.

I sat motionless, my dinner dagger clutched in numb fingers. I laid my knife down, so that I would not drop it.

Our corner of the table was plunged into silence. Only then did one of the men glance my way and remember I was there, and who I was. He shook his head once, and the other man glanced at me furtively, before looking away.

"Well, it's all in God's hands."

"And the king's."

"Amen."

I drank deep from my wine, though it was sour and unwatered. I tried to imagine what King Henry must be like, that he would order his own archbishop killed in the sacred precinct of a church. I tried to convince myself that even such a man would never turn on his own son. I almost managed to do so, until I met Marie Helene's eyes.

The fruit was brought out, and a minstrel stood with his lute to start the dancing. Marie Helene squeezed my hand beneath the table as if to offer me an assurance of Richard's safety, an assurance I was certain she did not feel.

I smiled when a young man from the lower tables asked me to dance. I did not accept or refuse, but looked to the queen for permission.

Eleanor had not spoken to me all evening, apart from greeting me when I arrived in the hall. I saw that in this place she was queen but not ruler. Even with Henry a day's ride away, his presence was felt at Windsor as if he were but in the next room. I wondered how Eleanor would fare when the king arrived, and how I might be of help to her when he came.

The queen smiled when she saw the request in my eyes, and beneath her court reserve, the Eleanor I knew peeked out at me. She made a great show of being delighted with my obedience and modesty, so that all might take note of it. I filled my role as if born to it, as indeed I was, and it became a game between us.

When each man asked me to dance, I would wait and catch her eye, so that she might nod and give her permission. I forgot the dinner talk of Thomas Becket and the king's anger. I lost myself in the motion of the dance, the steps that had been taught to me by Eleanor herself.

The queen winked when she sent me to the dance floor with a particularly good-looking young man. He was a lord from the north, a younger son who had just inherited unexpectedly. I knew from her ladies that he had come to court for the queen to arrange a match for him.

"At least I am spoken for," I said. "You don't have to fear that the queen will saddle you with me."

The young man laughed, his blue eyes sparkling with mischief. He looked over at Eleanor, who was still smiling at us indulgently. "I would never be so ungallant as to call your company a burden, Your Highness."

"Not for one dance," I said. "But for a lifetime . . . that might be more cumbersome."

He flushed, and I laughed. "Don't worry," I said. "She will make you a good match. The queen has excellent taste."

"The Lord Richard is surely a fortunate man."

Marie Helene and I left for my rooms soon after. When I curtsied to bid her good night, Eleanor drew me close. "Lead men a merry chase," she said, "but never let them catch you."

"Not until the wedding night," I said, speaking low, so that others would not hear me over the music.

Eleanor smiled her wicked smile, and let go of my hand. "No, Alais. Not even then."

PART II

❧

WINDSOR

Chapter 8

༜

ELEANOR: QUEEN OF SPIES

Windsor Castle
May 1172

My spy network, while still active at Windsor, had to go underground. So I took my waiting women out for a stroll in the forest, that I might do my true work as queen unencumbered.

The great trunks of the king's forest rose above our heads as they had done since long before the Norman dukes had conquered these lands. Spring was well advanced by that time, and the green of the trees had not yet darkened to opaqueness, but shone with hints of sunlight through the leaves.

We brought men-at-arms to guard us, though the king's peace was secure here, as it was in all of southern England by that time. Henry and I had seen to that.

Windsor was Henry's palace, more than it would ever be mine.

Though Winchester's royal seat was held by the bishop, my network found it easier to maneuver there, far from the king's eye. At Windsor, when the king was not in residence, his ministers were, and they all kept close watch over me.

It was a bond between us.

So to take my spies' reports, I had to hear them outdoors. Spring had blossomed with May, the month of the Blessed Virgin, as Alais was quick to remind me. I still had not weaned her from her father's religion. She clung to it as she clung to the memory of France. France I would never take from her, but Louis' blind obedience to the pope and all his teachings was something I would cure her of.

I left my adopted daughter with the elderly women of my court. She alone had the patience for them. Perhaps it was her convent up-bringing; she would sit with them, content to read aloud while they spun wool for hours on end. I left them to it. I put Alais out of my thoughts, for I had the business of the kingdom in hand, business that I wanted her to know nothing of.

Amaria caught my eye. When I nodded, she drew my waiting women away to watch a man on the tiltyard, not far from where we stood. He was one of Richard's men, a great, brawny specimen that in my youth I would have favored. No doubt he had little talk or music to recommend him, but those things were not what such men were good for.

Only Angeline and Mathilde were reluctant to leave me, but when the young man's horse leaped over an obstacle on the tiltyard, even they were drawn away, as flies to honey.

My spy met me as I stopped beneath a myrtle tree. The river

flowed nearby, and I could smell clean water on the air. For a moment, I almost wished that I were free, and a young girl once more, that I might go and sit beside that river, and leave the work of the kingdom to another. Of course, this fancy was nonsense, and I dismissed it as soon as it entered my mind. Still, it was not only Alais' youth I envied, nor just my son's love for her. Alais was sweet and unspoiled enough to enjoy a day by the river, with no thought for anything else. I had never been.

My spy, the lady Clarissa, bowed to me beneath the myrtle tree and smiled as if she had come to discuss the young man on the warhorse. We pretended to watch him from where we stood. I bowed my head as if looking at the flower in my hand while she made her report.

"Your Majesty, I bring great news."

"Indeed. Don't keep me waiting."

Clarissa had just returned from Normandy with her husband, where she waited on my eldest son's wife. I took in the girl's blond curls and winsome smile, and thought once more how deceiving perceptions are. Though she seemed a pious, empty-headed girl, she and I knew otherwise.

She was a spy for me, and one of Henry the Younger's lovers. How many other masks she wore I did not know, for I did not ask. She served me well, which was all that concerned us.

"Your son has joined with the King of France in an alliance."

My heart leaped for once at the thought of Louis, as it had not since the first year of our aborted marriage. I had sent a letter by my favorite priest to Louis over a year before, broaching the subject of my eldest son. In that letter, I said nothing specific, only that I feared for young Henry's soul, and prayed each day that he might be led by a good man to find strength in the Church.

Louis loved to hear lies from me, even now that he never saw my face. I had no doubt that he kept the letter I wrote to him, and wore it close to his heart, beneath his hair shirt. He had loved me when I was his wife, no matter how I humiliated him. He loved me still. I was not above using his love for me to shore up my power in Normandy.

"It is nothing formal," Clarissa said, laughing when Angeline noticed we had stepped aside. Clarissa twirled for me, as if to show off the dress my son had bought for her, a deep blue silk that cost as much as three hectares of land, and brought out the blue of her eyes.

I applauded her, as if we were only at some foolish game, but kept my applause quiet, so that Angeline and her sister would not draw near, bringing the others with them. As it was, we had little time, and I knew it.

Clarissa moved closer to me, taking the flower from my hand with a curtsy. "King Louis has begun sending young Henry prayer books, with political strategy in the bindings."

I laughed a little at that, and rolled my eyes. Henry the Younger would do better to take his politics from me.

"There is talk that the Lord Henry might spend a week with the king in Rouen, so that they may speak of the Church, and its place in the life of a ruler."

"And my husband knows nothing of this?"

"Not yet. Not unless he has spies as good as I am."

Clarissa smiled, and her eyes gleamed with the intelligence I hired her for. Of course, Henry's spy network was just as good as mine, but as one of the pieces on my chessboard, Clarissa had no way of knowing this.

However, Clarissa had a good grasp of political strategy, and she knew as well as I did that any alliance between Louis and my son set a wedge between Henry and his heir, while enhancing my power. Henry had always had his namesake's loyalty, but once Louis had our eldest's ear, I would ask him to speak well of me. Before many months, if all went well, I would have power in Normandy through my eldest son, as well as in the Aquitaine and in the Vexin through Richard and Alais.

One more step on the road that had no turning. My sons began to line up, one by one, farther from their father, and a little closer to me.

Amaria called to me then, asking me to come to my ladies, where they clustered like a gaggle of geese. I moved toward them with Clarissa at my side. I could not speak to her long, for her status was not high enough to warrant it.

Once we joined my women, she left me at once with a curtsy, her look of blond innocence in place as if the intelligence behind her eyes had never been. Later, Amaria would slip her a purse of gold. What she spent it on, and how she kept it hidden from her husband, I did not ask. Such things were not my secrets to tell.

When my ladies and I returned to the castle, Richard was waiting for me. I did not bat an eye when I found him alone in my solar. Alais was entertaining the elderly ladies in her own room, and Richard would never go alone among my old women, not even for her, not on pain of death.

He looked like a great bear left adrift on an inland sea. I sent my women away, and held out my hands to him. Though he had defied me by returning too soon, I was overjoyed to see him.

"Mother, I could not leave you to him."

He did not kneel, as he would have done had we not been alone. Richard kissed my cheek, and I took in the sun-warmed scent of his skin, and the beauty of his youth, like that of a young god. How such a creature had sprung from the last happy days of my marriage was beyond my comprehension.

"Leave me to whom, Richard?"

"My father. The king."

My son's face darkened when he spoke of Henry, as it had since he was a child. They had never embraced each other, not as Henry embraced the other boys. Richard held himself aloof; Richard had always been mine.

"Henry is still at Southampton, Richard."

"No, Mother, he will be here by sunset."

I wanted to ask the question: if such a thing was true, why had Richard not gone on to secure the Aquitaine, while I dealt with his father here? I knew his chivalry, and knew also that my words would wound him, so I said nothing. For Richard, as for Alais, I sometimes held my tongue.

"I could not leave you and Alais alone here to face him, after what I have done."

I did not point out to Richard that he had indeed done nothing yet. That he needed to go to Aquitaine to actually be invested as duke, and as such was still simply a prince. But he knew this already. I saw in his eyes that he had come back for Alais.

My pain pierced me like a well-honed dagger, sharp and true. I had not felt such pain since Henry first took the woman Rosamund as his mistress, so long ago. Richard thought me faint, and gripped my arm.

"Mother . . ."

"I am all right."

I took hold of myself, and smoothed all sign of distress from my face. My pain lay unheeded beneath my breast. "You must stay silent at the feast tonight, Richard. Leave your father to me."

"Mother, I will. But I will defend you, if I must."

I saw his love for me then. In spite of his newfound fascination with his betrothed, he loved me, too, just as he always had. I comforted myself with that knowledge. I even leaned my cheek against his shoulder for a moment, before I pulled away.

"I thank you, Richard. You are my knight, as you have always been, as you will always be."

He kissed my cheek first, and then bowed over my hand, as if swearing fealty. I looked down at his red gold hair, so much like Henry's, and knew that I would have to prepare myself for the night to come.

There were still hours of daylight left when I went to seek Alais. I found her, as I expected to, still reading to the old women of my court, all of whom looked at her as if she were the Second Coming of the Christ.

I dismissed them, and they moved quickly to do my bidding, as all my women knew to do. Alais came to me at once, and kissed me.

She smelled of the rose water I had sent her the night before. She had bathed her hair in a touch of it, so that her curls smelled sweet.

"Your Majesty," she said. "Did you enjoy your walk?"

"I did, Princess. Thank you."

The last woman left us so that only Marie Helene remained. Alais raised one hand, and her woman withdrew as quietly as if she were still one of my own. I was impressed, but knew better than to say so.

Alais wrapped her arms around me without my leave, and drew me close, her sweet affection spilling over as it often did when we were alone. I had never been one to caress or fondle outside of love play, but I could never turn Alais or my son away. I kissed her hair, and she drew back, satisfied.

I knew that she could not stay in the palace or Richard might come seeking her. I would watch them, and try to keep them apart, unless I was in the room. My favorite son would cause enough trouble that night without being left to make mischief with his betrothed. With the news of the Aquitaine hovering between them, Richard would irritate Henry with his very presence, even if he never opened his mouth.

"You have been indoors too long, Alais. You must go out and get some fresh air. One of my younger ladies will take you for a walk by the river, and then to the stable to see some puppies, if you would like."

Her eyes lit up as with a sunrise. I remembered, for all her poise, how truly young she was, and how little joy her life had held, save in my presence.

"I would love that, Eleanor. Thank you."

"Rest here, and Margaret will come for you by and by."

"I will pray while I wait," she said.

I thought at first she made a jest, but I remembered to whom I was speaking.

"I pray to be a good wife," she said. "I pray to the Virgin that I will make you proud of me."

I felt tears rise to my eyes unbidden, and I drew her close so that she would not see them. This daughter of my heart spoke so openly when we were alone that it almost took my breath. Her sweet, undivided love made me wish that I had once had the luxury of loving as purely and as openly as she did. If I had, perhaps my life with Henry would have been altogether different.

"I am proud of you already, Alais. Never forget that, whatever comes."

I drew back from her and saw tears in her eyes. Before I could chide her, she reached up with the kerchief I had given her, and wiped them away.

I was sewing with my women when the king arrived at Windsor. Or rather, I sat idly by while they finished the tapestry for my father's cathedral at Poitiers. It was all I could do not to go look for him myself, so impatient was I to make the next move on the chessboard that lay between myself and Henry.

Before the afternoon sun fell below the castle walls, I was pacing the floor like a tigress. My ladies watched me as I moved. No one spoke, but they all kept sewing the last flowers on the great tapestry.

I heard Henry before I saw him, before my spy came to tell me that he had arrived. Henry bellowed in the bailey for someone to take his horse. His voice echoed on the stone walls so that I heard it from my open window.

Amaria stopped reading aloud and my women stopped sewing. They all turned to look at me. "You may leave me," I said. "I will see you all at the evening meal."

They rose at once, leaving the tapestry unfinished on its frame. They all saw my face, and even Angeline knew better than to linger. Amaria stayed, for she knew that my order was not meant for her.

We left my solar through the secret door that led directly to my bedroom. There, Amaria helped me dress from head to toe in emerald silk, the gown Alais had worn before she had received her own dresses from my hand. Amaria dressed my hair carefully, then drew my wimple over it, leaving enough bronze along my cheek to show that the color had not faded with the years.

I had never used paint or powder, as the women did in the East, for I had never needed to. I gazed at my reflection in my bronze mirror. Though I had spent fifty years on this earth, my cheeks were smooth and lit with youth, as they had been the first day I ever saw Henry. This was a trick of the light perhaps. I wondered if he might think my beauty a reflection of joy at seeing him again.

I smiled to myself in my gilded mirror. My own emerald eyes stared back at me, holding all my secrets.

I walked alone down into the main hall, and heard Henry shouting even before I stepped into the central corridor. I realized at once that he must have heard already of young Henry's correspondence with Louis.

I stepped into the hall, and saw him there in the torchlight, for there were no windows in that hall, and no sunlight. The rushes had been recently changed, and the torches were fresh and did not smoke. As I looked at Henry in that feeble light, he reminded me of the way he had looked in his youth, when all the world lay at his feet, ready to be conquered, myself included.

"Ungrateful whelp! If the young master thinks I will sit idly by and do nothing while he takes tea with the King of France, he had bloody well think again. Christ's wounds, have I even one son who will not vex me at every turn, who will not throw every gift I give him back in my face?"

I laughed, and Henry heard me. He turned to me, his face still puce with anger, and I saw that I had taken a chance, and had won. His anger receded as he looked at me, a great tide drawn back.

He was dressed for the road in some of the ugliest clothes I have ever seen. He thought nothing of them, for he knew his kingship came from more than silk and gold. They were merely the settings for his greatness, as he had always been quick to tell me.

Henry stared at me across that darkened room. His gray eyes took me in, as no other man's had ever done. Even though it had been years since he had touched me, he still had the ability to steal my breath away.

Henry raised one hand, and his ministers left the hall, though no doubt they stayed close in the corridor outside, to hear what we might say. I crossed the room to him, but not too close, as if he were a lion that might maul me with one sweep of his arm.

For the first time in years, Henry smiled at me.

"Eleanor."

He did not kiss me as he once would have done, but when I

extended my hand, he came to me and took it, pressing it between both of his. He searched my face, as if to see what changes time had wrought. He saw my beauty, still untouched, and my strength, the strength that had always drawn him to me when we were alone.

"Henry," I said. "You are a welcome sight."

He did kiss me then. His lips lingered on mine for a moment, asking a question that I did not answer. When he drew back, all evidence of his anger had fled as if it had never been. He held my hand in his.

"You are still beautiful, wife. How is that possible?"

"Perhaps we are both the devil's spawn, my lord, as all the legends say."

He barked, his laughter echoing off the stone of that hall as his shouts had done only minutes before. He released my hand, but his eyes still held me. Just as he had once held power over me, I still held power over him.

"It is good to see you, Eleanor. I'd rather a woman I know than boys who won't take gifts from my hand without biting me."

"Which boy would that be, my liege?"

Henry's eyes narrowed, but his smile did not falter. "Richard, for one. He has taken the Aquitaine, and at your request."

"My lord king, the prince waits here on your pleasure. You will see him at the feast tonight."

"Indeed." Henry knew me well, and knew that my conciliatory tone did not change the fact that Richard would take the Aquitaine. It was clear from the look on Henry's face that he did not know of my involvement in the alliance between Louis and Henry the Younger. I would make certain to keep it that way.

I knew of one more way I might amuse Henry, one small thing I might do to draw his anger away from Richard and young Henry. Louis and his piety had long since been a joke between us. Even before we married, Louis' goodness had been inexplicable to both of us. I thought of Louis' daughter then, and how I had raised her to be a woman after my own heart, the kind of woman of beauty and intelligence who was rarely if ever seen in France. That I had worked such magic on our son's betrothed might amuse Henry, as it amused me.

"My lord, you might take your ease before the dinner hour. Perhaps a walk to the inner stables would do you good. One of your hounds has whelped, and the puppies are not yet weaned."

Henry laughed once more, and I was glad to see that I could still amuse him. "Indeed. It is kind of you to look after my bitches while I am away."

I laughed, as he meant me to, for I had always taken his bastards into the royal nursery, and raised them well, as if they were my own children. All bastards but that woman Rosamund's get, the woman who even now waited for him. As always, Henry and I did not speak of her.

"Richard's betrothed walks in the stable," I said, my voice smooth, as if Rosamund had never crossed my mind. "I thought I might tempt you to go and have a look at her."

His eyes sharpened, and I saw that though he would never share my bed again, I might once more gain his ear. "Nothing will ever tempt me as you have, Eleanor."

Henry took my hand in his, and raised it to his lips. He kissed not my fingers but my palm, the way he knew I loved. His breath was warm on my skin. His tongue flicked once, and I felt its touch like a sorcerer's wand. All the while he stared up at me, into my eyes. Neither of us looked away.

I did not betray the fact that I felt his kiss in the deepest places of my body, places I no longer thought of, unless a particularly beautiful young man crossed my path. I never acted on such impulses; it would have been just the excuse Henry needed to lock me away for the rest of my life.

I did not turn from him, nor did I give him any indication that his trick had moved me. After a long moment, he let my hand go. "I will view this French princess who has time to waste wandering among my horses."

"I do not mean for you to devil the girl," I said. "But no doubt, she will amuse you."

"No doubt." He stared at me, and once more I felt caught in the heat of his gaze. "Until tonight, then."

"Until tonight."

He moved to leave me, but stopped before he had taken three steps.

"Eleanor."

"Yes?" Only through years of hard training did I keep my voice even, and my tone light.

"I am glad to be home."

Henry meant not Windsor Castle, with its old drafty rooms and fires that smoked. He walked out of the hall to meet Alais, simply because I had asked him to.

Even now, with our happiness so many years behind us, when Henry spoke of home, he referred to me.

Chapter 9

༒

ALAIS: A STABLE HAND

Windsor Castle
May 1172

The queen's lady Margaret came for me as soon as Eleanor left. She was trailed by a hulking man who carried a great basket that held more food than an army could eat, much less two small women. Marie Helene stayed behind in the palace on business of her own, and I walked out with Margaret to picnic down by the riverbank.

We sat on a grassy knoll not far from the palace gates, where Margaret said we would be able to see the king when he rode past with his men. Margaret was a pretty girl just two years older than I, with soft blue eyes and blond hair that kept slipping down from beneath her wimple. She was too shy to take her wimple off and leave her hair to fall across her shoulders and down her back, though there was no one but myself and our guard to see. She kept pushing her fine blond hair back up, beneath her linen headdress.

As we ate our bread and cheese, I raised my face to the sky. Blue arched over our heads like the protective hand of God. Birds darted down from the trees by the roadside, searching for their own dinner in the grass.

Margaret was a good companion. For all her youth and beauty, she knew when to hold her tongue. The afternoon passed in blessed silence, except for birdsong. When I was sated with food and wine, I lay back on our blanket, while the hulking guard cleared up the remains of our picnic. Before long I fell asleep, the warmth of the sun on my face.

Margaret woke me gently when the shadows had begun to fall. "I must go back," she said. "But the queen wanted me to show you the puppies in the stable. Will you go with me?"

I rubbed sleep from my eyes. The servant and the picnic things were gone. Only Margaret and I remained, our blanket a raft on a vast sea of green.

"Of course," I said. "I am sorry to have kept you here."

"No matter." She smiled, her dimples showing. Her shyness was beginning to fade a little, and I saw that she was eager to get back to the keep for some reason of her own. "The king rode by with his men. How you slept through all that noise is beyond me."

We came to the stables within the walls of the castle. They had just been mucked, so the smell of manure was strong. I raised my scented handkerchief to my nose and mouth, grateful that Marie He-lene had made me bring it.

"I will leave you," Margaret said. "I have much to do in the castle now that the king is here."

I did not ask what one of Eleanor's waiting women had to do with the king. I had heard of King Henry's fascination with women, and thought it better not to know.

She left me with a curtsy and a smile, off to meet her lover, perhaps. My mind was full of such things, ever since I had seen and known Richard.

The inner stable was dimly lit, and I could see that no one else was there. I could hear the sound of iron striking metal in the smithy not far away, but the stable stood empty of all but horses.

I knew that I should return to the palace. But I loved puppies; I had not seen one since I was a small girl, at home in France.

I stepped into the dappled shade, surrounded by horses in their stalls on both sides. I looked around once more for a groom, but saw no one there. So when my veil slipped, I did not right it, but let it hang down my back.

I saw no dogs at first, only horses in their stalls on either side of the central hall. I found the puppies finally tucked away in an empty stall, set behind a barrier of wood so that even their mother could not escape. The hunting hound eyed me at first, but when I let her sniff my hand, she licked me. Only then did I turn to her pups, who lay with their mother on a soft bed of hay. The dogs were so small that they had not yet been weaned. They were some breed of hunting hound I had never seen before. They would grow to be large someday, for even as newborn puppies they were each as big as my hand, with flopping ears and large paws. Heedless of my silk gown, I knelt in the straw beside them.

One puppy bounded over to me, far bolder than the rest, his long ears almost brushing the straw, and yipped. I reached into the pen and drew the little dog up against my breast.

He rested against my heart and nuzzled me, as if looking for warmth or milk. I laughed. "Sorry, little one, I am not your mother."

"You're much more beautiful."

The voice sounded a little like Richard's, and at the sound of it, my heart leaped. But when I rose to my feet, I saw that though the man who spoke was large like Richard, and had Richard's dark red hair, that was where the resemblance ended. It must have been a trick of the fading light, for after first glance I saw that this man was poorly dressed in leather leggings and an old woolen tunic, rags Richard would never allow into his presence, much less wear.

The man moved toward me. I stepped back, but the wall of a horse stall blocked my path. I stood still with my back against it.

The man stopped moving and raised his hands as if in surrender. "Princess, I mean you no harm. I'm just a simple man, come to tend my dogs."

I raised my chin, angry with myself that I had shown this peasant fear.

"These are the king's dogs," I said.

"That they are. And I have the caring of them, from time to time."

My mask of dignity crumbled at the warmth of his voice. As he smiled, the skin around his eyes creased. His gaze reached for me, and held me, as if it might shelter me were a storm to come.

The dog in my arms distracted me, for he had begun to gnaw on my veil where it fell across my breast. I wrested it from him, and gave him the edge of my hair to chew instead.

"You are Alais, Princess of France and Countess of the Vexin?" the man asked, watching me.

I eyed him warily, but saw no harm in him. Perhaps he was simpleminded, and that was why he was left to care for dogs.

"I am," I said, informing him of what all the castle knew. But before I could stand on my dignity again, I heard a yelp from the bed of straw at my feet. Another puppy had come forward at the sound of our voices, crying to be picked up.

I turned from him and knelt, drawing the second puppy into my arms. The man watched in silence as I played with the dogs.

"Am I interfering with your work?" I asked. "If you need to tend them, I will go."

"No." He held up one big hand to stop me, so I stayed where I was, my skirt and veil trailing in the straw.

The puppies turned back to their mother to be fed. I set down the two I held, who quickly found a place at their mother's teats. When I looked up, I found the man still there, watching me.

"You are different than I thought you would be," he said.

I did not point out that it was impertinent for him to think anything of his betters.

I saw that his eyes were a light gray. He had come no closer, but I could feel the strength of his gaze on me.

"I am as God made me," I said.

"We can all say the same," he replied. "But not all are as beautiful."

I frowned and got to my feet. He raised his hand again, and I froze, for he stood between me and the stable door.

"I am sorry," he said. "I did not mean to frighten you."

I faced him squarely so that he could see that I was not lying. "I am not frightened."

He smiled, a long, slow smile that made him almost handsome. "So I see."

"Good day, sirrah."

I stepped forward, but still he did not let me pass. I reined in my temper, for even then I did not have the sense to be afraid. He was just a man, a servant, and he was in my way, as no servant had ever dared to be in all my life, not in France and not even in England.

Still he watched me. I thought that he might not let me pass. I felt my heart kick against my ribs, but I stood my ground and did not drop my gaze from his. Finally, he laughed, and stepped out of my way.

"Good day, Your Highness."

I only nodded to him, for I did not trust my voice. I walked into the castle, moving fast, for night was falling. I did not want to be late to the meal in the great hall. The queen was to present me to the king.

I knew that I would have to bathe again, for now I smelled of the stables, and of the puppies I had held in my arms.

I did not want to think of the man I had met, though his face stayed with me as I bathed and as I dressed in my new red gown. When Marie Helene went to put my hair up under a wimple, I stopped her, and called for a red veil.

It was the man I thought of as I left my hair trailing down my back to my waist. It was his eyes I felt on me as I raised the veil over my curls and pinned it in place myself.

"Your Highness, you cannot wear your hair that way. It is not the fashion."

"We will set a new fashion, Marie Helene."

As I stepped into the great hall, I found it abuzz as I had never heard it. Fresh rushes were strewn on the floor, and gave off the scent of thyme as they were crushed beneath my feet. I felt as if all eyes were on me; I looked to no one but Eleanor.

The hall seemed larger that night as I walked to the high table, with its gray stone walls covered in tapestries. The king's table was set on its dais above the rest of the company, so that all might see Eleanor and the king as they ate their meal.

The high table at Windsor was long, and seated over twenty people. Everyone had already taken their seats when I arrived. I did not look at them, knowing I would find King Henry's ministers, and Eleanor's ladies. I took a moment to wonder where Margaret was, but I did not turn from Eleanor to look for her. I knew that Angeline and Mathilde would be staring at me intently, as if praying for me to trip and fall. There was no danger of such a thing, and their rancor usually amused me, but that night, I kept my eyes on the queen.

Eleanor was seated in her place at the center of the high table. I went to kiss her, but the queen extended her hand to me. I took it, surprised by her formality. I curtsied, bowing over her hand, while she sat on her gilded throne. I thought perhaps she would offer the empty chair beside her, and invite me to eat from her trencher.

I stood in silence and waited for this invitation, with Marie Helene two steps behind me. I felt Marie Helene's hand on my sleeve, but I ignored her and did not take my eyes off the queen.

Eleanor leaned back against her cushions and took her hand

away from me. "Princess Alais, I present you to Henry, King of England and Duke of Normandy."

I looked to the high seat at the head of the table, the seat that had always been vacant, and found the man from the stable staring back at me.

All the manners of my childhood flew from my head as if they had never been. I did not even curtsy. My father would have been ashamed if he had seen me.

The English king was not displeased at my obvious shock but instead seemed to think it a great joke that I had not known him in the horse stable. He beamed at me as if I were a party to his joke, as if he had not made a fool of me, and was not making a fool of me now.

He said nothing about our earlier meeting, his gray eyes warm on mine.

I gathered my wits and took another step toward him, so that I might kneel before him where all the court could see me. I knew how to do this prettily, without giving offense with overt servility. I had been taught obeisance as a very young child. I fell back on those lessons now; whatever he was and whatever he thought of me, this man was king.

"Rise, Princess," he said. "You are welcome to our court."

I was surprised to find him suddenly before me, offering a hand to help me stand. This was gallantry I had not looked for. His hand was warm on mine, and welcoming, though welcoming me to what, I did not know.

"Perhaps, my lord king, you will seat the Princess Alais at your right hand as a sign of favor," the queen asked in her public voice.

"Yes, my lady Eleanor, I thank you. I will."

Something passed between them down the length of the table, a bolt of fire. Eleanor wore the bland mask she often wore in public, but I wondered what she was thinking as she looked at the king.

Henry's huge peasant hand dwarfed mine, and his wide shoulders seemed to block out half the room. His eyes never left Eleanor.

King Henry did me the honor of escorting me to the head of the table himself, one hand under my own. He helped me sit beside him before he took his own gilded chair. His trencher was wide and long, full of venison and smoked fish. It was too far from me, and he took care to bring it closer to the edge of the table, so that I might eat.

He took the first bite, as was proper. The rest of the hall picked up their conversations. Once the king began to eat, everyone else could eat as well. I looked to Eleanor at the center of the table. Marie Helene had taken my place beside her.

The queen did not look to me or to the king, but fell into conversation with the man on the far side of her. He was a young lord new to court, who seemed overwhelmed to be seated at the high table, let alone next to the queen herself. I watched as she put the young man at ease. In only a few minutes, she had him laughing at something she had said.

"Is it my wife you look at, or the young man beside her?"

The king leaned close so that no one but the server behind us would hear. Startled, I met his eyes. Their gray was like the sky after a rain. I saw for the first time that there was also gray threaded through the red of his hair. The scent of him was sweet, sweeter than I would have imagined, like the sandalwood that burned in the braziers back home in Paris. He wore blue silk now, with a band of gold at his temples. Seeing him among his courtiers, I felt as if the man I had met in the stables had been a phantom of my imagination.

"At the queen, Your Majesty. I do not make it a habit to stare at strange men."

I heard my own voice, and winced at how prudish I sounded. The scent of him had thrown me off my guard, as had the touch of his breath on my cheek. I wondered at myself. Even Richard's nearness had not put me so on edge.

The king did not notice my discomfort. He seemed pleased with my answer.

"As well you should not. As my son's betrothed, you have your reputation to think of."

"Yes, my lord," I said. "And that of my father."

"Ah, yes. Louis."

The king gestured, and a servant brought more mead and filled his tankard again. "We must not forget the honor of your father."

I spoke as if we were back in the stable, as if he were not king. "I never do, my lord."

As I had earlier that day, I felt his eyes on me. He said nothing vulgar, but his gaze moved over my curls where they were displayed more than hidden beneath my thin veil of silk. His boldness went beyond any compliment Richard had offered me. I felt his gaze on my body like hands, and my temper rose, as it rarely did. I found myself breathless with an anger I could not express.

Henry smiled, pleased with my reaction. He gestured that I should eat.

"You are too thin, Alais. Here, take a morsel from my knife."

He offered me a bit of meat on his dinner dagger, and I stared first at it, then at him, to see if he was testing me. I found no mockery in his eyes, only watchfulness. I did not take the meat into my mouth, as it seemed he expected me to, but drew it from his knife with my fingers.

I swallowed my anger as well as my pride, and I ate the morsel, chewing carefully so as not to choke. Henry watched every motion of my mouth. My hands felt heavy, and the hall felt warmer than it was.

I swallowed the meat and took a sip of my wine, which had been set out too long and had begun to sour. At Windsor, where Eleanor did not rule, the English court thought little of these things. Marie Helene was careful of the wine that was brought into my rooms, but when I sat at the high table at the king's court, I had to take what came.

After I finished the bite of venison, I looked at the king, once more in control of myself, my gaze mild.

I passed his test, whatever it was, for he smiled at me.

"The dogs are thriving, Alais."

"I am glad to hear it."

"They seemed to take to you. I wonder if you might visit them again with me."

"Of course, Your Majesty. If you wish it."

Though Eleanor was still speaking with the young lord beside her, she was looking at me.

"Do not concern yourself with Eleanor," the king said. He saw where my gaze was tending.

"My lord king," I began, weighing my words with care. I had

heard of his legendary temper. "I am in the queen's care. It is meet that I ask her permission, no matter what I do."

"Even if I order you otherwise?"

I thought perhaps that he was making another jest at my expense.

"My lord, I obey you in all things, as I would my own father."

This statement displeased him. His gray eyes darkened, and I tried again.

"Your Majesty, I have been brought here to serve my father's treaty. I am here as a princess of France. I will serve you always, in whatever way you require. For my honor is bound to your house, and will be for the rest of my life."

I thought this speech a pretty one, and watched his face as he took it in. Henry did not smile as I had hoped, but looked at my hair, at the way the curls fell across the front of my red gown. The firelight hit the silk and made the color shine like a small sun. The red caught my eye as I looked down at it, and I saw for the first time how beautiful that color was.

"You would serve me out of duty."

"Of course," I said, thinking that finally he understood me.

"I would have you serve me for love."

I sat very still, my hand on the goblet of my soured wine.

"Love is not given blindly. Love is earned, my lord king."

Henry looked at me for a long moment, his beaker of mead in his hand. He rolled his mug along his palm, and I braced myself, expecting him to order me from his presence. I was sure that he called for protestations of love from all those around him, and I was equally sure that all but myself had given them freely, whether true or not.

I glanced across the hall, and found Richard staring at me. I had not known he was at court; I had thought him long since gone to the Aquitaine.

Henry was speaking to me again, and I turned away from Richard.

"You are not a liar," Henry said.

"That is so, my lord."

He laughed at my earnestness, a great booming laugh that filled the hall. Conversation stopped all around us as people turned to look at the king, to see what had set him off in merriment. They saw only the king and myself, sitting before an almost untouched trencher. Some courtiers also laughed, though they did not know the joke, as indeed I did not.

The king caught his breath and wiped his eyes on his sleeve. "Well, little princess, that makes one of us."

I could not believe that he had just called himself a liar. He laughed again, and I smiled in spite of myself, for Henry was charming, whatever else was true about him. When he smiled, it was as if the sun had come out after a heavy rain, and shone over all the court. All in his court lived by his moods, as I began to learn that day.

The day I met him was an auspicious one, for nothing I said angered him, until the last. I was fortunate, for his moods could turn without warning, and what was a jest in one instant could send him into a black rage the next.

Henry reached out and touched my cheek. He wore no gloves, and his hand was rough with calluses from riding and from sword-play. As once with Richard's, I found myself caught and held by the warmth of his hand.

His eyes met mine, and still he did not take his hand away. It was as if we were alone, though all the court watched us, Eleanor included.

"Well, little princess, we will see if I can earn your love, if you will not give it freely."

A sudden hush fell over the hall. At first, I thought the rest of the court shocked by the king's boldness. But they had not heard what he said to me. Silence had fallen because Richard had risen from his place at one of the lower tables. As one, the court turned to look at him, as did I, Eleanor, and the king. I wondered why he was not seated at the high table with us, but I had no time to ask.

"I have written a song for my betrothed," Richard said.

A young man rose to stand behind the prince, and strummed the lute he carried. One note echoed across the great hall. There was no other sound. All I could hear was that note, and the sound of my own heart beating.

Richard lifted his voice. A prince of royal blood sang a song he had written for me in front of his father, his mother, and all the court. Such a thing would never have happened in France.

After the first note, he turned to me and met my eyes, and my nerves subsided. All I could see was him.

Richard sang of a rose without thorns that grew in darkness, in a courtyard where light rarely shone. He sang of the rose's soft petals and sweet scent, of how all who saw it wished to pluck it, though no one had yet done so.

The double meaning in that verse brought snickers here and there across the hall. Richard turned his eyes on them, and the laughter stopped. He raised his voice to sing the last verse in his beautiful tenor.

He sang of the rose once more, of how the sun would shine on it, gild its leaves and petals, protecting it always even as it fed its growth.

He fell silent, his song finished. The applause began. Many stood, offering the prince glasses of wine, extolling him. They were courtiers, trained to fawn, but there was a note of sincere admiration in their praise. Richard nodded graciously, but otherwise did not heed them. He looked only at me.

Richard bowed low as if to offer me fealty. Tears rose in my eyes, and I blinked them away.

His eyes shone as he sat down once more. Beakers of wine and mead were offered him, but he took none, his eyes never leaving my face. Only when he looked away did I turn to the king.

Henry did not smile, his feelings well hidden behind the gray of his eyes. I saw the wheels of his mind turning, but I had no idea where his thoughts were tending.

"Well, Princess, it seems you have given your love to my son already."

I heard the accusation in the king's voice, but I did not have the sense to be frightened. "The Lord Richard has made me welcome. I am grateful for his kindness."

"Are you indeed? Well, he is not the only one who welcomes you. You will find that the kindness of a king extends far beyond that of a prince."

"I thank you, my lord."

Henry's face softened when I said this. As he met my gaze again, I heard the bells chiming for vespers, and I asked, "My lord king, may I go to the chapel?"

"You would go to meet a lover?" he asked.

I saw his gaze shift to Richard, where he sat among the young men. Richard met his father's eyes, and a flash of hatred passed between them. I forced myself to stillness, until my horror passed.

"No, my lord. The call to prayer just rang. I have need of praying."

"By all means," Henry said. "If God calls you, do not let me keep you. I am only your king."

I searched his face. Though he did not smile, his eyes sparkled with mirth. I could see nothing of the hatred that had lurked in his gaze only a moment before. Perhaps it had been only a trick of the light.

I stood and curtsied to him. Henry waved one hand, and I turned from him to curtsy to the queen.

Eleanor raised her glass to me, and winked. She was pleased, both with Richard's song and with the king's reception of me. She had taught me to speak well and to hold my own with royalty. I could see, even with the distance between us, how proud she was of me.

Richard stood when I did and simply looked at me. When I curtsied to him, he did not nod or bow in return. He watched me as I passed.

Only as Marie Helene drew me out of the hall did he raise one hand to me. I gave him one more smile before I left him standing among his father's courtiers.

Chapter 10

❧

ELEANOR: THE LION'S DEN

Windsor Castle
May 1172

As Alais left the hall, Henry's eyes followed her. Richard did not sit again until she was gone, but it was Henry I watched from the corner of my eye.

As I did so, I raised one hand, and my footman stepped forward with my wine. He refilled my goblet from my private silver urn. At Henry's court, to take care to avoid poison, I drank my own wine. Also, one could never trust Henry's steward at Windsor to keep decent wine at table, as Henry himself drank only mead. I let Amaria spread the gossip that I drank a special draft for my health, but all knew why I took care at Windsor. There were many at Henry's court who did not wish me well.

Only after I had drunk deep and taken a last morsel of squab did

I turn to Henry. I was pleased to see him fawn over my daughter, as if she were some housemaid that he might take up against a wall. I thought of Rosamund, and wondered if she had spies in my court, as I would have, had I been in her place. I wondered if those spies would carry tales to her of Alais that night, and if so, how my old rival might receive them. The thought made my smile deepen, and it seemed Henry was caught in the light of my eyes. For all his attentions to Alais, now that she was gone, he had eyes only for me.

I smiled my old, wicked smile, and Henry laughed, raising his tankard. The musicians began to play the first measure of the first dance. Henry rose to his feet, and I wondered which woman he would choose to partner him. He walked, not down the steps to the dance floor, but across the dais to me.

"My lady Eleanor, would you honor me?"

Henry held out his hand to me. He pitched his voice low so that the court could see him approach me but could not hear his words.

Not for the first time, I wondered what had happened to the love that once had been between us, the great love that I had cast aside a crown for, more than a lifetime ago.

"My lord Henry, it is you who honor me."

I, too, kept my voice low, to keep the matter private between us as I laid my hand in his. Of course, nothing for a king is ever private. I had lived as a queen since the age of fifteen. I had long since grown used to the eyes of others always on me.

He said nothing more, but led me onto the dance floor. The musicians stopped playing when Henry offered me his hand, so shocked were they to see us together. We had not danced with one another in years, since Henry first touched Rosamund de Clifford.

The musicians Henry employed were ill trained and had not the sense to start playing again as soon as we took the floor. But Henry and I had heard the first bars of the song, and knew what steps it called for. It was a dance we had enjoyed long ago, when we had both been happy.

Henry met my eyes, as if in defiance of all who watched us. The entire court was silent, and for the first few steps of the dance, we were alone on the floor, moving as one. Our bodies remembered each other.

The musicians started playing then, first the mandolin, then the lute, the tabor catching up with a crash before they all settled together into harmonious time. Henry laughed under his breath and I joined him, my merry laughter filling that cold hall, touching even the dark corners with my own brand of fire.

"It is good to hold your hand again, Eleanor."

"I am glad to see you, Henry. I missed you while you were away."

Henry believed me, for his face softened as he looked at me. Had we been alone, he would have kissed me. As it was, he drew me closer in the dance.

"Eleanor, I am not myself when I am not with you."

"Stay, then, and let us bide a while together."

He did not turn from me, but his emotions were engaged, and he did not like it. He changed the subject, a gleam of mischief coming into his eyes. I had forgotten how well matched we once had been in mischief making, too.

"Your French princess is a beauty," Henry said.

I laughed again, and Henry smiled to hear it, the warm music that had been denied him for so long.

"She is not mine," I said.

"Well, she did not learn to tempt a man that way in the convent," he said. "You saw how Richard would follow her, like a hound come to heel."

I watched him, my eyes still gleaming with laughter. My smile did not slip; my expression gave nothing away.

His face darkened. "I should not have brought that boy's name into our conversation."

I changed the subject back to Alais before we could quarrel. "And how did you like the morsel I sent to tempt you?"

Henry laughed, as if he had forgotten Richard, though I knew he had not. "Your morsel is tempting, but not one I can digest."

"I knew that, Henry, or I never would have put her in front of you."

"Perhaps it is war I have no stomach for. I am growing old, Eleanor. I want peace."

The music stopped, and the court applauded us. Henry kissed my hand. He did not raise his head at once, but let his lips linger on my skin, before all the court, as if to swear me fealty, as Richard often did. When Henry raised his head and met my eyes, Richard spoke.

"My lord king."

Henry straightened. Though his hand stayed on mine, his eyes sharpened like a hawk's. His predator's gaze swept the hall until his eyes fell on Richard.

"My son," Henry said. "Or should I say, one of the jackals that would feed on my carcass before I am dead?"

A woman gasped, and her man shushed her, drawing her quickly from the hall. I felt the color fade from my cheeks as the bloom fades from a rose once it is cut. With Henry's hand still in mine, I silently cursed Richard for refusing to stay quiet when I ordered him to.

"There are no jackals here, my lord. Please, come and sit with me," I said, though I knew it was too late.

I pressed my hand to Henry's arm, hoping to placate him as I once could have done so easily. He hesitated while he considered my soft voice, as he had for many years before strife fell between us. Hope rose in me, if only for the space of a breath.

The court waited to see which would win, my voice of calm, or his hatred for my son. As always with Henry, hatred won out.

"You thankless whelp!"

His voice was like the thunder of a god. More than one grown man flinched, wishing themselves anywhere but there.

"You should join your cursed brother in Normandy. Henry, my eldest, scheming with the benighted French king. And you, taking the Aquitaine without so much as a by-your-leave. I am still king in this hall, by God. And in this land. I will be damned if I succor traitors who call themselves my sons!"

The word "traitor" almost made my heart stop. Never, in all the years I had known him, had Henry ever referred to one of our boys in such a way. He had spoken of Becket with that kind of rancor, and look what had happened to him.

My plans had not advanced far enough for hostilities to mount so quickly between Henry and my sons. I knew I must make the peace.

Richard must have seen the look on my face, for before I could speak, he went down on one knee in front of Henry.

"My lord king, it pains me that I have offended you."

Henry's face was still red, his temper high, but his pallor had not risen to the color of puce. His hand was still in mine. He had not yet pulled away.

He stared at Richard. Though Henry did not speak, he also did not order our son from his presence.

"I ask that you support my rise, that I might serve you in the Aquitaine as I serve you here," Richard said.

Henry held my son's eyes for a long moment. The silence in the hall was deafening. Even the least loyal of courtiers felt nothing but fear.

"Very well, Richard. Then let all be witness. You take the Aquitaine from my hand. Have it, and guard it well. I gift it to you, out of my royal largesse."

Richard, being Richard, could not let the slight go.

"My lord king, I thank you. But I remind you here, in the presence of this assembly, that the Aquitaine comes to me through my mother, as sanctioned by my overlord, the King of France, three years ago. Only now do I reach out my hand to take it."

I looked to Henry, as we all did, certain that he would send Richard from him now. I cursed Richard for a fool for not obeying me. He should have been well on his way to the Continent this night, and not at Henry's court, deviling the king.

Henry did not turn from me, even then, and I saw that we were safe. I realized what Henry was about: Richard and I had given him an opportunity to strike back at young Henry in Normandy. My husband was going to let Richard keep the Aquitaine to spite our eldest son.

But there was something in Henry's smile that I did not like as he turned it on Richard. It was not warm but calculating. And for once, I could not see behind the calculation in my husband's eyes.

"All here may bow to my son Richard, Duke of Aquitaine. He holds the land with his mother's blessing, and with mine. God speed him on his journey hence."

I heard the order behind the blessing, and this time I would force Richard to have the sense to heed it. My son bowed to the king, and the court applauded Henry's words. Everyone present was grateful that the scene had ended so well, but I was still uneasy.

Henry met my eyes only then, and bent to kiss my hand. Then the king released me, and moved to leave the hall. I took an unsteady breath, unable to do anything but watch him go.

The tension in the room did not dissipate when Henry left. I heard one old man say, "Christ's blood, God help the prince. The king smiled like that on Becket, too."

Richard came to my side. He heard the man's words but chose to ignore them, as he had chosen to ignore my advice. He took my hand, and led me into a dance.

I raised my skirt in one hand, and we moved together in a dance of Richard's choosing. He did not tell me the dance he thought of, but we moved together without thinking, in sympathy as we always were whenever Henry was not in the room.

The musicians, behind three beats once more, soon caught up. Richard's favorite men-at-arms took up partners and surrounded us, so that our conversation could not be overheard by Henry's courtiers.

"Richard, for God's sake, never do such a thing again."

"Mother, I'm sorry. I lost my temper. I should—"

"Have spoken with me first. Richard, you cannot beard the lion in his den. There is a strategy to politics, as there is in war. If you will not use your mind for chess here as you do on the battlefield, you must trust to me to make your moves for you."

"Mother, you're right. I'm sorry."

The contrition in his voice moved me, just as I had hoped to harden my heart, to make him see how close we might have come to disaster. His blue eyes met mine, as they had when he was a boy, guileless and full of love for me.

I turned to him in the dance, and pressed my lips to his cheek.

"You must go to Aquitaine tomorrow. Do not turn back, even if you hear that we have all fallen to a plague. I have sent word to the bishop. He will be waiting for you in Limoges."

"Yes, Mother."

"While you are gone, I will find some way to distract your father. We want peace with him, until we choose otherwise. We have won this round, Richard. Let me see to it that we do not lose the next."

The music ended and he kissed my cheek there on the dance floor, with all of Henry's court watching. "I swear, Mother, I will be ruled by you in this, as in all things."

Richard led me back to my chair. With Henry gone from the hall, he sat down at the high table beside me. He poured more wine for me and courted me for the rest of the night. Three troubadours sang to my beauty, a record at Henry's court, and Richard, too, raised his voice in praise of me.

Like all good things, those moments were not to last. Before long, one of Richard's men signaled to him, and he kissed me and left the hall. I wondered if he went to meet a lover.

I chided myself for being jealous of my son's attention. Soon he would marry Alais, with her sweet eyes and her long, rose-scented hair. She would hold him for me.

Chapter 11

✣

ALAIS: THE KING'S JEWEL

Windsor Castle
May 1172

That evening's mass was attended by only myself, Marie Helene, and one of Eleanor's elderly ladies as well as the priest who sang it. Vespers followed, and I knelt on the stone floor, my gown tucked under my knees as the sisters of St. Agnes had taught me, long ago.

Marie Helene knelt beside me, though I could feel her thoughts were far from prayer. I turned my own mind to God, and stayed on my knees long after the priest had finished and blessed us. I heard the elderly lady withdraw. Marie Helene rose and stood by the stone wall, where candles in sconces gave the only light.

I stayed on my knees, and prayed for my father and my brother, and for the future of France. I prayed for the Reverend Mother and all the sisters at the abbey, and I prayed for Richard and Eleanor. I even prayed for the king, though something about him vexed me, even as it drew me as the moth is drawn to the flame that kills it.

I tried to turn my mind from Henry altogether, from the warmth of his gray eyes. I tried to forget the way he had tempted me into losing my temper in front of the entire court, though I had been raised to self-control and obedience all my life.

I brought Richard's face to the forefront of my mind, Richard and the song he had written and sung for me himself. The song had been beautiful, as he was, but for some reason I could not understand, no matter how I disciplined myself, my mind kept turning to the king.

As if I had conjured him with my thoughts, I found Henry standing by the altar of the chapel when I rose from my prayers. He had come in silently, and alone. He must have sent Marie Helene away, for she was gone.

I reached for my father's prayer beads, their smooth pearls calming me, their cold diamonds and amethysts reminding me of my father, and all the training of my childhood.

The king came no closer. Henry seemed almost handsome in the dark of that chapel, the dull light from the sconces catching the red of his hair. His eyes did not move from my face, except once, to take in my hair under its red veil, and my breasts beneath the red silk gown his wife had given me.

"Do they not miss you in the hall, my lord?" I asked, because I could not bear the silence.

A strange heat had begun to mount in my belly, and it grew as Henry's eyes returned to my face. I strained my ears to listen for the sound of the priest in the sacristy. As I listened, I knew there was no one there.

"They miss me whenever I leave them, but like the sun, I always return."

Henry did not move closer, nor did he touch me. There were still at least five feet between us, but I felt as if he had stepped toward me. I remembered how it felt to have his breath on my cheek.

"I hope some of your prayers were for me, Alais."

My voice did not fail me, though it sounded strangled, not like my own smooth tones at all. "They were, my lord. And for the kingdom."

Henry's face softened when he heard my earnestness. I am sure that no matter how young he once was, he had never been earnest in his life. But my words must have reminded him of my youth, for the spell was broken as if it had never been. As Henry retreated behind the gray of his eyes, I wondered if I had imagined the connection between us.

"I will leave you," he said. "I hope to see you tomorrow."

I curtsied, my sore knees protesting, my voice still thick in my throat, as if I had swallowed honey. "Good night, Your Majesty."

Henry did not speak again, and left me as silently as he had come. I held my curtsy until he had gone, then stood once more as Marie Helene rushed back into the chapel.

"Are you well?" she asked, fear on her face.

I took her hand. I would never betray to her or anyone the way I was drawn to him, nor the power his gaze held over me. "Of course, I am well, Marie Helene. He is no ogre. He is only the king."

She crossed herself. I took her arm and led her into the hallway. It was dark, the cold gray stone reflecting very little light from the torches that were lit here and there along the walls. I was not sure that I would be able to find my way back to our rooms.

"Do you know the way?" I asked.

Before she could answer, Richard stepped out of the shadows. My voice stopped in my throat. The sight of Richard standing near me, the blue of his eyes searching my face, reminded me that any idea of a connection with the king was foolish fancy. This man was my future.

"I will lead you," Richard said. "Come this way."

We followed him in silence. It was not a long journey, for Richard knew a quicker way than I had taken earlier that evening. Marie Helene went into my rooms before me, to check the fires and to see that the bed was turned down. I stopped in my doorway.

"Thank you," I said. "If you had not come, I would still be stumbling in the dark."

"Alais, I am going to France tomorrow."

"Yes," I said. "I thought you had gone already."

"I was delayed."

"I am glad."

He smiled then in spite of himself. He seemed to remember that I did not dissemble, nor did I lie.

"I will be gone for some time."

"I hope that you will write to me," I said.

"I will."

Richard stood staring at me, as if trying to communicate without speech. I could not read his face.

"I will not be here to protect you," he said.

I did not ask what he meant, for surely there was no danger for me in his father's court.

"Take care," he said, "while I am away."

"I will."

"Promise me."

I stood in the dark hallway, the only light the fire from my room behind us. I looked into his eyes, but I could see nothing, for the shadows were long, and hid the blue of his gaze from me.

"I promise, Richard. I will be careful." I raised my eyes to his. "Thank you for my song."

He said nothing more, but only took my hand. I thought he would kiss the back of it, as he had done once before. Instead, he turned my hand over in his own large one, and kissed my palm.

The softness of his lips and the bristles of his beard made my breath come short. I waited for the hot warmth to pool in my stomach again, as it had done when Henry simply stood and looked at me. But it did not come.

He left me and I stood cradling the hand he had kissed. Marie Helene found me like that and brought me inside. She made me drink the warmed wine she had heated, and gave me a little cold meat and bread, for I had eaten little at dinner.

I lay in bed a long time without sleeping, while I tried to convince myself that the liquid heat Henry inspired in me was some strange alchemy that would have no power in the light of day. I drew my mind back to Richard, to the song he had sung for me, to his kindness. But as I slept, it was King Henry who came to me in my dreams.

At breakfast the next morning, I sat at my small table, my knife biting into the stewed pears the palace women brought. I laid a slice of pear on the soft fresh bread and savored the taste with my eyes closed.

Even in the light of morning, the memory of Henry's eyes stayed with me. I had hoped sleep would cure me of this folly, but so far, it had not.

"The king said that I could see the puppies in the stable," I told Marie Helene.

"The king said that?"

"He said they are fond of me."

"They are only dogs, my lady. They are fond of everyone."

I laughed. "Marie Helene, I am glad that I do not have to worry that you will try to turn my head with flattery."

She smiled wanly. "I am sorry, Your Highness. I fear for you."

Guilt pressed on me. I should not look on the king as I did, and I knew it. I would have to confess my sin, and be shriven. Perhaps once I did that, the heat of the king's eyes would fade for me, along with memory of the scent of sandalwood on his skin.

"There is nothing to be afraid of," I told her. "I am a princess of France."

Tears came to her eyes, and I offered her the linen handkerchief I kept tucked in my sleeve, the cloth that bore Eleanor's crest. As she wiped her eyes, I said, "All is in God's hands."

After breakfast, we found the puppies and their dam where I had left them the day before. No one else was with them when Marie Helene and I ventured into the stable.

One great gelding stood at his stall door, and blew at us when we stepped in from the sunlight of the stable yard.

I rubbed his nose, and he looked at me with his great brown eye, turning his head so that I might scratch his favorite spot.

"Come away from there, my lady. He might bite," Marie Helene said.

"He never bites. Sampson is a good horse for ladies."

Marie Helene knelt in the straw at the sound of the king's voice, but I did not have the good sense even to curtsy.

"My lord, do you spend a great deal of time in your stables? I thought the business of the kingdom would keep you elsewhere." I said this with a smile, as I felt Marie Helene tugging on the hem of my gown.

The king came down off his horse, clothed this day not in the rags he traveled in but in fine brown velvet. Two men-at-arms flanked him, but I barely noticed them. I had never seen the king so well dressed in the light of day. The sun from the stable yard caught the red of his hair, and dazzled me. I did not move, but blinked at him, all my fine court manners forgotten.

Marie Helene tugged on my gown again, and I finally had the sense to kneel in the straw with her.

But I had seen how broad Henry's shoulders were, how his strength could shelter as well as intimidate. I drew my eyes from his narrow hips and the leather boots that encased his thighs. Confused, I chastised myself for my thoughts. I would need to see a priest before the evening meal. I would go to confession at once, as soon as the king gave me leave.

"Rise," Henry said, his voice unreadable.

I stood, and Marie Helene helped me not to stumble. Henry stood before me in a short gown good for riding, his cloche hat set at a rakish angle over one eye. His hose and high boots covered hard muscled thighs that were well shaped in spite of his age.

Henry caught me staring and quirked an eyebrow at me.

The silence that had fallen between us whispered to me. His eyes seemed to speak to me of possibilities undreamt of, of things that could lie only between us, and no one else in the world. Though I could not take my eyes from his, I spoke to break the spell that had fallen over me.

"Good day, Your Grace. It is a fine day for riding," I said.

Henry answered formally, acknowledging that Marie Helene and his own men-at-arms were there with us. His eyes seemed to tell me that he had more to say, but that it could wait, until we were alone.

"And a fine day for lolling in the straw in good silk dresses, I see. Silk does not grow on trees, Alais. You might have a little more care."

Marie Helene tensed beside me, but I knew that the king was teasing me. He meant to make me laugh, not to chide me. I felt the new warmth rising within me, and my laughter with it.

"Then Your Grace will simply have to buy me a new gown."

Henry did not join my laughter as I had thought he might, but stared at me, searching my face.

"Indeed, Alais. The kingdom is not made of silk dresses."

"No, my lord. The kingdom is made of gold and warhorses and land."

He laughed then, and I felt Marie Helene relax where she stood behind me. I found myself wishing that she were not there, that no one else were watching us.

But kings are never private. We stood before our audience, neither able to say what we wished to the other. I chastised myself once more. By now I was so steeped in sin the priest would no doubt give me many prayers for penance.

"I have brought you a present," Henry said.

I felt Marie Helene's warning hand on my arm, pressing hard. But what I said was, "Your gifts are always welcome, Your Majesty."

His eyes lit up beneath his stylish hat, and Marie Helene's hand became a claw on my arm, pinching me. I did not heed her, but kept my gaze on the king's face.

"I am glad to hear it, Alais."

Henry gestured, and I saw that one of his men-at-arms stood in the doorway. Now he stepped forward carrying a box. When he set it on the ground, I heard the box whimper.

I shrugged Marie Helene's hand from my arm. I did not look at the king or at his men, but knelt by the box and opened it.

I found a little dog inside, with white fur and a soft, cold nose. The puppy yipped in joy to see me, and tried to scramble into my arms. I picked her up before she hurt herself.

Her white fur was soft and spongy, her eyes black and set wide apart. I had seen such dogs at my father's court as a child, and had always longed for one. But only court ladies kept lapdogs. I was a princess bound for England and marriage to an enemy. There had been no time for dogs.

How had Henry known of my secret longing? I had never told another soul of my childhood desire for something to care for, something to love that would be mine alone.

She leaped in my arms, licking my face. I laughed and soothed her with my hands, telling her to settle down, that she would be sure to get good scraps for supper.

"She had better get the finest scraps my table can provide," Henry said. "She cost a pretty penny."

I stood beaming at him, my arms full of scrambling puppy. "Thank you, Your Grace. She is beautiful."

"Not as beautiful as you are, Alais."

It was as if no one else were there with us, just Henry, myself, and that little dog. But Marie Helene cleared her throat, and Henry's men-at-arms turned away. I saw them do it, and tightened my hold on the puppy so that she whined. I kissed the top of her head, drawing my gaze away from the king. My puppy was quick to forgive, licking my nose when I got too near.

I laughed, and looked up to find the king watching me as a cat watches a mousehole. I froze at the sight of such naked longing. I felt the warmth in my belly again, heating with the strength of his gaze. In the next moment, the look on his face changed to one of such bland interest that I wondered if I had seen the other look at all.

"A Bijon for my bijou," Henry said.

He turned from me, calling for the groom to give him a leg up onto his horse. As if he held us both under an enchantment, Marie Helene and I followed him out into the stable yard.

Henry mounted and stood over me, his horse making him tower high above my head. As I looked up at him, his puppy in my arms, I saw again that he was king. I wondered how the day before he could ever have seemed otherwise to me.

"Good day, Princess. I will see you tonight at supper."

"You will, Your Grace." I knew that he did not offer an invitation, but issued an order.

Henry rode away without another word, his men behind him. Marie Helene and I stood staring after him.

My little dog barked to get my attention. "Well, little one, what should we call you?"

"Bijou," Marie Helene said. "It will please the king."

I ordered myself to set aside my thoughts of him, the warmth he made me feel, and the way he made me laugh. I would go inside to the priest, who was always waiting in the chapel, sitting with the Presence between masses. I would make my confession. Marie Helene offered to take Bijou from me, but I held on to her. I did not yet want to part with Henry's gift.

Chapter 12

ॐ

ELEANOR: TO DANCE WITH THE KING

Windsor Castle
May 1172

I caught Alais alone with her waiting woman on her way to the priest. I considered it my duty to do all I could to discourage her predilection for constant praying, and for confessing imagined sins. I called her into my solar as she passed by, and she could do naught but heed me.

From the guilty look on her face, I could see that she was glad to have some excuse to avoid the dark cavern of the chapel. She no doubt longed for the sunlit expanse of my solar, as I did whenever I was indoors. When she stepped inside, her waiting woman dismissed, I saw the little dog clutched under her cloak.

"What have we here, Alais? A puppy from the stable?"

"No, Your Majesty. She is my puppy. The king gave her to me."

"Did he indeed?"

I took this in, thinking of Henry's face the night before as he watched her leave the hall. He had joked with me about her while dancing last night. But he had seen her since, and had planned the meeting with no assistance from me.

"The king just happened to have an expensive lapdog about his person?"

I saw the guilt on her face for what it was: Alais knew as well as I did that such gifts were not common, nor warranted, to the betrothed of the king's son.

"Well, let her down, Alais. There's no need for you to clutch her close. There's nothing here that will harm her."

"No, Your Majesty, I fear she will harm something of yours."

I laughed, and Alais smiled for the first time since I had called her to me, her look of guilt fading a little, but only a little. I pressed on, curious to see what else might lie behind her unease. It was not like her to hide things from me. Her priest was in my pay, and from what he told me, she confessed only the usual things a young girl might: speaking harshly to a servant, moments of imagined disobedience, or occasional impure thoughts. I wondered now if there was something else, something her priest had not told me. I would have to increase his fee.

"There is nothing here she can damage, I think. The tapestries are off the floor for the summer, so let her go."

The little dog yipped in joy at her freedom. As all dogs and children did, she ran straight to me.

"There now, little one. What is your name?"

"Bijou," Alais said.

"What a lovely name for a lovely creature." I caressed the puppy's ears. Satisfied with that tribute, she raced off to smell the myriad joys of my solar.

As I watched, the little dog started chewing on one of my women's discarded embroidery frames. Alais at once set it out of her reach, and gave her something else to chew on. I saw that it was a bit of leather from one of Henry's gloves. It must have been in the box with the dog when he gave it to her.

Alais sat beside me when I bade her, and poured us both a cup of watered wine. We drank in silence, watching Bijou worry the bit of leather as if it were a rabbit she had by the throat. This little dog shared more traits with Henry than just the remnants of his glove.

My daughter watched the dog, unbridled joy on her face. I rarely saw her face so open, even when we were alone. I was reminded of the fact that she was still almost a child.

So I reined my jealousy in, and kept my voice even. "Alais, you know, of course, that Bijou was meant to be the gift for another."

She looked at me, a little of her joy dimmed, but I had to remind her of the realities at court. Henry was what he was. She could not give in to fantasy and foolishness where the king was concerned.

"Even kings do not keep expensive lapdogs in their saddlebags," I said. "Your Bijou was intended for his newest mistress, a girl just come to court from the country, some chit he picked up in Anjou."

I wondered what the illustrious Rosamund thought of Henry's newest doxy. I suppressed a smile. I might even ask my spies to look into it, simply to amuse me.

Alais turned pale as she took in this unwelcome news. She looked at her little dog, and I wondered for a moment if she might march out then and there, and cast Henry's gift back in his face.

But Bijou noticed her mistress looking at her, and bounded over, scrambling against Alais' legs, threatening to snag the good silk of Alais' silver gown. Alais raised the puppy into her lap, and kissed her, and caressed her head. If tears came to her eyes, she did not shed them. After a moment, Alais turned to me.

"I did not know that."

"I thought you did not."

I reached out and took Alais' hand. It lay still and cold in mine, distant, as if she were far from me. I squeezed it, and she grasped my hand in return, her palm warming at once over mine.

"You must not trouble yourself," I said. "Henry is given to extravagant gestures. I simply did not want you to read more into it than there was."

Alais met my eyes. I saw at once that she fancied Henry, perhaps because he was king, perhaps because she missed her own father and longed for the attentions of a man, though Richard had given her plenty of that when he was at court.

Or perhaps it was a girlish crush, as I once had on a traveling minstrel when I was twelve. Alais had never had the time or opportunity for such a thing, locked away in her nunnery.

Whatever her feelings were, she would follow my guidance in this as all else. I would watch over her fascination with the king, to make sure it did not become overblown, and confuse her wits. We had come too far with her marriage to my son to turn back now over some benighted folly.

Alais sang for me at my request, so that I could watch her face without encumbrances, so that I could think. She sang a sweet song of spring, of a girl whose love has gone away. I know she thought of

Richard as she sang it, for her face took on a softer look, the kind of look she got when caressing Bijou.

I saw then that I could cast the die either way. If Henry continued to support the alliance with France, and allow Richard and Alais to marry, I would gain power in the Aquitaine and the Vexin both. But if Henry turned his eye on Alais, with a covetousness I knew he possessed, I could secure Richard against his father for all time. If such a thing was to happen, there was nothing I could not persuade Richard to do.

My mother's instincts rebelled in horror at this idea. But if I ever thought that Richard looked to attach himself to Alais above all others, even me, then it was an option I would have to consider, and carefully.

Alais fell silent, her song finished. There was a long moment of quiet, when she looked at me. I feared that she read my eyes, and the evil thoughts that lurked behind them. I loved this girl, more than my own daughters, more than anyone but my son. But I knew that if need be, I would betray her. I had been a politician longer than I had loved anyone. Self-knowledge was a hard thing, but I could bear it. Self-knowledge and the strength to bear it had made me queen, not once, but twice.

I reached for her and drew her to me. Alais set her dog down and came into my arms as sweetly as she ever had, as if she had never cast a lustful eye at my husband, as if she had never threatened to take my favorite son from me. I had no god to pray to, but I prayed anyway. I begged a god I knew did not exist to shield this girl in the days to come, to harbor her, even from me.

In the great hall that night, I made certain that Alais was seated next to me, at my very trencher. No one else shared it, and in this I showed her such high favor that it was remarked on. No one had ever shared my trencher at Windsor but Richard. My food had all been tasted beforehand, and Alais shared the wine from my own silver goblet.

Henry raised his glass to me in greeting, but his glance was cool, the look he might have given anyone, with no calculation behind it. He turned at once to the man beside him and spoke of the kingdom's business, as if Alais and I were both forgotten.

Alais was disappointed that the King of England did not drop all he was doing and welcome her. I laid my hand over hers.

"Try this mutton," I said. "It is very tender."

I spent the entire meal speaking to Alais, often feeding her from my own hand. Before long, she was smiling once more, Henry forgotten. She even lowered her voice and made a joke about one woman's ill-fitting wimple, and I laughed, so long and low that even Henry turned to look at me. Alais did not notice him then, and I thought perhaps my work was done. She could not allow herself to be distracted by the king. She had my son to think of, at least until I decided otherwise.

The whole court noticed the favor I granted her, and smiled on her with more warmth than they had before. Though Windsor held plenty of my enemies, I had friends there, too.

As soon as the dancing started, I beckoned a young man to my side. I think Alais assumed that I would dance with him. I hid my smile, and laid her hand in his. Alais met my eyes, startled, and I winked at her.

"It is time you danced at Windsor, Alais, as you did at Winchester. You must dance, and be joyful, while you are young." I lowered my voice. "Richard will be back in a month. Until then, we must make merry where we can, must we not?"

Alais smiled at me, and it was as if the sun had come out in that dark hall. I simply smiled back at her, and let her go.

The boy I had called over bowed graciously and led Alais onto the dance floor, any thought of another partner forgotten in his duty to the queen. I watched Henry; his earlier indifference was feigned. His gaze never left Alais as the boy I had chosen led her in a reel, hand to hand, spinning slowly on the floor below the dais. I raised my goblet so that he could not see my eyes.

Alais wore her emerald gown that night, cut from the same bolt of silk as my favorite gown. I was dressed in cloth of gold, the only green on my person the emeralds on my fingers, and my eyes. Emerald was a color that suited Alais well.

It seemed Henry noticed, too, for he did not turn from her for even a moment. I had seen that look in his eye many times before, for the first time when it was turned on me.

He did not move on her at once as I thought he might, but bided his time. He watched as one man after another led her out onto the floor. Before accepting the hand of each one, Alais would look to me. I would nod my permission, and smile if the man was particularly good-looking, keeping my face smooth of care, my hand light on the goblet of my wine.

I listened to the jokes and gossip at the table around me, and laughed whenever it was appropriate, letting the music of my laughter compete with the music of the tabor, the lute, and the fife. Henry did not hear me. He had eyes only for her.

It was almost an hour before he rose and left the table, when the man who was speaking to him was in the middle of a sentence. A song had just ended, and before Alais could take the hand of yet another young man, Henry stepped between them.

Alais moved to one side deftly, almost as if her step was unplanned, and she was simply taken aback at the honor of the king's presence. But she had her wits about her. She looked to me, as if I had the power to deny Henry, even on the dance floor. My smile widened, and I nodded. Her face lit with relief, and she accepted Henry's hand.

I wondered if, at my prompting, she might have refused the King of England a dance in his own hall. She turned to me without thinking, without hesitation, as if either she or I had a choice. Her courage warmed my heart, as did her arrogance.

Alais and Henry moved together, the rest of the court forgotten. They stepped forward, then back, weaving in and out among the other couples as if Alais was the prey and Henry, the hunter. Henry was graceful, his movements measured and stately. Like a lion, he matched her pace at every turn, watching not for signs of weakness but for signs of strength. Alais stared back at him, the only woman in the room who could have held his eyes in such a moment, save one.

He seemed to find pleasure in her grace, for his gaze never left her, even when they were separated by the movements of the dance. I saw the fire that drew Henry to her, the same fire that had called to me when she first came from France so long ago. Alais' fire was banked, but it burned strong, and warmed all who came near it.

When the dance ended, they stood close, her hand in his. Henry seemed in no hurry to release her. Alais was first to remember where they were, and who.

She turned to the high table, trying to find me. Henry stepped between us, blocking me from her sight. He brought her hand close to his chest, as if he had no intention of releasing her. A spark of fire arced between them. It did not begin with him.

Henry smiled, his long, slow smile, the smile he had not turned on me since he left my bed. He bowed over her hand, and let her go.

She curtsied low. When she rose again, Henry was gone. He left the hall quickly, as if he wanted to carry the sight and smell of her with him, the touch of her hand in his. I knew he went to his mistress. Alais had forgotten the girl's existence in the heat that had risen between them. No doubt, that night when my husband took the girl from Anjou, he thought of Alais.

She met my eyes across the crowded hall. Everyone was pretending that they had not seen the exchange between her and the king, as if they were not speculating whether he would make her his mistress, and when.

For once with Alais, I revealed nothing of my thoughts. My face was as smooth and seamless as the silk I wore. In one graceful motion, I raised my glass to her.

She curtsied but did not come back to sit with me at my empty trencher. She left the hall, her lady-in-waiting trailing behind her.

I stayed another hour, and called for a song to go with the dancing. I laughed, and ordered more wine brought. I even took the floor myself, when a handsome young man bade me. I had learned years ago, before I ever went to Louis' court in Paris, how to make merry in adversity, how to hide my thoughts and feelings while in company, even from myself.

Chapter 13

ත

ALAIS: A CROWN OF FLOWERS

Windsor Castle
June 1172

"My lady, you are called to go on a hunt."

I sat in the simples garden, doing my embroidery. It was the only place where the ladies of the court would not follow me. The kitchen servants knew me by then, and paid me no heed, thinking me odd. Knowing that I was in high favor with both the king and the queen, they did not turn me away.

A month had passed since Richard left for the Aquitaine. After our dance in the great hall, I had not seen the king alone again. My fascination with him lingered even after I confessed the sin of it, and was shriven. I had confessed the sin only once, but the memory of it stayed with me, though Henry had not so much as looked at me in almost four weeks.

I had spent the time dancing with young men the queen chose for me, and improving my embroidery among her women, though I would never show as fair a hand at it as Marie Helene. I sat for long afternoons with Eleanor when she could spare the time away from her ladies and away from the court.

I would read to her, not from the Bible, but from old Roman texts that she drew out of her trunks, left over from her travels in the Holy Land with my father. We never spoke of my father, that old tie between us, but it gave me comfort to read those books aloud, as odd as they were, and to know that, once, my father had read them, too. They were pagan texts, every one of them, so I could not believe that he had ever liked them. I imagined that he had read them aloud, as I did now, for Eleanor's sake.

On this afternoon, the queen was out riding. She let me stay behind, as she knew I hated hunting with falcons. She had been very kind to me in the last weeks, since the king's interest in me had faded. She said nothing more of our conversation about Henry and his mistress. Whenever she saw Bijou, she greeted her kindly, as if my dog had no connection to the king at all.

When I confessed my interest in the king, the priest dismissed my fear of sin, though he had absolved me and given me penance for it. He said that it was natural I should feel awe in the royal presence, and that not all thoughts of admiration were impure. I tried to comfort myself with this, but I knew the priest was wrong. I was thinking of Henry as I sat in the simples garden, my embroidery forgotten on my lap, Bijou asleep at my feet.

"A hunt?" I asked. The sound of my voice woke my little dog. She leaped up against my knees and scrambled frantically to reach me. I hoisted Bijou onto my lap, where she began to gnaw on my embroidery frame.

I gave her a strip of leather that had once been my shoe, and put the embroidery out of her reach.

"The king's hunt, my lady."

"It seems rather late in the day to start a hunt, Marie Helene."

"I know that, Your Highness, but nevertheless, you are sent for."

I dreaded such hunts and avoided them when I could. I could still see the dove's bloody, beating heart in Richard's gloved hand as he reached up to offer it to his hawk.

I had never been called on to hunt in the king's party. The thought of Henry sent a frisson of joy down my spine, but I knew that such joy was foolish.

"Do I have time to dress?"

I kept my voice even, as if I had no thought for Henry at all. Marie Helene met my eyes. I could not tell if she believed my indifference.

"No, my lady. You must go as you are." Marie Helene took up my things and placed them in their velvet bag. Bijou scrambled from my embrace into my waiting woman's arms.

I ran my hand over the red silk of my gown. "Well," I said, "I hope I keep to my horse."

"Be careful, my lady."

She did not mean to warn me of my bad riding, but of other dangers. I chose to not acknowledge her fears, or my own desires.

"Do not fear for me. I will not fall."

No other ladies waited for me in the stable, nor gentlemen, either. Henry was nowhere to be seen; only a groom stood by to help me onto my horse.

Sampson had been saddled for me. He seemed to remember me from the time before, for he whinnied when I came near. I rubbed his nose before the groom put me on his back. I struggled a moment with my skirts, for I was not used to riding. I had always traveled by litter before coming to this court.

I was still struggling when the king came from nowhere, as he always seemed to do, and took hold of my foot. I froze in place, sure that if I moved, I would fall from Sampson's back and disgrace myself.

"Alais, you are not seated properly."

Without waiting for my answer, the king pulled me down off the horse, so that I stood next to him on the straw. I stared up at him, taking in the smell of sandalwood for the first time in weeks. I welcomed the scent, as well as the touch of his hands. I lowered my eyes so that Henry would not see my face.

Henry's hands stayed on my waist. I felt the warmth of his palms through the layers of my clothes. My tongue fastened itself to the roof of my mouth, dry as dust. I looked down at his hands to keep from looking into his eyes.

The king held me, and the groom turned the other way. I could not catch my breath; Henry was too near.

Just as I thought I must say something or step away, Henry lifted me onto the horse's back, checking the girth himself. His hand lingered on my foot as he placed it into the stirrup. He was wearing a new tunic; the blue offset the gray of his eyes.

I still did not speak, though I savored the sight of him. Once Richard returned, who knew when I might see the king alone again? I would take pleasure in each moment, then put them aside, never to be spoken of. I sat my horse in silence and kept my tongue between my teeth.

"Well, then," he said, in a voice too loud and hearty for indoors. "Shall we go?"

Henry did not move, but seemed to wait to hear me speak. I answered him with difficulty, loosening my tongue against my will and better judgment. "Yes, Your Majesty."

"You might call me Henry," he said.

Though this was what I called him in my thoughts, it was not worth my life to show such familiarity openly. He did not wait for my answer, but climbed onto his own horse, leading mine out of the stable.

It was good that Sampson knew his business, for any skills I had learned my first time on horseback were gone. I did nothing but keep my seat as we rode out into the courtyard and over the drawbridge. I kept the reins firm in my hands, but Sampson ignored me and simply followed the king.

We did not ride hard, though I knew that the king was fond of a good ride. I had been told that we were going on a hunt, but there were no other ladies present and only two men-at-arms. The king brought no hawk; I was grateful not to have to see such a bird again.

We rode until we came to the river, where ash and myrtle trees met with willows at the water's edge. There was tall grass by the river, dotted with purple irises and daisies.

Sampson stopped when the king's horse did, and stood still while the men came down off their mounts. I waited, paralyzed. Henry did not cross the expanse of green at once. As he met my eyes, I was struck by the warmth between us that seemed to rise from nowhere, and come from nothing.

I tried to bring to mind Richard's face. All I could recall was the red of his hair where it gleamed on his shoulders in the sunlight. I remembered the rose he had given me, the rose without a thorn. The flower was long since dead, but I had pressed its petals and saved them in a little drawstring bag. The fragments of the flower he had given me still held their scent.

Henry came to my side, squinting up at me. The sun was high; it was just past noon, and I had not eaten since breakfast. When my stomach growled, I closed my eyes and prayed for death. The king only laughed.

"It's a good thing I thought to bring some dried meat, Princess. We can't have you hungry this long before supper in the hall."

Henry drew me down from Sampson's back. He did not keep his hands on me this time, but let me go almost as soon as my feet touched the ground. When he turned to look in his saddlebags, I caressed Sampson's nose and thanked him for being so careful with me. The great horse lapped at my hair, but did not chew it.

"Is there anything for Sampson, my lord?" I asked.

Henry handed me a crab apple, which Sampson ate in one bite. He gave me some venison wrapped in lettuce, and I tore the lettuce off and ate the meat as soon as the king gave me leave. I stood close by Sampson, as if he might protect me from my own thoughts. Even next to the sun-warmed horse's hide, I could still smell the sandalwood on Henry's skin.

Henry watched as I ate, and I thought I would choke. I ate each bite carefully, chewing slowly, so that I would not disgrace myself. I felt his eyes on my lips and on my throat. I was not embarrassed now, but warm. I opened my palm, and Sampson ate the lettuce right out of my hand, his lips tickling, making me laugh.

I caught Henry's eye, and he laughed with me.

"Will you walk a little way with me, my lady?"

I took the hand he extended. He had taken his gloves off, and I felt the heat of his palm on mine. I did not flinch or shrink from his touch. If I had any sense, I would have been afraid. But for two men-at-arms, we were virtually alone. I was many things, but I was no coward.

Henry smiled when I did not back down, or pull away. He raised my hand to his lips. "You will make fine sons, Alais."

"God willing, my lord."

He looked at me a long time before he spoke again, the sunlight playing in the red gold of his hair. "Yes, Alais. God willing."

We walked down to the shore of the river. The king threw his cloak down for me to sit on. The sun was warm, the grass cool against my hands. He stood looking down at me before sitting a few feet away.

"My lord, you will ruin your clothes."

"I have more."

I did not speak again, but leaned back on my hands, sunlight on my face. The grass smelled sweet, and the purple irises by the water's edge glistened in the light.

It was a stolen moment. I knew that it was nothing, and could lead nowhere, but I decided to put Richard from my thoughts, and Eleanor. I would take them up once more, the people I loved above all others. But for this afternoon, I would sit alone, and enjoy the king.

"This is an enchanted place, my lord. Thank you for bringing me here."

Henry smiled, pleased that I did not dissemble. He heard no false tones of court speech in my voice; as always, I was myself with him.

"And the little dog," he said. "How is she faring?"

I smiled at the thought of what little Bijou might be tearing up even as the king and I sat there. Marie Helene would keep her out of my silks, but that was as far as my assurance went.

"She is delightful. Thank you again, Your Grace. She has brought me nothing but joy."

"It has been only a month, Princess. Do not count your chickens."

I laughed at the king's use of such earthy language, knowing that if he had ever seen a chicken up close, it had been on a plate.

"What have you named her, then?"

"Bijou."

Henry colored with pleasure. When he brought me the dog, he had called me his jewel.

I reached for a flower, and started to twist it around my fingers. The king, too, took hold of a daisy, and started plaiting a chain.

"I did not think kings knew how to make wreaths from flowers," I said.

"Every May Day of my childhood, I made one of these for my mother."

He wove another flower into the thin wreath in his hands, and I watched him do it with practiced grace.

"Did you love your mother?" I asked. After the question escaped my lips, I bit my tongue.

The legendary Plantagenet temper did not show itself, however. His hands simply stopped moving.

I saw that Henry was no longer with me. He had gone back down the corridor of years, and was looking once more on his mother's face.

"She was as beautiful as a spring rain after a winter of nothing but snow," he said. "She was a hard woman, and fierce, but I loved her always, until the day she died."

He seemed sad to think of her. I knew better than to touch him, though in that moment I wished I might.

"I never knew my mother. She died the day I was born."

"I remember."

Our eyes held above the wreath in his hand. The only sound was the river moving beside us, and the sound of the wind in the grass.

"Your Majesty," I said. "Why did you take my father's queen?"

I wondered where my caution had gone, the good prudence, the silent wariness that my nurse had worked so hard to instill in me when I was very small. I thought Eleanor would have slapped me for a fool had she been there, though she had never raised her hand to me in my life. To take such a risk, and for nothing, went against all she had ever taught me.

The wreath of daisies and irises fell from his hands, and he did not reach over to pick it up again. There was no anger in Henry's face, only a question, one that I could not hear or understand.

"I did not choose her," the king said. "She chose me. You will understand the difference someday, Alais."

I did not answer him. I had known him long enough to see that no one's choice would have overridden his own. I thought of the fertile lands of the Aquitaine, and wondered if that was why he had chosen her; I had seen them together at court. There was only a fragment of their old love left between them.

Henry took my chin in his hand so that I could not look away. His eyes were a light gray, and the lashes that fringed them were peppered with ginger and gold.

"We will not speak of Eleanor again," he said. His eyes settled on my lips, caught as if against his will.

I opened my mouth to agree, to say anything that would break the spell that had fallen between us. I could no longer hear the horses or the men-at-arms where they sat away from us, playing cards beneath a tree. I could hear only the sound of the river, the sound of water on rocks, a soft, clean sound that made me want to turn to it and away from him.

But I did not turn away and I did not speak, for Henry's lips were on mine, the first kiss I ever received from a man. I jumped under his hands, but he gentled me as he would a fractious horse.

He did not come any closer or touch me in any way except to hold me still between his hands, and to kiss me. His lips were like fire on mine. When I drew back, my lips still burned where his had touched them. I looked at him, at the fire in his eyes, and wondered if I was damned already.

I had seen lust directed at the women of the court all my life, both in France and in England. I had never before felt it directed full force on me. It took my breath away, that a man and a king could want me with such unswerving desire.

It was electric, that first false sense of power.

Henry did not touch me again. He only offered me his hand and helped me rise from his cloak. He did not say a word.

He raised me once more onto Sampson's back, then gestured to me. I leaned down, thinking that he meant to kiss me again.

He placed the wreath of flowers on my hair, fragrant with the smell of broken stems and the scent of the jasmine nestled by the irises at the river's edge.

I straightened the wreath on my head, feeling the soft petals of the irises and daisies under my fingertips. Henry smiled, and spoke the last words that he would say to me that day. He whispered low, there by the river's edge, so that even his men-at-arms could not hear.

"Someday I will place a different crown on your head."

I clutched my horse's reins. Henry's eyes never left mine. I heard his words for the offer they were, a siren's song, the suggestion, however unlikely, that he might one day set Eleanor aside, as she had once set aside my father, and marry me.

Guilt and horror mingled to gnaw at me. I said a silent Act of Contrition before my horse even began to move. I had sinned once more, against the queen and my betrothed. Though I rejected the idea that Henry had planted in my head, the seed took root that day. I remembered it later, when I was alone.

As my horse followed Henry's mount back to the keep, Henry's scent was still with me, and the touch of his soft lips on mine. I could taste him still, even as we rode away.

Marie Helene saw that I was disturbed when she helped me dress for dinner. The dark guilt Henry had planted within me had not gone, though it was no longer in the forefront of my thought. Still, the shadow of it lingered, even as I tried to keep my mind from it.

I did not speak as she bathed me. Only when I was dressed once more in my dark blue gown did I reach out, and take her hand. I knew what I must do, the only act that would settle the question, the only act that would assuage the guilt I felt for even listening to Henry's idle offer.

"I must write to the king," I said.

"My lady?"

I lowered my voice, so that the walls might not hear. "I must write to the king, my father."

She did not answer, but her face grew pale. Her blond hair was soft against her cheek, her blue eyes staring back at me. I knew she would not betray me.

"I must ask him to call for my wedding date to be set."

"My lady, when you rode out with the king . . . did you fall into sin?"

I remembered that before she was my lady, she had been the queen's. I smiled, though I did not feel it.

"Of course not. All is well. May God bless His Majesty." I said this last loud enough for any spy to hear.

"No." I lowered my voice once more. "But I would be married. I do not want to wait any longer."

"And your father will help you?" Marie Helene asked.

"Yes," I said. "As will the queen." I looked into her eyes; I could see that Marie Helene, too, would stand with me. "But I must ask my father first."

I went to my table, and Marie Helene drew out my parchment and ink. Eleanor had given me such things so that I might write to Richard, and practice my Latin. I drew a chair close to the table, wishing I had my writing table from the abbey. Marie Helene placed the lamp at my elbow, for the sun had set, and the shadows in my room grew long.

"The French ambassador is still at court," Marie Helene said, her voice low, her breath warm against my ear. "I will deliver your letter to him tonight."

From the gravity of her eyes, and the calm purpose behind her gaze, I knew that she understood. To seek help from my father in secret, behind the back of the king, was treason. From the moment I set foot in England, I belonged not to my father's house but to my husband's.

Though I owed my allegiance to Henry and to Eleanor, I would write to my father. As soon as possible, I had to place myself in an honorable marriage, away from the king, for my own sake as well as Richard's. I would hear no more secret offers. Marriage to Richard would protect me from them.

I wrote a short letter, wishing my father well, and asking blessings on his health, and that of Philippe Auguste. In addition to this, I asked only that my marriage date be set, that my father use his influence with King Henry to see that it was done.

I signed this letter and sealed it, using a ring Eleanor had given me just the day before. The ring was gold, and set with the fleur-de-lys of my own crest. Eleanor would help me marry, just as my father would, though I could never tell her why.

I saw the question in Marie Helene's eyes. She served me well, and deserved an answer. "I must marry, before the summer is gone."

"Did the king . . . ?" The horror on her face brought the depth of my sin home to me as nothing else could. My shame rose up from the floor to clutch at me, and I fought it down. I had listened to the king when he made his offer; I had not turned away. I had done wrong, but I would be shriven. I would confess my sin, and see to it that I did not fall into sin again.

"No," I said. "Nothing as bad as that."

She crossed herself, but did not look comforted. She took up my hand where it lay next to my letter on the table. She knelt beside me, offering me fealty, as I once knelt to my father, so long ago.

"I will help you, my lady."

I kissed her, tears rising in my eyes. I blinked them away. Eleanor taught me well: tears fed no gardens; the salt blighted the flowers of my cheeks, and left my eyes an ugly red.

Marie Helene rose with me as I stood to go. She took the sealed letter, and slipped it into her velvet alms purse. She gripped my hand. As we turned to leave for the great hall, Eleanor swept into my room, her women trailing behind her.

"Alais, why do you look so grim? Did you not have a nice afternoon, riding with the king?"

Her eyes glittered. I felt them accusing me, as if she could see into my heart, as if she knew my guilt already. I swore then that she would never know. Such pain would never come to her by me.

I knelt to her, as Marie Helene had just knelt to me. I did not lower my head in supplication, but met her eyes. I raised my voice to be sure all her women heard me.

"Your Majesty, I am yours, now and always. May God be my witness."

I saw that she wanted to ask me why I had to call on God, for had I not always been hers? But Eleanor was politic, and felt the eyes of our audience as heavy as I did. I thought for one horrible moment that the mother I loved would keep me kneeling, that she would turn from me, without giving me leave to rise. She had heard of our ride, perhaps even of the kiss Henry had given me. I saw in her eyes that she knew nothing of the offer he made me, and I thanked God. I held her gaze; I did not flinch or look away.

Admiration for my courage dawned on her face. Eleanor extended one long, elegant hand. Her jewels were like cold fire on my skin as I gripped her fingers. I did not need her help, but she drew me to my feet.

"Come down to the hall, Alais. The table would not be merry without you."

I went into her arms, heedless of the women standing by. I could feel her shock as my arms reached around her and drew her to me. For one long moment I clung to her in silence.

In the next, Eleanor murmured into my hair. "Come away now, Alais. We cannot keep the king waiting."

I heard her true words, *I love you,* beneath this. My eyes filled once more, but I blinked my tears away. Eleanor took my hand, and we walked down to the great hall together.

Chapter 14

✛

ELEANOR: A LETTER

Windsor Castle
June 1172

My ladies were dancing for me in my solar, one playing the tabor and another, the lute, when Amaria signaled for my attention. She went to my prie-dieu and knelt instead of genuflecting. After she blessed herself with holy water, she stayed kneeling. This signal meant that the news she brought was dire indeed.

I waited until the song was finished. Angeline and Mathilde, Margaret, and Joan all bowed before me, flushed with laughter. I applauded them, standing, and they bowed lower, sensible of the honor I did them, not knowing that I had a different motive. When they had taken their fill of my praise, I raised one hand. "Ladies, I must ask you to leave me alone. I feel the need to pray for my son's safe return."

The whole court knew that Richard had been invested as duke

in Aquitaine, and that he was expected to return to Henry's court on the morrow. Alais was waiting for him. Even when sitting in my rooms, she always dressed her hair with the gold filet I had given her to match her ring. The filet was decorated with fleurs-de-lys cast in electrum. It looked well on her dark curls. Though she loved my son, in the hall at each evening meal, I saw that her eyes tended toward the king.

My women bowed and left me, save Amaria, who made my prie-dieu ready for my devotions. I knelt as my women left, drawing the door closed behind them. Amaria knelt beside me. We prayed together for two long minutes, long enough for anyone standing by my door to withdraw. Only then did Amaria reach into her gown and draw out a letter.

"Clarissa sends this, my lady, with her compliments."

"How charming of her. She has no need to send me missives."

I knew the letter in my hand was not meant for me. I did not turn it over and look at the seal. I found, as I knelt in the sunshine as I had seen Alais do, that I did not want to know whose letter it was. Not yet.

"As you know, Your Majesty, while she is at court, Clarissa makes it her business to be your eyes and ears at Windsor."

"Yes."

The news must be bad indeed, if my dour Amaria was loath to tell me.

"Clarissa had the good fortune to spend the night with the French ambassador."

I knew then whose letter I held, but I did not allow myself to think on it. "Good fortune for him," I said. "Louis' courtiers were never much for love play."

Amaria laughed, as she knew I meant her to. "No, madam. So I have always heard." She kept her hands clasped together, in case anyone was to peek in and see us there. "The French ambassador handed that letter to Clarissa as soon as he saw her. He asked her to give it to Your Majesty."

"He gave it to her before he had her?"

"Yes, my lady."

"We must pay him, then."

I rose from my cushion, and turned the letter over in my hand. The letter's seal was the fleur-de-lys from the ring I had given Alais only two days before. She was writing to her father, in secret.

My mind felt like one large bruise as I looked down at that seal. I thought of Alais as a little girl, how she had loved her father when she first came to me. No doubt she loved him still. Her love, once given, was never taken back. Or so I had always assumed.

"Pay him in ducats," I said, "so that the money cannot be traced back to me."

"Yes, Your Majesty."

Amaria stood by, waiting for my next command. She would not send the money herself, but would have one of Henry's men do it. A young and foolish boy, one who would think nothing of doing a service for the queen's majesty. One who himself would never speak of it, and thus make himself useful to me again in the future. There were many such men in Henry's train, more even than he knew of.

Amaria left me then. She had been in my service many years,

and knew without my telling her when I wanted to be alone. She drew the hidden door to my bedchamber closed behind her. She would not go far, but would wait on me, in case I had need of her. She had seen the seal, too.

I sat in my chair, the bright summer sunshine falling across my hands, making the emeralds of my rings catch fire. Louis gave them to me the day I returned to him from Raymond, when we left the Levant together, to make a fresh start once more in France.

I broke the seal, and read the letter. It was very short, and said almost nothing. Even the request it made was nicely phrased, and calm, almost blasé in its demand. The fact that it had been written at all spoke volumes to me. Alais was desperate indeed, if she would turn to Louis herself, without consulting me.

If Henry saw this letter, or even knew of its existence, he would lock the French princess away in a nunnery until all forgot that she breathed somewhere upon the earth. I could almost hear Henry's rage, as it had so often been turned on me, or on my son.

I thought of Richard; if Alais was banished from court for the rest of her life, it would break his heart. Henry brooked no treachery, not from anyone, not even from me. Richard knew this. Henry would never harm Alais, would never raise a hand to a hair on her head, but neither would he allow himself to be deceived.

I smiled as I read the letter over once more. Its calm, cool clarity spoke to me, and sounded more like my own writings than the church-bred missives I had seen her write to the abbess of the Sisters of St. Agnes. I would have expected that pious tone to enter into her letter to her father, but after asking God for a blessing on him and her brother, she did nothing of the kind.

And yet her style was not hurried or desperate. She called for her marriage as she might call for a basket of figs, as if it were a small thing, something her father might send by messenger, as if her marriage was only her due. Which, indeed, it was.

I should be horrified that Alais had moved against Henry, that she had taken such a foolish risk, not knowing that my spies, and Henry's spies, were everywhere. I thanked a god I did not know that her letter had fallen into my hands, that Clarissa had chosen last night to sleep with the ambassador, that after all these years there were still some people at Louis' court loyal to me.

Of course, my generosity was legendary in diplomatic circles. I made it my business to know what Henry paid for knowledge, and doubled his price. People found it expedient to do business with the king, but they were always sure to deal first with me.

Pride rose in me as I read Alais' letter over once more. She had stepped forward and taken her life into her own hands. I would have preferred that she come to me; in the days ahead, she very well might beg my assistance in bringing her marriage about. But her first instinct had been to strike out on her own. Her letter had failed, but she had written it, showing courage and a cunning I was proud she possessed.

I laughed, but the bruise over my heart did not fade. I was proud of her. I loved her. But not long ago, she first would have come to me.

I crossed the room to my bronze brazier, Alais' letter to Louis in my hand. If I loved her with my whole heart, as I had always told myself I did, I would cast that letter into the fire. But I had been a duchess in my own right since the age of fifteen. I had worn two crowns in my lifetime not because of my beauty, not because of my fire, but because always, no matter what the circumstance, I faced life as it was. Information did not get burned. Information got hidden away, unless and until, someday, I might have need of it.

I slipped the letter into my gown and rang the bell for Amaria. She stepped into my solar almost at once. As she looked at me, I could tell that she saw nothing of my emotions on my face.

I raised one hand, and said nothing, but she knew me well. She called my women back in once more, but this time they sat at their embroidery frames. The tapestry for the cathedral in Poitiers was finished, and now they worked on cushions for my bed. I would give away my old ones, once these new ones were done. I had thought to give them to Alais, but now I knew that I would not. I would have new cushions made for her, for Alais and Richard were to marry. I would give them my support, whether or not Alais asked for it.

I thought of Henry, of the light in his face when he smiled down at Alais while they were dancing. I thought of that expensive dog, and of how Henry had taken a new mistress in the last week, one with long curling hair, one with a sweet smile that made even me think of Alais.

She wanted Richard; whatever her true feelings for Henry were, Alais would wed my son. Perhaps I had taught her well enough. Perhaps she understood, as I had always meant her to, that she must value herself above all others, that she must take care and make her way in the world on her own. Treaties came and went, wars were fought and won, but always, a woman must look to herself.

As I sat among my ladies, Bertrand came to sing to us. I listened to my minstrel, all the while wishing he were Richard. Alais joined us, the woman beside me giving place to her.

Alais took my hand in hers and kissed it, as if she had never betrayed me and mine, as if she had never written that letter, or taken her ease with my husband down by the riverside. Her afternoon with Henry had cost me something, and I knew it. I knew every blade of grass they had sat on, every flower that had gone into the wreath he made for her.

I measured her with my eyes, and she sat serene under my scrutiny. Though I was proud of her courage, something was tarnished between us. I decided then that I would shield her from it. For as long as I could, I would protect the princess, even from this.

Chapter 15

༄

ALAIS: ANOTHER GARDEN

Windsor Castle
July 1172

I did not sleep that night, the last night of the month of June, but paced alone beneath my windows. The French ambassador had left that morning for Barfleur, and my letter with him. I said a prayer for his safe journey, and for my father to heed my request.

The wind came up from the river, touching my face as the king had done when he placed the wreath of flowers on my head. I kept that wreath. It lay drying on my table. The flowers had begun to wilt, and soon their petals would fall.

Marie Helene did not speak all that night, but watched me pace in silence. She offered me the good, sweet wine that Richard had sent from his lands in Anjou. I took one sip to please her, but the taste only pained me, reminding me of how precarious my position was as

Richard's betrothed, of how dangerous it was to catch the eye of the king.

Bijou stayed awake with me almost until dawn. She saw I was agitated, and she paced with me, up and down the length of my room, her little legs trailing behind me or running ahead, as if it were a game we played. She finally fell asleep, watching me from the soft nest of Marie Helene's lap.

I felt the guilt of a hundred deaths on my conscience. I sat beside Eleanor all the day before, and all through the evening meal after I'd ridden out with Henry, as if I had not betrayed her, as if I had not committed treason. Perhaps even she would be in danger if the king was to know of my letter. Though she knew nothing of my treachery, she had had the raising of me. The king might hold her responsible for what I had done, for I was in her keeping.

I felt guilty, too, that Richard knew nothing of my fascination with his father. He could never know. I myself must forget it. I prayed that I might, that this sin might pass from me. The Holy Mother watched me from Her niche above my bed, Her eyes patient, but I was not comforted. My mind whirled in a spiral, thoughts that led nowhere.

The sun came up; my guilt did not keep the dawn from rising. I stopped pacing as soon as the night sky lightened to the gray of Henry's eyes. I watched as light bled across the gray walls of his castle, and made its way to me.

Marie Helene let me stand alone for almost an hour by the window before she came to me, knowing that if she approached any sooner, I would start pacing again.

"My lady," she said. "You must dress. You are still wearing the gown from last night's feast."

I drew my thoughts back into the room. I looked around at the fine tapestries and the clean wooden floor, taking in the scent of the fresh herbs that burned in the braziers. My bronze goblet gleamed where it lay on my table, Richard's wine untouched but for one sip.

I met Marie Helene's eyes and saw that though she worried for me, she had begun to see my strength. I took her hand, and we stood in silence, united in the knowledge that my marriage to Richard would take place, and quickly. I would see to it.

Marie Helene raised my father's rosary between us. She pressed the figure of Christ into my palm, so that the gold bit into my flesh, as did the diamonds, pearls, and amethysts that led up from His Body in an unbroken line of prayer.

She said a Novena over me and called on the Holy Mother to guard my steps. I had never before heard a woman's voice raised in prayer except Mother Sebastian's in the nunnery. There was sanctity in it that I rarely felt in church, a level of commitment to God that I had not found even when a priest raised his hand to bless me in the mass. I did not consider that this was blasphemy, but accepted Marie Helene's blessing as a gift from the Holy Mother. I knew that I would need all Her gifts in the days to come.

Marie Helene opened her eyes, and there were tears in them. "Your wash water is coming, my lady. You must take off your gown, so that the servants do not tell the king that you were up all night, thinking of him."

I laughed at the irony in her voice, and I felt my heart lift.

I let her strip my gown from me and take it back behind the screen where my other gowns were kept. In the next moment, castle servants with my wash water scratched once at the door before letting themselves in. Marie Helene caught my eye before moving to instruct them on where to lay the water and fresh linens, as if they could not see for themselves that I had only one table, which served me in everything.

Perhaps it was the new link between us, or perhaps I had begun to grow more wary already. I knew that she meant for me to turn down my bed, so that the servants would not see that it had not been slept in.

I tossed the bedsheets, pressing my hand into my pillows to make a dent, as if my head had rested there all night. The servants did not see me do this, for I was quick.

Bijou seemed to know what I was about, for instead of running to play with me as she normally would have done, she leaped down from the bed and chased the servants' skirts, so that they laughed and made much of her. The women did not look at me at all until they curtsied in the hallway, closing the door to my rooms behind them.

Marie Helene met my eyes over the steaming wash water. "The Lord Richard has returned from Aquitaine," she told me.

I stared at her, not moving. "How do you know this?"

"The servant woman told me as she passed."

I felt as if a dam had broken over my head, washing me in a tide of hope. I knelt in the sunlight, wearing only my shift, my breakfast forgotten.

"God be praised." I asked forgiveness once more for all my sins, my father's rosary between my hands. I asked that God cleanse my mind of all thoughts of the king, and turn my mind once more to Richard, and forever.

Richard waited for me in the kitchen garden. He stood by the willow tree, beside the bench I always sat on. He met my eyes, but did not cross to join me. It was I who crossed the garden to him.

There was no one about, no servants from the kitchen, no women gathering herbs for dinner in the hall. We were alone but for Marie Helene, who stood well back, by the door to the castle.

I held out my hand to him, and he took it. His face revealed nothing but wariness, and I wondered if he still wanted to marry me at all.

"We must marry," I said.

He blinked, as if surprised to hear such words come from my lips.

I lowered my voice, and stepped close to him. I was being too bold, but I did not want to be overheard. Though there were no servants to be seen, someone, somewhere close, was watching us. We did not have long.

"I fear the king," I said. I could not tell him that I feared myself more.

His face darkened. Richard had never before turned such a look on me. I remembered in that moment the gray dove that had lain dying in his hand. That same knife was even now sheathed on his wrist.

"Has he touched you?"

If I told him of Henry's kiss, Richard might leave that garden and kill his father with his bare hands. The king's men-at-arms would stop him with their pikes. I would be without a husband, shamed before all the court, sent home in disgrace, or to a convent for the rest of my life. In my exile, I would know that I had brought about Richard's death. And I would never see Henry again.

"No," I said. "He has not touched me."

My conscience pricked me, but I ignored it. I saw that I had surprised him. Unless I was more specific, he might not move at all. I had no more words to give him.

So I offered what I never had, except to a crowned king or queen: I knelt at his feet, as I would at prayer. I said nothing, but lowered my head. If my words could not move him to act for both our good, perhaps my gestures would.

Richard lifted me to my feet, his hands on my arms. He drew me close and breathed in the scent of my hair.

I stood still in his arms, a bird who could not escape the net. Richard felt me stiffen. His grip loosened, but he did not let me go.

"You need never fear me, Alais," he said. He spoke no poetry and used no flowery phrases. He was a soldier, and not used to making his feelings known, except in song. He spoke simply, his blue eyes never leaving mine.

"I will love you, for the rest of my life. You, and no other."

Richard kissed me, there under the flowering tree. The willow's blossoms hung low, and caressed my skin as they fell from the branches above us.

He tasted of honey and sunlight. No fire burned me as it did with Henry—no warmth rose within me at his touch—but his touch was gentle. This was the path I had chosen as a child. Richard loved me truly, and I loved him. He would stand by me, and serve with me, for the rest of my life. He would be a haven for me when the rest of the world grew dark. He would shield me always; he would keep me safe.

"I must not touch you again," he said. His voice was hoarse with longing.

This time, Richard knelt to me. He grasped his sword, which was always at his side. He drew it from its scabbard, and drove its point into the ground at my feet. I stepped back, startled, but he took my hand in his, and drew me toward him.

He placed my hand on the hilt of his sword, where it formed the cross of Our Lord. This was the sword he had carried all his life, the sword he had been knighted with, the sword he had taken from the hand of his king.

Richard pressed my hands to the cross, his own laid over them.

"I swear I will serve you for the rest of my life. With this sword, I will defend your life and honor as long as I draw breath. This I vow before God. May He be my witness."

I accepted his vow as my due. The sunlight touched his red hair with gold. His eyes were the clear blue of some distant inland sea. His voice, low and honeyed, did not waver, as he swore an oath he would not keep.

Marie Helene and I went back inside. Richard bowed to me as I left, and I raised my hand to him. There was a sweetness about him that haunted me as I left him among the flowers of the kitchen garden. I prayed that I would be a good wife to him. I prayed that I would forget the king.

I went to the chapel, made my confession, and took the Sacrament, for it was almost noon. I stayed afterward and prayed, the sunlight falling into that chapel from the courtyard outside. Only at this time of day did the sun find its way into that part of the keep, touching the colored glass of that chapel with blue and purple fire.

I rose, certain of my purpose. My letter would be in Paris in a few days' time; my father would support me. I must ask for Eleanor's help before my father wrote to her. I would ask her to back me in my marriage to her son.

I left alone, sending Marie Helene back to my rooms to look after Bijou. I was safe in the keep, but with only one leather curtain between my little dog and my dresses, my silks and shoes were not.

I moved alone down the long corridor that led to Eleanor's solar. I walked quickly, a spring of joy in my step, for in that moment Henry seemed far away. My soul was pure, newly washed in the blood of Christ. My betrothed loved me and would stand with me before his father. I had only to secure Eleanor's support, and all would indeed be well.

As I stepped into the wide, torchlit hallway, I saw movement in a niche behind a tapestry. This tapestry covered a window and a little bench, where one or two people might sit concealed, and find a bit of privacy from the rest of the court. Often I had seen Mathilde duck into that niche with one man or another, a few times even with the chanteur Bertrand. I thought that one of the queen's ladies had hidden herself there with a suitor, and almost passed by without looking when I saw the flash of Richard's red hair, and the blue silk tunic he had worn in the garden when he knelt and swore me fealty for the rest of his life.

I moved closer, hoping to speak with him, as no one else stood by. As I came toward Richard, I looked behind the tapestry. There was a young woman deep in the alcove with him. They sat together on a low stool, and Richard was laughing.

The woman was Margaret, my favorite of all the queen's ladies. I had not recognized her at first, for I had never before seen her hair loose. Always before, she had worn a wimple, but now her soft blond hair spilled across her shoulders and down her back. She looked at Richard with adoration as he leaned close to her, one arm around her, his lips on her hair. As I watched, Richard kissed her, as Henry had kissed me.

I stepped back quickly into the shadows of the hallway. Only one torch was lit, for the hall was little used at that time of day. The shadows were deep, though it was only afternoon. In Windsor, without torches to light our way, shadows ruled the stone keep.

For once, the darkness helped and did not hinder me. The sunlight was bright within their niche. If Richard or Margaret had turned to look at me, the sun would have dazzled their eyes so that they could not have seen me hiding in the shadows. But they did not turn to look.

I moved away quickly, but I could not muffle my steps on the stone. I thought Richard might hear me and come out, but the tapestry only fluttered once, before Richard and his lover were completely hidden from my sight.

I do not know what told me that they were lovers. Perhaps it was the anticipation on Margaret's face, the look of unbridled lust that I had never seen in her blue eyes before. And Richard shared her lust. I could almost feel the warmth of it rising from him in a wave of fire.

I knew that fire well. I felt it for Henry. I had done everything I could to drown that fire within me, to quench it, to put it out. I had risked everything by writing to my father, to make our marriage come about, so that I might turn my back on my desire for Henry for the rest of my life. And now I saw that lust reflected on Richard's face, and the look of desire he wore was not for me.

I did not think, but went at once to Eleanor. I stood in the doorway to the queen's antechamber in full view of her ladies, the horror of what I had seen on my face. The thought that Richard would make love to another woman after kneeling and swearing fealty to me was almost my undoing.

Eleanor's hand was on my arm, her strength flowing into me.

"Alais, come inside. Sit with me. You look ill."

She sent her women away, and brought me to a chair. Mathilde and Angeline laughed at my distress behind their hands, but I did not heed them. If I had not known better, I would have thought that they knew Richard had a lover, and that they mocked me for a fool. I felt like a fool as pain rose in me, taking my breath. How could he have sworn love for me in that garden, and turned to another woman not even two hours later?

I sat down in the chair Eleanor offered me, the strength of my legs draining away. I thought of the look on Richard's face as he bent to kiss the woman I had thought of as my friend. Tears rose in my eyes, a scalding heat that burned my throat. I prayed to the Virgin for strength, that I might not shed them there in front of Eleanor.

Eleanor poured wine for me herself, though Amaria stood by. In the next moment, a look passed between them, as if they had stood in that corridor with me, and had seen what I had seen. I saw the worldly knowledge in both their eyes as Amaria withdrew.

Richard loved another. And Eleanor knew it.

Chapter 16

☙

ELEANOR: TRUTH TELLING

Windsor Castle
July 1172

Alais rushed into my antechamber from the outer hallway as if the devil himself were on her heels. I knew then that she must have seen my son with his lover. The niche in the outer hallway was a favorite of Richard's trysting places, as it was for half the court. Even Alais had known of this niche, though she had never used it herself. No, she took her ease with my husband by the riverside, in full view of his men.

Alais froze in my doorway, as a rabbit does before it runs. She, too, would run from her pain, but it would catch her in the end. Better to face it, and know herself. Men brought pain as the spring brought rain, my son included.

I remembered the day I had known that even Henry would stray from me. I had absorbed my pain, and lived with it, but in those days

Henry had known me well, and had seen the pain on me as he would have seen a bruise. I covered it from others, but then I could hide nothing from him.

"Would you rather return to Louis?" he asked me. "He would never take a lover."

"No," I said. "He never did."

"And yet you chose me," Henry said.

I had seen my choice, and knew what path I would take. I reached for Henry's hand, and drew him with me onto my bed of furs.

"I choose you," I said.

I took Alais' arm and she followed me, away from the sight of Richard hiding from the rest of the world with another woman. Alais sat in the chair I offered her, her face as pale as I had ever seen it. Her eyes were vacant, lost, and I knew that I would have to take her in hand. If she thought to marry among my men, she had better learn to take what comes.

"Alais," I said, "you saw something you did not like."

"Richard," she said. She closed her mouth and did not speak again.

I sat beside her and waited, sipping my own wine.

She did not drink her wine, but held the golden goblet between her hands, as if it were the last connection she had to earth. I took it from her and set it on my table. I drew my chair close to her, and took her hand.

"You saw Richard with my woman Margaret."

She met my eyes, and I saw that she was older than she looked. She understood me.

"You knew," she said. "You've always known."

"Alais, if you mean that I knew my son took women to his bed, you are correct."

I let her take this information in. She sat once more in silence, her great brown eyes wounded as they had been on the day I took her hunting, and that bird had bled out its life on Richard's glove. Fury rose in me, that she would be so weak. I had trained her to see the world as it was. I blamed the Church and all its teachings for this.

"Did you truly expect fidelity, Alais? Richard is a good man, the best man I have ever known. But what is true of all men is true even of my favorite son."

I sat back against the cushions of my chair and watched her, my anger behind my teeth.

I saw the political value of all this. I think I saw it first, as I see everything, as a tool to be used to shore up my power. This pain of Alais' could be used as a wedge. I might drive it between them, if I had the need. I might support their marriage while keeping them apart, separate from each other in any real sense, and both dependent on me.

I saw this, as I would see the next move laid out on my chess table before I lifted my chosen pawn. I felt my heart twist within me. I wanted Alais to be stronger than that. I wanted her to let it go, to become the kind of woman I had always been. The woman I had been since the age of fifteen, when I had looked in Louis' eyes and known that my husband loved me, and I did not love him.

She would join me in the here and now. I would see to it that she chose to live in the world. She was my daughter in truth, and I would prove it, both to her and to myself.

I spoke harshly to her, more harshly than I had ever spoken to her in my life. I watched as tears sprang into her eyes. She drew her handkerchief from her sleeve, the one that bore my crest. She wept openly, but I did not hold back. I loved her, but I loved Richard, too.

"All men take lovers. No man, save your sainted father, lives without whores. And Louis would barely rouse himself to sleep with me, his lawful wife."

Alais stood when I said that; fury blazed in her eyes, burning up her tears. For a moment I thought she would cast my wine in my face. But she was my daughter. She stepped back from me, her control fleeting but steady. Her goblet of wine stayed where it was.

"It means little to you who sleeps with my son," I said.

I stood to face her. She was a little taller than she had been a few months ago. She had grown since I had brought her out of the nunnery. She could almost meet my eyes without raising her chin. For some reason, this filled me with pride, even as I fought down my rage.

"Whether Richard sleeps with men or women or dogs, it can mean nothing to you. You will be his wife. You will bear his children, and give him an heir. You will reign as the Duchess of Aquitaine at his side. Your alliance is a political one. Alais, you have given your life to it. You knew that already."

"He said he loved only me."

Her tears were dry then, and my fury drained away, as water from a broken jar. I wanted to reach for her, but knew it was too soon. I held back, and watched her as she wiped the salt from her cheeks, and carefully folded the handkerchief I had given her, placing it once more in her sleeve. I watched her gain control of herself, her passion spent, her inner fire banked.

My heart surged within me, with pride and pain: pride that she was after all as strong as I had ever known her to be, and pain that she suffered so, as all women suffer, and I could do nothing.

We all must walk this path. Sooner or later all women must learn their place in the world of men. Only then can that place be remade, to suit ourselves. But we must first see the world as it is.

"Richard does love you, Alais. More than I have ever seen him love another, more than any woman that he has ever hoped to take into his bed. But Richard is still a man. Men are what they are. Even my son. You must learn to live in the world."

She met my eyes, and I thought for a moment that she would be reconciled, that she would sit with me and drink my wine, that she would let me hold her hand. But she did none of these things.

Instead, Alais walked to the outer door. I thought she might leave me in silence, without a curtsy, without being dismissed. But she turned back and looked at me, and I saw once more how truly young she was.

"I will not live in that world," she said. And then she was gone, my door left standing open behind her.

I did not move, but let my ladies come to me, surrounding me as an incoming tide. They brought chatter and fresh fruit. Amaria took my arm and led me back to my chair. Only when I saw her face did I know that my wound showed on mine.

I smiled then, and laughed, and called for more wine. Bertrand came in and played for us without being asked, and Angeline and

Mathilde got up to dance. I saw that my women meant to distract me; they knew something had passed between me and my favorite. As I watched, I saw that they did not know what. We had remembered ourselves that far, at least. We had kept our voices down, knowing always that the walls of every castle have ears.

Chapter 17

⚜

ALAIS: LOSS

Windsor Castle
July 1172

Marie Helene helped me dress for dinner in the hall. I did not speak, but she saw my face, and the pain there. She was kind enough to say nothing, but laced my gown in silence.

The door was always open, but this day Bijou did not try to flee as she had always done before. Her desire to explore the smells of Henry's castle was overwhelmed by the need to stay by me. She sat on her cushion and stared up at me as I dressed. She seemed to sense my sorrow, as dogs and children can. Bijou came to me, and licked my hand, not for her comfort, but for mine.

I wore cloth of gold, heavily embroidered, the most elaborate dress I had been given since being brought out of the nunnery. The gown

had been very fine fresh from the seamstress' hand, but Marie Helene
had a talent with a needle. She had added to the sleeves in gold thread
an embroidered crest, twining my father's fleur-de-lys with the lion of
Richard's house. I looked down at those sleeves that had given me so
much pleasure. I thought to wear a different dress, but I remembered
Eleanor's eyes, and how she challenged me to be the woman she had
raised me to be. I swallowed my pride, and left the gown on.

I remembered how proud I had been of that gown when Marie
Helene first showed it to me, and how I had looked forward to wearing
it. Now that joy was ashes in my mouth.

Marie Helene placed the filet Eleanor had given me over my
hair. Tonight my veil was a light gold. The fleurs-de-lys of my childhood blessed my temple where they lay on my brow, and gleamed on
my finger where Eleanor's ring winked at me in the firelight. I raised
my hand and crossed myself, though I had not been at prayer.

Marie Helene repeated my gesture before she followed me from
the room, down into Eleanor's hall.

I did not see Richard when I came into the great hall, though I looked
for him. Eleanor caught my eye and smiled, gesturing that I was to join
her at the high table. If she saw the embroidery on my sleeve, she did
not speak of it.

"Alais, what a pretty gown. You will outshine us all."

She met my eyes as if our earlier conversation had never happened, as if I had not stormed out of her rooms without her leave less
than two hours before. Instead of stoking the fire of my anger, her calm

regard gave me strength. As always, the presence of Eleanor reminded me of who I was.

My courtier's tongue loosened as it rarely did, and I spoke without thinking. "That would be impossible, Your Majesty, as long as you are in the room."

I coupled those words with a pretty curtsy. Eleanor laughed and clapped, admiration in her eyes. No doubt she thought I had given in to her point of view, that I would lie back and let Richard take any lover he pleased. I, of course, knew otherwise.

"Well said, Princess, well said. Come and sit by me, and tell me more of my beauty."

I sat beside her at once, and Marie Helene took a chair farther down the table, her worried gaze never leaving my face. I turned from her to the queen, wondering what I might say. I had never before spoken lies to Eleanor. In the end, I found that I could not. Between us, there had always been truth.

"My father loved you." I met the queen's eyes to show her I was no coward.

She faced my gaze, all traces of her smile gone. Eleanor watched me as I had once seen a man eye another over a shield at a tournament, gauging his opponent's strengths, and where he might strike first.

It was the first time she looked at me that way, her calculation naked and open before me. I did not flinch from her, as a lesser woman might have done. However foolhardy my words had been, I meant what I said.

"Your father spoke of me to you, did he? Did he tell you of my fine eyes?"

"No, Your Grace. He never spoke of you. He rarely speaks at all, as you know. But once, someone else said your name, and his eyes filled with tears."

Eleanor scoffed, waving one hand. Her footman moved to fill the queen's glass, and barely dodged out of the way in time to avoid having her select wine spilled across the table. "They were tears of horror, I assure you. Louis bears no love for me, nor I for him."

"I know you don't love him," I said.

She stared at me, her gaze sharp pointed knives, though she smiled. "And how do you know this? Do you claim to know the secrets of the hearts of all women, or only mine?"

"I do not presume to speak of secrets, Majesty. I know none. But if you had loved him, whatever came, you would never have left him."

Eleanor pushed herself back against the cushions of her chair, pinned by my words as I uttered them.

"I have seen it with my own eyes, Majesty, and I do not lie. All men love you. They do not stop loving you, when you are gone."

I looked up the table, to where Henry sat eating venison, his eyes on his master of the horse, who sat beside him. "The king loves you this way," I said, "though I think he does not know it."

"Alais," she said, her voice low, her tone so quiet that I had to lean close to hear her. "I think you are right."

She looked down the table. Henry did not feel her gaze, but kept speaking, uninterrupted, as his master of the horse nodded, certain to do as he was bidden.

"But since Henry does not know of it, his love does me little good."

Eleanor did not look at me again, nor at Henry, but sat and watched as each course came, taking nothing, smiling graciously at the server who brought each dish to her trencher, though she did not eat.

I thought that the king would notice her lack of appetite, and remark upon it, but he never looked at her. It was as if, withdrawn behind a mask of stone, she had become a ghost in her own hall. For without her vibrant laughter and ready wit to draw them, the courtiers all around us turned away from her, and kept their eyes only on the king.

When the meal ended, the musicians came down from their gallery to play the first dance. Richard's lover, Margaret, came to stand among the dancers as they gathered. I watched as all the court greeted her warmly, as Richard's friends and allies fawned over her. I saw clearly that all the court knew of her, and of who she was to Richard. All the court had known of Richard's lover, but me.

The courtiers rose and the king gestured with a smile for the music to start. Just then, with his men flanking him, Richard strode into the hall.

My heart twisted at the sight of him. He stood, tall and fair, his red hair a lion's mane around his shoulders, his eyes fixed on Henry. I stared at him, hoping that he might glance at me, but he had eyes only for the king.

"My lord."

Richard's voice was flat, but it carried well over the great hall. The musicians had sounded the first note, but at the word of their prince, the music died away. Richard bowed once, not low, and then raised his eyes to Henry on his dais. Henry's face hardened as he looked at his son. In spite of my fury at Richard, and the sick nausea that came upon me as I looked at him, I felt my breath catch in my throat.

"'Your Majesty' is the proper greeting to use when addressing your king."

Richard's face was like stone, and I felt his anger rising off him in waves. I saw his temper revealed to me for the first time. There were layers and layers to this man who would be my husband; it seemed that day they were to be laid out before me, one by one, that I might see them all, and know the man I was getting.

"Your Majesty," Richard said, his voice harder still.

Henry's eyes narrowed; I saw the beginnings of the legendary Plantagenet temper in his face. All the court held their breath as they looked at father and son, facing each other in the great hall as if they both wished for a weapon.

"It is also the custom to kneel before your king, especially when you come late to the king's feast, so late that you miss the meat, and break the mirth with your arrival."

Richard did not apologize, but stood his ground.

"Kneel," Henry said.

I saw Richard flinch, and I began to be afraid for him. In spite of my anger at Richard, a cooler part of my brain began to speak to me, to warn me that Henry was in earnest, and that his rage was stronger than Richard's, and farther reaching. I remembered the fate of Thomas Becket, and I started to pray. I prayed to the Holy Mother that Richard's pride might bend, that he might hide his fury and do as the king bade him.

"My lord king."

Richard lowered himself to one knee. He did not stay down, but rose again just as quickly, his obeisance and his rise one smooth motion.

"I come to ask that you honor your sworn word before God. I ask that you honor my betrothal."

Henry started to laugh. His laughter rose and filled the hall, the stone walls throwing it back at me until it seemed that laughter was everywhere at once. I bowed my head, and looked at the king. He was not full of mirth at all; laughter was the way he chose to vent his fury.

"Betrothal? Are there not women enough to slake your lust? And yet you come into my hall and make demands of your liege lord?"

"I demand nothing, sire. I ask only that you do as you have sworn you must."

"Must? Must?" Henry rose to his feet.

Men-at-arms stepped forward from the shadows, armed not with swords but with pikes. I started to rise, to stand between Richard and the king, but Eleanor gripped my hand so hard her fingernails dug into my flesh, and her rings bit into my wrist. I kept my seat.

"This is not a word one uses to God's anointed king. I must do nothing but my will. I am king in this hall. You will never be."

"Honor my betrothal, Father. Set the date for our wedding."

"It's the wedding night you crave, boy. And again I say, slake your lust somewhere else. For the Princess Alais is in my keeping, and she will stay in my keeping until I deem otherwise."

"She is in your power. Give her to me."

"Get out."

Henry's voice was not the shout I expected but a deadly calm that belied the fury on his face. "Get out of my sight, you miserable whelp. For now I tell you this: you will never have her. Not today. Not tomorrow. Not next year. Not for as long as I draw breath."

I clutched Eleanor's hand, and turned to her, that she might stand between them, and stop this. Her face was as pale as driven snow.

Father and son faced each other with such hatred that if one had held a weapon, the other would be dead. No one in the hall moved, or even breathed, in that long moment of silence.

Richard did not speak again, but turned on his heel and left the hall with his men following him. He left me there, clutching his mother's hand.

Henry looked neither right nor left, but strode from his own hall without a backward glance. He went out a side entrance, into the corridor that led to his private apartments.

The courtiers did not gossip or laugh when this scene was done. They stared at one another in the deadly silence, until, one after the next, they rose from their benches or moved out from the shadows, where they had gone to get away from the prince, and from the wrath of the king. Every one of the courtiers turned and left the hall, and the servants with them, until Eleanor and I were left alone.

"Stop him," I said. "Don't let Henry kill him."

She smoothed my curls back from my face. "He will never kill Richard," Eleanor said. "Not as long as I draw breath. Now let me go."

I saw then that my fingers were clinging to hers, our earlier rancor far from my mind. I forced my fingers to relax and release her. My hands were stiff with fear. Eleanor chafed them, drawing blood back into them. She stood and kissed me.

"Fear nothing, Alais. I will go to the king. Follow me in five minutes' time. Do you know the way?"

"I will find it," I said, meeting her gaze without flinching.

She left me then, and I sat alone. The hall was empty but for the

rats that moved under the tables, looking for scraps now that all
the court had fled.

I found the king in his antechamber, in the room that led to the royal
apartments where he slept. Eleanor stood facing him, and I could see
no traces of his rage, as if it had never been. The king and queen stood
together, a few feet apart, but close enough that they made me think
of conspirators, come together to weave a plot. Henry stood still, a letter of vellum in his hand.

I thanked God that the king was no longer angry as I knelt on
the hard wooden floor.

"You may leave us."

Henry's voice was calm, and almost sweet. I blinked, thinking
that he had ordered me from him already, when I saw a girl not much
older than myself cross the room to him. She wore little, just a shift
with a fur robe thrown around it, though spring had passed already
into summer.

Her hair was long and curly, like mine, and its blond length
reached her waist. Her eyes were blue like the summer sky, and I was
surprised how pretty she was.

I did not think to question her presence, until I saw her kiss the
king.

I felt my throat close with jealousy. I tried to force my eyes from
the sight, but I could not look away. The king had not kissed me that
way, down by the waterside. His lips had not devoured me as if he
would drink me in.

Henry caressed her hair, his hand coming to rest on the small of her back. He stroked her backside absently, as one might stroke a horse, his eyes never leaving Eleanor's face.

"I will come to you anon," he said.

The girl left him, closing the door to his bedroom behind her. The king turned to me at once, his paramour forgotten. There was nothing of the connection between us in his eyes, as if our time together by the riverside had never been.

"You come into my presence unannounced and uncalled for. What do you want, Princess?"

"I come to beg Your Majesty's forgiveness."

Henry's face smoothed to blankness.

I meant to speak for Richard, to call on Henry's kindness to me, but it seemed his son no longer interested him.

"I have a missive here. Do you know what it says?"

"No, my lord."

"That's odd, Alais. Because you wrote it."

My heart stopped in my chest, and my knees gave way beneath me. Henry held the letter that had been meant for my father.

He did not look away from me, and I came to myself, half kneeling on that stone floor. I would not let them stand over me in triumph. I rose slowly and faced him, trying to gather my scattered wits, the fury in my eyes held in check, but barely. I had been betrayed. My father would never read that letter.

Henry saw the calm courage in my eyes, and the fire of my fury behind it. He looked into my face, seeking me out. Had Eleanor not been there, I think he would have said something more. As it was, he walked to the brazier behind him, and cast my letter into the fire.

"Never write to your father again, Alais. I am your king now."

Henry stared at me for a long moment, as if waiting for me to speak. I said nothing; Eleanor stood watching us. I saw in his eyes not only his anger at me, but, beyond that, a deeper wish to go to his whore.

He walked away from me, his eyes on his bedroom door. The room was silent after he left. The only sound was the crackle of burning vellum, as the last of my letter bled out in smoke and ash.

"Alais," Eleanor said, "the next time you send a message, see to it that the courier is not in my employ."

I heard her words as if they had been spoken to another. She had betrayed me twice: first, by knowing of Richard's infidelity and saying nothing, and second, by handing my treasonous letter over to the king. Had our roles been reversed, I would have burned her letter as soon as it came into my hand. The knowledge of her betrayal was a distant pain. I had lost both Richard and Eleanor in the same day, almost in the same hour. I found I could feel nothing.

"I loved you."

It was my only thought. As I stood there, watching her smile at me, I could only speak the truth.

Eleanor's smile faded. "You love me still, Alais. You always will. Just as I love you."

I thought that she would leave me, but she stopped by the door to the outer hallway. "I betrayed you to Henry to save Richard. Your letter distracted him, and bought me time. Richard is gone from the keep, safe from Henry's anger. It was necessary."

I did not speak, but stared at the door the king had gone through. Behind its smooth panels, I could hear the gasps of his whore as he drove her in love play. Eleanor and I stood together and listened as Henry's whore called out his name.

The sound of their motions stopped, and there was silence. Eleanor stared at me for a long moment before she turned and walked away.

PART III

&

A WOMAN GROWN

Chapter 18

☙

ALAIS: TO BED A KING

Windsor Castle
July 1172

Marie Helene waited for me in my rooms, Bijou on her knee. My little dog tried to leap from her lap and come to me, but when Marie Helene saw the look on my face, she held her back.

Her sewing basket lay on the table; she had been embroidering the sleeves of my silver gown. I looked down at my arms and saw my own sleeves of gold, where the gold thread traced out my crest, and Richard's. Eleanor giving my letter to the king was the final stroke that severed my self-control. The anger I had been suppressing all day rose in me in one great tide, and my reason was swept away. I grabbed Marie Helene's scissors from her basket. She watched me, but did not move, for something in my face held her still.

I could not bear the touch of that silk a moment longer. The cloth

of gold reached around me, drawing my slender waist in its grip, chok-
ing me so that I could not move, could not breathe.

I did not wait to unlace myself, but cut the laces of my gown
with Marie Helene's scissors with one smooth sweep of my arm. She
gasped, frightened that I might hurt myself, but when I laid the scissors
down, there was no blood on them. With those laces cut, I could
breathe again, but only barely.

I tore the gown from my body, the beautiful, expensive gown it
had taken three women a week to make. I cast it onto the stone floor
of my room, and it lay there like my discarded hope. I thought to throw
the scissors down on it, to trample it, as I wanted to trample on Eleanor
and Richard for the way they had tricked me, for the way they would
still use me, for I was in their power. I was still to marry her son.

When the king's anger cooled, in a month or a year, I would
have to stand before God and swear to obey Richard for the rest of my
life. I would have to take yet another oath, and keep it, no matter what
came after, no matter how many women he thought to bring to his
bed. My jealousy almost overwhelmed me.

My love for him lay in shards around me like broken glass. I
could not walk anywhere for fear of cutting myself, not forward, nor
back. I thought of my father, and how he had endured such humilia-
tion at Eleanor's hands when they had been married. All the world
knew that she cuckolded him without restraint. And so would Richard
do to me.

I had known of such things all my life. To expect fidelity from a
man was to expect the sun not to shine. I found that though I had held
this truth in my mind, my heart had not known it. It was my heart that
bled now, and burned with fire.

I snatched my golden gown from the floor and tore at it. I was weak, and the dress was well made, for I only made a small rent at the hem.

I lifted Marie Helene's scissors once more and heard her say, "No, my lady!" But she did not move to stop me.

I used those scissors to start a tear, but I did not want to just cut the gown to ribbons with steel. I wanted to rip the dress apart with my own hands, and that's what I did, each tear feeding the next, until the gown lay in pieces at my feet, on the table, and draped over a chair. When I finally came to myself, I was holding one sleeve, staring at Marie Helene's beautiful embroidery in my hand.

Tears obscured my vision. I remembered Eleanor's admonition, to give my tears to no man, but to keep them for myself, for they were my own power, and no other's. I remembered those words, and I drew my tears back into my heart.

It was Eleanor's betrayal I thought of finally, as I came back to myself. The sight of my letter in Henry's hand stayed with me, the proof that Eleanor had used me for her own ends, without hesitation, without remorse. Perhaps she had always done so, and my love for her, and hers for me, had been an illusion. I knew that, in the future, she would use me again. I dried my eyes on the remnant of that golden sleeve before I cast it into the fire.

The charcoal in the brazier flamed high when the silk and cloth of gold touched it. My dress burned well, but gave off noxious fumes. I stood in that black smoke, until each and every piece of that gown was burned to ash.

I turned then to wash my face and hands in my silver bowl. Marie Helene set Bijou down and moved my brazier close to the window, so that the fumes would be carried away by the wind over the river. The wind blew in my favor, and carried that black smoke out of my chamber.

I stripped off my dirty shift, and washed myself as best I could. Marie Helene called for more water, and the castle servants brought it, though the hour was late and they all should have been in bed.

I stepped into that steaming tub, and Marie Helene bathed me without a word. She sang a sweet song, low under her breath. The sound of those words soothed me as nothing else could, as did the touch of her hands on my hair.

She had the smoking brazier taken away, and a new, finer one brought, one that did not give off noxious odors. She led me gently to sit beside the fire; she dried my hair so that it curled to my waist once more in waves of brown and gold and maple, hair like my mother's, the woman I had never seen. I longed for my mother, my real mother, for the first time since I met Eleanor.

Marie Helene stroked my hair, and it seemed to me that I felt my mother's touch behind her hand. Then Bijou, who had been frightened by my fury, came out from beneath the table and lay down on my foot. I picked her up and kissed her, and held her for the rest of the night.

I did not stay awake, as I had the night before. I said my prayers, asking for a blessing on my father, on my brother, and on the kingdom of France. Then I slept, with Marie Helene beside me.

Before I slept, I remembered the king's words to me, down by the waterside. I still had the wreath he had made me. He had crowned me with those flowers; he had told me that one day he would place another crown on my head.

I knew well that the king had spoken in the heat of the moment, when lust no doubt had overwhelmed his reason, or perhaps when his mood had been softened by our time together on the grass of the riverbank. Henry no doubt had forgotten his words almost as soon as he spoke them. But I remembered.

Tomorrow, I would see the king.

In the morning, I stayed in my rooms and Eleanor did not send for me. I took a little bread and cheese at noon, and then called for Marie Helene to dress me.

I was calm by this time, for I knew my purpose. I would step out on my own. I would leave Eleanor and Richard behind, and see what I might make of my life for myself. I had the clarity of thought that comes after great anger, when a woman knows she has nothing left to lose, and everything to play for.

My love for Richard still lay in shards at my feet. I would love him all my life, but it was a love fraught with lies, a love I could not live with.

I would not think of Eleanor. When she came into my mind, all I could see was her elegant, tapered fingers holding my father's letter, handing it in one graceful motion to the king. I knew her reasons for betraying me: she had handed over my letter to save Richard, as she would have betrayed anyone else to protect the son she loved. Her love for me had not stayed her hand; she had never loved me, if she could use me as just one more pawn on her chessboard.

As I dressed, I thought of Henry. I set aside all ideas of sin and loss, and thought of his gray eyes, of his wide peasant hands, and of how his hands felt on my waist, lifting me down from my horse.

I perfumed my body and my hair with the rose water Eleanor had given me, and donned my red silk gown. I paid close attention to my shift as well, and chose one embroidered by Marie Helene with red flowers at the hem and along the collar. I did not draw the string at the throat closed tight, but left the shift to drape over my shoulders. I knew that with one tug, it could easily be drawn off.

I wore my red silk gown, for it was the first dress Henry had seen me wear in his hall the night he fed me from his own trencher, the night he offered me venison from his own knife. I laid a light veil across my hair that covered my curls but did not hide them. Over that veil I wore the filet Eleanor had given me, the fleurs-de-lys of my father's crest riding like a crown over my brow.

I looked into my bronze mirror, and I did not recognize the woman reflected there. My face was the same except for my eyes.

"My lady," Marie Helene said. "You must consider."

"I have already considered."

"Your Highness, you must think of the queen."

"I do think on her, Marie Helene. I go to the king. Every step I take toward his chamber, I will think of her, and of her son."

Marie Helene did not speak again. As I watched, two tears formed in the shadows of her eyes. They fell in silence, marring her cheeks.

"Do not weep for them," I said.

"My lady, I weep for you."

I laid my mirror down, that I might not see my own bitterness. "Marie Helene, there is no need."

I left then and walked alone to the king's chambers, though Marie Helene asked to go in my stead. She hoped to call on him, so that

Henry might turn her, and thus myself, away. I knew better than to send another to do my bidding. I was nothing, and no one. I had not even Eleanor's love and protection; to her, I was just one more thing to be used and discarded. Whatever I was, and whatever I would be, I would have to make of myself.

The king was not alone, as kings never are. I stood outside the door to his antechamber, dressed in my red silk gown. The men-at-arms who kept the gate stared at me as if I were an apparition. I simply smiled at them, and asked to see the king.

They did not know what to do, so they sent a page inside with my request. I had chosen my time well, and carefully, for the daily business of the kingdom was winding down. In an hour, the king would go to the main hall, to greet his people and break his afternoon fast. There would be dancing and singing in the hall, as there was every night. Women would smile at him, offering him their charms, were he to choose to taste them.

If I had my way, Henry would not be there that night.

I did not wait long. Henry's chamberlain called me in almost at once, bowing to me, for he knew who my father was.

I saw Henry standing beside his worktable, which was piled high with scrolls of vellum. Lamps burned and smoked, for in the depths of Windsor Castle it was already night.

"So, Alais. You come for me."

I met his gray eyes without flinching. His face reflected none of his usual easy familiarity with me. I saw his anger, thinly veiled. He had not forgotten my letter to my father.

For a moment, I feared that the connection between us had broken, burned away in the fire of his lust for his whore or in the fire of his rage, as my letter to my father had burned to ash. But as I saw the flicker of anger take light behind his eyes, I knew that we were not done with one another, not yet. All was not lost. I still might play, and win.

I stepped into the room, and Henry's ministers made way for me. He watched me, standing by his table, a roll of vellum in his hand. His eyes did not leave me, though he feigned indifference before the men standing there. I felt the heat of his gaze first on my face, then on my breasts and hair. I had him, and I knew it. It was for me to play it out. I raised my first pawn, and knelt before him.

There was a deep silence then, as all his men stared at me. I felt that each man wished he were alone with me. Each wished that he might draw that veil from my hair, and cast my filet aside, the gold of my father's fleurs-de-lys tossed to the floor, my silk skirts raised above my waist.

I knew little of the act of love, but the night before, I had made Marie Helene describe it to me. At first she feigned ignorance, then modesty, but when I told her what I would do, she dropped all pretense and explained what would happen, and how it would hurt, and why a woman, once lost, was lost forever. I did not care. I did not mean to lose myself to Henry, as I had to Richard and Eleanor; I meant to find the road to my future in him.

The silence stretched on, and I neither moved nor spoke. Henry finally raised one hand. "Leave us."

Whatever business they had been about, whatever moment I had interrupted, was over. Henry's ministers filed out, one behind the other, each seeking the sight of me once more before the chamberlain closed the door behind them.

"What do you want, Alais?"

Henry came no closer, but his eyes were on mine, and the softness of my hair where it lay against the curve of my breast. I stared back at him. I did not lower my eyes. Henry liked boldness in women, and I was bold enough for anything that day. I would get what I had come for.

"I come to beg your forgiveness, my lord king."

Henry snorted, throwing the vellum scroll he held onto the pile on the table. He paced away from me, and moved to pour himself a cup of mead. I felt his eyes on me, even then, and the connection between us was as strong as it had ever been, even when he held me in his arms down by the riverside. I could feel the heat rising from his body, and we were more than ten feet apart.

As I knew he would, he circled back to me, until he was standing only a few feet away, his cup in his hand.

"Alais, what are you playing at? Has Eleanor sent you?"

I laughed, the music of my laughter rising to fill those gray walls. I did not hold it back, but let it surround Henry, and draw him closer to me, though he did not move.

"I am here at no one's bidding, Your Majesty. I come for love of you."

Henry scoffed again, but I had caught his attention. He did not even look at his cup as he set it down once more with not a sip drunk from it. He stared at me, his gray eyes boring into mine, seeking me out, searching for a lie. I stared back at him. I had no more lies to tell.

"I thought love had to be earned, Princess."

"It does. It has been. You have won mine."

"By not throwing you out on your ear? For not locking you away for high treason?"

"No, my lord. For seeing me alone when I have done you wrong. For letting me ask forgiveness, when I have thrown away the right to it."

"No one has the right to forgiveness, Alais."

Henry stared at me, and I did not take my eyes from his. I watched the wheels of his mind turning, and saw that he still was not ready to give in to me, not yet. We both knew why I had come. He simply did not believe it. I would have to show him.

"If it is forgiveness you want, you have it." He waved one hand, as if to dismiss me, as if to dismiss the heat that even then rose between us, like a tide that would not go out. "But most penitents do not seek forgiveness dressed from head to toe in red, Alais."

I rose to my feet in one graceful motion. I had been taught to rise smoothly as well as kneel gracefully when I was a child. I stepped toward him, my senses on fire, the scent of him reaching out to me, drawing me close. Henry was a man, and did not back away from me, but his eyes widened. He would have expected this from any other woman, but never from me.

"It is your favorite gown, is it not, Your Majesty?"

He did not answer me, but his face hardened. I saw that he would resist me, and I smiled. He was resisting himself, and for nothing.

I raised my lips to his, but did not kiss him. I took in the scent of sandalwood from his skin, and woodsmoke from the braziers that burned nearby. I breathed him in, as if I would devour him. I let him see that I favored him in truth, and not only because he was king.

"I wear this gown to please you, Majesty. Tell me, then. Does it please you?"

Henry gripped my arms and held me still. I could not tell whether he meant to hold me back or keep me near. I saw in his eyes that he was at war with himself, but I knew he need not fight a losing battle. I had chosen him already.

"You know it does."

Henry bent close to me, his lips over mine, his breath hot against my skin. But then he slipped the leash, and let me go. Before I could take my next breath, he was walking away from me, passing through the inner door to his bedroom beyond. He stopped in the door, and spoke to me over one shoulder.

"Go, Alais. I have had enough of childish games. Go back to Eleanor."

I crossed the room to him and caught the door before he could close it in my face. "No, my lord. I will not leave you."

His body squire stood at attention in the room beyond, his eyes wide, one of Henry's boots still in his hand. The other had been blacked already and sat warming by the fire. The boy saw Henry and myself and his face turned gray as ditchwater. He bowed when Henry raised one hand, giving him leave to go. I did not look at him, as if he were not there. I kept my eyes fixed on the king.

"Alais, what do you want from me? Would you have me take you, like some milkmaid, like some peasant in a field? You are a princess of France."

"Yes, my lord king, I am a princess of France. And I would take you."

Henry laughed, running one hand through his mane of red gold hair, so that it stood up in clumps along his temples and above his forehead. He laughed long and hard, but I did not back down or look away. He thought to humiliate me, to make me leave him in peace, but I would have what I came for.

Henry saw me watching him. He, too, felt the fire between us that would not go out. He sighed then, and sat down on his bed, his head between his hands.

"Alais, God knows you are beautiful. And I have wanted you since the moment I saw you, kneeling in the straw. But I will not take you."

He met my eyes, and I saw the truth of why he stopped, of why he held his hand, when any other man would have had me and been done with it.

"It would ruin your life."

I crossed the room slowly, as if he were the deer and I, the hunter, as if I did not want to startle him or frighten him away. I knelt once more between his knees, and raised my face to his, so that he might see my eyes, so that he might hear me, and know that I was in earnest.

"Henry," I said. "I want the life I choose, not one that was chosen for me. I want you."

Even then he did not reach for me, but looked down at me as if searching for the truth behind my eyes. No doubt he saw that my motives were not pure. And it was true that love for him alone did not drive me.

No doubt he saw my anger at Eleanor and at Richard. He saw the pain of their betrayal in my face, though I had spent a long night at prayer trying to banish such thoughts from my heart. He knew, as I did, that what I offered was a political alliance that might not last the month. Other tides could rise, and sweep him from me, and me from him.

He knew all this, so his touch was gentle when he laid his hand on my cheek.

"What of our treaty, Alais? Do you not think on France?"

"I always think of France, my lord king."

I took his hand from my cheek and kissed his palm, as Richard once had done to me. Henry held his breath, and I felt his desire rising even as I knelt before him. But he was not won, not yet. He was a man in control of his desires. I would have to meet his reason on common ground.

"Let us make a new treaty, Henry, between us. And if it fails, I swear to you that I will marry where you bid me, and follow your commands for the rest of my life. I am yours, now and forever, if you would have me."

I would like to say that Henry touched me out of thankful joy in my presence, that love conquered reason, and he swept me into his arms. This was not the case, for either of us. Even as I knelt before him, I saw his mind turning over the problem I presented him.

Before he so much as kissed me twice, he knew both the risks and the costs of what I offered him. But like me, he was willing to pay.

He raised me up and drew me to him, so that I sat beside him on the bed of state. I wondered how many of his sons had been conceived in that bed, legitimate and otherwise. I wondered how many mistresses had lain between those sheets, as I was about to do, and whether Henry would keep me long, once he had me beneath him. But these thoughts, all thoughts of politics and loss, were burned away in the heat of Henry's fire.

His hands warmed me even as he stripped me first of my crown and veil, then of my red silk gown. Henry left my shift on me, for it seemed he liked the sight of my body outlined against it in the fire-light. The fluid light on my young body held his focus for many min-utes, and I thought perhaps he would only toy with me, and not take my maidenhead.

I saw him wonder if I was a maiden at all, though he was too much a gentleman to say so. But as his hands raised my shift and toyed with my nether parts, a satisfied smile lit his face before his own gown was off.

"I see you are mine in truth, and not just in name, Alais."

"I am, Henry. I swear it."

He laughed, his lips against the skin of my breast. His tongue ran over me, even as his fingers entered me, and I gasped. Marie Helene had told me of what might happen, of the things Henry might do to please me, but hearing the words and feeling the king's touch were two very different things.

"Alais, if you are truly mine, I will hurt you at first. I cannot help it."

"I know, my lord," I said.

He laughed, his hand lingering over my breasts while his fingers laved at my inner wetness, bringing me closer to a tightening pleasure, one I had neither expected nor looked for.

"And will an entourage of your ladies come for you soon? Will they whisk you away to bathe you once you are done with me?"

I gasped under his hand, while Henry watched me, as a hawk does a dove, waiting for the sight of something on my face.

"No, my lord," I said, almost too far gone to speak. "I am yours all night."

Something in my words drew him, for his fingers increased their strength on me, and I moaned, a great wave of pleasure welling up inside me, cresting over my head. I could not get my breath even as it passed, for Henry was on me. He entered me in one hard push, coming hot on the heels of my pleasure, so that I barely felt the pain at all.

Henry moved within me, and I clung to him, my knees rising to take him in deeper, so that he moaned and laughed at once. "Dear God, Alais, you are a witch."

"No, my lord. I am yours."

He grimaced and convulsed within me, spilling his seed inside me as he had in countless other women, Eleanor and Rosamund included. I found I did not think of these other women after the first moment, however. I lay beneath Henry, and caught my breath, feeling the first pang of soreness as he withdrew from me.

"Alais, you are a deep river of pleasure."

"One that will never run dry, my lord."

He laughed again, and I heard the thought, though he did not voice it, that "never" was a word not to be spoken between us. Who knew what expediencies the next day would bring? For now, the king was mine, and the real game could begin. Now it was up to me to keep him.

The king and I lay together for half an hour, his hand in my hair. I lay across his chest, and rained kisses on his cheeks and over his forehead. He laughed at me, and it seemed to me his laughter held a hint of light, a trace of something he had not allowed himself in many years: a sense of ease and peace.

I thought that we might again fall to love play. Indeed, Henry's hand sought me, parting my thighs so that he might work his magic on me once more, and give me that pleasure I had no right to expect. He had opened the door to my pleasure, his body raised over mine, when his chamberlain came in after knocking, followed by his page and washmen.

Stumbling upon us, the man exclaimed, "My lord king!"

The chamberlain could have been no more shocked if I had been a nun, and Henry had me up against a wall in church on Sunday. I laughed, and Henry laughed with me, his lips on mine.

It was not he but I who spoke to his chamberlain. I rose from Henry's bed, drawing a fur about my shoulders. There was one left on the bed always, for even in summer the nights grew chill in Windsor Castle. I stood, and the fur covered me to my knees. I let one shoulder be seen, and drew my hair back, so that it hung down to my waist, a riot of curls that drew all eyes, even those of the young page, who knew better than to look at the king's whore.

"Sir Roland," I said, "please send word to the great hall that the king will not be down tonight. His Majesty will break his fast here in his room with me."

The chamberlain turned as pale as death, no doubt expecting a shout of fury from Henry, who never let a woman order his servants in his presence. I waited, too, to see which way the die would fall.

Henry said not a word, but nodded once to his man, who bowed deeply, his face to the ground. Sir Roland backed out of the room. I almost laughed at his show of abject humility meant only to hide his shock, and perhaps his secret laughter.

Before he left, I raised the tankard that sat on the king's table and found mead in it. I set it down at once.

"Sir Roland, please send up a pitcher of the queen's wine from Anjou. I would take it with my evening meal."

Henry smiled, leaning on one arm, still reclined in bed as I had left him. Sir Roland stopped dead in his tracks. He raised himself from his bow, and stared at me.

"Do as she says, Roland."

The man bowed once more, tearing his eyes from me, from the sight of my calves beneath Henry's bearskin, from the sight of my hair curled where Henry's hands had been playing in it.

The chamberlain left at once, his men with him. The youngest closed the door behind them all, casting one last look of horror and awe at me.

I laughed again, the music of it ringing off Henry's bedroom walls. I crossed the room to him, dropping the fur on the floor as I walked, so that for the first time Henry saw my nakedness, my youth and curves, the bounty that I had offered him, the bounty that now was his, and no other's.

"You played that hand well, Alais."

"I played and won, my lord, only because you let me."

Henry smiled at me, his hand running once more down my back, over my thigh, and between my legs, where he cupped my sex, and caressed it, his eyes always on mine. "As long as you remember that, Alais, we will do well."

I opened my lips over his, and kissed him. He took me under him and entered me, to make certain I knew who my master was. I moaned as he rode me, this time reaching that peak of pleasure without his fingers to guide me. He rode me hard, as a stallion rides a mare, and this time I found that pleasure beneath him for myself.

I left him gasping, as he left me. His body was warm over mine. I nestled down beneath him, reveling in the feel of his hard thighs, and the scent of sandalwood that surrounded me, now that I was with him.

Henry looked at me, his mind working as it always was. I kissed him, but he would not be drawn to me again.

"Eleanor thought she knew you," he said.

The pain of my adopted mother's name stabbed me as a dagger might, just below my breast. I did not gasp, for by that time I knew my own strength. Henry watched my face for a sign of weakness. He searched my eyes, but did not find it.

"No one knows me. No one but you, my lord king."

Henry kissed me as his chamberlain brought in our dinner. On a tray sat a silver ewer and goblet, holding Eleanor's wine. Water beaded along the edges of that pitcher, for all the castle knew that the queen took her wine cold.

I raised myself up, hiding my charms behind Henry, and behind the great thickness of my hair. "Thank you, Roland. That will be all."

The chamberlain looked to Henry, then back to me.

Henry raised one hand, and his chamberlain withdrew. I kissed Henry, but his lips did not move beneath mine. I drew back, and met his eyes.

"I wanted to send a message to the queen. Thank you for allowing me."

He did not speak, so I rose from his bed. I walked naked to our dinner, and set out chicken on a silver plate, and fruit, and honeyed bread. I brought that plate with his mead and my wine, and I set it on the bedclothes between us.

I offered his beaker; he took it and drank deep. I raised a choice bit of chicken from the plate, and held it up, that he might feast from my hand. His lips were warm and soft on my fingertips. Henry stared at me, and took what I offered him.

"You are good to me, my lord. I will endeavor to deserve it."

He kissed me, and I tasted the mead on his tongue. He set our plate down, along with his beaker and my wine. He raised himself over me and took me again, this time in silence, this time taking his own pleasure with no thought for mine, so that we would both remember that he was king.

Chapter 19

⚜

ELEANOR: THE KING'S HEALTH

Windsor Castle

July 1172

I sat in royal splendor at table with all the great lords of the kingdom arrayed about me like stars. Some sat at the high table with me, but many seats stood vacant: my son's, which would not be filled that day, and also Alais' chair, and the king's.

I called for my wine, because my steward had not brought it as he always did. There was some tumult among the house servants; it seemed my silver ewer had been mislaid, so that my wine was brought to me in a vessel of gold.

I raised one hand, and had my steward taste my wine there in front of me. When he did not fall retching, I let him pour it into the golden goblet that stood by. It was good to drink from gold, better than silver, except that I had not called for it, which meant that someone else had.

I drank my wine, but the food sat untouched on the trencher before me. All the hall waited, as I did, for the king to come in and begin the feast. No one would eat a grape or a morsel of squab until the king had come and seated himself among us, and raised the first bite to his own lips.

There was laughter in the hall that night, but to my court-trained ears, the sound was false, and rang with fear. I wondered if they feared for Richard still, for another confrontation between the king and my son. Richard was tucked safe away, half a day's ride from court. He would stay there until I called for him. I had yet to make his peace with the king.

So something else kept the courtiers on edge. The Earl of Hertford raised his glass to me in salute, but would not meet my eyes. One of my own ladies laughed behind her hand. It was then that I began to know that whatever these people feared had something to do with me.

I felt but did not see the eyes of the lower tables raised to me. They stared at me, and whispered, but whenever I turned my head their way, as if to ask one of my ladies a question, the courtiers at the lower tables shifted their gaze from mine, as if I might read their lips, or their thoughts.

Henry's castellan came to me, his piggy eyes averted out of fear. This man hated me, as so many of Henry's men did, especially the men who lived at Windsor. He thought me a whore and worse, no doubt, though I had never cuckolded Henry in all the years we had been married. I knew my husband. It would not have been worth my life to defy him in that way; Henry would not have killed me outright, but he would have locked me away if I had ever betrayed him.

This man was a fool, and hated me for no other reason than that I had held the king's ear for years longer than anyone else ever had. His eyes shifted away from mine, and I knew that he hated me still.

Henry's castellan bowed low to me, as if he respected me. I saw then his fear of me was real, and I leaned back on the cushions of my chair, smiling. Whatever was going on, it must be good news indeed to make this man bow so low.

"Your Grace," he said, his voice not even stumbling over my title, as if he honored me. "The king is not coming to the hall this night."

I held myself very still. My smile did not fade. "Indeed. Did His Majesty send word telling us why?"

He flushed, the pale skin of his sweaty face turning red with the effort not to breathe in my presence. He bowed again, very low. "No, Your Grace. I believe the king is taken ill."

"But you are not certain."

"No, Your Grace. I am not."

I raised one hand, and he withdrew, still bowing, backing away from me as if I were a lion that might maul him if he turned his back on me.

I caught Marie Helene's eye. She was sitting next to Alais' empty chair. I heard a muffled laugh from the end of the high table, and something in its tone touched my heart with cold.

I called Marie Helene to me. She came at once, her eyes averted, as everyone's eyes were averted from mine that night. Whatever news was being bandied about the court regarding my husband, everyone had heard already. Everyone but me.

She sat beside me when I gave her leave, in the chair that would have been Richard's had he been there. Still, she would not meet my eyes. I touched her hand, once, very briefly. Surprised, her blue eyes met mine.

"You served me, Marie Helene, for years before you served Alais. Is this not so?"

"It is, Your Grace. I serve you still."

"Indeed. But you serve her first."

This time her blue gaze did not drop from mine. "Yes, Your Majesty. I serve the Princess Alais."

I sighed, and sat back once more against my cushions, lifting my cup of gold, taking a sip of my newly watered wine.

"That is fitting," I said. "I would ask you a question, Marie Helene. I could ask it of another woman, to win her loyalty, to flatter her, so that in days to come she may sit close and flatter me. Or I could ask one of my spies, who serve me for gold, and for fear, and they would tell me. But I would rather ask you. Do you know why that is?"

"Because I do not lie?" she asked.

In spite of all the years she had lived in my court, she was still naive, as Alais was. She still believed in honor and in duty. No doubt, she even kept her given word.

I sipped my wine in its golden goblet, and wondered where my silver one had been taken, and to whom. My spies would tell me that before the meal was done, but for now, I spoke to Marie Helene, the woman to whom I had given my daughter's keeping.

"Marie Helene, I ask you because you love me. Am I wrong in saying that?"

I saw the pain on her face, the pain of divided loyalty. She knew, no doubt, as all the court did, that Alais and I had quarreled over Richard. Being close to Alais, she no doubt knew more than most. She met my eyes. I saw that, in spite of her other loyalties, she would not lie to me.

"You are not wrong, Your Majesty. I love you, as all men do."

I waved her attempt at flattery away. "We need not trouble ourselves with niceties, Marie Helene. I want only the truth. Will you give it?"

"If it lies in my power, Your Grace."

"Very well. Tell me what the court is whispering. Tell me, where is the king?"

She did not look away, though I knew she wanted to. She was honest, as Alais was honest, which was why I left her to serve my daughter without asking her to spy for me. I had plenty of spies, and Alais had needed a friend. She had found one in Marie Helene.

"Your Grace, it is news that will be hard to hear."

I laughed, setting my wine cup down. "I have lived many years in this court, Marie. Let me be the judge of what is hard."

I leaned close, as if to kiss her cheek, offering my wine cup, that she might sip from it. "Tell me," I said. "I would know it. And I would hear it from you."

"The king stays in his rooms abovestairs," she said.

"Yes, all the world knows that. But what do they whisper? No one wants to tell me, but I will know it."

Marie Helene swallowed her fear, and a sip of my favorite wine. I watched the movement of her elegant throat, the swanlike grace with which she set my cup down again without offering it to me. She met my eyes, and spoke the truth that no one else, even my paid spies, had the courage to tell me.

"The king is in his rooms. The Princess Alais is with him."

She spoke low, so that no one else might hear. I looked around my husband's court, an easy smile on my face. I did not feel the pain at once. I have heard it said that mortal wounds are not felt at first. Only later, after the blade is drawn out, does one feel the pain. The blade was still in me, and deep. I did not yet draw it out.

I needed to know only one thing more.

"Did the king call her to him?"

"No, Your Grace. The princess went to him herself."

I laughed then, so that all the court could hear me. I took a ring from my finger and pressed it into her palm. "I thank you, Marie Helene, for bringing me news that no man in my employ was brave enough to carry. Sit here at my side, drink my wine, and eat my food. We will make merry in the king's absence."

Louis' emerald set in gold sparkled in her palm. For half a moment I thought that she would not accept it, that she might actually set my favor aside. But of course, she did not. Whomever she served and whomever she loved best, she also loved and served me. I was queen.

I stood and raised one hand. All the hall fell silent at once. I knew then that our talk had not gone unnoticed; even now spies moved among the courtiers, giving out word that I knew of my husband's infidelity, and Alais' betrayal.

"Lords and ladies, gentlefolk all, welcome to my husband's hall."

They cheered me, as if I had announced a tournament. I heard in their voices the relief of sheep that sought a shepherd, the bleating of sheep that needed to hide from the wolf. Tonight they would find that safe haven in me.

"Word has been sent me that the king has taken ill."

Their cheers were silenced. A cup was dropped somewhere by some ham-fisted servant girl, and the sound echoed in the stone hall like the toll of a bell.

"We must all pray for the king's swift recovery. Please know that the Princess Alais, lately come from France, ministers to our lord at his bedside. Let us drink to her, and to his health, that what she brings our king may succor him, and raise him up once more."

There was another silence, as they took in my words, and their double meaning. A thunder of cheers greeted me, and almost salved the pain of my daughter's treachery. They called my name first, and hailed me as their queen. Remembering themselves, they called on Henry, as if he were a god that might strike them down if they did not.

They laughed, too, beneath their cheering, but none of them was laughing at me. I called for wine from my own private barrels to be sent around the hall. I had never shown this favor in Henry's hall before, and it raised yet another cheer, this one in my honor.

"So, let us make merry and drink deep, all the while keeping our lord the king in our prayers. Long live the king!"

I raised my own goblet as I said this, and everyone rose around me, one great sea of courtiers, called to attention by me.

"Long live the king!"

They cheered once more as my dancers came into the hall. Amaria could read my looks even from a distance, and she had sent for Bertrand and my musicians, as well as for my lesser ladies, the ones who danced with my waiting women for my pleasure in my own rooms. My musicians struck up a light and rousing tune as my ladies danced among the tables, and came to stand below the dais, bowing low to me.

I raised my hand once more, that the hall might see where this bounty of music and merriment came from. Amaria was at my elbow then with a sack of English coin, which I cast down among them. They danced across a shower of gleaming gold.

Henry was tightfisted and paid his musicians and dancers after the feast, and in silver. I paid mine in gold where all could see my largesse. They remembered then how rich the Aquitaine was, and that I still held it, no matter who sat as duke in Poitiers.

Amaria met my eyes once more, and at her bidding, favored ladies and gentlemen rose from the ranks of the lower tables to sit with me at Henry's board. No one took the king's place, of course, but the rest of the table was filled to overflowing with laughter and merriment, rich food and fine wines. A great peacock was displayed in the center of the table in my honor, although it was a display that had been meant for the king.

I took the court's worship as my due, as indeed it was. They saw then, if they had ever doubted it, that no matter who Henry took as mistress, I was queen.

Of Alais, I tried not to think. Marie Helene sat beside me, my ring gleaming bright on her finger, touching her hand with fire. I saw the pain in her face, and knew that she pitied me. To my surprise, I did not despise her for it. It was good that someone, somewhere, felt my pain that night, since I could not.

I could only smile, and raise my glass, and eat more than my fill of succulent pork and fowl. I could only rise to my feet and dance every dance with every fine young man and gallant swain who asked me. And when it came time to hear the songs, I sat and listened to each one sung in my honor with a smile on my face, as if I could hear them.

I shored up my power that night in Henry's court. Indeed, I had not been so powerful among his ministers since his mother died, before Rosamund had ever shown her face. I drank my wine, and accepted tribute from Henry's men, who bowed and kissed their hands to me. I knew that they would despise me on the morrow, for I was a woman cuckolded by her own daughter, in her own house. But tonight, they honored me.

At court, it was always best to live each day as it came.

Chapter 20

༄

ALAIS: THE KING'S MISTRESS

Windsor Castle
July 1172

Henry woke first, but he did not leave me. When I turned over, and drew my hair from my eyes, I found myself cuddled close to him in my sleep, his eyes on me.

I did not know that for the king to stay abed with me was a high honor. Any other woman would not have been allowed to sleep at the king's side, but would have been sent away when he was done with her. We had broken new ground. Already, I was more than I had been.

"Good morning, my lord," I said, my voice sleepy, my eyes still heavy with dreams.

Henry kissed me, his lips warm on mine. I felt his love for me behind them, and no trace of his lust, or mine. He kissed me, and I felt safe, safer than I had ever been. I knew that this safety was a slippery slope; I would have to tread carefully to stay in favor, move with care to stay in his good graces. But for that moment, and for as long as we were alone, I forgot all that. I would forget that he was king. He was the man I loved, the man I wanted; the man I finally had.

"Good morning, Alais, Princess of France."

I kissed him back, my lips lingering over his. I wanted him to make love to me again, though he had kept me awake with love play into the early hours of the morning, his hands on my body, his body over mine.

"In this room, I am no princess," I said. "I am only yours."

Henry laughed and moved as if to draw back, but I clung to him, my hand running down his thigh, and he stayed.

"You are always a princess, and I am always king."

"I know that, Henry. But here, behind the curtains of your bed, may we not be lovers, and nothing more?"

"No. You know we cannot."

I drew back from him this time, for he would not join me in love play. I saw that if I was not careful, he would leave me, and deny that this night had ever happened. Then I would still be no one, with nothing, with nothing left to play for.

So I used the weapon I always used with Henry when my wits and wiles failed: I spoke the truth.

"Henry, I am a princess of France and you are King of England. We are bound by treaty to keep faith with my father, to keep the peace between our two countries, between the lands you and my father hold. I know this. Last night did not change it."

I raised myself so that I sat before him. He listened to me, and his eyes never left mine for an instant.

"I have allied myself with you, now and always. I will live my life in your service, and in the service of France."

"And what of Eleanor?"

He knew me already. This pain was the worst, the most hideous truth he could throw back at me. I did not lie to him, even then.

"I love Eleanor. But I will serve you."

"From love?"

I did not lower my eyes. "I do love you, Henry. But with or without love, I am yours, for the rest of my life."

"And your father's," he said.

"By serving you, and serving this treaty, I serve the throne of France."

"And if you must marry my son, next week or next year?"

"I will do it if you command me."

"And for no other reason?"

"For no other."

He kissed me then, pressing me back against the soft sheets of the royal bed. He moved over me, and came into me before I could catch my breath. He rode me hard, and touched me deep, so that in moments I was gasping under him, filled with the pleasure that only he could give me.

When his man came in with his breakfast, I saw that he had brought enough bread and honey for both of us. I drew a fur around my shoulders, and cut into a pear, slicing it up on a silver tray. I took a bite, then brought it to the king, and fed him from my own hand.

"You must leave me, Alais. I have the work of the kingdom, and I must be about it."

I let the fur drape down past one shoulder, and offered him another bit of fruit. Henry laughed, and ate it, but I saw that he was not moved to change his mind.

"I would rather stay here with you," I said.

"You cannot."

I set down the silver tray, and licked the juice of the pear from my fingers. I raised my fingers to his lips, as if to wipe pear juice away. I leaned up and kissed him, taking his tongue into my mouth like a wanton, like a whore, the way he had taught me to kiss him in the dark reaches of the night.

"Henry, I would be alone with you."

His hands drew me close, clasping my hips so that I could feel the strength of his desire for me against my midriff. And I had thought him an old man almost in his dotage. My eyes had been opened. I was a woman in truth.

"Give me today, Alais. Give me time, and we will be together."

"How long?" I asked him, my clever hand slipping between us to clasp his desire in my palm.

He groaned and pressed himself to me, then withdrew at once, before either of us could take our pleasure again.

"Give me a day, Alais. Tonight, in the hall, I will see you again."

"I will sit at your trencher," I said. "I will eat from your plate, and drink wine from your goblet."

He pulled me close once more, as if he could not help himself, as if he would savor me, before he left to do his duty. "You will, Alais. You, and no other."

"All right, then. Until tonight."

I dropped my fur, and let him look at my naked body. Never before had I known the value of my beauty or my youth. In Henry's bed, under his hands, I had learned what Eleanor, in all her years as my mistress, had never taught me.

I felt his eyes on me as I drew on my shift and tied it loosely at my throat. My fingers lingered in his favorite places, at my throat, over my breasts, over the curve of my hips. I stepped into my gown and pulled it closed around me, taking my time to lace the side, drawing the red silk ribbons closed, as Henry had drawn them open, slowly, his eyes always on me.

Henry knocked on his outer door, and a man-at-arms came in and bowed low, first to Henry, and then to me.

"Matthew will take you a back way to your rooms."

I stepped toward Henry and met his eyes. I stood close, but did not touch him. I kept my voice soft, with a touch of servility, now that we were no longer alone.

"My lord king, I would walk the main corridors unencumbered. I am ashamed of nothing that has passed between us."

Henry's gray eyes examined mine, and he saw once more that I was not lying. I think he began to love me in that moment, when he knew my courage and saw it reflected in my eyes.

He drew me close, and kissed me. "Indeed, Princess. And so you should not be." Henry handed me my veil, as if he were my lady's maid. Once I pinned it to my hair, he placed my gold filet on my head.

He lowered his voice, and pressed his lips to my ear. "Give me until tonight. I will take care of you. You will see."

"I trust you, my lord. I will wait."

I curtsied, bowing low, so that my head rested at the level of his thigh. He chuckled, and raised me up. "You had better go, Alais, before I forget that there is a kingdom to see to."

I said nothing, but smiled back at him over my shoulder before following his man into the darkness of the hidden corridor. I walked away from the king then, and I did not look back.

I found Marie Helene alone in my rooms, dressed in the same gown she had worn the night before, my little dog drawn close on her lap. She set Bijou down as soon as she saw me, and my puppy ran to me, jumping on my knees. I knelt to pet her ears. She licked my face, happy to see me, and happy to catch the scent of Henry on my hair.

"I did not sleep, for fear of you," Marie Helene said.

"You should have," I answered. "All was well with me. I was with the king."

"I know, my lady. I thought you might return, and need me."

I crossed the room to her, and took her hand in mine. "I would have woken you." She still would not meet my eyes. "Are you ashamed of me?"

Her eyes flew to mine at once, and I saw the truth in them. "No, my lady."

"Then you fear the queen."

"No, Your Highness. I fear for you."

I squeezed her hand, then let it go. "Do not, Marie Helene. As I said, all is well with me. I am with the king."

"My lady, what of your father?"

I felt shame pressing on me, calling to me from behind the closed door in my mind, where all the teachings of my childhood lay. But the door stayed locked. I would see to my father's welfare. I would see to the kingdom of France, as was my duty and my right. My shame was my own business.

"Do not trouble yourself for my sake, Marie Helene. I have all well in hand."

She did not question me again, but went to fetch my bathwater. I saw on her right hand a ring, gleaming in the sunlight of my bedroom. It was an emerald set in gold. The queen had given it to her, to secure her loyalty, perhaps to spy on me.

"Marie Helene, I see her ring on your hand. Do you serve the queen?"

"No, my lady. I serve you."

Without looking down at her hand she reached for the ring, and drew it off. She moved to my window as if to cast it from her, out of my sight. I caught her hand in mine.

"No, Marie Helene. Keep her ring, and wear it. But if news of me comes to the queen, I will know it came from you."

She knelt, and her face crumpled, tears on her cheeks. "My lady, I swear, she will learn nothing of your doings from me."

I felt the sharpness of my own words pricking me, but I would not have my rooms divided against me. I raised Marie Helene and kissed her, for I saw how deeply she had been hurt by what I had said. I repented the pain I had caused. She was simply a pawn, as I had been, as I would still be had I not struck out on my own, and made a bargain for myself.

I dried her tears with Eleanor's handkerchief, then slid that bit of linen back into my sleeve. Even now it was dear to me, the dearest of all my possessions. The king might give me a dozen gowns in cloth of gold, and have his own people embroider his crest on my sleeves. Still, that bit of cloth would be the dearest thing I owned, because once it had been hers.

I bathed, and dressed in a dark blue gown. I strung my father's rosary about my waist, but I did not kneel to pray as I usually did in the morning. Marie Helene called for picnic things, and for a man-at-arms to carry them. I would not walk out alone, with only one woman to accompany me. I would be careful of my honor, and protect it, now that I was the king's mistress.

I set aside all thoughts of Richard and of Eleanor. I set aside all thoughts of my father. I still had a good deal to play for, and I could not do it if I thought of them. Henry was drawn to me, but I did not have him yet. I would have to secure him, and hold him fast, before I took the next step toward my chosen future.

We walked out of the castle, Bijou in my arms. It was still early, so we saw no one from the court, which was just as well. Our man cast down a blanket for us at the riverside, and we spent the day eating bread and cheese, and watching Bijou pretend to hunt in the tall grasses that grew there. She was small, but like her mother, she had the heart of a lion.

When we came back to the palace, night had begun to fall. The shadows grew long in the corridors at Windsor, and our man had to lead us by the light of a torch back to my rooms.

As we passed the courtiers in the hallway heading downstairs for the evening meal, they met my eyes. I thought they might simper or laugh at me behind their hands, pious Louis' daughter, the princess of France who had fallen into disgrace. But they did not. Instead, they all stopped as soon as they saw me. Each bowed low to me, almost as if I were queen.

We came into my rooms, and Marie Helene went to fetch new shoes for me to wear into the great hall that night. Eleanor's woman knocked almost as soon as I closed my bedroom door behind me. The queen must have known where I was, and had kept watch for when I would return.

Margaret entered my rooms when I gave permission, but she did not come close, as she once would have done. At the sight of her, my anger rose once more, and I almost ordered her from my presence. But Eleanor had sent her. It was a blow intended for me, and I stood under it.

The girl's face was pale beneath her veil. No doubt she had heard that I knew of her affair with my betrothed, and of my fury. But now I had no stones to cast at her. I was a mistress, too.

She curtsied deeply, and spoke to me with respect, fear shining from her clear blue eyes, as if I were an adder that might bite.

"Your Royal Highness. The queen requests your presence in her rooms before supper in the hall. If you would see her there, she would be most obliged."

I thought she would leave then, her message delivered. As Margaret stood watching me, I realized that she waited to take my answer back.

Marie Helene shifted behind me. I heard her hush Bijou, who had begun to bark, angry at not being allowed to run and sniff the new woman standing there.

I saw in Margaret's fear-filled eyes that the whole court knew of my fall, and that it did not make me less in their eyes. By taking my maidenhead, Henry had raised me in the esteem of this court, if nowhere else on earth. That would work to my advantage in the days to come. I still had everything to play for.

"Please tell the queen that I will come to her directly."

The woman curtsied again, this time with her eyes downcast. "As you wish, Your Highness."

Marie Helene looked at me, and I saw the fear on her face. I went to her, and kissed her cheek. Bijou leaped up between us, as if to free herself from Marie Helene's arms. I stroked my little dog's head.

"Shall I come with you, my lady?"

I saw that no matter how I reassured her, she would always fear for me.

"No, Marie Helene. Dress for dinner. I will see you in the great hall."

She curtsied as I left, Bijou in her arms. Even Marie Helene respected me more now that I was Henry's lover. We would see how much else I might gain, if all the court found respect for me after only one night.

Chapter 21

⚔

ELEANOR: THE QUEEN

Windsor Castle
July 1172

When Alais came to me, she did not knock, for the door was open and my women saw her coming. The tallest of my ladies beckoned her in with a smile, as if to welcome her into the ranks of the wicked.

I raised one hand, and my women withdrew from the room.

The door closed behind them. Amaria lingered, to see if I would have her stay, but my hand remained raised, so she withdrew as well. Alais and I were alone, but for Richard, who stood behind me. If she was affected by the sight of my son, her face showed no sign of it.

I stood before my daughter, before the woman who had betrayed me with my own husband in my own house. I looked for the little girl I had known, the little girl I had taken under my wing when she first came to me from France. As I looked into her eyes, a woman stared

back at me, a woman of my own devising. Had I not been so miserable, I might have laughed at the irony of Fate. As it was, I simply offered her a chair.

"Will you join me, Alais? Will you take some wine?"

"I thank you, Your Majesty. No."

Alais continued to stand, and continued to look at me. She did
not glance at my son or acknowledge his presence.

It had been a long day for me. I had endured scenes with Richard, who came back to court when I sent word, who now stood behind
me in sullen silence, having refused to leave the room. I had suffered
the silent consternation of my own ladies, which no doubt turned to
amusement when they were out of my sight. I still had the meal in the
great hall to face. I hoped to settle with Alais now, and to make the best
of what had happened.

"Alais, you must deny the king."

She stared at me, the daughter of my heart, and I saw her strength
as I had always seen it. Now I saw not only her strength but also the
will behind it.

I had thought to control this girl. She was only fourteen. But then
I remembered: I had been only fifteen when I first became queen of
France. I had asked no one's leave, either.

Alais held my eyes when she answered me. "I deny nothing."

I sighed, and sat down, raising my goblet of wine to my lips. It
was my silver goblet, the one that had gone missing the night before.
I found later that it had been brought to Alais in the king's rooms, at
her request, so that I had to drink my wine from another. I kept my
silver ewer and goblet in my own chamber now. No one would be
fool enough to take them from there, not even Henry's chamberlain.

Henry's people were allowed nowhere near my rooms, though no doubt he had spies among my women, as I had among his men.

"Alais, you have put me in an untenable position. You have slept with my husband, and all the court knows it. You must deny that it happened. If we stand together, we can save your reputation and our treaty with France. If you stand with me, I can protect you, even from yourself."

"I have the king's protection. I have no need of any other."

I felt my temper rise, and I clamped my jaw down on it. If we both gave up our reason, neither of us would get anywhere. I did not look to Richard. He stayed silent behind me, as he had promised me he would. I knew he did not trust himself to speak with her, that, even now, his heart bled as if she had stabbed him with his own knife.

My eyes moved to the hourglass and saw that there was little time left before the evening meal. I would have to secure her assent, and quickly. There was no more time for niceties.

I saw the stubborn set of her lips, and remembered where I had seen that stubbornness before. Louis had always looked like that when he was determined to get his way. Louis had given me that same look when I asked to be left with Raymond in peace. No doubt he would have worn that look the whole time he laid siege to Antioch, if I had not walked out of that city, and agreed to come home with him. The stubborn look sat strange on my daughter's face, but she had been Louis' daughter before she was mine.

"You are making a fool of me in my own court, Alais. I will not allow it."

She stared at me without answering. I saw that she had not forgiven me for handing over her letter to the king. Behind her fury, I also saw her pain. She felt Richard had betrayed her, simply because he was a man. She felt I had betrayed her. She was furious with me for acting against her, for handing over her letter to Henry. But she was my daughter. I could bring her back to me.

Richard stepped forward then, and came to stand at my side. Finally, Alais looked at him, at the man she had claimed so fervently to love before she cuckolded him with my husband.

When she saw his face, the pain in his eyes pierced her fury. Alais took a step toward him, as if drawn by a higher force, as if she could not stop herself. She moved only one step, for Richard flinched away from her as if she were a leper and might infect all who came too near.

"How could you?" he asked her, his own fury rising to fill the blue of his eyes. "How could you be so faithless, and with him?"

Alais drew herself up as if he had struck her. I saw the tears in her eyes, tears that I knew she would not shed.

"You keep a mistress, and sit in judgment on me?"

Richard blinked, stunned. No woman in his life had ever thrown his infidelity back in his face. No other woman would have dared. But Alais stood before him, her dark eyes blazing with an inner fire.

I saw in that moment that she refused to accept what I had understood all my life: men are unfaithful ever. She thought to hold the men she loved to a higher standard. I could have warned her to look elsewhere if she expected faithfulness from Henry.

"I thought better of you," Richard said.

Alais swallowed her tears, for they had risen once more, and vied with her fury for supremacy. Her fury won, if only barely. Her eyes grew calm, her voice cold, as if we were dead to her already.

"I will deny nothing, for I am ashamed of nothing, except that I called you beloved and meant it."

I did not know if she was speaking to Richard or to me. Perhaps she was speaking to both of us. I know I felt the pain of her words, and I saw my own pain mirrored on Richard's face.

She left us gasping. She walked away as if she had never known us, as if she might never see us again. I thought I might weep, for my heart was bleeding. Richard came to me then, and took my arm.

My strength flowed back at his touch. Alais loved me still, I knew that she did. I need only continue to chase her; I would run her to ground. What lay between us could not be undone.

Richard escorted me into Henry's hall, his eyes shadowed and his face grim. I smiled brightly for all to see, and greeted by name each person who called to me, with a graceful sweep of my arm.

Alais was there before us, seated at Henry's right hand. She shared his trencher, lifting a morsel of squab to her lips as her eyes turned to look at me. They had started the feast without us.

Henry saw the breach and regretted it. I was still his wife and queen. He smiled at me and bowed, first to me and then to Richard. My smile did not leave my face, though the knife twisted in my heart. The sight of my daughter seated next to my husband, as if her place were there and not with me, was almost my undoing. But I would not think of that. Instead, I pressed my hand down hard on Richard's arm until he bowed to his father, and drew out my chair for me.

"Welcome, wife," Henry called, sitting down once more and raising his glass to me. I thought at first he meant to rub my face in his triumph, but I saw soon that he meant only to make the peace. I was mollified. God knows, I had seen such mistresses come and go before. Never before had one of them been my daughter, fed from my own heart's blood. But I would not think of that, either.

Alais said nothing, but when I raised my glass to her, she bowed her head to me. I wondered if we still might play it off, for if Henry favored her only, but did not acknowledge her as his mistress, all public knowledge of this business could still be avoided. But little did I know her, and her plans.

Henry rose once more but gestured for the court to sit. He raised his tankard of mead to the whole company, and the idle talk fell silent.

"I am happy to announce that I will be going to my hunting lodge at Deptford. There I will see to the needs of the kingdom while indulging in some much-needed respite. While I am gone, Eleanor, my queen, will sit in state at Windsor, and keep you all in fine spirits, until I return."

I raised my glass to him as if I had known of this all along, as if he had consulted me, as indeed he once would have done. My dissembling was so skilled that even Richard was taken in, and glared at me until I pressed his hand beneath the table.

"My lady Alais, Princess of France, will accompany me into my self-imposed exile. She will give me comfort while I withdraw from public life, to deal with the affairs of state in private."

Alais stood with him then, and the hall applauded her. I was a beat behind, but as always, I was quick to pick up the tune. I set my goblet down and applauded her also, the knife twisting where she had stabbed me the night before. Still I smiled, while Richard glowered, but even he showed restraint. He did not stalk from the hall as he once would have done.

They sat down, and the king leaned close to fill her glass with wine taken from my own barrels. While he poured my wine for her with his own hand, Alais smiled at him, and rewarded him with a kiss. She did not give him a demure peck as a daughter might, but opened her mouth over his, welcoming his tongue, as he no doubt had taught her to do the night before. One of the younger men let out a whoop to see her do it, then turned pale as he looked at me.

I said nothing, but raised my glass once more to the princess and to my husband. She nodded to me, and I saw admiration for me dawn in her eyes, to live there with the anger that still controlled every move she made. As I watched, she made the mistake of looking at Richard. She saw the pain on his face, pain he did not know how to hide.

I thought in that moment that she would collapse under the weight she had chosen to carry. I thought that she would weep and run from the hall, that she would throw herself down at his feet and beg his forgiveness. But she did none of these things.

As I watched from the corner of my eye, Richard faced her and saw her pain. In my rooms he had been too blinded by anger to see it, to remember who she was, and who she had been to him. He saw it now. He clutched my hand under the table, this time drawing strength from me.

He raised his glass, and did not look at her again, his back straight and his shoulders squared under the heap of bitterness and gall that she and his father had laid upon him. Beneath the table, he still held my hand, but his grip loosened, so that my blood could flow once more.

Music began then, for last night I had started a new tradition of having music at dinner as the rest of the hall ate their meal.

Henry noticed where his lover's gaze was tending, but he did not rain fury down on her head. He only watched her, his gray eyes on her face, offering her a bit of venison, which she ate, no doubt without tasting it. When the bell for vespers chimed, she leaned close to him and asked him leave to go. Even carnal knowledge of Henry had not turned her from her father's religion.

Henry's face darkened, but she did not notice, so sunk was she in her own misery. Henry kissed her, his hand gentle on her cheek as he let her go.

Richard watched Alais leave the hall, but did not move from my side. Henry ate his dinner, but his appetite was gone. Only I would know that, though; of all the courtiers who ate in his hall, only I knew him.

When the dancing began, Henry rose as if to join them. I stood, and Richard stood with me, ready as he always was to support me, whatever might come.

Henry passed beside my chair and I spoke low to him, daring to make a move that I knew was foolhardy. But even I make mistakes; I made only one that night.

"My lord king, will you join the dancing?"

I all but asked him to partner me, there in front of the whole table. He knew what I was offering: an alliance with me and my son, no matter what harlot he chose to take to his bed. He could stand with me, and dance, as we had done the night when he gifted Richard with the Aquitaine.

I could tell from the gray of his eyes that he was thinking of that night, too. For a moment's breath, I thought I had him.

Henry bowed to me most courteously, and kissed my hand. "My lady wife, I must be gone. I have pressing business elsewhere."

Henry left the hall, and all the court knew that he went to her.

Richard took up my hand as soon as his father dropped it. The two men I had loved the most said not a word to each other, nor did they glance in the other's direction. Once Henry stalked out of the hall after the prey that had lately slipped his nets, Richard led me onto the dance floor, smiling down at me.

"Richard, you never smile unless you mean it," I said. "Has your heart healed so quickly?"

He moved with me in the dance, his smile in place, his eyes never leaving my face. "My heart will never heal, Mother. But do they need to know it?"

The music of my laughter filled that stone hall, so that others joined in, though they did not know the joke. Indeed, there was nothing funny. I laughed so that I would not weep as I took my son's hand and followed him in the intricacies of the dance.

There would be more moves to make and more dance steps to plan for, before I gave Alais up. That night the whole hall knew I faced yet another challenge to my power with a glittering smile and light laughter. All in that hall knew, as I did, that whatever came before, in the end, I would win.

Chapter 22

❧

ALAIS: TO BECOME QUEEN

Windsor Castle
July 1172

I went to the chapel, which that night was empty. The Presence was
lit on the altar and an old priest sat near, tending it. I knelt on the cold
stone floor, doubling my skirt under me to protect my knees.

I did not take the Mass, as I still had not been shriven. I could not
confess, for I did not repent. So I set thoughts of myself and my sin
aside, and prayed instead for Richard.

I had wounded him, more deeply than I would have thought
possible. As I knelt, my anger at him and his infidelity rose to choke
me, until it threatened to block out everything else. Once more I saw
the blue, beguiling eyes of Richard's lover, the warm welcome on her

face, her arms opening to draw my betrothed to her as Richard closed the curtain to the alcove behind them.

I turned my eyes on the statue of the Mother by the altar, and reminded myself how She had seen worse things done, and She had forgiven them. This was cold comfort, and blasphemy, so I said a few beads of my father's rosary, and crossed myself, praying both for France and for my own soul, that I might come to humility once more, that I might feel remorse for what I had done. I was far from remorseful, and I knew it. I was truly Eleanor's daughter now.

"Do you pray for Richard?"

Henry's voice drew me from my prayers, caressing me, bringing heat to my face and my loins as if he had touched me. I had not known it was possible to want a man as much as I wanted him. This must be what the Church preached against, this overwhelming lust that blocked out all reason and all prayer. Still, I did not repent.

I stood and crossed myself, turning only then to meet the king's eyes.

"Well, do you?"

"I do, my lord. And I pray for you. And for this kingdom."

"Do you regret what you have done?"

I saw the danger in his eyes for the first time. I wondered if, even now, after acknowledging me before the entire court, Henry would turn from me, blighting all my hopes. I stepped toward him, watching his face. He did not back away from me, but he did not move to meet me, either.

"I regret nothing, Henry. You know that."

"Do I? What I know is that as soon as I announce I am removing my royal presence and your lovely self from Windsor, you turn white like a milkmaid who had been tilted in a field, and you run to prayer for comfort. And I am not alone in seeing this. You ran from me in front of the entire court."

I heard his words unspoken: I had run from him in front of Eleanor and Richard. This was all he truly cared about. I cursed myself for a fool. I would have to remember to look to the king always, as I had once looked to Eleanor. I had no one now to guide me but myself. I would have to do better.

"Henry, I am sorry."

He raised one hand, as if to order me from him, but I did not stop. I moved toward him, until my breasts brushed against his chest, where his gown hid his body from me. I took in his scent, the sandalwood I loved, and his own scent under that, the scent of Henry, the most erotic scent I had ever bathed in.

He saw the honest pleasure on my face; that was what moved him more than my contrite words. For he did not love me for my obedience, nor for my old shows of modesty. He loved me for my fire, as Eleanor and Richard had loved me before him. But with him, my inner fire burned brightest. Only he knew how to stoke it, to make it burn.

I thought we might leave together. Perhaps he knew a different way to his rooms, a secret passage from the chapel that would take us up some hidden stairs, back to his bed. But he would not wait.

Henry drew me deeper into the gloom of the chapel, far from the altar, behind a choir screen. He pressed me back against the stone wall. I opened my mouth to protest, to ask him to take me to his bed, but I saw in his eyes that he would exact this price. If he was to let my desertion before the court pass, I would have to concede this.

I asked forgiveness of the Holy Mother in silence, then raised my lips to his. Henry's body blocked the chapel from my view but for some feeble candlelight still visible at the altar. All I could see was that light, and him.

Henry looked into my eyes. What he saw there must have satisfied him. I opened my mouth under his as he pressed me hard against the wall. The stone dug into my back as he raised me up. He hoisted my skirt, his hands under me. I reached down, but he wore no leggings, only a long gown, so he was ready for me, even as I caressed him.

He groaned, low and long, in my ear, and I thought he might drop me, so great was his pleasure. I fastened my teeth on his ear, and he laughed under his breath.

"You will be the death of me, Alais."

"God forbid, Your Grace."

He took me then, my back pressed to the wall, my legs wrapped around his hips. I was still sore, for I had been a virgin when he first touched me, but the pain was soon eclipsed by my own desire. I heard myself panting in his ear, and then I moaned his name.

The pleasure came to me even as Henry groaned and lost himself in me. He clutched me close, and set me down, breathing hard, as I was. I forgot how much older he was than me. He had the strength of a lion still. Someday, God willing, we would make fine sons.

This idle thought crossed my mind, and I let it go just as quickly. I did not want to think of politics, or of tomorrow. I stood in my lover's embrace, my skirt falling once more around my ankles.

I pressed my lips to Henry's throat. He laughed and leaned down to kiss me.

"I believe I was angry at you," he said.

I laughed low, and kissed him back. "God forbid, my liege."

He looked down at me, and though his face was soft with love and spent desire, I saw his intelligence there shining back at me. I could not make such a mistake again. I would remember it.

"Come to bed, Henry," I said.

He quirked an eyebrow at my presumption, but I pressed myself against him, and he did not contradict me. He drew me close, and led me out of that chapel by a back way. We made our way through a dark passage, until we emerged once more in Henry's rooms from a secret door hidden behind a tapestry.

I laughed. "Henry, is there no end to secrets in this keep?"

He kissed me, but his gray eyes were solemn. "No, Alais. And you would do well to remember it."

I was sick of politics. I wanted him over me in bed with no thought for any other, with no thought for the morrow. I drew him down with me even before his chamberlain and page had fled, kissing him deeply. I pulled his gown off him so that his naked skin was against mine.

I turned my mind from anything beyond the shadows of that bed. I took Henry in, body and soul, mouth and tongue and teeth, and banished all thoughts of Eleanor and Richard. Henry worked like a magic elixir over me. As long as the curtains of that bed were drawn, I could forget all else, even my own father, even that Henry was king.

When we left for Deptford, I expected a litter to carry me. Sampson was brought to the courtyard instead, already saddled and waiting.

Bijou peeked out from beneath my cloak, almost as if she was looking for Henry. I could feel her tail wagging against my side, and I wondered if I had been foolish to bring her.

The king saw her, and laughed. "I am glad to see that you are loath to part from my gift, my lady. I will have to give you more, to see if you will bear them all with you wherever you go."

"The gift of your presence is enough for all of us, my lord king."

I lowered my eyes as I said this, but not before I saw the approving looks from the men around us. Henry's smile broadened, and he rode beside me as we left the castle keep.

I waved to Marie Helene as I rode out, and saw her in conversation with a man-at-arms who was being left behind. I wondered if she might take a lover while I was gone. I thought to warn her from it, but we had gone too far, and already it was too late to turn back.

Henry met my eyes. "Don't fear for your gentlewoman. She will be safe in my court."

"Even without you near?" I asked, my voice pitched low so that no one else could hear.

Henry's open, sunny laugh warmed me. There was something charming about him always, a warmth that reached out to me all the days I knew him.

"The king's peace extends beyond my presence," Henry said. "I have worked hard to secure it."

I thought of the stories I had heard of the time before his reign, when his mother and King Stephen had torn the country apart with their civil war. No woman was safe in the kingdom then; babes were spitted on pikes, and good English cities fell to English armies; warlords ravaged the countryside without ceasing.

That dark time was the very thing that my father had spent his life and mine to defend France from. Henry gave his own country a strong rule of law that was rarely if ever seen in Christendom. Henry had been strong enough to make the peace and to keep it.

I wondered if his son young Henry would be as strong.

That was a dangerous road to travel, for thoughts of any of his sons led to Richard. So I turned my eyes back to Henry where he rode beside me, slowing his horse and the horses of the entire company for my sake.

"My father seeks to keep the peace in France, my lord."

"And is he successful?"

"You would know that better than I, Your Grace."

"I think he does well, Alais. Better than one of his nature is wont to do, for he is not strong, but only good. A good man is usually not fit to be king."

"My father is," I said, anger rising in me, filling my eyes with tears that I would not shed.

Henry saw them, and he leaned over and took my hand. "As you say. Your father is a good man, and a good king."

I knew that Henry did not mean what he said, but I knew also that he did not mean to start a quarrel. I watched him, but his face betrayed nothing of his true thoughts. He might have contempt for my father, as the rest of Europe did, for a pious man and a cuckold, but he needed the alliance with France, as France needed the alliance with him. It was that alliance I had given my life for. It was that alliance I would serve, even now.

As a concession to show that I did not hold his lies against him,

I smiled at him, distracted from all else around me. Henry met my eyes, and I could see that he was as eager to be alone together as I was. Bijou chose that moment to try to leap from my arms to his and I had to grab her before she fell.

"Lucky for your little dog, Princess, we have not far to ride."

"Lucky for me as well, my lord, for I feel the toll of riding horseback already."

Henry smiled at me, and I saw in his eyes that his thoughts tended back to my bed. "You will find, Alais, that you were born to be in the saddle."

I felt my face flush, but I did not look away from him. He had pitched his voice low, so that his men would not hear him. My lust rose, and I leaned closer to him, almost unseating myself from my horse. I did not care, though all the company watched us. I leaned as close to him as I dared, and he saw me do it. Henry drew his horse near mine and kissed me.

We stopped along the roadside at a pavilion down by the river that some of his men had ridden ahead of us to set up. There was a table and two chairs, and a feast of cold meats and cheese, fruit, and wine. Henry brought me down off my horse himself, and kept my hand in his.

"I am hungry, my lord. I am glad we stop to eat."

Henry smiled, for he knew I was not hungry for food. He hoped as well as I did that we might find a quiet glen somewhere, a place to lie down on soft grass, so that he might have me in the open air. This knowledge did not show in his face, but only in his eyes. His voice was bland when he spoke to me, conscious of the men who were present.

"The young are always hungry. And there are always dispatches to be signed."

He helped me to my chair, and as he seated me, his hand lingered on my back, and caressed my rump. I laughed and he kissed me, before he sat down beside me.

The royal clerk stepped forward, and before Henry broke his fast, he signed three scrolls in succession, reading them all before he signed.

I watched him without touching the food before me. I knew better than to eat without his permission.

Bijou had no such scruples, and whined at my feet. I picked her up and stealthily fed her scraps of meat before setting her down once more. She wandered off into the tall grass, but always came back when I called her.

I looked up to find myself alone with Henry, his clerk gone, the dispatches carried away by courier in their wooden box.

Henry watched me as if he was thinking of something else. I wondered if he might take up a bit of bread, so that I, too, could eat.

"Alais, do you despise me?"

"What, my lord?"

I kept my face smooth, as Eleanor had taught me. I leaned back in my chair, the soft river breeze on my face.

"Tell me, Alais. I will not be angry. Do you mourn the loss of your good name? Your father's honor?"

The thought of my father was like poison in my blood, like a fire that burned behind my eyes, making tears come. I blinked so that they cleared away. My father would bless me when I accomplished what I had set out to do. I could not think of him until then.

"No, my lord. I am not ashamed of us, or of anything we have done. What grieves me is the thought that war might come."

Henry raised a grape to his lips. "War troubles you? What does a pampered princess know of war?"

I took a deep breath to keep my temper.

"I know what my father taught me," I said. "If our treaty is to fail, if there is war again in France, the land will be plunged into darkness."

Henry's face grew grim. We had not spoken of the time before his reign, but the knowledge of it lay between us. He had been king for almost twenty years, and there were still parts of the realm that had not recovered from the fire of that civil war. There were villages razed to the ground that would never be peopled again. Every man, woman, and child in those villages had been killed by Stephen's marauding armies. Even I, foreigner that I was, knew that.

"You fear for the land, Alais?"

"No, my lord. For the people who live on it."

Henry did not speak for a time, but watched me as I ate. Since he had begun to eat, I could as well.

I said a prayer as I ate, though I was outside of God's grace, and unshriven for the sin of licentiousness. I prayed for the people under my father's rule, that war would be kept from them, that our treaty would not come to nothing. I prayed that I was strong enough, as Eleanor had taught me to be, to hold Henry to it.

"The queen causes strife among my sons."

I did not answer. Between Henry and Richard, there was a great deal of rancor that had not begun with me. There was also a struggle for supremacy between Henry and his eldest son. It had not occurred to me before, but now that Henry pointed it out, I wondered. Perhaps Eleanor had a hand in that, too.

"She keeps Richard always in arms against me, fighting with me when he should be in the south, protecting our lands in France."

Henry watched me, but my face revealed nothing. I allowed him to see my intelligence so that he would know I was not too simple to understand him, but that I kept my own counsel. He smiled, pleased with my self-control.

"I have it on good authority that not only did Eleanor watch while my eldest son and heir made an alliance with your father, but that she brokered the alliance herself."

A chill moved up my spine that had nothing to do with the afternoon breeze. Here was my chance. I would bide my time, and then I would take it.

"My lord, surely you are wrong."

"One of the horrors of being king, Alais, is that I rarely am. Especially when it comes to seeing treachery."

I crossed myself against the evil he spoke.

Henry caught my hand, and held it in his. He looked at me, his gray eyes seeing me as if for the first time.

"Trust me, Alais. Trust me to find a way to keep the peace."

"How, my lord?"

"Let me think on it, and I will tell you."

I would let him think, and hope that he might draw his own conclusion without me having to lead him to it. I saw in that moment that Henry remembered the words he had spoken to me by the riverside, when he had placed that crown of flowers on my head. It was all

I could do not to crow in triumph. We might yet make a new treaty, one that would hold as long as we both should live.

After we finished our picnic and rode on, I knew that I had the strength to draw Henry where I wanted him to go, if he did not go there himself.

Perhaps we were more alike than I knew, for as I brought my horse alongside his, Bijou in one arm, it seemed I saw my own thoughts in his eyes, mirrored back at me.

But Henry did not talk politics with me again that afternoon. He was attentive, and always watching me. He wanted me as much as I wanted him, but he did not reach for me, and his eyes held a calculating look.

We rode into the gates of his hunting lodge at Deptford before midafternoon. Henry himself helped me down before Sampson was led away.

He did not leave me even then, but took me into his lodge himself, a rustic place even by English standards. I could see that Eleanor had no power here, if she had ever been here at all. That was why he had brought me.

Henry kissed me and showed me the bed that I would sleep in. Some woman had been there before us, for the room was clean if very plain, and the tapestries on the wall had been beaten so that there was very little dust. I looked at the bed, and crossed the room to open a window, letting Bijou loose among the rushes. She loved playing in straw. Eleanor did not keep rushes on the floor in the private rooms at court, so it was a new treat for my little dog.

Henry's eyes were on me when I looked up from Bijou's antics.

I thought he might cross the room and take me against the windowsill; his eyes were so full of fire.

He did not approach me, though. "I will send wine and refreshment to you, Alais. Don't eat too much, for you and I will dine alone tonight."

"And where is your room, my lord? Will you send for me or must I come and find you?"

The fire in his eyes warmed me where I stood. I felt my own lust rise unbidden. I had always thought of myself as a quiet, modest girl before I first met Henry. Eleanor had taught me my strength, but I was beginning to see that there was more to me than even she had dreamt of.

"This is my room, Alais. You will share it with me."

Lust flamed in me when he said that, so that my legs weakened. I needed to sit down, but I stayed on my feet out of pride. I had not known what it was to want something as much as I wanted him.

Henry seemed to see this in my face, for he groaned and backed away from me. "I must go, Alais, and arrange the hunt for the morrow, or neither of us will leave this room until past dawn."

I simply stared at him. "Come back soon," I said.

He laughed, but I could see that his hunger for me was rising. He left without another word. I stood, breathing as hard as if I had taken a flight of stairs. I needed to have my wits about me, to ask the king for the boon I craved, to lead Henry down the path that I would have him walk.

I leaned my head against the stone casement of the window. I said a prayer, knowing that the Holy Mother would hear me, whether

I was shriven or not. The cool stone soothed me like the touch of Her hand, until I was calm again. I played with Bijou on the floor as if I were a simple girl, a girl with no thought for tomorrow, an obedient woman who always did her duty. I was not the woman I had been raised to be.

After an hour, I saw to it that the women of the house unpacked my trunk and hung up my clothes properly. There was no dressing room in those apartments, but there was a decent clothespress and the servants knew how to use it.

This did not take long, for I had brought little. I wandered in the orchard near the house for a time, looking at the apples on the trees that had not yet turned ripe. Bijou loved being outside, so we spent a pleasant hour under the trees, catching the scent of rain that soon would fall.

I returned to the king's rooms before long, and ordered bathwater brought to me.

I was still drying off when Henry came in, his movements quiet, as they always were. I knew that he was there only because the kitchen girl who helped me bathe stopped talking and knelt on the rushes by my bath.

"You may leave us," Henry said.

The girl ran out without a backward glance, and my hip bath and ewer were left standing in the middle of the room. I sighed, for I had grown used to the peaceful running of Eleanor's household.

I was naked but for the sheet I was wrapped in, and Henry scooped me up in his arms and carried me to the bed.

"I'm still wet," I told him, my heart racing.

He did not answer me, but laid me down across the wool cover-let. At least I did not have to fear we would ruin it. It was the last co-herent thought I had before his lips found mine.

After Henry brought me to the peak of pleasure, and followed me over the edge himself, we lay together, still tangled in my bath sheet.

"I meant to tell you that dinner will be served in here," he said.

"You forgot to mention that, my lord."

He laughed and buried his face between my breasts. I stroked his hair, the strands of it soft between my fingers where the sun had light-ened it.

"They will bring us venison, and cheese," he said, his voice muffled.

I bent down and kissed his temple. He looked up at me and gave me the sweetest smile.

"I'm glad that we're here, Your Grace. I'm glad we've come."

He did not make a vulgar joke as I thought he might, but stared into my eyes. Henry ran his fingers over the curls that covered my forehead. He leaned up and kissed my cheek.

"I am glad as well, Alais. We can be ourselves here, and have some peace."

He raised himself then, and I rose with him. I did not dress again, but only drew a shift on, so that he might still see my body in the firelight.

Even this distraction did not keep him from his evening meal. We sat alone, as he had promised. The cheese was soft and the deer meat well seasoned, just as he had said. I watched him, his eyes on me. I saw the wheels turning in his mind, and I knew it was time to speak, to take the next step on the road that had no turning.

"Henry, do you truly want peace?"

His eyes measured me, taking me in. He swallowed the last bite of bread, and looked at me without blinking. I could see nothing of his thoughts on his face.

"I have given my life to spread the king's peace. You know that, Alais."

"And I have given my life to keep the peace between England and France."

"Until two nights ago," he said.

"No, my lord. What I did two nights ago, I did for France, as well as for myself."

I rose from my chair and knelt beside him, the rushes on the stone floor catching on the hem of my shift. I ignored them, and the fact that they pricked my heels and ankles. I met Henry's eyes, and he did not look away.

"If Eleanor breaks the peace, if she causes strife between you and your sons, why not put her away?"

Henry did not laugh at me as I had thought he might. His eyes did not leave mine. I knew then with complete certainty that he had been thinking along this line already. His idle statement by the riverside had not been mere fancy. I grew bolder.

"As an abbess in a nunnery, Eleanor could do little to foment rebellion. In the cloister, she would see no one, hear nothing. Perhaps she might be at peace."

"There is peace only in the grave, Alais, and you know it."

I saw then that he was testing me, wondering if I would call for her death. The pain of that thought pierced me like a lance in my side. I almost could not breathe.

"Dear God, Your Majesty. God forbid any harm should come to the queen." I crossed myself, and prayed in truth, my hands clasped, though my rosary was far from me. I prayed for Eleanor's safety with no thought for my own. I prayed that she would be safe always. No matter what came between us, I loved her and I always would.

Henry saw my fear, and how deep it ran. He drew me onto his lap. He stroked my hair, and kissed me. "Alais, I would never harm Eleanor. You know that."

"I would never speak her name again," I said. "I would go into a nunnery myself and never see the light of day before I would draw harm down on Eleanor's head."

Henry stroked me, his hands on my body, but my lust did not rise, and his touch did not comfort me. "No, Alais, I will keep you by me a while longer."

I clutched him, and he held me, his hands gentle on my body and on my hair. He did not move to take me, and I felt my fear receding. All was not yet lost. I loved Eleanor, and I saw for the first time that Henry did, too. Perhaps we could speak together, and deal with one another, with this understanding between us.

He kissed me, and I drew myself up, so that I might meet his eyes. I drew my fear back into my heart, for I was strong enough to bear it. Henry saw this, and smiled.

"You will make fine sons, Alais," he said.

"God willing, Your Majesty, we will."

He stared at me, the smile fading from his face. His eyes were grave, but I saw at once that his thoughts had been tending this way, too. But he would not speak. He wanted to hear me give them voice.

"Your Grace, I would be your wife. Set Eleanor aside, as she once set aside my father, and marry me."

Henry looked at me for a long moment, drinking in the truth from my eyes. He pushed my curls back from my face, where they had fallen when I knelt to pray. He pressed his hand against my cheek and held it there. His voice was soft when he answered me.

"You have ambition, then?" he asked.

I met his eyes. I did not look away, not at the fire or at the floor. I did not dissemble, nor did I lie, just as I had promised him the night he first met me. From me, he would always have the truth.

"Only to serve you, my lord king. And our treaty. I wish to bind the peace for all time. I wish to serve you and this country, my father and France, all in one stroke. I would be your wife, obedient to your desires. I would keep my father in league with us, no matter what your sons wished to do in the future. I would stir up no trouble amongst your kin, but be a salve of peace over them."

"Your son would never sit on the throne of England."

"I know that. God preserve Henry and Richard, Geoffrey, and John into your old age, and beyond. Put our sons in the Church, or send them as diplomats to foreign courts, wherever you need them. I will raise them as I was raised, to serve my king. They will stand by you, Henry, as I do. As I always will. I swear it."

"And Eleanor would step aside? The most powerful woman in Europe would take the veil, and step down for you?"

"No, my lord king. She would be moved aside to keep the peace. Eleanor loves this country, as you do. In the end, she will do what is best for the people."

Henry did not share my confidence. I took his hand in mine, and kissed it, looking once more into his eyes. "She will step down because you tell her to. You are king."

"I will send her to the abbey at Fontevrault. Even Eleanor will make little mischief there. I will set her aside, and we will have some peace."

Speaking these words, he kissed me, drawing me close, lifting me as if I weighed nothing, as if I were a feather on the wind. He laid me down on his bed, on the sheets that smelled of apple orchards and summer sun. He pressed me back onto those sheets and entered my body almost without preamble, as if to seal the pact between us.

I gasped under him, the motion of his body washing over me as the waves of the sea. The pleasure took me, but did not swamp my reason. I kept my eyes on his, and he kept his on mine as his own pleasure took him, and cast him down once more. He clung to me, and I to him.

"Alais, Princess of France, will you stand with me against all others?"

"Henry of England, Normandy, and Anjou, I will stand with you, now and always, until I take my last breath on this earth."

He knew this was no idle oath. He knew it was not the aftermath of love play, nor the languor of love, that bade me speak. He saw the truth in my eyes, even as he stared down at me, and I saw the truth in his. Whatever else came after, on that day we pledged ourselves, one to the other. On that day, he became my husband in truth in my own mind, if nowhere else on earth.

Chapter 23

꿍

ELEANOR: ANOTHER LETTER

Windsor Castle
August 1172

Once Alais and Henry had gone, I made no pretense of joy among my own women. I stared out my window, as if waiting for Alais to come back, knowing that she would not.

They had been gone over two weeks already, and her absence in the palace and at table was like a hole in my heart. I spoke to no one about my own loss, for that was my concern. Richard still was brooding, more than I thought he might. Always before, at the first sign of betrayal, Richard cursed the offender, then forgot his existence. Alais, in all ways, was different.

Though Henry had run amok with his newfound lust, I knew that in the end he would see reason, as he always did. Even now, I wondered what the fair Rosamund thought of her erstwhile lover. No doubt she looked on all Henry's other doxies as simply the lusts of a vital man. I knew that she would hear of Alais, and I hoped the knowledge pained her.

For if Rosamund was my opposite in temperament, as so many people said, Alais was almost my equal in strength. No other woman in all of Christendom could say the same. She was the woman I had raised her to be. Only Alais was lit with that inner fire that rode above my own heart. Only she reminded me of myself when I was young, when my father had the teaching of me.

It was the loss of Alais that burned like acid on my skin, but I did not accept that loss. She was mine, and forever. An affair with my husband would not change that. I wondered how long it would be until she knew it.

Richard came to me from the tiltyard, his face newly washed, his red gold hair a mane around his shoulders. My women preened for him; Angeline even fawned, dropping into a low curtsy, hoping that she might be called on to succor him in his time of distress. Margaret paled at the sight of him. As I watched, I saw no spark between them. Perhaps, in his grief, he had turned her away.

"Richard," I said. "How fare you?"

"The same, Mother. I imagine I will be the same for a long time to come."

I raised one hand, and my women left us without a word. Richard saw Marie Helene among them, and stared. She averted her eyes, afraid to look at him. He watched Marie Helene until she left the room. Only then did he turn once more to me.

"Do you want her?" I asked. "I could have her in your bed by sundown."

He stared at me, almost as if my words came to his ears in a language he did not know. Then the light of understanding came back into his eyes, and I wished my words back. His pain was not dimmed by my offer but sharpened.

"No, Mother. Do not trouble yourself on my account."

I came to his side and pressed the softness of my palm against his cheek. "Richard, there is news."

"From Aquitaine?"

"No. From Deptford."

He flinched at the word, and stiffened under my hand, controlling himself with difficulty. He did not step away from me.

I moved across the room to allow him to gather his thoughts. On my table a letter lay, its seal broken.

"My spies have brought a letter that was meant for His Holiness the pope."

"Who wrote it?" he asked.

"Your father. The king."

I watched my son for some sign of spleen, for some sign that his wits were not about him, that his fury would overwhelm his common sense. After the first moment, when his fist clenched almost against his will, I did not see it.

Richard met my eyes, ready to hear the rest, his legendary temper dormant beneath the cool blue of his eyes. He had heard me name his father without cursing. Now I could tell him the rest.

"Henry has written to the pope to ask for his support in casting me aside. The king would like me to retire to the nunnery at Fontevrault. As the abbess, of course."

My smile was bitter, in spite of my attempts at self-control. This blow did not come from Henry, for he would never have thought of divorcing me on his own. This came from Alais, a barb that struck home. I had yet to draw it out.

"Kind of him, to make that small allowance, is it not?" I asked my son.

Richard turned pale, but still, he did not speak. At first I thought him considering the merits of his father's letter, as if Alais, a girl fresh from the convent and as young and green as spring grass, might actually be a viable alternative as queen. I saw, though, that Richard was merely stunned. He could not conceive of this level of betrayal in the woman he loved, the woman he loved almost as much as he loved me. He saw my strength in her. I had known that from the first. In Alais, Richard saw a woman of strength and fire, but strength tempered with compassion. Or so he had thought, before she spurned him.

I began pacing, the letter to the pope in my hand. I could not contain my rage. It began to spill out in my voice, though I fought for control. "Would you like to know who Henry wishes to set in my place? Who he would crown as queen, as well as concubine?"

He knew already, but stood still, his back straight, as I told him. "The Princess Alais."

I thought he would spit then, but he stood in my solar, not on a battlefield or a tiltyard, so he held himself in check. As I watched, his Plantagenet rage rose to consume all rational thought. I thought that he would not be able to hear me if I continued, but as I watched, he gained control of himself once more.

If only he had shown this restraint before with Henry, if only he had been more discreet with his lovers, perhaps we might have avoided this. Perhaps we might have married him to Alais before she knew of his infidelity, and she would have been neutralized.

But no one, not even I, had known what lurked beneath the surface of her convent leanings. Even I had not seen the depth of treachery Alais was capable of. Had she turned on anyone else but myself and my son, I would have been proud of her.

Richard swallowed his spleen. I saw his reason win the battle for supremacy against his fury. He stood under the onslaught, and faced me.

"My God, Mother. I never would have thought them capable of it."

My own bitterness rose, and I swallowed it, just as Richard had swallowed his anger. It was not a time for emotion. That time would come later, in the dark reaches of the night, when I was alone. I kept my voice even, my tone light, when I answered him.

"Anyone is capable of anything, Richard, given time and opportunity."

He took this in, his blue eyes steady on mine. I saw that he did not believe me, but his mind had moved on already, looking for a way out of the mess his father had created out of lust and blind folly.

"We must write to Henry my brother at once," Richard said.

I smiled that his mind moved to the correct answer so quickly, and with no prompting from me. Though there was no rancor between Richard and my eldest son, there was no love between them, either.

"I already have," I said.

He stared at me. "How long have you kept this news from me? How long have you known what the king planned to do?"

"Since three days after they left for Deptford."

I had been silent for weeks, and I saw that Richard felt my silence as another betrayal. He turned from me to stare out the window. The glass afforded light but no air. A breeze came through the arrow-slit window close by, a narrow casement built for war, as Richard was.

"Why did you wait to tell me?" Richard asked.

"I did not know what your brother would say. You are burdened enough."

"If we are allies, Mother, you must keep nothing from me. My private griefs are my own affair. This is a matter of state. I will not be coddled, not even by you."

"Richard, I am sorry."

I went to him, and laid my hand on his arm. I reveled in the knowledge that he was a well-honed weapon that I might wield against any enemy. For any enemy of mine was Richard's enemy, too. He loved me and me alone, now that Alais had betrayed us both.

I set my tone to soothe him, letting the warmth of my voice co-coon him, as I had done when he was very small. He relaxed beside me, even before I spoke. The tension went out of his body as soon as I laid my hand on his sword arm.

"I heard from your brother only today. I sent for you as soon as I had his letter in hand."

"What did he say?"

I smiled, and for the first time that day, bitterness did not color my expression. "Shall I read it to you?"

I held the letter up, another scroll of vellum from my tabletop. Richard grunted in assent, and I almost laughed out loud, so much did he remind me of my husband in that moment. Richard wanted his brother's help, but was loath to admit it. It would do him good to learn to act with his brothers, at least when I called on him to do so.

I unrolled the scroll and held it aloft, for Richard's sake. I did not need the letter, and used it only as a prop. I had read it over so often, and with such pleasure, that I had memorized it already.

"'God's grace to you, Mother, and my greetings. I must remind you that never, at any time in your life, have you needed anyone's help, least of all mine.'"

Richard took this in, even as I savored the words from my eldest son. Young Henry and I had never been close, but rarely, now and again, he gave me compliments, as all men inevitably did. I read on.

"'The old man has found a paramour? May she bring him joy. He wants to set his trollop on the throne? Once he is dead, let her try to keep it.'"

I savored those last words on my tongue as if they were fine wine and squab. Young Henry's letter brought me out of the sink of self-pity I had descended into. He reminded me of the reality of the situation, how all of Europe, even the pope himself, would see it.

Alais was a princess with a small dowry, a dowry that my husband already possessed. She would not marry the king, then or ever, for she brought nothing to the bargain. I brought the Aquitaine, as all the world knew. Even though my son was duke, that land and its people were still loyal first and foremost to me.

Richard, of course, missed the salient point of this missive: even Henry's favored son looked on this proposed union with disdain. Surely the rest of Europe, who had no interest in avoiding Henry's wrath, who stood to gain nothing from Henry's hand, would also see the proposed alliance for what it was: a dalliance that would run its course, and fade, as all things must.

"So he will do nothing to back us?" Richard asked.

His anger had mounted him again, the temper he could never shake off, except on the battlefield. Only when at war did Richard see clearly, and far. It was lucky for him that he had me to rule his politics.

"Not at this point," I said.

I did not speak of how deep my work with young Henry went. I did not mention to Richard the letters that passed across the Channel between his brothers and myself. I still was not certain that I would encourage them as far as they wanted to go in their hatred of their father. I bided my time, and waited to see if Henry might first come to terms with me. His antics with Alais indicated that he most likely would not. But before I turned my sons against him completely, I would be sure.

I tried to draw Richard's mind away from young Henry's letter itself, to its relevant point. "Your brother speaks the truth. Henry is a fool if he thinks he can win."

Richard did not speak, but stared at me. We both knew that Henry was many things, but a fool was not one of them.

"On what grounds would Father set you aside? The same ones you used to set aside Louis?"

I almost laughed, so ridiculous was Henry's reasoning. "Yes," I said. "Your father claims that our marriage is incestuous."

Richard snorted, and the sound of his derision was like a tonic to me. I felt more strength flowing into me. I knew he would leave his pain behind, and unite with me. He would leave off licking his wounds and stand against his father with me.

I went on to describe the letter my spies had intercepted, the letter Henry meant to send to the Holy See.

"Henry writes the pope that our marriage must be annulled, because I once slept with his father, while I was still Queen of France."

Richard laughed outright at that. "My God, Mother. He should try something someone might believe."

"Well," I said, thinking of my annulled marriage to Louis of France, "the Holy See will not be moved to such folly twice. Which is to my advantage."

"Our advantage," Richard reminded me.

"Yes."

I moved back to my table where Henry's letter lay. I had delayed as long as I might in sending the letter on to the pope. Henry had no idea how far my spy network went, nor how deep into his own household. If I hoped to keep the reach of my spy network intact, I would have to be careful to keep its true depths a secret.

If I held the letter any longer, or threw it into the fire, Henry would only send another. I met Richard's eyes as I lifted a bar of sealing wax. "I will send this letter on to His Holiness, while we make our own plans here. Trust me, Richard. We will win."

I folded Henry's letter carefully, then melted wax onto the place where the old seal had been. I reached into my gown, and drew out a seal of my own.

Richard stepped forward, and took the letter from my hand, so that he might see the impression in the wax. I had closed Henry's letter with the royal seal of England, which no one but the king was supposed to possess, on pain of death.

I started laughing. I owned a copy of the royal seal, unknown to anyone but me and the man who had made it, a man who was many years dead. I was in danger now that Richard knew my secret, but I did not care. The danger was worth it, to show Richard the risks I took for him, and how much power I truly held. No one else knew. Not Alais. Not even the king.

Chapter 24

⚜

ALAIS: QUEEN IN ALL BUT NAME

Windsor Castle
September 1172

When Henry and I returned to Windsor at the beginning of September, the entire castle turned out to greet us. We had stayed away too long, happy together as Henry had rarely been, even with Rosamund. What that woman thought of our liaison, I had not heard. Henry never spoke of her, and I knew better than to ask. But as happy as we had been together, we knew that we could not stay from court forever. Eleanor waited for us, just as we waited for word from the pope.

As we reached the castle gates, Henry told me that Eleanor still resided at Windsor. I had no time to ask him why she had not gone on to the Abbey of Fontevrault, for the court had seen us then, and raised their cries of welcome. And still, I wondered why he had not done as he said he would.

Men-at-arms stood at attention, their pikes raised in salute to the king. Ladies of the court stood in the mud of the bailey in jewel-colored dresses, their wimples snow-white against the castle's gray stone.

All the women held flowers. When I was taken down off my horse, one of them stepped forward, and laid a bunch of roses in my arms. The last of the summer roses, roses that bore no thorns.

Those flowers made me think of Richard, and I had to breathe once, deeply, before I could put the thought of him away. And I saw the message for what it meant. I was a rose that now had been plucked, and some woman thought to mock me with it. It was a piece of cruelty worthy of Eleanor.

I looked for her in the crowd of women, but of course, she was not there. I searched the faces of the men for Richard, but I did not find him, either. I turned my eyes on the crenellated windows of the women's solar, and wondered if perhaps Eleanor looked down on me.

Though Richard was somewhere in the keep, he, too, was gone from me, as all my former life was, by my own choice. I pushed Eleanor and Richard from my thoughts, and took in the faces of those around me.

I stood in the king's bailey and was gracious to the same women who once had dismissed me as a pious and obedient lapdog of the queen. In spite of the mockery of the roses I held, I saw in the eyes of the women around me that they feared me a little, now that I had the ear of the king.

False subservience shone in the faces of all who surrounded me. For the first time, the truth of what it would mean to be queen dawned in my mind. I would have to be careful, and guard against the sin of pride. I was used to patience and obedience, but I was not used to praise. Even false praise was a heady wine, and could be my undoing.

I thanked God Henry had made me wear my best blue silk. I wore no wimple; my veil was held in place by the filet of golden fleurs-de-lys Eleanor had given me. I took in the scent of red roses in my arms, trying to block out the thought of Richard as I smiled on the woman who had given them to me.

Henry took my hand. As I turned to him, all thoughts of Richard fled. I was enveloped by the touch of my lover, and the scent of sandalwood that clung to his clothes and perfumed his skin. Henry smiled down at me, and for a moment, the rest of the court seemed to disappear.

I raised my lips to his and he kissed me there in front of all the people. A cheer went up, and his men-at-arms called out his name. He waved to them, then smiled down once more on me.

"My lady Alais, I would present my son."

I blinked, my lips still warm from his kiss, and from the approbation of the court. Never in my life had I been made so welcome. I knew that it was false warmth, but it warmed my soul just the same. Once Henry and I were married, and took the realm in hand, perhaps in time the warmth of the court would become real.

Henry raised one hand, and a boy not yet ten years old stepped forward out of the crowd. I had never seen him before, but he had the look of Henry and Eleanor both, and something else, something that belonged only to him. He bore a sense of his own worth that marked him at once as a prince.

"Alais, Princess of France and Countess of the Vexin, I present John, Prince of England."

I noticed that there was no other title behind the boy's name, and I realized that this must be the famous John Lackland, Henry and Eleanor's youngest son. I knew that Henry had once thought to put this boy into the Church, and that even now young John spent most of his time in the Abbey of Fontevrault. A boy meant for the Church had no need of lands, when his father might gift him with a bishopric, or better. As I looked into John's eyes, I found myself doubting all I had heard. The shrewd gaze that stared back at me gave me pause. Even as a child, this boy was a political animal. Somehow I did not think the walls of a church would ever hold him, as they had once held me.

The boy bowed to me, and smiled. I caught a hint of mischief in his gaze, and the sight of it made me long for Eleanor. There was a touch of her green in the hazel depths of John's slanted eyes.

"Good day, my lord prince. It is an honor to meet my future husband's son."

John's smile turned wicked. "Indeed, Princess, the honor is mine. It is not every day that a man is given a stepmother as beautiful as you are."

I laughed, for I was not his stepmother yet, and well he knew it, nor, for all his self-confidence, could he be considered a man. I saw that Henry was not pleased with John's honeyed answer. I pressed the king's hand. "My lord, your youngest son has your charm."

Henry's face softened, as it often did now when he looked at me. "Indeed, Alais. Too much charm for my peace."

The boy bowed low, as serious as in a church on Sunday. "My lord, never on pain of death would I disturb the king's peace."

Though there was still a light in John's eyes, I saw that he did not mock Henry. The boy meant to offer his loyalty in front of all the court, child though he was, reminding everyone present of Henry's other sons who did not do the same. Henry the Younger, Geoffrey, and Richard were conspicuously absent, young Henry in Normandy, Geoffrey in Brittany, and Richard hidden somewhere in the keep. All the court knew that Henry's sons did not support our alliance, except for John.

Henry looked down at his youngest son, and saw what I did. This boy, though young, would follow Henry, while his other sons did not.

Henry clasped his shoulder. "Let us go inside. The sun is setting, and it will soon be time to feast."

John looked at me. "I feast my eyes on the beauty of your lady, my lord. But a feast in the hall is also welcome."

Henry laughed, drawing me close. "The princess is mine, son."

Some women standing by had the gall to simper at the prince, as young as he was. He cast an appraising glance over them, taking them in as if he knew what lay beneath their gowns already.

"My lord king, it would be my honor to escort the princess to her new rooms, if you will allow me."

Henry kissed me once more as Prince John took my hand. "Look after her for me, Johnny. I will see you both in the great hall in an hour's time."

I curtsied, as if I did not think it foolish for a child to escort me into the keep. This boy was the only son loyal to Henry, and I knew that made him precious, no matter what his age. John bowed, and

Henry walked into his keep, the rest of the court falling into step behind him. As I watched, his ministers stepped forward and began whispering to him. Henry had kept the business of the kingdom with him at Deptford, but it had not consumed him. Now that he was back at court, it would become his focus, and I would fade into the background.

For the first time since Henry had aligned himself with me, I felt the sharp bite of fear as I watched him walk away. There was nothing to hold him to his pledge to me, nothing but his word, freely given, and one letter he had sent by dispatch to the pope.

I remembered my father's words about Henry, words I had overheard once when I was a child. My father had said that Henry would swear an oath before God one day, and break it the next. Papa had told his courtier that Henry was known for such throughout Christendom. Any treaty with him was worth less than the vellum it was written on.

I wondered, standing in my lover's bailey, why I had not remembered that before. And I wondered now if Henry would break his word to me.

John saw a shadow come over my eyes, and he smiled at me as he led me up the wide staircase to the castle's upper levels. "Don't frown so, Your Grace. There are new rooms waiting for you. The king has been very solicitous on your behalf while you have been away."

"The king is good to me."

John raised one eyebrow, and for the first time I saw the light of skepticism reach his eyes, a perception that went far beyond his years. It was uncanny, that this boy saw so much, when at his age I had known nothing. What I knew now of politics, Eleanor had taught me. I wondered, watching the prince, who had taught him.

"Indeed, Princess. I am happy to hear it."

We came to a large set of double doors on a wide corridor that I had never walked down before. At our approach, the doors were thrown open and Marie Helene stepped out, Bijou in her arms.

She curtsied at once to John, who eyed her russet gown as if he was imagining all that lay beneath it. She did not take offense at his gaze, but she did not dismiss his interest as a child's bravado, either.

"My lad, I am glad you have returned."

"So am I." I caressed Bijou's head. "Has she behaved since they brought her up with the baggage?"

Marie Helene's lips quirked in a smile. "Indeed, my lady. I have not yet set her down. Your new rooms are quite fine, and I wanted you to see them first."

"Ladies, I will leave you." John smiled on us, then turned to me, taking my hand in his. "I will see you at the king's table, Princess."

"I look forward to it, my lord prince."

"Call me John, Your Highness. I insist that beautiful women ignore my title, and smile on myself alone."

I wondered how a boy could have such a silver tongue. "Thank you, John."

He bowed, taking in Marie Helene's curves once more before he strolled away.

"Be on your guard with the prince, Your Highness," Marie Helene said. "He is not as young in his mind as he is in his body."

I kissed her cheek. "I must be on my guard always, Marie Helene, whoever I am speaking to. But I am glad I have you to remind me."

I took Bijou in my arms, and stepped into my new rooms.

Those rooms were wide, with great glass windows that looked down on the bailey below. They were filled with beeswax candles, and the scent of wax mixed with the scent of clean herbs in the braziers.

The great bed was covered in green silk, and heavy drapes of satin hung from the canopy. I saw at once that the drapes and bed-clothes were new. I would thank Henry for them at dinner.

Three large braziers stood, the scene of a deer hunt carved into the bronze of their bowls. Between these braziers was the deepest tub I had ever seen, filled with water so hot, steam rose from it. Two women stood beside it, their sleeves rolled up, ewers of water in their arms. One ewer held warm water and another cold, so that they could keep my bath comfortable while I sat in it.

The tapestries on the walls depicted another deer hunt, and were beautifully rendered in brilliant colors, though I could not look on the final panel and still sleep. In it, a deer was impaled on a pike, then hoisted onto the back of a horse. The deer's glassy eyes were rendered so well that it gave me pause. I moved to cross myself, but I was still holding Bijou.

"I have spoiled her," I said. "She was with me all the time at Deptford."

"You needed a friend in that place," Marie Helene said.

I saw the darkness in her eyes, and the set of her mouth. She could not continue to be surly, or Henry would never let her stay.

"Marie Helene, the king was there. He is my friend, as well as yours."

She did not answer, so I set Bijou down and took her hand. "I love him. You will see. Henry loves me, too."

"Richard will be glad to hear of it."

Eleanor stood in the wide doorway, two of her ladies flanking her. She raised one hand, and stepped into my rooms. The women closed the door behind her. But for the bathing women and Marie Helene, we were alone.

Eleanor was as beautiful as when I left her over a month before. Any grief she felt over my betrayal had not shadowed her splendor. Her eyes were undimmed; the beauty of their emerald light still beckoned me. My heart seized, and I had to breathe slow and deep. I loved her still.

I turned to the women who stood by to tend my bath. "You may go," I said.

They set their ewers down, and left the room by a side door hidden behind a tapestry. Marie Helene made sure that the door was shut fast behind them.

I took off the filet Eleanor had given me, and drew my veil off. Marie Helene moved to my side to take them from me. I sat in one of the many chairs that graced my new rooms. The pillows in each chair were plump and beautifully embroidered with scenes of the hunt.

"Welcome, Your Majesty," I said. "Can we offer you some watered wine?"

Eleanor laughed as she stood by the outer door. The sound was beautiful, as beautiful as it had ever been, before I knew of her betrayal, before I had betrayed her myself. Soon, Henry and I would hear from the pope. Henry would be granted an annulment, and Eleanor would retire to a nunnery. I would become the king's lawful wife. I had begun to learn a new thing while at Deptford, something Eleanor had never taught me: the law was what the king said it was.

"You are making yourself at home here, I see," Eleanor said as she stepped into the room. She did not sit with me.

Marie Helene poured two goblets of wine, the first one for me, which she set by my elbow. After I had drunk, Marie Helene brought another golden goblet to the queen. Eleanor took it from her, and held it up in the firelight.

"It would seem that these, too, are mine."

Eleanor drank the wine that Henry had ordered for me from Anjou before she set the goblet down on a small table near the bed. She took in the giant bed frame with its elaborate draperies and dark wood. She eyed it for a long moment. If I had not known her better, I would have thought she was amused.

"Richard was conceived in that bed," she said. "I had almost forgotten."

Though hearing Richard's name on her lips pained me, my anger began to rise as well. She planted the seeds of dissent and war among her sons, and hoped to plant them now in me. In the end, she would see reason, and let the king go. I did not answer her, but took another sip of my wine.

"These rooms were mine, you see," she said. "Once, long ago."

Eleanor strolled through my new rooms, taking in the sight of the new tapestries, the new bedding, the gold plate on the sideboard. There was a large oak table in the center of the room, surrounded by braziers. It would be the perfect spot for private suppers with the king.

She stopped near my chair, and Bijou came to her at once, sniffing around the edges of her gown. I smiled, my dignity lost, and scooped up my wayward puppy.

"Pardon Bijou, Your Majesty. She does not know her manners. She takes everyone for a friend."

"As you used to, Alais."

"Indeed, Your Majesty. I did."

Eleanor sighed and sat down. I looked to Marie Helene and she went at once to fetch the queen's cup of wine from across the room. She set it on the table at the queen's elbow, as she had set down mine.

Eleanor saw that I gave this order without speaking, and that Marie Helene obeyed in the same instant. She knew us both well enough to see behind the ruse. We meant to show her that I was queen in these rooms, as I would one day be queen in England. The light of admiration came into her eyes, and she smiled at me.

"Princess, how far you have risen."

"Indeed, Your Majesty. I will one day be a queen."

Eleanor barked with laughter, the music of her mirth filling my rooms so that Bijou wagged her tail.

But I did not smile, nor did Marie Helene. We knew that she was laughing at me.

"Alais, forgive me." Eleanor wiped tears of mirth from her eyes and sat back in her chair, her wine untouched beside her. "I think of you as Louis' daughter, and he could never stand up to me. I forget that you had a mother. You must have gotten your strength from her."

Neither of us spoke of the deeper truth that lay between us: she had been both my mother and my father for the last few years of my life. And now, as I looked at the woman I loved more than anyone else on earth, I saw only my enemy.

"So you have taken my rooms, and scheme now to take my crown."

"I do not scheme, Your Majesty."

"Oh, no, not you, Alais. It would be beneath your father's honor, would it not?"

I kept my tone low, my voice even. "Your Majesty, I want only for there to be peace between the king and his sons."

Eleanor was on her feet in an instant, the fury she had been holding back flashing in her eyes, and raining from her tongue.

"How dare you sit in my rooms, drink my wine, and name my sons to me?"

I stood and faced her. My voice was calm when I answered her, the ice of my own pain behind my eyes. "Your Majesty, you would do the realm a service by stepping aside. Once you have taken the veil, your sons will abide by their father's rule. Plantagenet lands will be at peace, in England and on the Continent, and this strife will end as if it had never been."

Eleanor's eyes glittered with malice. Never before had she turned such a face on me. It was like a dagger in my heart to see her fury directed at me. But she had helped me make this bed, with her own lies and treachery. Now we would both lie in it.

"You are a fool, Alais. As big a fool as your father ever was. Henry has fed you a pack of lies, and you have swallowed them whole. God help you when you see it."

My own fury rose to meet hers, and now I welcomed it. I had made a play for the throne, and I would take it. I would preserve the treaty with France, and remake my life. Eleanor would have to move out of my way.

"What I see, Your Majesty, is that you will step aside and take up the position as abbess at Fontevrault. What I see is that there will be peace between the king and his sons."

Eleanor turned on me, but I stood my ground. In these rooms, and in Henry's court, I was now her equal.

"Hear this, Alais, for I will only say it once. I will never take the veil. Not now, not thirty years from now. I am queen in these lands. No decree from the king, and no prayers from you, will make it otherwise."

Eleanor moved to the outer door. Her women must have heard her steps, for they opened my doors from the corridor, so that she stood framed in my doorway.

She turned back and raised her voice, so that anyone in the corridor might hear. "Do you really think you can defeat me, Alais? Even now, have you no idea who I am?"

All my doubts of Henry were buried now in my anger at Eleanor. I crossed the room until I, too, could be heard in the corridor. When I spoke, my voice was strong. I did not hesitate to strike for blood, knowing that I would draw it.

"Your Majesty, it is not I who fights you. It is the king. And he always wins."

Eleanor stared at me, the color draining from her face. The only color left beneath her wimple was the green of her glittering eyes.

Her women stepped forward, and took her arms. If they had not come to support her, Eleanor might have fallen.

It was the sharpest pain of my life, to see her brought so low. But there was triumph in that moment, too. She had used me as one more pawn on her chessboard, when I had done nothing but love her. If I had wanted revenge for her treachery in turning my letter over to the king, for the deception of her son, I had it then.

I stood in silence as her women met my eyes. They curtsied to me, before they led her away.

Chapter 25

ELEANOR: LOYAL SUBJECTS OF THE KING

Windsor Castle
September 1172

I had no time to recover from my meeting with Alais, for the meal in the great hall would take place, whether I willed it or no. And I did will it, for it was the only chance that day that I would have to see Henry, to remind him of our old alliance, and of his love for me.

Whatever Alais did for him behind the curtains of his bed, I had done more and done better in my time. I had borne him living sons, and daughters to shore up his power, and the power of the realm. Henry and I had been partners on the throne of England far longer than Alais had been alive. I knew that even now he might still be brought to reason.

I was late coming to the hall, but when I stepped inside, I saw that all my arrangements had taken place just as I had ordered them.

Jugglers and musicians performed below the high table, careful to include the king in their revelry, but always keeping their focus on the foot of the table, where Richard and I would sit.

Richard was waiting for me. He had never found such things amusing, and as he sat across from Henry, gazing at the woman who would have been his, he drank bitter dregs along with his mead. But I had coached him well, and he knew his role. He stood when I entered, and bowed to me, as if I were an empress.

The rest of my people took up his gesture, bowing as if they had never seen me before and I had just come down to earth from the right hand of God. They did not kneel, for that would have been pushing things too far. As it was, Henry raised a sardonic eyebrow at me, meeting my gaze above everyone's heads.

Some of Henry's own men took up the conceit, and bowed to me as well, though not as low or as long. Henry almost laughed to see them do it, and to see their confusion as they rose once more, looking first to one another and then to him for guidance. Never before had our court been so openly divided. No one but my own people knew how to handle it gracefully, and they knew only because I had instructed them.

Just when it would have begun to seem defiance of the king and not love of me, my people rose from their obeisance and took their places at the high table and at the tables below the dais. My musicians began to play a softer tune, one more conducive to taking a meal, gentle, light music to aid digestion. There was much for me to swallow that night, and well Henry knew it.

Henry stood to greet me with honor, and I faced him.

"Welcome, Eleanor."

I had covered myself in splendor that night, wearing a new gown of the deepest green that brought out the emerald brilliance of my eyes. I smiled at him as if it were any other night, and raised one jeweled hand, acknowledging his words.

"I thank you, my lord king. You are kind to welcome me into my own hall."

Henry did not smolder. Anger did not rise behind his eyes. I wondered if he had heard from the pope already. Clearly, he had planned the next move in his game, and did not fear any retribution from me.

"It is my hall, Eleanor. It would do well for you to remember that."

I knew that if Henry and I might speak alone, even now, the political situation might be salvaged. But I saw from the set of his clear gray eyes that he would not see me alone, that night or ever. We would have to play out this farce, as we had played out so many before, neither giving way.

Always before, I had deferred to him in the end, for always, he was king. But this time, I could not, and he knew it. This time we played for all or nothing, no middle ground between us. I saw that it saddened him a little to cast me aside, but when he turned to Alais, and took her hand, I saw that he would do it.

I said nothing more, but curtsied to Henry, letting Richard take my arm and seat me at the end of the high table. I sat at the very foot, facing Henry directly. My presence elevated the lowly spot to one of beauty and graciousness. Even in defeat, I smiled as if I knew it.

My women came and sat around me, the ones who knew they would never gain position with the king. Richard shared my trencher and his men flanked him.

Alais sat by Henry, eating off his trencher, dressed once more in cloth of gold. Henry had his dressmakers working during the weeks he and his lover were gone to Deptford; my spies had reported back to me of the fortune Henry was spending on new silks for the princess, the multicolored gowns that were cut from her old measurements. Alais did not seem overweening in her pride, in spite of the fortune in jewels and silk she wore; she simply sat at Henry's side as if she belonged there.

Henry sat beside my rival and waved one hand. Servers came at once and laid fresh meat and greens on my trencher, setting down a golden goblet full of my favorite wine. Henry smiled on me as if I were his guest, and not his wife of over twenty years.

Prince John came into the hall then, drawing my eye away from the king. He had waited in the shadows to see how the scene between us played out. Now that all was calm once more, he stepped forward onto the dais.

John came to me first, bowing courteously to me and kissing my hand, as any good son might. But after he greeted me, he turned at once and knelt to the king.

Henry smiled, his eyes softening. I could see that John was still his favorite son. There was no dissembling in John's face, no ploy to play one parent off against the other. A flash of irritation lit Richard's eyes, and Henry noticed it as I did. He gazed down the table at his elder son before he gave John leave to rise.

"You are welcome, John. Come here and sit by me."

The gentleman at Henry's side vacated his position at once, and John sat down, his slanted eyes smiling at Alais, as I had instructed him.

"Good evening, Father. I see your rose is as lovely as she was an hour ago."

"Two hours ago, John. No rose, even one just cut, would fade so quickly."

John served himself some pork. "The princess is as lovely as a fresh bloom, my lord. That is not merely a pretty courtesy."

The meal passed slowly as I paid my people the compliments they deserved, and as my musicians played on, knowing that I would pay them as well, once the meal was over.

Henry eyed me over the rim of his cup of mead. I still hoped that I might persuade him to speak to me. I raised my goblet to him in a mock toast, and Henry laughed, raising his tankard to me. For a moment, the ember of the old love that had always been between us glowed once more.

But Henry turned from me almost in the same instant, and moved his hand beneath the table. No doubt he was caressing Alais there in front of me. He raised his voice to be certain that I might hear him.

"Alais," Henry said, "will you not stand up for a dance with my son?"

For one horrible moment, I thought he wanted her to stand with Richard before all the court, dancing under his eye, as if they were still together, and happy.

Alais thought the same thing, for she turned pale, her color returning only when Henry spoke again. "John, take my betrothed among the dancers, if you are willing."

I heard the word Henry used to my face, as did all the company. All my people looked away, or called for wine or mead. Henry met my eyes. He was set on this course, for good or ill. Whether or not Alais' hand had put him there, he walked that path now of his own free will. I listened as my son answered him.

"It would be my honor, my lord king."

John stood and bowed, first to Henry, then to me. As I tried to regain my balance, to keep my smile in place, I wondered where John had gotten his worldly calm. It did not have a hint of Henry behind it, nor of my own false warmth. John was a man unto himself, though he was still only a boy.

John looked down on Alais, his hand extended, then looked to me. As I met his eyes, I saw nothing in their hazel depths. A mask of smiling pleasure covered his thoughts as Alais laid her hand in his.

Richard sat helpless as his brother led Alais onto the dance floor. He watched them move together, his face a mask of misery.

His man-at-arms John of Northumberland spoke for him. "My lord. The king."

Richard looked down the table and saw Henry gloating at his pain. Richard drew on all the powers of dissemblance I had ever tried to teach him, for he did not flush with fury, nor did he reach for the dagger at his wrist. Instead, Richard bowed his head to the king, then turned back to his tankard of mead. John was but a child, after all.

Henry moved to join my son and Alais on the floor below our dais. He extended his hand to her, and Alais took it, John bowing to them both as smoothly as any courtier, as if Henry's presence was just one more step in the dance. Richard watched his father and his betrothed together, and I saw the pain behind his eyes, and the hatred behind that. Henry saw it, too.

Henry took Alais out of the hall. I rose to my feet when everyone else did, to watch him pass. Alais did not meet my gaze, nor I, hers, yet in the moment before she disappeared, she was the only other person in the room for me.

Once they were gone, I sat down, heavily. Henry had not spoken to me, nor even nodded, as he took his paramour out of my sight. But the night was still young, and I had my own moves to make.

Richard swallowed hard, taking in this poison, as I had taken in mine. It was a hard road we walked. He had not yet put his love for Alais behind him. I began to see that he never would, for now she had become attached to his hatred for his father.

Gregory of Lisle and John of Northumberland were never far from my son's side, especially in this court of his enemies. They sat on Richard's other side, as if to flank him, to protect his back as they would in time of war.

I smiled my wicked smile at them, knowing that smile had brought many men to their knees over the years. Both young men blushed, and I was well rewarded. My son kissed my cheek as if his pain was not deep, as if the poison inside him did not hinder him. I saw his pain, but I saw also that it might be remedied. He would always love Alais, for she was the only woman on earth who was so like me, but there were other women who might comfort him.

I leaned across Richard and spoke to Gregory. "You must see to it that Richard takes a lover. He cannot moon after the princess any longer."

"Madam, I have already told him so." Gregory met Richard's eyes, and tried not to smile.

Richard had done all he could for one night, and would take no more advice from me. "I am going to my rooms, Mother. Unless you have need of me."

"Go, Richard. I will see you in the morning."

"Who will escort you to your rooms?"

His solicitousness was sweet, as he always was. He was the greatest warrior in Europe, but Richard had a soft heart. He would shield me from the dark, as if that were all I had to fear.

I smiled at Richard's man. "The Lord Northumberland will be kind enough to see me safe home."

John gulped, and a blush suffused his fair skin. "Your Majesty, it will be my honor."

Richard looked into my eyes, searching for my motive. He did not find it. He kissed me once more, swiftly on the cheek, then turned to leave, as if he could not bear the sight of his father's hall a moment longer.

Gregory followed him, for we all knew that it would not do to have the prince left alone in the dark halls of his father's castle. Gregory would bring my son a woman that night, and Richard most likely would have none of her.

I caught the eye of young Margaret, who was still at court, though not as openly welcomed by Richard as she once had been. I nodded to her, and she flushed, honored by my attention, for she had been banished from my women for over a month now. I raised one eyebrow, and inclined my head toward the door Richard had departed from.

Margaret colored visibly, and leaped to her feet as if scalded. She bowed low to me, and hurried after Richard. Perhaps she was one woman my son would not turn away.

John of Northumberland then led me out by the hand in front of my husband's court. All the world knew that I had never taken a lover since marrying Henry. All knew that it would not be worth my life to defy the king in such a way. But tonight would be different. Tonight I would indulge myself, and Henry be damned.

John of Northumberland took me back to my own rooms, and my women withdrew as they had done in the past when Henry would visit me, as silently as if John were the king himself.

The young man stood tall, and looked frightened, as if he had never been alone in a room with a woman before. I thought at first he was simply overawed, for I was queen, the most beautiful woman in Europe, the only woman to hold power in her own right in the whole of Christendom. I thought to offer him some wine, to ask him about his adventures in war at my son's side, but then I saw the truth. He honored me, but did not desire me. I was old enough to be his grandmother.

I had never been one to lie to myself. I sighed, and drank my wine. "That is all, John. You may go."

He left at once, bowing low, knowing that I had gifted him with a reprieve. He knew, as I did, that all the court would believe him my lover, though he had not so much as touched my hand. I hoped it raised his standing among his comrades, as it once would have done. I would never know, for I would not ask my spies to tell me. Though I had to be honest with myself, I did not have to listen to the honest opinions of others unless I wished to. One more advantage of being queen.

So I sat alone, without my women to attend me, as I had always done since Alais left me. No longer did I have her soft hands in my hair. No longer did I feel the gentle pull of her brush as she sat behind me, keeping my feet to the fire, that I might be comfortable as she tended me. Alais had cared for me from love, and not from fear. She was the only woman who had ever done so. Even my daughters feared me. Even my sons.

I lay down on my bed, but I did not sleep. I stared at the shadows that ran across my ceiling, the shadows that once would have shown the motion of me and my chosen lover, moving together in the half-light. Those shadows once would have shown Henry standing over me, leaning down to take my lips with his.

Tonight Henry did attend a woman. Once more, as it had been for many years, that woman was not me.

Chapter 26

❧

ALAIS: ANOTHER PRINCE

Windsor Castle
September 1172

"How like you my son?"

The king was baiting me as he had at dinner, purposefully naming Richard to me, under the auspices of John. It had been a long meal, and painful. Now I saw that Henry meant to sound out my loyalty, as if he doubted me. I, too, had begun to doubt him. I had returned to find Eleanor still at Windsor, and not on her way to Fontevrault as Henry had promised. Henry had not yet sent her away, as he had sworn to me he would. Whatever else was true, I did not now think to allow Henry to bait me further.

Marie Helene saw that I wanted her gone. She curtsied first to the king, and then to me, taking Bijou into her arms and leaving us alone.

"John is very pleasant, my lord. I cannot decide who he takes after, you or the queen."

"You still call her the queen, do you?"

"She is still queen, my lord. She still wears your crown. She sits at your table and drinks your wine and raises her glass to you. She has not yet been thrown down."

"Eleanor sits at my table and drinks my wine because I will it, and for no other reason. In time, she will go to Fontevrault, and take up the veil there, just as I have told you she would."

"When, Your Majesty? For there cannot be two queens in this keep."

"No," he answered. "There cannot."

I heard the suggestion behind his words, that if he was to change his mind, to turn from me even now, letters to the pope or no, I would be cast aside with nothing but my shame. I tasted fear, but swallowed it whole. I kept my face blank, my eyes serene, as both my father and Eleanor had taught me.

I smiled at Henry; he saw no hint of my fear as I drew the laces of my gown between my fingers. I had become adept at dressing and undressing myself at Deptford. Tonight I did it slowly, knowing that Henry savored the sight of my clothes falling off me as he savored little else. But tonight, though I watched the lust rise in his eyes, he would not be distracted.

"Eleanor is not the queen, Alais. I made her queen, and now I withdraw that privilege from her. I give it to you."

My gown slipped down my shoulders, onto the stone floor. I stepped out of it, leaving the beautiful gold silk where it lay. I drew my hair down over one breast, laying my silk veil on the table next to the wine that Marie Helene had left for us.

I still wore my fine linen shift, but it was very thin. I made sure to stand between the king and a brazier, so that he could see the shadow of my body in the firelight.

Henry stared at me, but he did not move to touch me. I poured wine into the same golden goblet Eleanor had drunk from that afternoon. I offered the wine to Henry first, but when he did not take it, I drank it myself.

"You have changed, Alais," he said.

"No doubt, my lord. Loving you has changed me, and for the better."

"But Richard . . ."

I raised one hand, as I never would have done anywhere else, at any other time, to silence him. I would let him win that night regarding Eleanor, for I had no choice. But I would not stand by while he named his son to me. I had lost Richard, and the loss pained me. As much as I had gained from Henry, as much as I stood to win, I loved Richard, and my pain over his infidelity burned in my breast, right above my heart. My own disloyalty had not lifted that burden from me. Revenge was not the tonic I had hoped it would be.

"My lord, your sons are well and good. In time, they will learn to serve you better. But in these rooms, I do not want to hear of them. I would rather hear of you."

Henry's eyes narrowed. I stepped forward, and stood close to him, so that I could feel the heat of his body through his gown.

"John is charming, Henry. But he is not you. No one is like you. No one will ever be like you."

"Because I am king," he said, his eyes drawn to the outline of my lips.

I pressed myself to him, my hands running up his back, until my arms were wrapped around his neck. I watched as he felt the softness of my body, how I yielded to him here, as everywhere, as Eleanor did not.

Just before his eyes caught fire, just before he took my lips with his, I said, "Because you are Henry."

We went on that way for a month, Eleanor keeping state at the lower end of the king's table in the great hall, making each feast merrier than the last, the merriment more forced as each day passed. Henry stayed in thrall to me and to my young body, as I stayed in thrall to him. We heard nothing from the pope. Though we had not yet expected to, Henry grew more restless, so that I had to work harder to tame him, and to draw him down onto his bed with me.

I kept my own fears hidden, even from myself. My memory of my father's words about Henry and the oaths he would not keep came back to me, when I was alone in the dark. But in daylight, and while I slept by Henry's side, I kept these fears locked in my heart, out of sight. I did all I could not to think on them, but they plagued me, as did my father's warning.

Henry was a hard man with a quick temper, but he rarely spoke a harsh word to me. He enjoyed watching me in the firelight at night, as I drew a brush through my long dark hair. He loved to watch me play with Bijou, and ride Sampson farther and faster than I ever had.

My time with him taught me not to fear horses, so that Sampson became too sedate a mount for me, and Henry gave me another.

Henry and I went on a hunt two months into our love affair, and though I had no falcon of my own, I did not shrink from Henry's hawk as I had from Richard's.

Henry cut a piece of dove for his hawk to feed on, a reward for bringing the bird down. I watched without flinching as Henry fed the hawk the bloody bit of flesh, fresh from the kill. He must have heard the story of my other hunt—whether from Eleanor or Richard, I did not know. Or perhaps he had made it his business to know all he could about me, and about my time with Eleanor, before he had come to court and seen me for himself.

Henry eyed me over the sleek head of his hawk, the great bird hooded once more before it could turn its eye on me. Henry watched me for a long moment without speaking as I reached out and caressed the hawk gently, one more reward for its faithful service.

"You do not like a hunt, Alais. Or so I had been told."

I smiled at him, my face open as if my heart were light, except for my eyes. "So it was, Your Grace. I did not savor watching a smaller bird killed."

"And yet that is the way of the world, Alais."

"I know." I met his eyes. "I have become more of a falcon myself, Your Grace. I do not feed on others. But neither do I stand still and let others feed on me."

He laughed then, handing his hawk to his squire, who took the bird and withdrew, his eyes cast down, as if he could hear nothing of our speech. I had gotten used to being listened to at every moment. Only between the curtains of his bed or mine were we truly free of others. I accepted that as a necessity, for he was king.

"You have changed, Alais," he said.

"I have, Your Grace. I have come to know myself."

Henry drew his horse beside mine and led me beneath a willow tree down by the river, where the water still ran clear and cool, even in the unseasonable warmth of that September. He came off his horse and handed the reins to a groom, taking me from my horse as well.

He did not speak a word, but his men seemed to know him, as I did, for they did not follow us. Henry brought me into a copse of willow trees, where the spongy ground near the river was fragrant with clover, and a hint of honeysuckle, though those flowers had long since fallen.

Henry threw his cloak on the ground and drew me to him without speaking, his hands ranging over me as they did when we were alone in his room, the door shut behind us. I pressed myself against him, reveling in the hard contours of his body, for he was fit for a man almost forty, his hair as thick as it had ever been, his hands as strong. Those hands cupped me, and drew me hard against him, so that I could feel his desire through the thickness of his gown.

"My lord king, it seems you have something for me."

He laughed low, his lips trailing from my cheek to my throat, and down onto my breasts through the soft silk of my gray gown. He drew me down, and mounted me, until we were joined as one, our clothes pushed aside but not drawn off, his breath hot on my cheek and in my hair.

He brought me to the peak of pleasure as he always did, but for some reason, that day, the pleasure made me sad. Before long, winter would come, and time would continue to slide away from us, as the river made its way inexorably to the sea. I felt my mortality for the first time with Henry beside me, his passion spent, breathing gently into my hair.

"I love you, Alais."

It was the first time he spoke those words to me, though I had seen his love for me in his eyes since the night he first had me. I kissed him, savoring the taste of him, not wanting the moment to end. Like all things, this spell, too, would be broken.

For that moment, I cast aside all thought of the future, all thought of Eleanor. I would sit on her throne, wearing her heavy golden crown, doling out death and judgment at Henry's side, as I must if I was to be queen. I pushed away all thought of Richard, and my childhood hopes. I kissed Henry until I could think of nothing but him.

"I love you," I whispered, so that only he could hear me.

In the next week, my courses were late. I waited until I was sure before I planned my next move on the chessboard my birth had set me on.

I took no one into my counsel now, not even Marie Helene. She knew, as I did, that my body was changing, but instead of filling her with triumph as it did me, my pregnancy filled her only with fear. She watched me constantly, as if I might shatter. I allowed her to bring me mulled wine and warm furs, though it was not October yet. I accepted her solicitation but did not tell her of my thoughts.

On the day I planned to go to Henry with the news, I watched Bijou play on the new silk bedding. I caressed my dog, but she ran from me, happy to frolic under the sheets, trying to draw me beneath the bedclothes in some strange game of chase.

I met Marie Helene's eyes, and caught her staring at me. "My lady, you must tell the king."

"I know, Marie Helene. I will."

A woman came in from the kitchens then, bearing a tray with fresh bread so hot I could see the steam still rising from it. With it, she brought a crock of fresh-churned butter, late apples, and a hunk of English cheddar. The scent of that good bread turned my stomach, but I had a will of iron. The nausea passed.

The maid set it on the table, no doubt thinking that it was for me.

"Thank you, Maude," I said.

She colored visibly, grateful that I remembered her name.

I had dressed carefully that morning in my royal blue gown, one of the first gowns Henry had given me. I wore my father's rosary at my waist, the gold and pearls set against the indigo silk. I wore no veil, for Henry liked to see my curls uncovered when we were alone. If I was successful, we would soon be alone, though it was the middle of the day.

"Well, Marie Helene. May the Holy Mother bless us."

"Amen."

Marie Helene crossed herself. Only then did she see what I was about. She knew me well by now, and knew that I would not allow her to walk with me. This day would be yet another move on my chessboard. Today, Henry would stand with me or cast me off when he heard of the child I would bear. I took up the tray, and Marie

Helene opened the outer door for me. She did not follow, and I went on alone.

Henry's men-at-arms knew me at once, and bowed, each taken with the light as it fell on my chestnut curls. I smiled at them.

"Brian. Fitzwilliam. May I see the king?"

They stared at me, as if in a stupor. I had not come to the king unannounced since the day I first had him.

"I have brought him this good bread," I said. "It is fresh from the bakehouse. I fear that the day runs on, and His Majesty does not eat."

This concern struck both of them dumb. Never, in any time or place, would Eleanor have shown such solicitude, or such womanly grace. I knew this and smiled, even as they opened the door for me.

Henry was surrounded by his ministers. I had not yet been introduced to any of them, but to a man they bowed to me as if I were queen already.

Henry crossed the room to me, taking the tray from my hands.

"Alais, what is this feast? Did you bake this bread yourself?"

His men laughed, as he meant them to. He looked down at me, and I could see love in his eyes in spite of the dismissal in his tone.

"No, Your Majesty. I simply sent to the kitchens for it. But I learned to bake in the nunnery. If you would have me bake bread for you with my own hands, it would please me above all things."

The men stopped laughing, struck dumb as the men-at-arms had been. No doubt they had never seen a princess of the royal blood humble herself. Certainly Eleanor would never have done so.

A man-at-arms came forward and took the tray from Henry's hands. The king made one gesture, and moving as one, all his ministers and men-at-arms left us alone. As they went, they bowed first to the king, and then to me. I noticed that the bows they offered were almost equally deep. Henry noticed as well, and he quirked a brow at me.

"So, Alais, what are you playing at?"

"Nothing, my lord. I wanted only to feed you, and to have a moment alone."

I pressed myself against him, and his arms came around me. He had taught me well, for my kiss took his mind from his men, from the bread on his table, from everything but the touch of my body against his. I kissed him until his eyes were drowsy. Before he could draw me with him into his bedroom beyond, I said, "My lord king, I have news."

Hope began to dawn behind his eyes. I watched as he fought it, for hope was a luxury he no longer allowed himself. Until now. I would give it back to him.

"I am with child."

Henry searched my eyes to see if I was lying, if this might be some trick, some ploy, as it could have been from Eleanor. I stood under his gaze, my eyes on his. He remembered then who I was, and what I meant to him.

He swept me up and cradled me, clutching me close as he sat down on his favorite chair. The cushions were plump to support his back, which pained him now and then, though no one but me and his page knew it. I kissed his cheek. When he looked at me, his eyes were full of tears.

"A son," he said. "A son for England."

"God willing," I said.

"Amen."

It was the first time I ever heard Henry utter a prayer, and the last. My own relief washed over me, like a tide that would never go out. He would claim this child, and me. I was one step closer to the throne.

He held me close, and I pressed a kiss to his temple. His hand rested on my still-flat belly. We sat together in silence, both filled with the unexpected hope of a new beginning, the beginning that our unborn son might bring.

Through the marriage he might make with me, through this unborn child in my belly, Henry hoped to capture his youth once more. Like all older men who sought a younger wife, he wanted to pretend that the choices he had made in his life were not binding, that there was still time left to him to make things right. He might truly cheat death, make me his wife, and begin again, as if the world were new, all rancor with Eleanor and her sons a distant memory.

We stayed together all afternoon, and that time alone was like a blessed season. Neither doubt nor fear entered my mind as I sat alone with Henry that day.

Henry sent word that his ministers need not wait on him until the morrow. He ate the bread and cheese I brought, then sat munching an apple as I sipped gingerly at my favorite wine. During my pregnancy, I was nauseous for half the day, but as the afternoon began to turn toward evening, my stomach settled, and I was myself once more.

"There is word from the pope, Alais."

"Will he support us, Henry?"

I sat once more on his lap, his hand caressing my hair. "He does not say."

My fear of Henry's oath breaking did not rise to taunt me as I sat wrapped safe in his arms. I tilted my head to look at him, and Henry pressed a kiss to my lips. "His Holiness waits to see which way the wind blows. Eleanor is powerful, and until a few months ago held the Aquitaine in her own right. His Holiness does not want to make an enemy of her and, through her, my son."

"Richard?"

I spoke the name without thinking, and Henry's back stiffened. I ignored my own pain at the thought of Richard. It was a wound that still bled in me. I kept my voice light as I kissed Henry, caressing his hair. "My lord, the Prince Richard is surely too devout to question the decisions of the pope."

Henry's lips quirked in mirth, but he did not laugh at me. "Surely."

"Write to him again, my lord. His Holiness will want to keep the peace in these lands, as we do. He will support you."

"Us, Alais. He will support us."

"To support you is to support me, Henry. I will be your wife. We will be one flesh before God. I am yours, for the rest of my life."

He kissed me and lifted me in his arms. I savored the taste of him as I savored little else in those first early days of my pregnancy.

Henry carried me into the room where he slept, and pressed me back onto the softness of his bed. Henry brought me to ecstasy with his strong, wide hands.

We took pleasure in each other until after the sun had set. We were late coming to the great hall that night for the evening feast, but it did not matter. For he was king.

The autumn came on and my belly grew, rounding nicely though the rest of my body stayed slender. I displayed my belly even before it had grown much, proud of the heir I carried, one more son to shore up Henry's power.

Even the sight of me did not give Eleanor pause. She raised her goblet to me from the other end of the high table. I did not see her alone, then or ever, and we did not speak of it. She was kind enough to send fresh pears to my rooms when they came in from Anjou. They were one of the few foods I could eat in the mornings without being sick.

She did not act from kindness alone. Eleanor meant to remind me of how far her arm reached, and of how much her spies knew of the intimacies of my life, but I was still touched. I stayed in a haze of goodwill regarding her until eels were served at dinner the next night, and I had to leave the hall or vomit in front of all the court.

I caught Eleanor's eye as I ran from the hall in disgrace, and I saw how she smiled to her lady Amaria at my expense. The eels had been brought to table by Eleanor's steward in honor of my pregnancy, and my roiling belly.

My temper flared, and as my women attended me over my silver bowl, I quipped, "The Lady Eleanor will no doubt retire soon to her nunnery. Her womb is dried up, and can no longer serve the king. Perhaps her prayers will aid the kingdom where her womb cannot."

The ladies who attended me laughed appreciatively, but I saw a look pass between them that said perhaps King Henry had too many sons already. I bent over the bowl, retching again. When I raised my head once more, the look between them had fled. Marie Helene frowned at me, the only woman among my ladies who would dare to show disapproval.

Eleanor's spies no doubt numbered among the women who served in my rooms, for the next day Richard came to me alone.

I was shocked to see him there, standing in my rooms as if he belonged in them. My ladies tittered behind their hands, all young women just up from the country, eager to serve at court and to make good marriages. They had been sent to serve the queen, but now attended me.

I raised one hand, as I had always seen Eleanor do, and those ladies withdrew. Marie Helene stayed for propriety's sake, though I knew that Richard would not touch me. Our old friendship, our old affinity and affection, born from loneliness and the joy of finding more in each other than duty, all that was gone. Even now, months since we had broken with each other, the sight of him pained me. I grieved over all we had lost. In spite of my own disloyalty, I was furious that he had tossed our love away for a moment of pleasure with Margaret.

I breathed deep, my hand on my rounded belly. I had made my choice, and now I must live with it.

"Richard, you are welcome here. May I offer you wine?"

My betrothed looked at me as if he did not know me. I was dressed from head to toe in my new silk finery. Henry had more elaborate taste in clothes than Eleanor, at least for his mistresses, for I wore cloth of gold almost every day now, with gilt trim and sable. I kept my habit of wearing a simple veil held in place by Eleanor's gold filet. The fleurs-de-lys of my father's house pressed into my brow, reminding me always of who I was and why I walked the path I had chosen.

Richard took in the sight of me, and bowed low, almost as low as he bowed to his mother. I could see even then that he was angry, and I waited for him to speak.

"You spoke ill of my mother, and all the world heard you. You spoke of her dried-up womb with contempt. She has borne the king many sons, and healthy daughters. To speak so of her is a disgrace, both to the king and to you."

I felt shame rising to engulf my face in fire. I swallowed tears. His face softened, but he did not speak to comfort me. I regained control of myself, the easy tears of pregnancy banished behind my eyes. I placed my goblet down.

"Richard, I spoke harshly of the queen to the women in my own rooms. No doubt word of my folly spread, and tales are being carried of me that are worse than the truth that spawned them."

"The queen has heard what you said. It grieves her."

My heart contracted as I thought of Eleanor, the only mother I had ever known, and of all I had brought her to. She had not backed down; not for one moment had she considered becoming a nun, as any other woman would have done in her place. I admired her strength, and the strength she had fostered in me. But I would make this alliance for France, to save my own life, and the life of my unborn child. I would not back down and go into disgrace. Henry would be mine, as would her crown.

Whatever I was, whatever I would become, Eleanor had made me. She had shown me the way to my own strength. Without her, I never would have begun to know myself.

"Richard, please tell the queen that I am sorry. I spoke out of turn, in a fit of retching."

Richard's blue eyes sharpened on my face. "You call her the queen, even as you seek her throne?"

Henry had warned me of such slips. So far, I had made them only with him, when we were alone. Now I had called Eleanor queen in front of her favorite son. I knew she would hear of it.

I did not flinch from the accusation in his eyes. I had betrayed Eleanor, but she had betrayed me first.

"I would not have thought you capable of such duplicity," he said.

I laid my hand on my belly, and my child gave me strength. I fought not just for myself now but for him.

"I have never lied, nor will I. But know this, Richard: I will be queen in these lands. I wish it. Your father wishes it. In time you will come to see it as I do."

"I will not."

We stood, caught in the eyes of the other, until he blinked, and looked away.

I thought he would leave then, but he had one more question for me. "How could you be so faithless?" he asked me. "How could you leave me for him?"

I knew I could not explain all his mother had done to force my hand, all the deceit that lay between myself and the queen. I could not tell him of the letter she had given over to his father to save him, nor of the fact Richard and I were both pawns on her chessboard until I struck out on my own, for myself. I knew he would never believe me.

"You were unfaithful first."

I watched my barb hit home. His face grew pale and his blue eyes reflected the truth that he could not deny what I said. I saw that he had never before considered that just as he had expected fidelity from me, so I had wanted it from him.

Even then, he did not leave me. He raised his eyes to mine once more, and this time, I saw his pain, bereft of all anger and hatred, bereft of all but sorrow. I saw in his eyes the words that he had spoken as we stood alone in the kitchen garden, words that even now hung between us. I had closed my heart to them, and to him; I had told myself that I had forgotten. But standing there, facing him, alone but for Marie Helene, those words came back to me.

"I will serve you for the rest of my life," he had said.

I saw now that such a vow was folly. No man could be held to such an oath. But when Richard spoke those words, my heart had believed him. My heart believed him still, even now, after all I had done. I had closed the door of my heart to him, turned my back on the love we shared, out of revenge, and spite, lust for his father, and my own ambition. I had turned my back on him for what I thought was forever. But I saw, as he stood there with his heart in his eyes, that I loved him still, just as he loved me.

Even with the pain of this new knowledge on my heart, I would turn away from his love once more. Whatever my fears, whatever my folly, I had joined with Henry for good or ill. I could not now turn back.

Richard did not speak again, for he had seen the pain in my eyes, the pain that matched his own. There was nothing left to say. He left me standing alone with only Marie Helene to attend me. She came to my side and took my hand.

My women came back into the room, bringing lutes and tabors with them, that they might make music to pass the afternoon, as they might once have done in Eleanor's rooms.

Marie Helene brought Bijou to me, so that I could sit with my little dog and hear the music. I had no heart to sing myself, for I could not find my voice, but my women sang for me.

Chapter 27

ॐ

ELEANOR: A MOMENT OF TRUCE

Windsor Castle
October 1172

I sat alone in blessed silence. I was supposed to be at prayer, but unlike Alais, I had no god to pray to. I had just heard from my spy network that Henry had word from the pope. His Holiness was cautious, nothing like the man who had set me free from Louis. This pope would wait, and bide his time, to see which way the wind blew, before he moved against me.

The pope no doubt knew, as I did, that though Henry had sworn to go on Crusade, he would never stir from his own borders to begin a foreign war, especially a war of someone else's devising. It served no purpose but to waste money, and Henry had the business of the kingdom to consume him; that, and keeping his sons at bay.

Richard was another matter altogether. I knew it was the secret wish of his heart to go on Crusade for the Church, to raise the banner of Christ once more over the city of Jerusalem. No doubt the pope had heard this, too. From all accounts, his spy network was almost as good as mine.

So His Holiness would not move against me, or my son. All I needed to do was bide my time, and wait for Henry to tire of her.

I crossed my solar to my window, where the breeze and sun touched my face. It was almost winter, but still I kept my windows unshuttered. I loved the feel of the wind, and kept them open as long as I could, mewed up as I was in my husband's keep. I could not go far, either in hunting or in merriment. I had to keep my eye always on Henry, to see what move he might make next.

I did not think on Alais. I missed her as I missed nothing and no one else, but I kept my mind from her, except when she was before me. Like the pope, I would bide my time there as well. Before long, an opportunity would present itself, and I would bring her back to me.

Richard barged in without knocking, the only man alive who would have dared. He crossed the room to me, his hair disheveled, his eyes wild. For one horrible moment, I thought something might have happened to Henry, or to Alais.

I was wrong.

"Mother, he will discard her."

"Richard."

I raised one hand, and Amaria drew the door closed behind my son. She raised an eyebrow, and I shook my head at her, telling her that there was nothing truly to worry about, reminding her that Richard was emotional, especially where Alais was concerned. His news had to do with Alais, the only subject that could upset him during those dark days.

"Richard, what ails you?"

"Alais, Mother. She is bearing the king's bastard, and he will toss her aside as he has all the others. What will she do then? Who will protect her, when I cannot?"

I waited, but the old jealousy did not rise as it once would have done.

"Hear me, Richard. When Henry casts Alais aside, as indeed he must, I will care for her."

"She will be disgraced before all of Europe. Her life will be over."

I smiled. My son was strong and brave, but naive, as all men are. The loss of reputation did not ruin a woman unless she had no one else to succor her. Alais would always have me.

"Richard, do not trouble yourself over this. There is nothing you or anyone can do to help her. She has chosen this path, and she will walk it to the end. But know this: when he casts her off, I will take her in. I will give her shelter."

"And her child?"

The words were like bile in my throat, sharp and foul, but I meant them. "And her child."

Richard knelt to me and pressed his lips to my hand. He felt things so deeply; he always had, even as a child. I saw how much he still loved her, how much he would always love her, as he knelt there at my feet.

"Richard, enough of this. Come and sit with me. Keep me company. I grow lonely without you near."

He rose at once, and crossed the room, my hand in his. He seated me in the best chair, and arranged the cushions behind my back. He kissed my forehead as if in blessing, before he sat beside me.

"Wine, Mother?"

"Please. Thank you, Richard."

He poured a glass of Anjou wine for me, and I drank it, though I was not thirsty. I watched him, my beautiful golden boy, and cursed Alais for hurting him as no woman ever had, as no woman ever would again.

I swallowed my bile, and smiled at him. "What brings Alais' plight to your mind, Richard? Have you been praying for her again?"

"Yes, Mother. But I also went to see her."

I raised one eyebrow, but said nothing.

"She said something vile about you, about . . ."

He flushed, not willing to repeat the phrase that was on all the court's lips. My dried-up womb, indeed.

"Yes, Richard, she spoke foolishly."

"She spoke against you," he said.

"Richard, things are said at such times that are not meant. No doubt Alais forgot in a moment of pique that every word she says is open to the speculation of others. The court cares for what a queen has to say, as they do not a princess of France."

"She is not queen," Richard said, his face darkening.

"Nor will she be. But the court does not know that. They must be cautious, and play both sides, until one comes out a clear winner."

"It is despicable."

"It is politics, my son. You would do well to heed it."

"I would rather be run through on the battlefield than force my-self to such womanish tricks."

I laughed out loud at that. He forgot that I was a woman, too.

"I'm sorry. . . ."

I raised one hand, still laughing. "No, Richard, you do me honor. I know in your world to be thought womanish is a weakness. But women have deviousness, and ways that men do not, to see to it that their will is done."

"Yes, Mother."

"Do not trouble yourself, Richard. Leave the politics to me."

His face was still dark, his blue eyes shadowed. "Mother, she is sorry that she hurt you."

I felt my breath catch in my throat, as if he brought me news of a lover, and not of a young girl.

"Is she?"

I kept my voice from trembling, but I held my breath as I waited for his answer.

"Yes. She is sorry for what she said."

I pressed his hand, and forced myself to smile. "Don't think on the princess anymore, Richard."

He kissed my cheek, and rose to his feet. He had been too long indoors already.

"I love you, Mother."

He left me, and my women came in, bringing fruit and fresh wine, smiling at me as if I had not fallen into disgrace with the king, as if no usurper sought my throne.

"Send for Bertrand," I told Amaria. "Let us have some music and be merry, while we may."

She obeyed me, and my women laughed and clapped, for they loved to look at my troubadour, at his shapely thighs and calves, his broad shoulders and muscled arms, which more than one of them had felt around them in the dark.

As for myself, I wanted only peace. Music was the only way to get that during that dark, benighted time, when I had nothing and no one but Richard.

I sat alone that night after the meal in the great hall. Alais had gone to bed early, for pregnancy made her tired. I sent rose water to her rooms, and a snifter of brandy to help her sleep. She sent no reply.

I sat before the fire, my hair trailing down my back. It was still bronze, but silver had begun to make its inroads, the march of time across my forehead, and into the glossy depths of my hair. I was growing old. So be it. I was not dead yet.

Richard had gone off with his lover, Margaret. Though they saw little of each other now, Margaret was to leave court on the morrow. Her father had heard of her disgrace and had asked me to arrange her marriage. I had done so with little difficulty, for I had settled some money on her, and had chosen for her an older man. Sir Ralph of Nottingham was happy to overlook the fact that Margaret had once been a favorite of my son's.

No doubt Richard and Margaret wished to have some lovers' talk, about old times that would not come again. Richard was not quite sixteen years old. It amused me that he thought he had old times to speak of.

The fire was burning well, and the charcoals gave off their feeble heat. I was not one for melancholy, but for some reason that night my regrets lingered with me, all the losses of my long life, and precursors of all the losses yet to come.

I was musing to myself, deep in self-pity, when there was a scratching at my door. When I called, Henry answered, and came in.

I did not stand and greet him, so surprised was I to see him, there in my rooms, alone. I watched him as he came to me, moving like the lion he so often made me think of, the predator that I had matched my wits against for so many years, the man I had loved.

"Henry, you are welcome."

When I moved to stand, finally remembering the protocol that should govern us even when we were alone, Henry gestured to me to sit, drawing another chair close to me, and to the fire.

"Eleanor."

He sat, staring into the fire, and I did the same. For that moment, it was as if we had both slipped into old age, with lust and fire behind us. As if we watched and waited for death together, as I once thought we might.

Henry reached over and took my hand in his. In his strong grip, my hand looked feeble and old. My rings gleamed in the lamplight, and my fingers tapered in elegance into his palm. Time was what it was, and had left me as it left me. I would not be ashamed.

As if he could see these thoughts behind my eyes, Henry smiled at me. His smile was full of grudging admiration as his looks always were, now that we were enemies. But that night we sat together, a moment of détente in the middle of a war. Neither of us knew yet which of us would win, but sitting alone, the court banished from our presence, we saw for the first time what both of us had lost already.

"Eleanor, I am sorry it has come to this."

I did not answer right away. I knew, even then, that nothing would change between us.

"You have only to raise one hand, and this war would end, Henry. You know that."

The gray eyes I had loved for half my life did not leave mine.

"But you will not," I said.

"No," he answered. "I will not."

He did not release my hand, even then. Still we sat together in peaceful silence, the firelight flickering across our faces, and over the silvered bronze of my hair.

"Your hair shines like electrum in this light, Eleanor. I had forgotten."

I felt my tears rise then, for all that we had once been to one another, for what we would never be to each other again. I knew, even as my sorrow rose, that my pain was part of our love, just as the joy once had been. Even now, at the end, I would not have had it any different.

"Ah, Henry, soon you will be singing me love songs."

He laughed, as I had meant him to, and my tears receded.

"And would you have me fetch you barley cakes, and apple butter made with my own hands?"

Henry barked once more with laughter, but I heard the seriousness under that. "Dear God, Eleanor, stop it. You are a queen."

"And so I shall remain, until my days pass from this earth. You know that, do you not?"

Henry met my eyes, his temper dormant. That night I might

have said anything to him, and he would have loved me just the same.

"I know that you will try."

I inclined my head. My hand still lay in his.

"You are a queen, Eleanor, and not because I made you one."

"I am surprised you know it," I said.

"Ah, Eleanor, I have always known it. I knew it the moment I met you. The day I met you, I knew that if I could make you mine, the world would be at my feet, the throne of England mine for the taking."

"I knew it, too."

We sat once more in silence, both taken back to that magic time, when all the obstacles that stood in our way were as nothing: my husband, Henry's mother, the war he fought for his inheritance. When we stood together, looking at each other in the light of my husband's court, he had known, as I had, that together we could do anything.

"I love you," Henry said.

"I know that, too."

As he stood, even then, he was reluctant to let go of my hand. In the end, I took it from him, to remind him that he had made his choice already. We walked a path of his own devising. We could not now turn back.

But at my door, Henry did turn back. He saw me, sitting where he had left me, my green gown drawn around my shoulders against the evening chill. He saw my hair, shining like bronze in the firelight, the silver strands heightening its beauty, the light soft on my face.

"Henry," I said. "Why did you come?"

"I missed you, Eleanor. I am not myself when you are not with me."

He left me then, and closed the door. My women did not come in to wish me a good night. Though I had no god to thank, I was grateful, for there were tears on my cheeks. I did not want to shed them in front of another. Not even him.

Chapter 28

ॐ

ALAIS: A CHOICE

Windsor Castle
February 1173

As the months passed, I displayed my belly proudly, setting aside all my fears and misgivings, reminding myself to stand fast and to take what comes, as Eleanor had taught me. Eleanor pretended that she did not see my growing belly, but of course, all the court knew.

Henry gave me a cloak made of dark blue silk, the blue of the French royal crest. The deep bell sleeves were embroidered with golden fleurs-de-lys, and the waist was gathered with a fleur-de-lys clasp cast in gold. The blue cloak was my prize possession, lined in the softest white seal fur; the sleeves and throat were trimmed in ermine.

The court saw me wear that cloak and began to realize that the king was not acting on a whim; he truly meant to make me queen. Only the king and queen wore ermine.

Henry would not let me write to my father. I was to remain silent, and let the king handle all political dispatches. This troubled me deeply, but as my pregnancy advanced, a mental torpor seemed to spread over my mind, and I did not fight for this concession from Henry. I knew well that Eleanor wrote to the Continent often, and never asked for Henry's leave.

In spite of my pregnancy, in spite of the fact that she still had not been removed to Fontevrault, it seemed that Eleanor and I had declared an uneasy truce. That winter, Eleanor smiled at me from down the table, and sent me dishes of squab braised in herbs and butter. Marie Helene brought her decanters of the wine my father had given me, but Eleanor and I did not speak alone.

As my pregnancy advanced, I missed Eleanor more and more. I wished to go to her with questions, but had to settle for the information gleaned from the midwives by Marie Helene. I longed in the evenings, when Henry did not come to me, to sit with Eleanor and have her comb my hair, as I had once combed through hers.

Though I could not sit alone with Eleanor anymore, from time to time, Henry indulged me. One afternoon deep in winter, Henry and I sat alone together, his hand on my belly, his head on my knee. Such times were rare, and I savored them, as I had savored nothing else in my young life, except the lost presence of Eleanor. During that afternoon, I had no fear for my future, no fear that Henry would turn from me. That day, even the pain of losing Richard had fled.

I had brought in a musician to play for us, and the sound of the lute was sweet. For once, with my lover next to me, and my child moving within me, the sound of the lute did not remind me of Richard.

I fed Henry a piece of cheese, for he still did not eat enough to please me. I leaned down and kissed him, almost forgetting that the musician was there.

"This is lovely, Alais. Thank you."

"You work so hard, Henry." I lowered my voice so that the musician would not hear me use his given name. "You work long hours to protect me, and our child. You need a time of peace, when we can be alone."

"Sometimes I think the only peace I have ever known in my life has been with you."

Henry's gray eyes stared up at me, and I knew he meant what he said. I kissed his lips, putting all my love for him into it. He tasted of the bread I had fed him, and the English cheddar I had pared for him alone. The touch of his hand on my hair was sweet as he reached up to hold me to him.

"My lord king!"

John burst into the room, coming in past Henry's men-at-arms, who looked grim. I was surprised that they did not stop him at my door as they should have.

I thought at first that John, like any child, was running in pell-mell to see his father. But I remembered then that John was no ordinary child, but a prince of the blood. He was a creature of politics already.

Henry's hand fell from my hair, and he sat up, looking at his youngest son. He was not annoyed, as I was. Henry knew, even in the first moment, that danger, not rudeness, brought John to us without warning.

I did not move from my chair. Marie Helene came to stand behind me.

"My lord, Richard and Geoffrey have deceived you. They have formed an alliance behind your back, and now they will turn their armies on you."

John extended his hand and held out a letter to Henry. I watched as Henry took it and read it quickly, his face darkening, as if the sun had set in his soul, never to rise again.

Henry's rage did not surface, as it had always done whenever Richard challenged him. As I watched, Henry grew very still; then he stood to face his son.

"You did well to come to me."

I saw that he would not discuss the matter further with me in the room. Henry's gray eyes were far from me, even as he leaned down and kissed my hair. I felt the world as I had known it slipping away. I was frightened when I saw that Henry's rage ran not hot but cold.

"Alais, I must see to this. Be a good girl, and stay in your rooms until I call for you."

"Henry, what will you do?"

He turned to me, all the soft looks of the afternoon gone as if they had never been. When he met my eyes, his gray gaze was bitter. I shivered beneath it.

"This is an affair of state, Alais. It does not concern you."

Had he struck me, I could not have been more surprised. I sat, my belly large in my lap, and watched him go.

The man I had thought would be my husband left my rooms without looking at me again, his young son at his heels. John, while only a child, had his father's ear. I saw at once that I never would. When Henry left the room without another word to me, I knew that I would never be his partner on the throne, as Eleanor once had been.

As he left to go about the business of the kingdom, as he left to arrest his son, Henry dismissed me, with as little thought as if I had been Bijou, and unable to understand him.

I saw myself in that moment for what I was, a girl who had nothing and no one but a bastard child soon to come. Henry would no more make me queen than God might one day make me pope. I had been a fool. Eleanor had foreseen it.

I had deceived myself, but there was still time. In spite of all I had done, I might still save myself, and my unborn child.

Even now, Richard sat in his rooms, surrounded by the king's men, surrounded by enemies. Any one of those men with pikes might push past Richard's guard, and strike him down, as a knight of Henry's had struck down Thomas Becket.

I faced a choice, and I made it without hesitation, without remorse. Once more, I would step out on my own, but this time to defy the king.

Henry had left me, and Richard might never take me back. Both the men in my life might abandon me, leaving me with nothing. But I remembered Eleanor, and the love she bore her son. If I saved Richard, Eleanor would shield me, even from Henry.

I rose to my feet. "Bolt my door after I leave and do not open it except to the king himself," I said.

"My lady," Marie Helene cried as she tried to clutch my arm. She reached for my trailing sleeve, but I slipped from her grasp. I could not stop to comfort her. While Henry would not harm Richard, his men-at-arms might.

I remembered well what Henry's knights had done to Thomas Becket. They had struck the top of his head clean from his body, leaving him dead and bleeding before the altar of God. If Henry's knights would do such a thing to an archbishop before God's very altar, what might they do to a treasonous prince?

I opened the door behind my tapestry. It led into the hidden corridor behind the wall of my room. I had never walked that path alone. Always before, Henry had been with me.

I took up a lamp, and stepped into the darkness of that passage, closing the hidden door tight behind me.

Chapter 29

⚜

ELEANOR: AN ESCAPE

Windsor Castle
February 1173

Richard and I were sitting in his rooms, whiling away the long, dark afternoon in my husband's keep, when Alais burst in on us from the hidden door. I could not have been more shocked if she had risen full-blown from the stones of the floor the way Henry's ancestor was said to have been raised straight from hell. Richard was on his feet in an instant, trained for war as he was. He had his dagger in his hand before he realized that it was not an assassin who came to us but Alais.

"Richard, you must leave this place," she said.

"Alais." Richard spoke only her name.

My son had the sense to put away his weapon, but I saw that he was slain already. Pain and love lingered on his face, at war with each other, vying for precedence. I saw then that he loved her far more than

I had understood. For the first time, I saw that between these two, there were no politics, no talk of war, or lands, or gold. Between these two, they had found something I had never sought. A love based not on necessity, politics, or power but on the simple, personal bond between them. The loss of Alais had cost him not an alliance with France, or the lands of the Vexin, but something that was to Richard more precious.

Alais seemed as struck by the sight of my son as he was by her. She blinked, swallowing convulsively, though she was too strong to weep. As I watched, she rallied, and found her voice once more.

"You must go. John has brought Henry a letter that tells of your alliance with Geoffrey. Even now, the king musters his men-at-arms."

Light began to dawn behind Richard's eyes, a light of joy I thought never to see again.

"You have betrayed him," Richard said. "You have risked yourself, for me."

Alais reached for him, and he caught her hand. "I will not stand by and let them kill you."

Henry would never raise his hand to our son. But I remembered Becket, and how Henry's knights had murdered him in cold blood. I knew that Richard could not tarry here.

Richard kissed Alais' hand as if swearing her fealty, as he so often had with mine, but he held it longer, and lingered over it as a lover might. She let him hold her hand, but she turned to me. I rose and went to them.

"Eleanor, Henry is coming. Before he gets here, you must forgive me," Alais said.

"For what, Alais?" I asked, thinking that she meant to ask forgiveness for trying to steal my throne.

"For taking the king's love from you."

The princess spoke low, her voice barely above a whisper. I knew then that this was what she feared, the one thing that had plagued her the whole time she schemed to take my place. It was love she craved, love she valued. She served France blindly out of love for her father. I took her other hand in mine and kissed it.

"Alais, you never stole Henry's love from me. For a long time, there has been no real love between us."

I saw the question unasked in her eyes, and I answered it. I did not make her pay for it, but gave it freely, gift for gift. For when faced with the choice, she had saved my son. "I have not loved him truly, Alais. Not in many years. Not since long before I met you."

She came into my arms then, and I held her. Richard dropped her hand, and turned away. At first I thought he was sorry to see her in my arms again, but as he donned his chain mail, I saw him swipe at his eyes. He was as softhearted toward her as he had ever been.

"Eleanor, will you shelter me? Me, and my unborn child?"

My grip on her tightened, and I breathed in the rose scent of her hair. Finally, the war between Henry and myself for the love of this girl was over. Finally, I had won.

"Alais, I will protect you. You need not even ask."

Richard gestured, clearing his throat, his squire springing into action as if on a battlefield. "Bring my light armor. We ride for the coast."

My love for Henry had died long ago, and for the first time, I had admitted it; that admission had set Richard free. His pain was lifted as if it were a dream gone at morning. His anguish had been, not just jealousy over the princess, but fear that I had been suffering, and horror that he could do nothing to save me pain. With that burden lifted, he looked light again, the bright young prince I knew him to be.

Richard had seen me hold the woman he loved, and heard me promise to shield her. It was no idle boast. I had protected him from Henry all his life; I would protect her now. Leaving Alais safe with me, Richard would be strong enough to hold his own with Geoffrey and young Henry when spring came, when all my sons rose as one against the king.

"Go to Geoffrey," I told him.

"Will he receive me?" Richard asked.

"Geoff is waiting for you," I said. "That is why Henry is coming for you now."

Richard was clothed in his travel armor. His men-at-arms, John of Northumberland and Gregory of Lisle, were ready to follow him. Richard came to me, and pressed my hand.

"Stay at my keep in Oxford," I said. I rang a bell, and Amaria stepped into Richard's rooms from the hall outside. "Go by river. I will have the ice-breaking barge ready for you."

Amaria heard my command and left at once to see that the barge was prepared.

"Henry can't move troops in winter, but as soon as there is a thaw, he will come after you. Wait for word from me. Come spring, we will all be ready."

"If it is war Father wants, I will bring it to him in Anjou."

I kissed my son. I saw that the time for counsel was over. I would have to trust Richard now to act for himself. On the battlefield, he knew no equal.

Richard turned to leave and passed Alais then, going out the door by which she had entered. He stopped and took her hand. He raised it to his lips.

"I will remember this, Alais. In the end, you chose me."

She did not speak, but he saw her love for him on her face. He and his men left, and the hidden stone door closed behind him.

There was no longer a question in my mind. For months I had debated with myself whether to mount a full-scale rebellion, a complete uprising of all Henry's sons. I had hesitated, wondering if Henry might someday see reason, if he might release his stranglehold over our sons, and the lands they held only in name. Each was a lord in his own land: Henry the Younger in Normandy, Geoffrey in Brittany, and Richard in the Aquitaine. But always, Henry kept his far-flung empire under his control. No matter what titles and honors he grudgingly granted our sons, he refused to let them rule. Now Geoffrey's letter had tipped the balance.

Henry knew nothing of my involvement, and nothing of young Henry's desire for war. He had only veiled references from Geoffrey to Richard, which I knew he would be too overconfident to heed.

Once Geoffrey wrote again and placated Henry, no doubt Geoff's lies would be believed. It was only Richard whom Henry hated with an unswerving passion. Once my favorite son was safe, I would wait, and take my time to spring the trap I had built so carefully.

I would take action to protect my sons, and myself. Henry understood only force, so let that be. Come spring, we would show him force, my sons and I together.

Chapter 30

ↂ

ALAIS: THE PIPER PAID

Windsor Castle
February 1173

I prayed to God for Richard's safety, standing there steeped in sin, my father's rosary in my hand. I thought of all I must be shriven for, but I turned that thought aside. There was more to do before there was less. There was a piper to be paid, and I would pay him.

Eleanor and I stood alone in Richard's rooms. His men had fled with him, down the hidden corridor. I thought I saw her reach for me. Then Henry was there, and I saw nothing else.

His eyes fell on me, and his men-at-arms stopped short behind him. He stared at me, at the betrayal he had not expected, from the last person on earth he expected it from. For I had warned Richard of his coming, and now Henry's rebellious son had once more slipped his grasp. I saw the bitterness rise in his eyes, the same bitterness he had always turned on Richard. Now, for the first time, Henry turned that bitterness on me.

"Alais."

He said nothing else. I saw that he would never forgive me. I had betrayed him to the son he hated most. Nothing, not even our unborn child, would succor that.

I moved toward him and stood before him, in case he ordered his men to take me up, as he would have ordered them to take up Richard. The pain on his face cut me, but I stood firm under it, for I deserved it.

Henry raised one hand, his gray gaze boring into mine. I saw his rage build behind his eyes, a great wall of red that swept his reason from him, until there was nothing left but his fury. I did not move even then, but waited for his hand to fall on me.

Eleanor stepped between us.

"Henry," she said.

His eyes did not leave mine, but his hand did not come down to strike me.

"She feared for his life, Henry. You forget, she is only fifteen years old."

Henry's face contorted with rage. I thought he would spit at her, but he did not; his eyes never left mine. He did not speak, but turned and left me there, standing in Richard's rooms. He did not say a word, but stalked away. His men followed him like dogs, their pikes in their hands.

"What have I done?"

"What you had to do," Eleanor said.

My knees buckled. I would have fallen had she not caught my arm. Eleanor held me up until she could get me to a chair.

Marie Helene came in then, looking stricken. She came to me at once, and took my other hand. Eleanor had not let me go.

"My lady, the king is calling up his men to ride after Prince Richard," she reported.

I felt my stomach tighten as a wave of pain washed over me. I gasped under it, as if I had been swept up in a tide.

Eleanor squeezed my hand and looked into my eyes. "He will not catch them, Alais. They have gone by barge to my keep in Oxford. They will be safe there, until they can go down to the coast. Henry will not have them. They have slipped his net. Thanks to you."

I felt light-headed, and I could not answer her. Eleanor knelt beside me, and pressed her lips to my hand.

"Thank you, Alais. Thank you for saving my son."

Pain in my abdomen struck me then, taking my breath away. Eleanor saw something in my face that she recognized, for she stood at once.

"Marie Helene, call my chamberlain. Have him take the princess to her rooms."

My waiting woman moved to obey as the dull ache in my abdomen receded. I had felt dull pains off and on all day, but had thought nothing of them. As Eleanor watched me, I realized that these pains were something else altogether.

Eleanor's man lifted me in his arms. He tried not to jolt me, and I was grateful for his help. I was suddenly very tired, and I knew that I had a long night ahead of me. Her chamberlain brought me back to my rooms, and set me not on my bed but on a chair, as Eleanor directed him.

As I thanked him, I saw the certain knowledge on Eleanor's face: my child was coming two months early.

Another pain came then, stronger than the last, and in the midst of that fire, Henry, Richard, the court, and my place in it faded as if they had never been. As my agony gripped me, all thought of the loss of Henry vanished. I released my grip on the chair and knelt on the floor of my room, my pain taking me as Henry once had done. I knew that I was truly in the hand of God.

Eleanor called for a midwife, and for a birthing chair. Both were brought at once, though the keep was buzzing like a kicked wasp's nest. All had heard of my betrayal of the king. No woman wanted to tend me in the midst of my disgrace, but one came, for she feared the queen.

Henry left Windsor, riding out to his hunting lodge at Woodstock, which was within striking distance of Oxford. I had lost him, and forever.

Amaria whispered this news to Eleanor, but I heard what she said. When the queen turned back to me, she did not speak of Henry or of Richard, but nodded to the midwife, as if my birthing was the most important business to befall her that day.

"Alais, between us, you will do well. God knows I've borne Henry enough children. I ought to know by now how it is done."

I took heart at her matter-of-fact tone, and felt my fear recede. Eleanor gripped my hand and helped me stand, so that Marie Helene could strip my silk gown off me. I wore only my shift, so Marie Helene then built up the fires in the braziers, and brought them closer so that I would be warm.

Eleanor would not leave my side. She spoke to me of the doings of her women, and of the foolishness they had gotten up to in the presence of her minstrel, Bertrand. Her soothing voice took me back to that simpler time, when I sat with her women, listening to him sing. The time before I ever saw Henry, when Eleanor and her son had been my whole world.

Three hours later, I was walking a circuit around the room with Eleanor when my water broke. Fluid gushed down my thighs, and I felt much lighter. The midwife and her women cleaned up the small pool of liquid from the floor, while Eleanor made me drink a glass of my favorite wine.

She helped me walk between pains all that night. For hours she stayed with me, and walked with me in a slow circuit around the room. For the first time, I saw that room as it truly was: an old chamber filled with Eleanor's castoffs, as my place at court had been from the time I first moved against her. The pillows, the tapestries, the plate, all belonged to her, as Henry did. As Henry always would.

Somehow, in the midst of my childbed pains, this knowledge did not wound me. The world was reduced to what it had always been: myself, alone with Eleanor.

As my pains got worse, I bit down on the fine linen cloth Marie Helene gave me, but it was too thin to do me good. Eleanor's woman, Amaria, found me a piece of leather, and I bit down on that. Between contractions, I laughed. "I am just like Bijou now."

Bijou did not chew her leather thong, but lay beneath the table, wide-eyed, looking up at me as I walked in circles around the room.

Agony rode me, over and again. In another hour, I could not walk at all, and Eleanor brought me to the birthing chair, from which

I did not rise again. I gripped the arms of that chair, praying as each pain passed. Eleanor pressed a damp cloth against my face, and its coolness soothed me.

I laughed even as pain gripped me, and Marie Helene looked at me as if I were demented. Only Eleanor smiled. She understood.

"It is time," I said.

As my pains came upon me harder and faster, there was only Eleanor. Henry now was gone, as was Richard, off to fight over power in the kingdom. As each contraction took me, Eleanor stood by me, or knelt with me when I was laid low, the agony too much to bear.

I pushed, gripping the arms of that birthing chair, and Eleanor held me up. It was as if we were one flesh, as if she gave me her strength to bear the agony. Her very presence reminded me that childbirth is a triumph, a field of war that men have no part in. Whenever I laughed, she laughed with me, her beautiful bronze hair falling from beneath her wimple, her emerald eyes on mine.

The pains ran together, but always I felt my child moving toward me, a fish in a stream that would never run dry. This stream flowed beneath me, and through me, and was bringing my child to me.

This stream crested, and my daughter came into the world. She slid out of me, into Eleanor's waiting hands. My baby was very small and she was blue, except for where she was covered in my blood.

Marie Helene washed me, and Amaria helped me to my bed. Eleanor brought my daughter to me, clean and dry, wrapped in one of the queen's furs against the cold.

"Here she is, Alais. What will you name your firstborn?"

I saw my daughter's face, her rosebud mouth and red-tinged hair that was so like Henry's. "Rose," I said. "For Our Lady."

"And for our garden," Eleanor reminded me.

When my baby lay in my arms, I was shocked to find her as light as down, as if she were not truly in the world at all. Rose was still blue, so I kissed her, and laid my mouth over hers, until her breath deepened and her color cleared.

My daughter cried then as I held her close to my breast, soothing her. She was so small, smaller than any child I had ever seen. When she stopped crying, her eyes opened. She looked at me as if to say, "Finally. There you are."

I kissed her. I was sore, but my young body had been made for birthing. I felt elated, as if I had just conquered London single-handedly and handed the keys of the city to my father.

"This is why men fight and kill," I said. "So that they can feel like this."

Now I knew why I was not afraid of the future, though I had lost the favor of the king, though I would be cast aside, as my father once had been cast off by Eleanor. I got to have my child.

My triumph did not linger, as nothing on this earth is meant to last. Eleanor saw before I did that my daughter had trouble breathing. Rose's sighs rattled in her chest, so that Marie Helene had to turn away. With tears on her checks, my waiting woman brought me the holy water that I kept on my prie-dieu.

I sprinkled the water on my daughter's head, bathing her in the salvation of God. "I baptize thee Rose, in the name of the Father, of the Son, and of the Holy Spirit. Amen."

I had spoken this last in Latin, and Marie Helene and Amaria crossed themselves. Eleanor simply reached out and caressed my baby's head.

"And my blessing do I give you, daughter of my daughter. May your spirit fly free and far, to the paradise your mother so fervently believes in."

Rose did not cry when the cold water touched her skin. She smiled at me, and at Eleanor, as if we knew a secret.

For that day, it seemed that the world was not what I had thought it was. It was not a world that belonged to kings and princes, to queens and pawns.

It was a world that belonged to God, but to a God nothing like the one I had known in my childhood. As I lay awash in this truth, I watched my little girl take her last breath, Eleanor's hand in my hair.

Chapter 31

ༀ

ELEANOR: ENDGAME

Windsor Castle
February 1173

Alais had the strength of a lion. I had always known this, but I saw it clearly on the day her child died. My daughter stood strong in the face of the loss of Henry, and the loss of the Crown. I saw at once that such things were as nothing to her, compared to the love she bore her child.

Alais came back to herself as she held her daughter in her arms. She did not weep when her child's spirit flew, but dried her eyes on the fur the babe was wrapped in, as if my furs were made to dry her tears.

Her waiting woman brought from her clothespress the deep blue gown that had come from Henry. Alais took the scissors from Marie Helene's workbasket, and cut away the skirt. The royal blue silk gleamed in the light of the lamps. Alais fingered it, and decided that it was soft enough to touch her daughter's skin.

She wrapped the child in that blue silk, until only the baby's face was visible above the cloth. She leaned down and kissed her daughter's brow. Already, it was as cold as stone.

After she laid her child down, we both looked at that little girl. All my own lost children came back to me, one by one: Charles, who had died stillborn in the Levant; little William, who had not lived to see his third birthday; and Isabelle, Louis' infant daughter, buried and left behind long ago in France.

At sunset, we stood together in the churchyard in the cold wind of that winter day. Rose did not rest in a box, but was laid directly into the earth, still wrapped in blue silk. The sight of her child laid in the ground was Alais' undoing. She almost dived into the grave, to bring her baby out of it, but I held her back.

"It is hard," I said. "Nothing will ever be as hard as this. But you must bear it."

The priest made the sign of the cross. When I nodded my permission, he went into the chapel to prepare for the mass that would be sung for the child's soul. In spite of all my teachings, I still had not wrested from Alais her childhood religion. That day, for the first time, I was glad I had not. Perhaps her religion and her prayers would bring her some consolation, when I myself could not.

That night, Alais and I sat alone in the rooms that once had been mine. Her waiting woman, Marie Helene, would not leave us; only when I ordered her, and made it clear that I would brook no refusals, did she obey me. She saw that then, as always, I was queen.

My own Amaria went to find her bed at my prompting. She knew me well, and knew that I would sit alone with my adopted daughter, keeping vigil that night, and for the nights to come, should Alais have need of me. Our rancor was gone like a dream cast off at morning. We sat together, two women who loved each other, for now Alais was a woman indeed.

The scissors from Marie Helene's sewing basket lay on the table, the blades Alais had used to make her daughter's shroud. They were heavy, for they were made of steel, polished to a fine sheen.

Alais picked up those scissors, and cut into her hair. A great sea of curls fell at her feet, all around the table where I sat. When she was done, her hair was only an inch long, as a nun's would be.

"Ah, Alais," I said. "Ever and always, you are a woman of extremes."

She smiled at me. Her mouth shuddered, as if she could not remember how to form a smile, as if she might weep. But she steadied, and her smile grew, until it almost reached her eyes.

"Come here, daughter, and let me trim it."

She knelt beside me, and I combed her short hair with my fingers, tidying the strands of it, so that it lay over her skull more like a cap, and less like a nun's devotion.

"There," I said. "You are a beautiful woman. The loss of your hair does not dim it."

Her eyes filled with tears, and she clutched my hand. I thought she might lose control then, but she did not. She pressed my hand to her lips. I felt them quake against my skin; then she pulled away.

Alais sat beside me in a second chair, lowering herself gingerly, still sore from giving birth. Her body spoke of her labor, even if she wished to forget.

"Perhaps someone might use it to make a wig," she said.

I laughed as she had meant me to. I poured her a cup of Anjou wine. When she took it up, I placed my hand over hers.

"I love you, Alais. Now and always, no matter what comes after."

She did not shed tears even then. Instead, she spoke in a steady voice, undimmed by pain. "And I love you, Eleanor. I always have. I always will."

It was my turn to swallow my tears as I turned my face toward the firelight, her hand warm on mine.

I sent word to Henry as soon as the baby died, but he was in London planning the hunt for Richard, and did not come. We heard soon afterward that Richard had left England, and had made safe landfall in Barfleur. It was April now and the cold of winter had broken. I knew that spring would bring war. But not yet. I had not yet given the order that would set my sons in motion.

As Richard mustered his troops in the Aquitaine, Henry received final word from His Holiness the pope. The Holy See would not support his marriage to Alais.

My spies brought the knowledge to me, secondhand. I, in turn, gave it to Alais, who accepted it, pale and unmoved. She spent all her time at prayer when she was not with me. Alais' short hair shocked my women, and they withdrew from her. I found I did not want them by me, either, so Alais and I spent a good deal of time alone, with Bertrand to play for us.

Alais was quiet, as she had been when she first came to me as a child. But day by day I saw a little of the light of her soul coming back into her eyes. She was brokenhearted by the death of her daughter, but her spirit had not been broken. I had never been prouder of her than I was during those dark days.

On a day in mid-April, Henry rode into the keep at Windsor. The sky was a bright blue, and the wind was from the south, and warm. It promised joy, a sense of hope that Alais did not feel. I saw in her eyes that she thought her life was over. She was so very young.

Henry came to me first in my solar. He did not announce himself, nor did he knock, but walked in past my women, raising one hand so that they knew to withdraw.

I stood looking at the husband who had tried to rid himself of me. We had been parted only a few months, but already it was as if I did not know him. As I looked at Henry, standing aloof and remote before me, I saw that I would never know his mind again.

"Henry," I said. "I am sorry for your loss."

His gray eyes met mine, but I did not feel their warmth. He stared at me, cold, remote, as he might stare at a stranger.

"Thank you," he said.

Alais came in, and I was grateful for her presence. She moved slowly, as an invalid might. She felt the loss of her daughter keenly.

The princess did not hesitate, but went straight to Henry's side. Despite all that had happened, she still felt drawn to him, as if she had the right.

And I suppose, if the right was something Henry gave her, she did have it. He opened his arms to her as if they had never been apart, as if she had not betrayed him to Richard.

I saw the love between them. I looked beyond their lust, beyond politics, and saw that they were kindred spirits, just as Alais and I were, just as Henry and I once had been.

Henry held her gently, close to his heart, as if she were made of Venetian glass and might break at the slightest touch.

"Henry." His name was the only word she spoke. She drew the heavy wimple and veil from her head, so that he might see her shorn hair.

His features darkened when he beheld the small cap of dark brown, all that was left of her glorious curls. He held her face between his hands, staring down into her eyes. He kissed her gently on the forehead, his lips as soft and fleeting as his love. He kissed her once, then let her go.

The pain in his eyes receded, drawn back into his heart, where he would never look at it again. I saw the shutters of his eyes close to her, as they already had closed to me.

He stared at Alais for a long moment, then took a step away from both of us. Though he loved her almost as much as he had once loved me, he had decided her fate already.

"It is good that you have shorn your hair, Princess. For in two weeks' time, you will return to the Abbey of St. Agnes, to pray for your sins, and to think on the good of France."

Alais listened to her lover as if he spoke of someone else. I do not think she believed him. She was so used to having him come to terms with her. She had never seen this side of Henry, the implacable king, the man whose mind, once made, was set in stone.

Alais did not beseech him, nor did she beg for mercy. She turned from him and came to stand by me.

"So you have won her back, have you, Eleanor?"

Even then, Henry's eyes were cold as he looked at me. I would have welcomed hatred, even anger, even bile, but in his eyes there was nothing. Just cold gray emptiness, like the sky before dawn.

And then he spoke in a voice as empty as his eyes. "She was the last pure thing in my life, before she turned back to you."

He left us without another word, without even a glance at Alais. She leaned against me, and I took her hand in mine. She needed my strength to hold her up.

"He never loved me," she said. "He never loved me if he could leave me like this."

I drew her into my arms, pressing my lips against the softness of her hair.

"Ah, Alais. It is because he loved you that he leaves you like this. If he had not loved you, he would have sent someone else. He would not have come alone."

My words did not comfort her. But she was living in the world now, by her own choice. She, like the rest of us, must learn to face what comes.

Alais was full of sorrow at the loss of Henry. She might have been young enough, even after all she had seen, to still think herself living in a fairy story, where princesses are rescued, even from the folly of their own choices. But the death of her daughter had taught her the truth: life is fleeting. We must take what gifts it brings us, and enjoy them while we can.

So we sat together, in my rose garden at Windsor. It was a small garden, but it had a view of the river. Spring came upon us early that year, and the warmth of the season rose up from the ground itself, as if to comfort us.

As many hours as we could, we spent in that garden. Those two weeks in April were blessed by the Virgin, Alais said, for it did not rain even once. And yet the flowers still bloomed as if under an enchantment.

Our idyll did not leave me quiet, as Alais was. I wrote to Richard at once, as soon as Henry was on the road to Southampton. I asked him to contact his brothers, that they all might be ready when I came. In two weeks more, I would meet Richard in the Aquitaine, and ride with him from there, into a battle Henry did not yet know was coming.

But during those last two weeks with Alais, I resolved not to think of politics. I did not know how long Henry would hold Alais in the prison of her abbey. I knew well that he would never let Richard marry her, even if my son had been willing. But I was certain that I could convince Richard to do my bidding, even in this. Someday, Henry would release Alais, and I would be ready.

I arranged a marriage for Marie Helene, since she would not be going into the nunnery with Alais. We saw her off, with Alais' little dog in her arms. She went to her mother-in-law in Anjou, who would preside over the wedding in my stead. Marie Helene wept to leave the princess; after shedding a few tears of her own, Alais kissed her, and let her go.

Alais was calm, much calmer than I would be if I had been consigned to a nunnery for who knew how long.

Henry still loved her, for he was kind to her, even then. He sent her to the religious house I had chosen for her when she was a child. She knew the women there, and the Reverend Mother. Perhaps she would be safe there, as well as happy.

She was not happy to leave me. But after I assured her that she need not fear, that I would come for her once I had the king's leave, we did not speak of her nunnery again. We spoke instead of Richard, of his prowess in war, and of how we both loved him.

There was no jealousy between us, which six months before I would not have believed. We had been reduced to the essentials of our lives: our love for Richard, and our love for each other.

We sat, our chairs drawn into the sun. Birdsong was thick along the branches by the riverside. The roses had bloomed early, though the Persian roses I had brought from the Levant still had not yet budded. They would bloom in June. I would be on the Continent, and would not see it.

I watched Alais as her gaze drifted over the rose garden and down to the river. She had her rosary of diamonds and pearls between her fingers. Though her lips did not move, I knew she was praying in silence for the soul of her daughter.

The next day, she was to be taken away to her nunnery, and I would leave for the coast. I had forestalled the rebellion among my sons until May, for love of her.

"Alais," I said, "I gave your father that rosary."

The princess looked up from her prayers, her mind finally drawn from the Virgin and the child she had lost. Her attention did not waver from me. I smiled, lifting my hand to my forehead. The bronze of my hair peeped out along the edges of my wimple, just as I liked it to.

I settled into storytelling mode, but found I did not have the patience to tell the whole tale, of how my lover Raymond had gifted me with that rosary when first we met, thinking me genuinely pious. Once he knew me better, we laughed over it, and I gave the rosary to Louis.

"Your father and I rode together on Crusade."

"You did not want to return to France with him," she said.

I smiled. "Yes, that is true, Alais, but that is not part of this story."

Her eyes gleamed with a little wickedness, but she did not refer to her father again. She settled back against the rose embossed cushion I had given her to hear my version of the tale.

I raised my goblet of wine. Alais watched me as I leaned back in my chair, savoring the moment. She realized, as I did, that we must make the most of this one day.

"That rosary was given me by a great knight in the Levant, a man who held the kingdom of Antioch against the infidel."

Alais loved tales of great knights in the Holy Land, so I exaggerated slightly when I spoke of Raymond's piety. He was a soldier of Christ, of sorts, which I suppose was all that Alais ultimately cared for.

She listened, wide-eyed, and once more I was reminded that for all her recent loss and heartbreak, she was but fifteen years old. Alais seemed younger than I had ever been, even in the happy time before my father died, when I had been cherished and cared for. I leaned across the arm of my chair, and touched the soft skin of her cheek. I wished that I had protected her better. I wished that I had kept her safe.

She saw the tears in my eyes, and followed my thought, though I did not speak it and had lost the thread of my story.

"I love you, Eleanor. What I did, I did for myself. You could not have stopped me."

I laughed, tears standing in the emerald green of my eyes. "I tried to stop you, Alais, as you well know."

She took my hand in hers and pressed her lips to it. I saw that she would love me for the rest of her life, just as she loved me now.

"Eleanor, you are the mother I never knew. I am sorry for all the pain I caused you. I will never be able to thank you for the succor you have given me."

"You are the daughter of my heart, one of the great loves of my life. That was always true, even at the darkest times, even when we were apart."

Alais came out of her chair and knelt at my feet, as if she were a servant, or a child. She leaned her head on my lap. I drew off her wimple, that I might run my fingers through the short silk of her dark hair.

"Do not fear, Alais. We will be together again. I have foreseen it."

She did not answer, but her tears dampened the silk of my gown. We sat that way a long time, her head in my lap, my hand in what was left of her hair. We rose only when the sun had set, and Amaria came out to bid us come in, for the night grew damp, and we might catch our deaths.

Alais and I both laughed as we stood, my lady-in-waiting frowning down on us, pecking at us like a mother hen. Alais wrapped her arm around my still-slender waist, and we went inside to see what the cook had made for us. I knew supper would be good; he was also in my employ.

Epilogue

༄

ALAIS: A ROSE IN SPRING

Abbey of St. Agnes, Bath
May 1178

I became myself again, living the next five years among the nuns of St. Agnes. Mother Sebastian welcomed me back with open arms. I wondered at first if she had not heard of my affair with the king and of all that followed. But when we prayed together alone in my room, in front of the prie-dieu that they had built for me so long ago, she commended the soul of my daughter to heaven. I knew then that she had heard the whole story of my time with the king.

I prayed for Marie Helene, safely married to Charles of Anjou at the queen's bidding. I prayed also for Bijou, though she was only a dog. Marie Helene had taken my puppy away with her when she went by ship to meet her husband. Even I could keep no dogs in the nunnery.

I prayed for Henry and for Richard, the men I would always love, the men I could not keep.

And always, I prayed for Eleanor.

I took to painting again almost as if I had not left it. I found my-self fascinated with the Birth of the Holy Child, and I would paint nothing else. I worked with deep colors, leaving the dark tones of the vellum to stand in place for the skin of Our Lord. I painted Him always in the manger, surrounded by His Mother and singing angels, His limbs swaddled and His mouth smiling. Always, when I was done, the Christ Child wore her face.

These little vellum paintings became valued by the sisters as objects of devotion, and in the last year there had been a call for them even out in the world. The wealthy women of the county would come by litter in person to take one of my paintings from the convent, leav-ing a healthy gift of gold or silver in its place.

The Mother said that these paintings caught something of the joy as well as the sorrow in the birth of Our Lord. She said also that I was not the only woman ever to lose a child. I was old enough by then to understand her.

I sat in the garden on a beautiful spring day, five years after my daughter had been born and died. I wore a simple black gown and veil. My hair had grown back long past my shoulders.

The sun was high and warm, and I worked with my paints laid in the shade so that they would not dry out. I had brought my high table into the yard, as no one else would have been allowed to do. Though I lived among the sisters, I was not one of them.

I added the smallest touch of blue to the Christ Child's eye where He looked out from my painting, smiling as Rose had smiled at me.

I laid my brush down and looked at the face of my daughter where I had painted her on the vellum. It was intended for a squire's wife down the road in Bath, and her retinue was coming for it on the morrow.

As I sat among the flowers of the simples garden, Richard came to me. He had met with my father the year before at Rouen. He had stood as witness to the lie Henry swore was truth: that Henry had never touched me. My father and King Henry had confirmed my betrothal to Richard once more. I wondered now, and not for the first time, what Richard thought of this, of the whole world pushing me into his arms, when all but my father knew I had been the king's mistress.

Richard was as tall and straight as I had ever seen him, and it seemed that his shoulders were even wider than I remembered. His red hair was touched with gold in the sunlight. I had forgotten how beautiful he was. He seemed older than his twenty-one years. I knew that he still bore the burden of his father's enmity, and the loss of his mother.

Just weeks after I had last seen her, Eleanor had led her sons in a rebellion against their father, a war that even I, as close as we had been, could not have foreseen. Even Henry had been caught unaware, but he had known, as I did, that his sons would never have united against him without Eleanor urging them to it.

The rebellion had ended with each of Henry's sons falling one by one, as pawns on a chessboard, to Henry's superior strength. Henry had forgiven each of them, going so far as to offer them additional incomes and castles on the lands they held by title only. But Henry, being Henry, gave up none of his political power.

Just as he had been unable and unwilling to have a partnership with me or with Eleanor before me, Henry would brook no half measures with his sons. Though all three held title to their duchies, both by right of birth and by oath to their overlord, the King of France, Henry conceded nothing. Then, as always, Henry held his power close. I wondered if he found his power cold comfort, as my prayers were cold comfort for me.

Despite his largesse to his sons, Henry had not forgiven Eleanor. As the architect of the rebellion, as the mind who had united her sons against their father, Eleanor had been locked away.

I did not stand to greet Richard as I once would have done. I shaded my eyes from the sun with one gloved hand and smiled.

"Well met, my lord prince. You are welcome to this place."

There was a stone bench near my high table, and he sat down on it.

"That is beautiful," Richard said.

"Thank you. Painting soothes me as nothing else can."

His hair was longer, and reached his shoulders. This lion's mane suited him, and brought out the electric blue of his eyes.

"I have come to say that I am sorry."

I came down from my stool and sat beside him. Though it was no longer my right, I reached out and took his hand in mine.

Richard's hand was large, with long fingers and blunt-cut nails. The calluses rose on his palm where his sword bit into it, and made it stronger.

"I am sorry for your loss, though I know it is years past," he said. "I am sorry I could not come to you sooner."

"You are here now," I said. We sat for a long time, his hand in mine.

"Eleanor is still locked away at Sarum?" I asked, hoping perhaps she had been set free, and I simply had not heard of it. I knew that Henry would never let me go, but I prayed always that for Eleanor's sake he would relent. Confinement would prey on her much more than it did on me.

"She is at Winchester now. It is better for her there, but still, she is not free." His face was closed to me, as it sometimes was when he spoke of her.

"I am sorry to hear it. I pray for her always."

"And will you pray for me, Alais?"

For a moment, it was as if we were back in the kitchen garden at Windsor Castle. I could see his sword, driven into the ground at my feet, his blue eyes staring up at me, full of a love that neither of us would ever lay down completely.

"I always pray for you, Richard. You will have my prayers with you until the day I die."

He looked away from me, and I knew that he swallowed his tears. But then he smiled, and it was as if a second sun came out to warm the garden.

He spoke then of the reason he had come to me. "Mother sends her love." Richard swallowed hard, as if suddenly shy, and met my eyes. "She reminded me of the conversation we had at Windsor, just before I was forced to leave. You saved me that day. I have never forgotten it."

"Richard, I did what I had to do."

"No," he said. "You did much more."

Richard stood, and drew me to my feet. "I tell you now that I have forgotten no vow that lies between us."

I saw his love for me in his eyes, undimmed by the evil I had done.

"I will love you, no matter how long you sit alone in this house of God. When my father is dead, I will come and fetch you out."

I heard his words imply all he could not say. He would one day marry me, even though I had spurned him, even though I had borne his father a child. Our love still lived, untouched by politics and loss. I saw that it always would, no matter what might come to tarnish it. Our love would gleam bright again, once we lifted our hands to polish it.

Never had I hoped for such a reprieve. When I was released from the prison of my nunnery, Richard would come for me. He would honor our betrothal, not for politics or for the power my father's lands might bring him, but for me.

I pressed my lips to his cheek, taking in the sun-warmed scent of his skin. His arms came around me, and drew me to him.

For a long moment we did not speak, cherishing the revived possibilities between us. I knew that he would not be faithful, as no man was. But I knew he loved me. I knew that I loved him. We could start again, and make a true marriage, with nothing else to come between us.

Richard spoke finally, and his voice was hoarse with his longing for me. His grip loosened, and I stepped back, so that I might once more see his face.

"Mother is allowed no letters, but she instructed me to give you this message. She will bless our union. Nothing will give her more joy."

He reached into the pouch at his belt, and drew out a red rose with a shortened stem, a rose that bore no thorns. "The queen asks that I give you this, that you may not forget her, and her pledge."

I took the flower he offered me, its petals like velvet on my fingertips. It was a Persian rose, one of the strain Eleanor had brought back from the Levant years ago, when she was still married to my father.

Richard drew me close and I felt his lips on my hair.

"The king will not let me come again, I think, not for a very long time. Remember what I have said to you."

"I will remember."

I could feel his reluctance to leave me, but his arms fell away. He strode away from me, as if afraid what he might do were he to linger. Richard turned back once at the gate, raised his hand, and smiled at me.

I saw his red hair shining in the sun. When the day came for us to be married, I wondered if our children would wear his hair or mine.

I saw Eleanor in his smile for the first time in that sun-warmed garden. I had never noticed before how his slanted eyes were so like hers. We would all be together again. Eleanor had said so; she had foreseen it. Now so could I.

Richard left me then, but his presence lingered, and that of Eleanor. I felt them with me as I stood alone in that garden, holding the rose Eleanor had sent me.

I would have to give up the painting of my daughter's face on the morrow. But I did not need a painting to remind me of Rose, and of all she meant to me. Tomorrow, I would start a new painting, and this one, I would keep.

Mother Sebastian came to me then, bringing lay sisters with her to clean up my painting things, and to take me into the chapel for prayers. I was glad to go. I was certain now that, one day, I would be free. I would enter the world once more, a woman of strength and power, as Eleanor had raised me to be.

Afterword

The rebellion referenced at the end of *The Queen's Pawn* between Eleanor's sons and Henry began in May 1173, and raged on until 1174. Henry fought each son on a different front: Henry the Younger in Normandy, Geoffrey in Brittany, and Richard in Aquitaine. One by one, each son fell to his father's superior military strength, but Henry was not cruel in victory. He forgave them all; he gave castles and additional income to each son in turn. But their war was fought in vain: Henry kept tight political control over all three of their duchies.

The king was not as forgiving of Eleanor, since she was the driving force behind the rebellion in the first place. Henry no doubt knew that if left with her freedom, Eleanor would not accept defeat, but would rise in rebellion again, and bring their sons along with her. To separate her from their sons, especially her favorite son, Richard, Henry locked Eleanor away for the rest of his reign.

In my novel, I have offered the possibility that Alais and Henry's liaison was not all Henry's idea, but an attempt by Alais to take the throne. I enjoy the idea that Eleanor of Aquitaine was not the only woman in Henry's life that faced him as an equal. While the events of my novel occur from 1172 to 1173, the chroniclers of the time suggest that Henry took Alais as his mistress in 1175, and their liaison continued at least until 1177. In 1175, Henry also began to press the pope for an annulment of his marriage to Eleanor, which was never granted.

Though in history, Alais was sent to Henry's court at the age of nine, in *The Queen's Pawn* I have made an adjustment to her age. Though most of the book is set in 1172–1173, I have made Alais fourteen and fifteen during those years to approximate her historical age when she and Henry engaged in their affair. Setting the novel during the years 1172–1173 served my book in one important way: it allowed the reader to watch Eleanor of Aquitaine's machinations as she set the rebellion of 1173 in motion, while adding spice to Alais' bid for the throne. *The Queen's Pawn* simply asks the question, what if Henry and Alais' affair had happened before the rebellion, and not after? How would the landscape of history and politics have changed? In my novel, though Alais' play for power comes before Eleanor was locked away, the political landscape did not change because of her affair with Henry. No matter what the year, or how many letters Henry wrote to the pope calling for an annulment, Eleanor was queen, and remained so until Henry's death in 1189.

Beyond the Plantagenets themselves, Alais, Louis, and Eleanor's lady-in-waiting Amaria, all the other people in this novel are fictitious.

For simplicity's sake, I have narrowed the action in my novel to only two of Henry's holdings: Winchester Castle and Windsor Castle in England. Throughout Henry's reign, the court was almost constantly on the move, and a great deal of time was spent in Henry's larger holdings on the Continent, in Normandy and Anjou.

I chose Windsor Castle for much of the action of this novel because it was the seat of Henry's power in England. I chose Winchester Castle as the second setting for the novel because Eleanor was sent there once Henry imprisoned her. She spent the last years of Henry's reign at Winchester Castle under guard, and additional years at Sarum on Salisbury Plain.

Also for simplicity's sake, I created the Abbey of St. Agnes near Bath as both a haven and a prison for Alais, Princess of France. The historical Alais knew many other prisons and havens throughout her years in Henry's court; her historical whereabouts are known when others remember to make mention of her. In my fiction, I have given her a haven among the sisters of St. Agnes, a refuge that, as far as we know, she did not find in her life as a princess living among her father's enemies.

The unrest among the Plantagenets did not end with the events of my novel. Henry never allowed Eleanor freedom from her various prisons. She stayed under guard until Henry died in 1189. Young Henry died in 1187, and in 1189 Eleanor's favorite son, Richard, became king. Though Richard was his father's heir, he was at war with the king the winter Henry died. The first act of Richard's reign was to set his mother free.

Eleanor went on to advise her son throughout his kingship, with varying degrees of success. Though Richard clearly loved her, he rarely took her political advice, marrying a woman not of her choosing, going on Crusade in the Holy Land, and getting captured by fellow Christians on his way home so that Eleanor had to pay his ransom.

Alais' historical fate is less certain. It is logical to assume that after Henry died, Alais would be released to return to France. Though Richard did not marry her as his betrothal agreement called for, neither did he send her home. Instead, for years Alais remained in Rouen, in the heart of Richard's territories. Only after Richard married Berengaria of Navarre and returned from his Crusade was Alais released to return to Paris. At that time, her brother, King Philippe Auguste, arranged her marriage to his vassal the Count of Ponthieu. Sources say that Alais and her husband had at least one child, but the date and cause of her death were not recorded.

Richard fought his last battle at the castle of Châlus, conquering the French stronghold only to die from a festering arrow wound in his shoulder. Eleanor buried him at Fontevrault, near his father, next to the spot where she would one day lie. Eleanor sent Richard's spleen to be buried at the site of his last battle, perhaps as a gesture to symbolize that his temper killed him in the end. Richard's heart was buried in Rouen, the city where Alais spent years at the beginning of his reign.

Photo by Pamela Afesi

Christy English has a bachelor's degree in history from Duke University. She lives in New York City. *The Queen's Pawn* is her first novel. Please visit her at www.ChristyEnglish.com.

THE QUEEN'S PAWN

CHRISTY ENGLISH

QUESTIONS
FOR DISCUSSION

1. During the medieval period, young girls were often shipped abroad to make marriages of state. When Princess Alais' marriage is arranged during her childhood, how does she face leaving her family behind? How is her reaction different from what a modern child's would be?

2. When Eleanor greets Alais on her arrival in England, Eleanor is surprised by what she discovers in the young girl. How is Alais different from what Eleanor expected? How is Eleanor different from what Alais expected to find in her father's former wife?

3. In *The Queen's Pawn*, Eleanor of Aquitaine has a very cynical view of religion and the Church. How does this view influence her dealings with Alais? How does Alais feel about the role of religion in her own life? Which character do you think represents the common perception of the Church during the medieval period? Why?

4. When Eleanor introduces Richard to Alais, she expects Richard to be "brought to his knees." When Alais also is trans-

formed by her meeting with her betrothed, is Eleanor surprised? What events unfold because of the mutual and immediate bond between Richard and Princess Alais?

5. Even at fifteen, Richard the Lionhearted is known for his prowess in war, and for his patronage of poetry and music. When Richard stands up to sing for Alais at the feast in the great hall, how does Alais react? How does Eleanor? Does this scene foreshadow any of the conflict to come?

6. Eleanor of Aquitaine claims to love both Richard and Princess Alais, but she also uses them to further her political ends. Throughout the course of the novel, did you believe that Eleanor loved them both? If so, whom did she love more?

7. Eleanor has a spy network that reaches across her husband's lands, both in England and on the Continent. How does Eleanor maintain this spy network? What methods does she use to keep information flowing into her hands?

8. When Henry and Eleanor are first reunited, they share a moment alone in the great hall. In this scene, did you feel that Eleanor and Henry are speaking the truth, or are they both lying to each other? What are some of the things that Eleanor is trying to hide? Do you think she succeeds?

9. When Princess Alais meets the king in the stable, she does not know him. What factors do you think contributed to the fact that she did not recognize him? When she sees Henry again in the great hall that night, she is shocked. What might Henry seek to gain by deceiving Princess Alais, by not revealing who he is in the stable with the dogs?

10. Princess Alais and King Henry are drawn to each other, long before Alais seduces him. Do you think they are bound by anything beyond lust? What other factors, if any, might draw Henry and Alais together?

11. Richard swears an oath to Alais in the kitchen garden, only to be caught a few hours later making love to another woman. Do you think Richard's infidelity makes his vow to Alais null and void? If not, why not? How is Alais' reaction to his infidelity different from a modern woman's? How does Alais' reaction to Richard's betrayal differ from Eleanor's reaction when King Henry takes mistresses? Why?

12. When Richard confronts Henry in the great hall, both Eleanor and Alais fear for his safety. Once Eleanor is alone with the king, she betrays Alais by handing over the letter the princess wrote to her father. Would Eleanor have used Alais' letter to her father under any other circumstances? Why or why not? Which gives Alais a deeper feeling of betrayal, Richard's infidelity or Eleanor putting Alais' letter into Henry's hands?

13. Alais goes the next day to seduce the king. What are her motives for trying to take Eleanor's husband from her? Over the course of the next few chapters, do you agree that Alais wants to become queen to protect the treaty with France, and the people of France from war? Why or why not?

14. When Alais seduces Henry, and asks him to make her queen in Eleanor's place, Henry agrees almost at once. Do you believe that this idea was in the back of Henry's mind all along? If so, what made him decide to take Alais up on her offer of an

alliance? Do you believe that Henry intended to keep his word to Alais?

15. During the medieval period, men often put away wives who did not please them. What are the political implications of putting a reigning queen into a nunnery? What factors kept Eleanor out of the nunnery, and the crown of England in her hands? What are the differences between Eleanor of Aquitaine and the scores of other women whose husbands sought to make them take the veil?

16. Once Henry and Alais return to court, they are greeted by Henry's youngest son, Prince John. Though not yet ten years old, John is well versed in politics and holds his own among adults. Was this portrayal of the young prince surprising when you read the novel? How different is Prince John from children of a ruling leader today?

17. When Alais becomes pregnant with Henry's child, she sees her unborn child as one more link between them, one more thing to support their alliance. Do you think Henry saw her pregnancy in the same light? Why or why not?

18. At the climax of the novel, Alais turns her back on her alliance with Henry and asks for Eleanor's protection once more. What factors motivated her to switch allegiances? Do you think she made the right choice? Why do you think Eleanor took her back?

19. Henry sends Alais to the nunnery at the Abbey of St. Agnes at the end of the novel. Do you think he did this to punish her for her betrayal, or was the abbey simply a convenient place

to put her once she had outlasted her usefulness? In your opinion, did Henry ever love Alais? If so, do you think he paid a price, emotionally or politically, for letting her go?

20. At the end of the novel, Richard comes to see Alais in the nunnery near Bath. In spite of all that had gone on, Richard still loved and forgave Alais, as she loved and forgave him. What factors made the relationship between Alais and Richard different from any other relationship in the novel? If Richard had not later become king, do you think he would have married Alais as he promised at the end of *The Queen's Pawn*?